The Fountains

THE FOUNTAINS

by Sylvia Wallace

WILLIAM MORROW AND COMPANY, INC.
NEW YORK   1976

Library of Congress Cataloging in Publication Data

Wallace, Sylvia.
  The Fountains.

  I. Title.
PZ4.W1887Fo   [PS3573.A432]   813'.5'4   76-1007
ISBN 0-688-03040-8

BOOK DESIGN: H. ROBERTS

For Irving, David, and Amy
with love

Doth a fountain send forth at the
same place sweet water and bitter?

Epistle of James 3:11

Faces we see, hearts we know not.

Old Spanish proverb

I

It was a rotten day.

And it shouldn't have been, not now, not when all the pieces finally were in place: her perfect, hard-won job, better than ever since her advancement to contributing editor, the man she adored striding at her side proclaiming his need for her, the early-spring sunshine reminding her of the promising adventure ahead.

Yet it was a rotten day, growing worse.

She heard her slim heels clicking on the Fifth Avenue pavement—noisy, rhythmic—dim reminders of the subway sounds that had accompanied her long ago when, as Rita Slavonovich, she had ridden the shuddering, dirty BMT from faraway Brooklyn to her magazine job in midtown Manhattan.

She could sense Peter's irritation as he quickened his footsteps to match her own. "What's the rush?" he wanted to know.

She did not respond. Her thoughts were still on the BMT, on the old days, before she could afford taxis, before she became Rita Sloane.

Guilt nipped lightly at her conscience, then

vanished as she recalled the moment she had discarded the name of her Slavic ancestors, that turning point in her life when she had made the symbolic break with her Brooklyn past.

It had occurred in the calculatedly chic office of Elizabeta Stanford, editor-in-chief of the noted fashion magazine, *Caress.*

"Look, Rita," Elizabeta had said. "You don't have to do this. The entire editorial board approved your promotion. Your name goes up on the masthead either way. Sloane, Slavonovich, it doesn't matter to us."

Elizabeta had leaned forward across her improbable desk, a wondrous slab of Lucite suspended from the ceiling by four gleaming brass rods. Elizabeta's high-backed, cream-colored leather chair had tilted with her movement and she had squinted at Rita through owlish glasses. "Why are you doing this?"

"My astrologer recommends it."

"Crap," Elizabeta Stanford had replied. "You don't have an astrologer."

Rita had remained silent.

"Then Sloane it is," Elizabeta had said. "I'm sure you have your reasons."

However could she have told a sophisticated DAR-descended woman like Elizabeta Stanford her reasons? How could she have explained that over in Brooklyn there were good, dear people whom she deeply loved, her mother, her father, two older brothers and their wives, and a row of husky, bland, blue-eyed children, all of them decent and devoted and stubbornly average? Elizabeta would think it was snobbishness that led her to this break. But it wasn't snobbishness, and it wasn't really a break. She still visited Brooklyn once a week because she wanted to, because she loved everyone there. No, it was something else— a lingering childhood fantasy that twenty-five years ago she had been the victim of an absurd hospital mixup, that some careless nurse, after swaddling her in blankets that concealed her true identity, had inadvertently handed her over to the wrong family. Too tiny to protest, she had gone home with the Slavonoviches and remained with them for more than twenty years, growing up as one of their children, yet always feeling a little apart. Not better, only different.

How could she explain to Elizabeta and the others on the staff that at *Caress* magazine she had found her real home, that she belonged here among them, restored at last to her natural family, returned forever from her long exile in Brooklyn?

"Congratulations on the promotion," Elizabeta had said. "You've done a great job in beauty and fashion, but that's the lightweight stuff. With your talent you'll shine when you get down to harder journalism like some of the features we have in mind for you."

Two years ago. Since then she had written at least a dozen articles for *Caress* under her new by-line. Since then she had met and fallen in love with Peter Welles, an intense, burly economist working in a think tank on the Hudson River nearby New York City. And since then rival fashion magazines had come forward with alluring offers to Rita Sloane, Elizabeta Stanford's gifted young discovery.

She had resisted all overtures, including Pete's of marriage. Her devotion to *Caress* had been rewarded with lavish raises in salary and, more important, with better and better assignments. Like the one to do a story about The Fountains.

Recently, Elizabeta Stanford had summoned Rita to her corner office on the fortieth floor of the Madison Avenue high-rise that housed *Caress* and told her about The Fountains assignment.

"The Fountains has become one of the great beauty spas in America," Elizabeta had said. "Right up there with The Golden Door, The Greenhouse, and Maine Chance." Elizabeta had fussed with some papers on the floating Lucite desk, then looked out at the grimy buildings and the dismal day. "If I weren't so tied up with fall couture, I'd go myself. Think of it, start dreaming. You'll have a whole week under a sky so blue you'll want to hug it. And the air, it's so soft and balmy it'll feel like arms around you. You won't want to come back to New York."

"I'm sure it's bliss. But I'll be there as a journalist. After I pick up the rites and routines of The Fountains for our panting public, what's left? What about the guests? Except for me, twenty rich, idle women, all stamped from the same cookie cutter. What do I write about?"

Elizabeta had shaken her head. "I've been to those places. The women are as different as snowflakes, only not as pure. You're in for some surprises."

That had been ten days ago. Around the time Peter told her he was accepting the new job as economist in a think tank in Florence.

"And you're coming with me," he had announced gleefully. "Can't you see us, cavorting in the Tuscan hills, hand-in-handing through the Uffizi, weekending in Venice and Rome!"

"Hold it, Pete. What about my job?"

He had looked at her blankly. "Your job? What about your job?"

"You're asking me to leave *Caress*."

"Well, yes, in a way. But we'll be together. We'll study Italian, we'll ski in the Alps, expand our horizons." And he had taken off again, exuberantly.

"Pete," she had interrupted, "I'm not leaving *Caress*."

He didn't believe her. "It's just a job," he had said.

"So's yours."

Now, with Peter hurrying beside her, she turned abruptly into the entrance of Bonwit Teller.

"Hey, what's happening? I thought you had to get back to the office."

"I forgot the leotards. I'll need them for the exercise classes." Her voice muffled as she disappeared into the curve of the revolving door.

"You're mind's still on that damned spa," he complained, slipping into the compartment behind her. "You're not listening to me."

When they were inside the store she took a few steps, then stopped halfway between Scarves and Jewelry.

"Pete, I've listened to you for weeks. Over breakfast, lunch, and dinner. In bed and out of bed. At your apartment and mine. In taxicabs, in bars, on the telephone, in theater lobbies. You've listened to me, too. But Pete, you haven't *heard*."

The saleswoman behind Scarves was enthralled, then disappointed as she watched Rita, followed by Pete, turn away and march toward Hosiery.

At the hosiery counter, Pete's face reddened.

"Rita, this is *it*. In a few days I'll be gone. I'm ready to be reasonable. Go to The Fountains. Get the stupid story finished. Then join me in Florence."

"Pete, for the last time, I'm not coming."

"Say it, you don't want to be with me."

"I *do* want to be with you. Here in New York City. In Italy I'd wither, and not because of the heat. You'll be occupied, stimulated. What does my head do?"

"You're a writer. You can write in Florence."

"You're a thinker. You can think in New York."

He tried to cool his anger. "What about the leave of absence? Did you tell Elizabeta we'll be back some day?"

"I did. And she said 'No leave of absence. Stay or go. A career is a commitment. You don't pick it up and put it down and expect to find it waiting for you like a faithful dog.' Pete, there are hundreds of would-be journalists breathing behind me. If I walk out now, the door shuts. Slam, bam. Everyone in publishing will know Rita Sloane is unreliable. And little Rita Slavonovich will be standing on the outside looking in again."

"You're making a mistake. I'll phone you tonight."

"Don't do that, Pete. I'm going to bed early. I'm catching the first flight to San Diego."

His smile was grim. "This must be history's most poignant scene of parting. Poets will record it. Rita Sloane and Peter Welles renouncing their love in front of the hosiery counter at Bonwit's."

"Pete, be fair."

But he was on his way.

The saleswoman was gentle. "What can I help you with?"

"Leotards," she said. "Size medium. Dark green leotards. And where does Bonwit's stock the hemlock?"

II

Driven by a howling wind, the rain swept up from Lake Michigan and crashed against the windows of the penthouse apartment. The impact startled Charlotte and instinctively she stepped back deeper into the warm living room. Still looking out across the open, rain-drenched terrace to the churning water of the lake, she began to swear under her breath.

"Sonofabitching flying weather, too. Another gift from my gods. Thanks, friends, you never fail. *Well, the hell with you.*"

Turning away from the window, she crossed the room, passed through the library, and entered the bedroom where Grace, her housekeeper, was busily folding clothes and layering them into a suitcase. A second suitcase, firmly strapped, stood ready near the door.

"Don't let the storm upset you, ma'am," Grace said. "You'll be away from it soon enough. A few hours and you'll be standing out there in the California sunshine."

"There's no sunshine anywhere in the world."

"That's how you feel now. But one week at that

place and you'll think you're a girl again. Remember the last time? You came back to Chicago five pounds lighter. And all those exercises. Remember how they slimmed down your waist and hips and everything, and you felt so good?"

Charlotte smiled into the housekeeper's plump, anxious face. "Maybe this time they'll give out samples. I'll bring back some Instant Gorgeous for you."

"Better get your coat on, ma'am, the driver's on his way."

"Nina! I almost forgot to call Nina!"

Seated on the edge of her bed, she reached for the telephone and braced herself for the annoying playlet that invariably awaited her on Nina's line.

Predictably, a little voice answered the telephone.

"Whosis, whosis, whosis?"

"Charlie dear, it's Grandma Charlotte."

"Whosis, whosis, whosis?"

Sternly now. "Charlie, get your mother. Immediately!"

In seconds she heard her daughter's voice. "Charlie loves to answer the telephone," Nina apologized.

"And I love talking to Charlie," she lied, "but I'm in a rush. The car is coming and I didn't want to leave without saying good-bye."

"California," Nina sighed. "Mother, I envy you. Off again, free as a bird."

"Uh-huh. Nina, I want to remind you that Grace will be away for the week also. I can't depend on those clerks at the reception desk to keep an eye on my messages. You'll come by every day, won't you? I gave you a card with the address and telephone number of The Fountains. You haven't lost it, have you?"

"Relax, darling. Everything will be taken care

of. Enjoy yourself. Forget Chicago. I wish I could.
This miserable weather and more to come, and here I
am, stuck. Christ, how did you and Dad ever stand it?"

"We liked it, Nina, for quite a while, you know."

"Oh, Mother, that was tactless of me. It's just
that—well, you're managing so beautifully, sometimes
I forget it can still hurt."

"It doesn't hurt, Nina. I'm not the least bit upset.
How is your father?"

"Dad's fine. Ned and I saw them last night.
Mother, you're sure you're all right?"

"Of course, Nina, don't be silly. It's been two
years. You can get over anything, you know."

"Mother—" Nina hesitated.

"Yes, Nina?"

"Mother, I have something to tell you."

"I'm listening."

"Dad and Marcy—they're going away."

"How nice for them."

"You'll hear about it when you get back. You
might as well hear it from me."

"Hear what?"

"Remember that trip you always wanted to take
with Dad, that camera safari in Kenya? Well, Marcy
found out about it. She said she wanted to go and Dad
said Sure, why not. They're leaving next month."

For a moment there was silence between them.
Then—

"I'm not too surprised. It should be clear by
now that Marcy can be persuasive."

"Mother, I think it's mean of him." Nina sounded
tearful.

"Don't go gulpy on me, Nina. Your father and I
traveled a good deal together."

"Where *he* wanted to go. I shouldn't have mentioned it—"

"It's nothing, Nina, forget it. I have to hang up now. The limo will be here any minute. 'Bye, dear."

Charlotte returned the receiver to its cradle and prayed she wouldn't be ill. *Her* trip to Africa. She had yearned for it, brought it up dozens of times, and each time Arthur had waved it off citing the pressure of his work or his own frank disinterest. And now, Marcy, with a wiggle of her finger or her ass was taking an uncomplaining Arthur on *her* safari. She wanted to cry but she was damned if she would fall apart again. If she could just get out of this apartment—away from the pity in Grace's eyes, the sympathy in Nina's voice, away from Chicago, from the fear of running into Arthur and Marcy on Michigan Avenue, in the Pump Room, at the theater—she would be fine, she knew it.

She had been a fool to stay on in the apartment. But Arthur had insisted. It made him feel better, he had said, to know she wouldn't be uprooted. She was the one who had loved the penthouse, its spaciousness, its eclectic blend of Art Deco, Biedermeier, French and English antiques, and the view of the lake. She deserved to have it, he had said. And she, frozen with shock, had foolishly agreed to remain. It had all been a terrible mistake. She should have cut out immediately, left Chicago right after the breakup. To go where?

She heard Grace calling to her. "Mrs. Caldwell, the doorman says the car is waiting. You'll have to hurry."

She sat gathering her forces, then came to her feet quickly. At least today there was someplace to go . . .

The journey from Lake Shore Drive to O'Hare Airport was long and wet. Huddled in the rear of the rented Cadillac limousine, with the mink coat Grace had insisted she take piled on the seat beside her, she could no longer repress the suffocating wave of panic, despair, and abandonment. *Even in this car I rattle around, the way I rattle around the apartment, the way I rattle around the days of my life.*

Wretched, lonely, she slumped lower in her seat. Dismally, she recalled other excursions, escapes actually, to the airport since the breakup with Arthur.

There had been the hastily arranged cruise of the Caribbean, urged upon her by friends who thought she needed to get out of town. The trip had been a monumental error. Thrown together with a covey of young people who were seeking immediate sexual activity among themselves, she had felt like an intrusive den mother.

Soon after, she had made her first visit to a beauty spa, choosing the famed Greenhouse near Dallas because someone who knew Lady Bird Johnson said the former First Lady found it a soothing retreat. The week at The Greenhouse had fulfilled its promise, toning her body and lifting her spirits. On her return to Chicago, when Nina and Ned had invited her to join them on a skiing trip to Vail, she had accepted eagerly, only to wind up in the lodge as a baby-sitter for little Charlie who was stricken with a head cold and wailed each time his parents went off to the slopes.

Exhausted, she had sworn off further family entrapment and had determined to find a niche of her own. Untrained, unschooled, except for two college years in the East, she was still at loose ends when summer arrived. Longing for a change of scenery, she had sought another beauty farm, this time in California. The luxurious Fountains near San Diego had delighted her. The shrewdly planned regimen of diet, exercise, and recreation had restored her vanished vigor and feeling of femininity. In peak condition, hoarding her well-being, she had set off for Paris.

That had been last summer. A season of promise. Hopefully begun, disastrously ended.

As the limousine hummed along the rain-slicked

Kennedy Expressway, she struggled to put the memory
of Paris from her mind, to concentrate instead on the
sights beyond the car window.

She saw nothing to lighten her depression.
Dreary clapboard houses and ugly factories constructed
of gray and brown bricks were strung mournfully along
her route. Roadside billboards exhorted the passing
populace to find solace in Johnny Walker, Black Velvet,
Old Forester, and Budweiser. Trees and bushes, strag-
gling up the narrow slopes, stood gaunt and bare-
twigged, unaware that it was spring.

She shuddered. Tears, painfully withheld from
Grace and Nina, came at last.

The driver looked back. "Only five more minutes
to O'Hare, ma'am," he said.

Aboard the 707, the Mai-tais were cool and
strong. Sipping her second drink, toying with the dreadful lobster Newburg the stewardess had placed before
her, Charlotte waited for the familiar disembodied
feeling to reach her brain. Her limbs felt airy but her
mind, weighted with ravaging memories, remained
leaden.

Twenty-five years ago *she* had been Arthur's
bride—lithe, slender, with mahogany hair and glowing
olive skin, and optimism that couldn't be stopped. And
Marcy, Arthur's new bride, where had she been that
year? Probably in her crib. Or maybe in a laundry
basket. Marcy came from one of those families that
scraped by just above the poverty level. As a typist in
Arthur's investment firm, Marcy had had her first
glimpse of executive wealth and power. The sight had
pleased her. In due time, as Arthur's second wife, Marcy
had proved herself a quick study. The social columns
lauded her graciousness, the gossip columns attested to
her glamour, and all the department stores, as Char-

lotte's friend, Monica Rice, reported, appreciated her charge accounts.

Pushing aside the miserable lobster, Charlotte decided to concentrate on the Mai-tai. She was feeling better now. Glass in hand, she caught her reflection in the plane's window. "Not bad for an old duck," she told herself. Peering again, she smiled. Did she or didn't she? Only her surgeon knew. Her dark eyes looked back at her, the skin surrounding them smooth and unwrinkled. Her small chin, held high, rose above a neck that was taut and unlined. "Not bad, not bad at all. Dr. Faust, or Mephistopheles, or whatever-your-name-was, you did a beautiful job!"

Looking back, she tried to recall exactly when she determined to have her face lifted. A number of people she knew had "been to the well," as Monica Rice put it. Charlotte and Arthur had been amused by the vanity that afflicted their friends but fortunately was passing them by. Smugly, they had noted that it was not only the women who were succumbing. Arthur had come home from his club one Sunday afternoon and told her that a golfing companion, Judd Russell, a research chemist who spent his working hours in near seclusion, had recently had the bags removed from under his eyes "for professional reasons." She and Arthur had had a great laugh over that one.

But gradually the idea had taken hold in her own head. She supposed it began after Nina and Ned were married. The event had fatigued her mentally and physically, and the message from her mirror was that overnight she had aged ten years.

Prodded by Monica Rice, who was a devotee of the plastic surgeon's knife, she had telephoned nervously for an appointment with Josephus Lester, M.D. "The best in Chicago. Probably in the world," Monica had said. *"He'll* never admit it, but they say he has operated on socialites and movie stars from all over the world. And—" Monica's voice had dropped here, "—also on the wives of three former Presidents of the United States."

The first visit to Dr. Lester had been a mind-blower. The brass doorplate marking his high-rise office suite was discreet, announcing only that therein labored someone known as "Doctor." With Monica leading the way, Charlotte fairly stumbled through the doorway, prepared for instant confrontation with Dr. Lester. What awaited her instead was an intimate, almost a cozy room, a movie-set version of a Cape Cod cottage. Botanical prints in fruitwood frames hung against floral wallpaper, dried flower arrangements brightened old pine tables, and chintz-covered benches lined the walls. From their seats on the padded benches a half-dozen persons stared at her entrance. Deeply embarrassed, she followed Monica to the reception desk at the far end of the room.

"This is my friend, Charlotte Caldwell, right on time," Monica announced loudly to the receptionist and to the room. "Tell Dr. Lester to make her beautiful."

"Monica, for godsakes, lower your voice," Charlotte pleaded.

"Whisper? In this place?" Monica laughed. *"I'll* never tell a soul, but in this office we're all in it together. Sit down and fill out the form Miss Asner has for you. Me, I'm staying right here with Miss Asner." Monica turned back to the receptionist. "Miss Asner, does the doctor have anything new? See, I have this droop—"

Charlotte found a place between two women wearing dark glasses (the eye jobs). Opposite her was another woman, wearing dark glasses in addition to an incongruous beach hat that tied under her chin (the full face job). In a corner, flanked by worried-looking parents, sat a small boy who gave her a crooked, hare-lipped smile.

Hastily, with six pairs of eyes upon her, she filled in the form. Name, address, age, occupation, that sort of thing. Almost like a passport application. She returned the form to the desk, ignored Monica who was lamenting to the receptionist over the lines around her mouth, and picked up a magazine on the way back to her seat. She had barely turned a page when the receptionist, calling her name, brought her to her feet again. Once more, the bruised eyes behind the dark glasses stared at her. From his corner, the little boy gave her another harelipped grin and his parents frowned. With a cheering section like this one, she thought, how can I miss?

Trailing the receptionist, she entered a dimly lit office at the end of the corridor. Dr. Lester, dressed in a blue crew-neck sweater and rumpled cords, and surrounded by family snapshots and trophies of his achievements on the tennis court, rose to greet her. His office possessed the same movie-set prettiness of his reception room and Charlotte found herself glancing about for blazing logs in the fireplace and a drowsing dog at his feet.

But his manner, once he had seated her—in a chintz-covered chair—was crisp and to the point. It must be understood, he explained, that she was not to depend upon the surgery for major life changes. All he could promise was an improved appearance.

"It's nothing like that, Doctor," she assured him. "My marriage is an extremely happy one. My husband knows I'm here. He thinks none of this is necessary but he's willing to go along with what will please me."

Satisfied, Dr. Lester led her down a new corridor to a room that looked, at last, as though it belonged to a serious practicing physician.

In an enameled examining chair, Charlotte faced a mirror and watched, fascinated, as Dr. Lester's smooth fingers manipulated the loose skin on her eyelids, her cheeks, and her neck. A white-clad nurse stood by making rapid notes as Dr. Lester dictated his findings. "It's unreal," Charlotte said softly. But no one responded.

Finally, feeling dazed and detached, she heard herself thank Dr. Lester for his kind attention. She was about to follow him from the examining room when the nurse took her arm.

"Time for pictures," the nurse said.

"Pictures?" The disorientation was overwhelming now.

"We always take pictures. Occasionally a patient is disappointed. It helps to have a reminder of how things were before the surgery. Don't look so frightened, dear. We keep our rogues' gallery under lock and key."

Weeks later, alone in her hospital room, Charlotte hoped there were no hidden cameras recording the aftermath of the main bout. The area surrounding her eyes was swollen and discolored. Her head, from chin to crown, was wrapped thickly in cotton gauze. The few tufts of hair that had broken free were matted with dried blood. Lowering her hand mirror, she tried to smile but the effort hurt. Recalling the doctor's admonition that it would hasten the healing process if she didn't move a muscle, she lapsed into immobility.

Thinking back, she understood why Arthur had fled after five minutes. He had arrived earlier that evening laden with books and magazines and flowers and she had settled deep in her pillows, prepared for a long visit. Instead of pulling up a chair, Arthur had dropped his offerings on the bedside table, smoothed her blanket, reported some office gossip and then, to her surprise, he had squeezed her hand, mumbled something about a dinner meeting, and departed.

Poor Arthur. Maybe she should have kept him away from the whole ordeal. One could push the for-better-for-worse thing too far. Well, at least he would be spared any further visits to the accident ward. To-morrow she would leave the hospital and, with only Grace for company, she would hide out in their country house on Lake Geneva until she was sufficiently healed and ready for reentry. Nina, as well as friends, had been told she was going to New York to shop. Arthur, at her insistence, was to remain in Chicago and spend his evenings and weekends as he chose—with or with-out social engagements—exactly as he would if she really had gone to New York.

The two weeks at the country house had been good ones. The dreaded operation was behind her. With the bandages gone and her hair clean and shining, she began to revel in the results of the surgery. Each day, as the bruises faded and the swelling receded, she actually felt the years drop away. A renewed sense of *future* animated her. Moving toward forty-four, she had forgotten how thirty and thirty-five felt—the anticipa-tion, the plans, the awareness that life was *ahead.*

Her only disappointment in those weeks was that Arthur did not drive out to visit her. He performed exactly as she had asked him to, and she was vaguely piqued. He telephoned several times each day, he kept busy, and he stayed away.

Her first evening at home, after Grace had served their dinner, she followed Arthur into the library for their ritual liqueur.

Usually, he poured quickly, mock toasted, and sat down across from her to continue their table talk.

But this time he stood over the serving tray without moving, uncharacteristically quiet. Puzzled by his silence and inaction, she looked up at him questioningly.

Then he poured slowly and she saw that his hand shook.

He did not bother to serve the drinks. Almost inaudibly, falteringly, he began to speak. "Charlotte," he said, not meeting her eyes, "there's something—I—I've been wanting to talk about it for some time—something serious, very serious—about us. I hardly know where to begin—"

But he had begun, and now he did not stop. He rushed on.

He told her about Marcy, about Marcy and himself.

Stunned, she offered no protest. She had known for years theirs was not the most exciting of marriages. She had known Arthur's restlessness, moodiness, stretches of noncommunication. But she had never dreamt they spelled out the word he now uttered. Divorce.

She stared dumbly at his thickening middle, at his handsome, tanned face, heavily lined below the beautiful gray hair.

Arthur, dear husband, she thought. We're at the same place. Only you want your whole life lifted.

III

Outside the Beverly Hills medical building, the sun was shining.

Leaving Dr. Karl Lorenz's soundproofed office, Gillian Crain had remembered to put on her dark glasses. Without them, it was a dead giveaway, Dr. Karl had said. Something about the pupils of her eyes growing larger or smaller. She didn't remember which. Any one of his colleagues encountered in the elevator would know at once, he had said. Not that *she* cared. But, to accommodate him, she had promised always to wear the glasses.

Dr. Karl had been marvelous this afternoon. It had been their best session yet. Almost a year since she had gone into therapy with him and in these recent months his artfulness had grown unbelievably. Four orgasms today, and she could have gone on and on had the light near his office door not shone red and had the accompanying buzzer not announced that his next patient was waiting.

She stood uncertainly in the bright California sunshine that glinted down North Bedford Drive. Two

P.M. One hour until she was due to pick up Bitsy at her private high school. She thought of turning south toward Wilshire Boulevard to buy some socks for Jason. The idea amused her. There was a certain ironic appeal in performing a wifely chore with the fresh ejaculation of another man warm inside her.

To hell with Jason, she decided. Let him get his own socks. Someday soon, after she talked to him about the divorce, he'd have to run his own errands. Or train one of his quickie lays to add that to her services.

No, definitely, she would not get the socks. She had a better idea. She would turn east and go to Juel Park's over on North Rodeo. Although she was tall and blond and willowy, today she felt lush and fleshy and musky like a Rubens model brazenly exulting in her womanliness. Juel Park had the finest lingerie shop in Beverly Hills. She would go there and find a new negligee, something outrageous, something so sheer it would barely conceal her firm, round breasts, and the soft, shadowed places of her body.

Dr. Karl had never seen her in anything but the understated, well-cut skirts and sweaters and shirts and pants she wore into his office three times a week. The fancied image of herself standing before him in the filmiest of substances, of his fingers reaching to remove the tantalizing garment, aroused her deliciously. The throbbing in her vaginal area, not fully subsided from their lovemaking only minutes before, declared itself like a persistent demon. The movement of her thighs as she walked up Rodeo Drive accentuated her awareness of her still-unsatiated need and she hoped she was not attracting stares.

Months earlier she had walked this same street after leaving Dr. Karl and, with the first wonder of true arousal, she had been the one who stared. She had searched the face of each man and woman she passed

and, stranger in a new land, she had asked herself if
they knew what she knew. The cloddish faces and the
bright ones, the sullen salespeople standing in store-
fronts, the expensively clad matrons window-shopping,
the slim-hipped, brightly dressed young people and the
mournful elders, had they ever known, even once, what
it was like to be so richly in love, so completely alive?
She doubted it then and she doubted it now.

Before Dr. Karl, had anyone questioned her
about her sexual performance with Jason or her variety
of premarital lovers, she would have rated herself as
good-excellent, shading perhaps a bit toward excellent.
When Dr. Karl began to know her, he had made one of
his infrequent comments. "Spasms," he had said mock-
ingly. "Spasms. That's what you've had all these years.
Routine contractions, not true orgasms." She had resented him at the time. "This funny old man," she had
thought. "How can he even *remember* sex?"

This funny old man. Bitsy's analyst had suggested she see the noted Dr. Karl Lorenz for personal
consultations when all the catfighting broke out between her and the then post-pubescent Bitsy. Dr. Karl's
voice on the telephone had been youthful, vibrant,
strong. Reflexively she had anticipated their first meeting as she might have a first date. Initial impressions
were important, she had been taught, so she had
dressed carefully and rehearsed a few speeches that
would make it clear to the new doctor that, as far as
Bitsy's problems were concerned, she was not only
blameless but an intelligent, understanding mother as
well.

She was totally unprepared for Dr. Karl Lorenz.
Her first view of the gnome of a man who opened the
door stopped her cold. Dr. Lorenz was white-thatched
and paunchy, with wire-rimmed spectacles resting on a
thick nose. And he was elderly. Pushing sixty-five at

least. Older than her father. Yet, incredibly, he emitted
a force and energy that dominated her immediately.

"There you were," she told him many months
later, "looming below me."

He had smiled without injury. "You are here,
my dear, to change your perspectives."

It happened so gradually, their falling in love.
Bitsy and her problems became early casualties of their
meetings as Dr. Karl, seated opposite, urged her to talk
about herself.

"I really can't. I never have. There's nothing to
tell anyway," she insisted in the beginning.

"Try," he said. "We'll both try to find out what
is hurting you."

The next time she appeared in his office she was
carrying an eight-by-ten laminated plaque under her
arm.

"It's all there, on that thing," she said, offering
it to him. "Everything you want to know. The complete story of my life."

He accepted the plaque gingerly. It was an ugly,
walnut object backed with stiff brown velvet.

"A wedding gift," she explained. "An announce-
ment of my marriage to Jason. In *The New York Times.*
Sixteen years ago. Mother's cook had it made up. So
Jason and I would never forget that happy day."

She sat back in her chair and watched him as he
read from the plaque.

> Miss Gillian Kathleen Delman, daughter of Mr.
> and Mrs. Lawrence Delman of New York City and
> Paris, France, was married here today to Jason Donald
> Crain, son of Mr. and Mrs. Aubrey Crain of Benning-
> ton, Vt., and Palm Beach, Fla.
>
> The ceremony was performed in the Manhattan
> residence of Mr. and Mrs. Delman by Judge Oscar

Kayden of the Supreme Court of the State of New York.

The bride's father is the internationally known art dealer. Her mother, the former Margo Royce, is a daughter of the late Benjamin Royce, founder of Royce Steel, Inc., of Pittsburgh, Pa.

The bridegroom's father is a former board member of the Vermont State Bank.

The bride, who is 20 years old, graduated from the Dunwiddie School in Massachusetts and attended the École des Arts Décoratif in Paris and the University of Grenoble. She has been associated with Delman-St. Honoré et Cie, her father's art gallery in Paris.

Mr. Crain, 26, graduated from the Woodstock Country School in South Woodstock, Vt., and from Princeton University.

After a honeymoon trip abroad, the couple will live in New York City where Mr. Crain is a stockbroker with the firm of Scott, Swanson and Little.

When Dr. Karl was finished reading, he thrust the plaque into her hand.

"Take it home." His voice was disdainful. "Here we do not deal with birth announcements, obituaries, or other public notices."

"I thought it would be helpful."

"A few paragraphs on a piece of paper, that is your life? And nothing else? Is that your life—nothing?"

She attempted a feeble smile. "There's Bitsy, of course. And Jason isn't a stockbroker anymore. Too confining, he said." She wrinkled her forehead. "In fact all of New York got to be too confining for Jason. As long as my parents—well, as long as Lawrence and Margo were around. And they were around more and more after Bitsy was born. Lawrence and Margo loved being glamorous grandparents. *Vogue* and *Bazaar* had run out of ideas about how to feature Margo. They'd had years of her as Celebrated Beauty and Fabled Hostess.

Then they came up with Youthful Grandmother and
Margo adored it." Gillian compressed her lips and
smiled meagerly. "Lawrence's ego likes stroking, too.
Once, he got a woman at *The New York Times* to
sneak him a copy of his own obituary. You know how
newspapers write them up in advance. Lawrence read
his obituary and glowed for weeks. He was thrilled
because it ran so long." Her smile vanished. "No, Lawrence wouldn't stand aside either. He forgot Jason was
Bitsy's father. Jason resented the whole scene. Jason is
an only child. He was used to having attention focused
on him."

"And you?"

"What about me?"

Dr. Lorenz rubbed his hands impatiently. "Have
you forgotten so soon? We are here to talk about *you*."

"I'm sorry. I'm always apologizing to you—" Her
mind reached for long-ago feelings. "I guess I was
having a pretty good time. Everyone I cared about was
right there. It was fun until Jason became so difficult."

"In what way did he become difficult?"

"He began to pick fights with me. He said he
felt emasculated. He was sick of being on the fringe.
When an old classmate from Princeton told him marvelous things were happening in California real estate,
he asserted himself. He insisted we make the break and
come out here. Bitsy was ready to start school and
Lawrence and Margo were taking charge of that, too.
To hold us together, I agreed to the move."

"And the situation became better between you?"

She smiled grimly. "Hardly. Jason had a lot of
getting even to do. And he's still getting even."

Dr. Lorenz saw her eyes mist and her fists
tighten as she fought to maintain the rigid control that
had marked their earlier sessions.

"Ah, the ice floe moves slightly. Go on."

"Jason came into his own all right. He joined a large Beverly Hills firm as a real estate broker. He was an immediate success. It didn't take very long to discover that his Ivy League charm could dissolve buyers and sellers alike. He became a specialist in luxury homes. And he made a lot of new friends."

"Friends?"

"Female friends. Willing, available women. There are plenty of them around, aren't there? Plenty of beautiful women. Jason found them. Recently divorced women, an occasional widow. All kinds of women whose life patterns were changing. For whatever reason, they were selling their homes. And there they were, waiting for him—sitting alone in their plush Beverly Hills houses with the bar stocked and the bed empty. Maybe the kids were away at school or sent off to relatives. I've pictured it a thousand times, those hungry women, avid for sex. And in walks Jason, tall, smooth, ballsy. A perfect setup. No, Jason wasn't confined anymore."

"He told you this?"

"He never had to. He had his own telephone in his study. His business phone. Sometimes I'd answer it. It was always a woman and Jason would drop whatever he was doing and rush out. To meet a client, he said. Oh, he sold the houses all right. He made a great deal of money and after a while we bought one of those big houses for ourselves. From one of Jason's clients. A beautiful two-story Colonial, twelve rooms, swimming pool, tennis court. For all I know, I'm not the first woman Jason slept with in our bedroom."

"And now—"

"Jason has moved on to more sophisticated aspects of real estate. Land development projects. Industrial centers. All over the State. He's gone for days at a time. Sacramento, San Francisco, Northern California.

If I object, he's the one who becomes angry. He claims he's doing it for Bitsy and me. When he's home, he pretends he's worn out. And he probably is. By other women who are happy to tumble into bed with a virile specimen like Jason."

"And you stay with him? Why?"

She began to cry. "I—I—I have no place to go. What I mean is—I have no *one* to go to. I've thought about it so many times. I'm afraid to ask for a divorce. I have nightmares. I see myself as one more of those rich, hungry women, sitting alone in my living room, waiting, waiting for someone like Jason to wander in . . ." Her tears embarrassed her. "Lawrence and Margo would be horrified if they could see me now. We Delmans never bleed or sweat or cry."

Dr. Lorenz handed her a box of Kleenex and sat back in his brown leather chair, silent, watching.

She wiped her eyes and nose and tried to smile. "Now you know our best-kept secret. Delman noses run."

Dr. Lorenz's expression was somber.

"This is not a comedy hour, my dear Gillian. There is a frightened, lost little girl inside you. Together we will free her to grow, to be one with the ripe, beautiful woman I see before me."

She looked up at him, curiosity surfacing on her face, not certain she had understood him correctly. She had first heard that approach in boarding school. A math teacher, not much older than Gillian herself, had volunteered to transform her overnight from un-awakened maidenhood to gloriously fulfilled womanhood. She had complied uncertainly, achieving something less than rapture. Without doubt, that little child inside was a tough nut to crack. Many men had followed, dredging up the same line and many times she had cooperated. Obviously to no avail—for here to

her wonderment, was Dr. Karl Lorenz, eminent psychoanalyst, repeating what she had been told so often
before. Yet, it was unthinkable that he could be trying
to seduce her. Totally unthinkable.

Months later, after she had sniffled her way
through many boxes of Kleenex, Dr. Lorenz surprised
her by leaving his chair and moving forward to comfort her. Gratefully she accepted the quick hug he
gave her. At the door he raised himself on his toes and
his lips briefly brushed her cheek. She told herself she
must read nothing into his actions. He was a married
man, a grandfather. When he spoke of his family it was
with respect. She was still the little girl he was treating.
It was like a visit to the pediatrician's. Only Dr. Lorenz
wasn't handing out toy balloons.

How it began, she couldn't really say. She
poured out her hurts and her needs, she exposed her
weaknesses and flaws. And through it all he was compassionate and uncritical. As she talked, the Toad
Prince, hunched in his leather chair, became the most
desirable of lovers. Encapsulated with him in that quiet
room, no other reality existed for her. She loved him
and she told him so. He verbalized no response, merely
nodded. Sometimes he held her in his arms until her
crying stopped, or gently massaged the back of her
neck until she relaxed.

In time, the physical interludes with him became
more important to her than her emotional outpourings.
She began to dress for those moments when he would
touch her. Button-front sweaters replaced the turtle-
necks she had favored. And he understood. Nearing the
end of a visit, he would rise from his chair, draw her
to him, and take her in his arms. Then his stroking
fingers would find their way to the smooth crevice between her breasts as, one by one, she released the

buttons on her sweater. His fingers would drift slowly over her bared breasts to the rising nipples and he would take them to his lips and suckle them gently. Her groping hands, with a life of their own, would glide to his sheathed crotch and caress him until he hardened. Only the soft buzz at the door, signaling the arrival of his next patient, would make them break apart. It became the way they said good-bye.

The day she abandoned her usual pants and appeared before him bare-legged and wearing a pleated skirt her message was apparent. Wordlessly he pulled her to him. As she opened her sweater, his fingers rose on her thighs with unbearable slowness. When, finally, they found her vagina it was wet and eager. Ignoring the couch, he guided her toward the carpeted floor. Dropping to her knees she grazed her cheeks and then her lips against his exposed, arced penis. When he entered her, her joy was total. She was complete at last, physically and emotionally. The voice she heard, the voice she dimly knew to be her own, was babbling crazily. "Fuck me, fuck me, fuck me. Please, my darling, don't ever stop fucking me!"

Unexpectedly, her sex life with Jason, never very good she realized now, began to intensify. Returning from ecstatic sessions with Dr. Karl, her flesh gave off a new warmth and receptiveness that Jason sensed, and it aroused him. Too mellow for disputes, she submitted when he wanted her. Although her head told her Jason was the wrong man, she delighted him by releasing herself freely to the sensuality that flooded her body. But to her Jason remained an instrument, barely perceived. Dr. Karl was the reason for her existence.

Sometimes, after Jason had returned to his own side of their bed, she listened to the metronomic rhythm of his breathing and pleasurably re-created the highlights of her affair with Dr. Karl. She enjoyed forming a mosaic of the incidents that made up their story. And always she sought to find the piece that would make the picture whole, that would answer the question that teased her. Who, she wondered over and over again, who had seduced whom?

The declarations of love had come from her, as had the whispered confessions of desire to touch more intimately. Yet it was he who had initiated their physical contact, however innocent it may have appeared at the time. Still it was she who had decided on the provocative sweaters and the inviting exposure of her skin. Although it was he who, while adroitly maintaining the doctor-patient relationship as they talked, had concluded their meetings by darting in and out of her clothes. Adding to her confusion, it was he who had issued a sharp rebuke when she laughingly called him her "lay analyst." Yet it was he who, that same afternoon, had introduced her to an exotic new sex act that sent her into the street dazed.

The day he told her they would have to miss a couple of sessions in the following month because he had accepted an invitation to lecture before the guests at the exclusive Fountains near San Diego and that he would remain in the area overnight, it was she who had suggested she needed a vacation and might like to spend a week at the beauty spa. In response, he had dipped his white head, peered over his wire-rimmed glasses, and casually mentioned the name of his motel. Later, when she told him she had made her reservation at The Fountains and that, to avoid arousing Jason's suspicions, she had persuaded her friend Drucilla Jennings to join her, he had made no comment at all.

Now, heading up Rodeo Drive toward Juel Park's lingerie salon, she mused about what she might purchase that would excite Dr. Karl when they met in his motel room. Something spiderweb sheer, that was certain. And something with a single fastening. When she stood before him in the provocative negligee, she wanted it to fall away easily at a touch. If they were to have just one night together, she was determined it would be a total celebration with no time-wasting fumblings.

In the salon, while a honey-voiced saleswoman volunteered unwanted suggestions, she finally found what she was seeking. It was a subtle, foamy, lilac-colored negligee with one tiny button just beneath her bustline. Below the button the lilac froth fell free, exposing her as she moved.

The saleswoman frowned. "Perhaps you need a nightgown, too."

"I'm the one who knows what I need," she said with annoyance.

"Of course you do, madam." The saleswoman turned away, offended.

Gillian wanted out of there. "Thank you for your help," she said, her voice softening. "I have a matching gown at home. If you will please box the negligee."

A glance at her wristwatch told her it was three o'clock and she would be late meeting Bitsy. She sighed as Bitsy reentered her thoughts. Hurrying back to the parking lot adjoining Dr. Karl's medical building, she claimed her car and locked the box containing the precious negligee into the trunk.

Waiting on the street corner, fat and sloppy in her patched jeans and dirty Salvation Army cape, Bitsy Crain slouched against a street post and grumbled to herself because her mother was late. All the other kids had left for home, or the neighborhood juice bar, or their shrinks. She was the only one still hanging around. She wished the bitch would get here.

Bitsy hated being only fifteen years old. She hated even more her real name which was Marilyn, and she hated her nickname even more than that. She was tired of the dumb story of how she had got her nickname. Bitsy had been a premature baby, weighing in at New York Doctors' Hospital at three pounds, eleven ounces. Viewing her granddaughter in an incubator, Grandma Margo Delman had been reminded of the delicate "itsy-bitsy" Japanese ivory miniatures called netsukes which she collected, and she had promptly and ebulliently dubbed the baby Bitsy. The name had stuck, to Bitsy's disgust. She was fat. She was a fat person, and that was that.

Bitsy was a student at a small private school attended by bright rich kids, children of movie and television stars, famed athletes, and wealthy professional people. These children were the offspring of hapless parents who gamely came up with the high tuition fees because they hoped that an intimate learning environment would make their sons and daughters more acceptable human beings. Going to the school was fine with Bitsy, but she knew it hadn't done much to fix up the trouble between herself and her mother, that bitch. True, things had been a little better since Gillian got her own shrink, but things weren't *that* good, not by a long shot.

To Bitsy, Gillian with her long legs and slender, well-dressed body looked like one of those waxy creatures in I. Magnin's fancy windows over on Wilshire Boulevard. Bitsy knew Gillian could *die* for having such a messy, overweight slob for a daughter. The bitch took it as a personal failure. She nagged about exercises for Bitsy and shoved all that low-calorie junk at her. When nothing happened, Gillian just got madder and madder.

Compounding Bitsy's weight problem was the fact that secretly she was on the Pill. In her French class Bitsy sat alongside Jerry whose father traveled a lot, and whose mother was a big wheel in fashions somewhere in downtown L.A. Jerry had the key to the nearby family duplex so that he could go home at lunchtime to make himself a sandwich and feed his dog. Bitsy had soon fallen into the habit of strolling home with Jerry. Bitsy didn't wash too often and her mother complained about that, too. But it never bothered Jerry. One day, almost a year ago, after setting the egg salad and the sandwich bread on the breakfast table, Jerry had flung himself at Bitsy, kissed her hotly, and led her unprotesting to his unmade bed where he introduced her to the Big Mystery.

It had been as simple as all that. Every school day, except when they had to go on some stupid field trip like to the La Brea Tar Pits or the County Art Museum, Bitsy went home with Jerry and they messed around. Mildly concerned about pregnancy, Bitsy had consulted her friend Diane, who was sixteen. Diane had told her how to get the Pill.

"Just go down to the Free Clinic in Hollywood," said Diane. "No questions asked. Some nurse will make you sit through a long rap about how not to have a baby. But they don't care how much you ball."

Bitsy didn't care either. It was a nice break in the school day. Afterward, she and Jerry would eat their sandwiches and walk back to school together. At the end of the day, when Gillian came by to pick her up, Bitsy usually managed to look sullen. It drove her mother crazy. After a few snapped words they would finish the trip in silence. Bitsy was sorry for Gillian then. It made the atmosphere pretty heavy. But it did keep Gillian from asking nosy questions and that suited Bitsy just fine.

Now she was aware that Gillian had finally appeared at the corner in her little red Mazda. Sighting her mother, Bitsy knew at once that something was different. The creep was smiling, even happy, as she leaned across to unlock the car door for Bitsy. And there was none of the usual crap about the torn blouse and dirty feet. Then Bitsy remembered. Her mother was leaving for a week, going off to one of those funny fat farms where she would exercise day and night and get high on cottage cheese and yogurt. Well, that was agreeable to contemplate. The ding-a-ling would be away for a week and her father would be in charge. If *he* didn't decide to cut out, too. No, he had said there would be just the two of them and Bitsy looked forward to the change. Poor old Jason, she thought. She was sure her father screwed around a lot when he was off on his business trips, and she couldn't blame him. Gillian, that tight-assed bitch, could freeze the balls off any man.

In the car, Bitsy kissed her mother on the cheek for a change, and dutifully answered all questions as they pointed toward home.

Jason's Jaguar, parked under a leafy sycamore in the semicircular driveway, was a sight for which Gillian was unprepared. Jason seldom came home so early in the day. Although his office was only a dozen blocks away in the heart of the Beverly Hills business district, he was generally tied up till evening—or so he said—with clients or bankers or someone's investment counselor. Now he was behind the bar mixing a drink as Gillian and Bitsy crossed the large entry hall and entered the walnut-paneled den.

"Hi, women!" he called out gaily.

"Hi, Dad," Bitsy called back. "Excuse me. I'll leave you two boozers alone. Gotta get something to eat."

After Bitsy had disappeared, Gillian eased onto

a barstool. "What's the supersalesman doing home at this time of day?" she asked.

He pretended to be hurt. "How about a drink?"

"No, thank you. You didn't answer my question."

"My wife is leaving me to take a trip. Did you think I'd let you go without a personal send-off?"

"Really, Jason. We went through our good-byes this morning. This is you and me, not Héloïse and Abelard."

His good humor persisted. "Believe it or not, I'm going to miss you."

Moving from behind the bar, he let his eyes rove over her. "You're one great-looking chick. What are you up to, going off to a shape-up farm? If there's one thing you don't need, baby, it's an improvement in that body."

"Jason, you know I need new scenery, too. Dr. Lorenz thinks it will be good for me to take a week off, to be more in touch with my physical self. Get my mind off my mind, he says, or something like that."

"Okay, okay, if the old coot says so. But don't forget, I love every inch of you just where it is."

He studied her again, his eyes narrowed. "Funny thing. You're getting better looking all the time. Not doing any free-lance fucking, are you?"

"Jason, that's disgusting."

He was enjoying his own joke. "Let's go upstairs, lover. A quick one for the road."

"Jason!" She was horrified. "Bitsy's in the kitchen. Ada can probably hear you in her room. You really are crude."

He took a long gulp from his glass and dropped into a chair, indignant. "Forgive me, Ice Cube. I forgot the ground rules. A good woman never climbs in the hay while the sun is shining."

"Jason, you're being ridiculous. I still have to

pack. Then I'm picking up Drucilla. It was nice of you to come home and I'll miss you, too. But don't expect me to be available like one of your sex-starved matinee numbers whenever you decide to drop in."

He squirmed, not liking the direction their talk was taking. He reached for a familiar ploy and rescue.

"But I love you," he said, handing her the words, smiling, trying to silence her like a parent forcing a pacifier into the mouth of a fretful child.

"Jason," she sighed, "the old line's not working today. You dropped in. Thanks for the gesture. I'll carry it away with me."

"Dropped in?" He was infuriated. "I live here. Somewhere on a piece of paper it says you're my wife. Twenty-four hours a day. Not just between midnight and one A.M. Pacific Coast Time."

"Bitsy. She'll hear you."

"Don't Bitsy me." He raised his voice. "She knows what goes on here. Remember what her shrink said? 'A sponge with antennae.' She's been picking up on the whole scene for years. No wonder she's screwed up. What kid wouldn't be, with a walking Popsicle for a mother."

"Jason, you're detestable. Simply because I don't warm up whenever you—"

He was at the door. "Have a happy week, my puritan bride. And mind what the good doctor said. Get in touch with your physical self. Because, baby, you're the only one who can!"

After the Jaguar had roared out of the driveway, Gillian leaned against the wood mantel, shaking. When Bitsy reappeared, crumbs sprinkled down the torn blouse, cookies clutched in her fist, Gillian managed a weak "Hi there," for her child.

"What happened to Dad?" Bitsy asked. "Did I hear his car leave?"

Gillian put her arm around Bitsy's shoulders. You lying, spying monster, she thought, you heard it all. What she said was, "He had to get back to the office. He said to give you a kiss and tell you he would see you at dinner."

IV

Every time Dru entered the three-story C.B.S. building, pure-lined and multiwindowed, on the corner of Fairfax and Beverly in Hollywood, the thought occurred to her that it resembled a Brooks Brothers refugee who had blindly wandered into the wrong neighborhood.

Dru loved the C.B.S. building. Her own presence there meant that she belonged, that she had made it at last in the cutthroat world of commercial television. First as a writer, now as an associate producer in charge of scripts, she was *in*. She felt at home within the building, just as she felt at home within the colorful Fairfax district that surrounded it.

Born and raised in the gentility of Missoula, Montana, Dru savored the vitality of the Fairfax neighborhood, an ethnic enclave, largely elderly, unmistakably Jewish, abounding in hodgepodge produce markets, fragrant delicatessens, and temptingly stocked bakeries. A shy woman, she marveled at the camaraderie that existed between the established Jewish community and the last survivors of the hippie movement. She envied the ease with which the two groups mingled as they found common comfort and acceptance in the few blocks of the Fairfax district.

Eavesdropping on the crowded streets, talking with shopkeepers, Dru had been touched to discover that the locals were intimidated by the C.B.S. building. To them the building, austere and impressive, was like a foreign embassy they dared not enter. Behind the facade, they were convinced, labored the *truly* Chosen People, the gifted, the powerful, the rich.

Dru knew better.

This early afternoon as she wheeled her car into the parking area designated for executives and headed toward the far end where a slot was reserved for her, she had to admit she did feel chosen. Unfortunately, it was for her own brand of misery. Normally the sight of her name, Drucilla Jennings, painted in bold black letters on the white bumper rail, could give her a charge. This time not even that well-earned symbol of success came to her aid.

Walking rapidly in the direction of the building, she waved to the uniformed guard, entered the waiting elevator and, minutes later, was nestled in a lounge chair across from Patrick Smith's jumbo-sized desk. As she waited for Patrick to come off the telephone she toyed with the briefcase that lay across her lap. Patrick had encouraged her to remain at home today, to take it easy before leaving for her week at The Fountains, but she had insisted there was still work to be done. Finally they had agreed upon lunch in his office.

Observing Patrick—large, handsome, blustery, unconsciously gesturing for the benefit of his unseen caller—Dru knew that despite his heartiness Patrick's appraisal of himself bore little resemblance to the stereotype projected upon him and other television producers by the overawed Fairfax residents.

Patrick *was* gifted, she thought. As the executive

producer of two current network hits and three series in reruns, his talent could not be denied. And he did have power, even if it was limited to the few dozen people who were directly accountable to him. But Patrick was honest too, and painfully aware that in the television hierarchy there were other men, stronger men, who could crush him if he faltered. As for money, Patrick had made heaps of it. "Where did it go, Dru?" he would wail. She never answered because they both knew. Patrick had divorced one wife who had cleaned him out in the process. He had promptly married a loudmouthed nag whose extravagances added nothing to her appeal and whom he despised.

Around the studio it was common knowledge that Patrick was having an affair with a young doe-eyed set designer with whom he spent every possible hour. Once, speaking to Dru, he had lowered his head and appeared close to tears. "Migod, I want to be free," he said. "But I can't face a divorce, not again. Can anyone explain why a wretched marriage can make me feel like a success at the game, while a happy divorce would make me feel like a loser?"

She hadn't attempted to answer that one either. It was a question she was still asking herself.

She was staring out the window when she heard Patrick end his phone conversation.

"Actors," he snorted as he hung up the receiver. He moved around the desk and fell wearily into a chair near Dru's.

"Trouble?" she asked.

"Always, but we won't talk about it now. Rule number one: Never discuss actors before lunch."

"Discuss away if it'll help you feel better. I don't want any lunch."

"Not even hot pastrami? The deli is sending it up on rye."

"Not even hot pastrami."

"That's not like you, Dru, you're a pastrami freak." He leaned forward. "What's bothering you, baby? Tell Uncle Patrick."

"Nothing's bothering me. Yes—something is. I feel guilty. I shouldn't be walking out on you, even for a week. I should be right here, working with the staff on the new scripts."

"Nonsense," he replied. "We'll manage. You were due for this holiday. We agreed the timing was perfect. Just because our schedule suddenly gets advanced is no reason to shake up your plans."

"I can still cancel—"

"No way. Besides, a week among the healthies will bring the color back to your cheeks. In the end, it'll help the shows."

"That bad, huh? You can level with me. I've been a slug lately, haven't I?"

"You haven't been your usual hotshot self. But what the hell, we all have our dippy times. God knows, I've had mine. So you hit a period that's a bummer. No big deal. Don't be too hard on yourself."

"Thanks, Patrick, you're nice. Sometimes I think, you and me, we're like an old married couple." She began to open her briefcase.

"Keep that damn thing closed," he ordered. "No business today."

"Oh?"

"Let's talk about old married couples. How's Tim?"

"Fine. Still out of town."

"Where'd he go this time?"

"Washington."

"Not again?"

"What's that supposed to mean?"

"Not much, except he seems to spend more time in Washington than at home."

"What of it? You know that's where the big stories are. Ever since he won his Pulitzer, the paper has wanted him to travel. I've told you that. They insist it helps his column and his reputation, and his lecture tours. They must be right. Last time we counted, Tim was syndicated in almost two hundred papers."

"So that's all he does in Washington—work?"

"Patrick, don't be nasty. Yes, that's all he does." She bristled. "Except right now he's helping Jonny Ring with his reelection campaign. You remember, Tim managed Jonny's school campaigns when they were prepping. Later, after Dartmouth, Tim advised him right into Congress."

"Jonathan Ring should be a shoo-in. He's been a good Senator."

"True, but in Arizona it's no help with the voters when your wife files for divorce in an election year."

"I suppose not. Whatever happened to Nancy Ring? I thought she was lovely."

"She's still living in the Georgetown house with the children. Jonny moved to an apartment on K Street. He sees the kids once a week. The split was a big blow. In a way, I'm happy Tim is in Washington. Jonny depends upon him."

"And you, Dru, whom do you depend on?"

"Myself, mostly. But Tim is here when I need him."

"Apparently you don't need him very often."

She jumped to her feet. "Patrick, you are a bastard!"

"Simmer down, baby," he said, coming to her side. "I'm sorry if I've hurt you. It's just that I don't want anyone else hurting you."

She tried to smile. "I forgive you. You mean well, but you sure as hell are clumsy."

He raised her chin with his fingers. "Get your sad little face out of here," he said. "Enjoy your vacation. If it'll ease your conscience, I'll give you an assignment."

"Name it."

"You did tell me there would be a bunch of rich broads at The Fountains?"

"I guess they're rich. It costs a thousand dollars a week to stay there."

He whistled. "That's what I thought you said. And you did say there would be twenty guests in all?"

"Right."

"Then please, Dru, find me a woman who can afford to stay a month. It's my only hope."

She laughed. "I'll do that. And you do something for me."

"Anything."

"Put the pastrami on ice for a week."

Driving out Sunset Boulevard from the studio usually soothed her. She loved hitting the speed limit and guiding her car over the smoothly banked curves, past the evergreen lawns that fronted the fashionable houses of Beverly Hills, and the tangle of bushes and trees that concealed the large estates of Holmby Hills and Bel-Air. At the studio there were endless abrasive conferences and draining conflicts and always, always, people.

Alone in her car at the end of the day, her destination the small house in a wooded cul-de-sac in Brentwood, she could begin to unwind. This afternoon the familiar tonic wasn't working. She was annoyed with Patrick for needling her about Tim. And she was —admit it—angry with Tim for placing her in a situation she could not defend. "Damn you both," she said aloud, and her own voice startled her.

Pausing for the red signal at Beverly Glen, she glanced to her right at the heavily treed road winding into the canyon. Somewhere up there, she knew, behind handsome wrought-iron gates and dense hedges, still dwelt those unlikely—and unwitting—matchmakers of her marriage, Hannah and Harry Hastings. Crazy, how they had come into her life. Her friend Lucy Lerner had been running for her first important State office and Dru had volunteered to write her speeches. To their mutual surprise, Harry Hastings, a well-heeled attorney of doubtful antecedents and fierce political drives, and Hannah, his brittle, ambitious wife, had attached themselves to Lucy's campaign. Migod, how long ago had that been? Six years, almost seven? She thought back . . .

It had been a picture-postcard day—rare, smogless, sparkling. A good omen, they agreed. She and Lucy had left their car with the parking attendants at the foot of the hill and were hurrying up the driveway toward the heavy oak doors of the Hastings Mexican-style hacienda. ("The real thing," Hannah had told them. "Those doors once belonged to Maximilian and Carlota.")

Like vivid sentinels, birds of paradise in full bloom lined the long driveway, and orange hibiscus clung to the natural brick facade of the main house. Beyond the porte cochere they could glimpse the famed Hastings rose garden, bordered now with bright blue lobelia.

Pausing for breath, Dru surveyed the landscape.

"So much for the theory that plants thrive best in a warm, loving environment," she remarked irritably. "If that were true, every living thing on the Hastings property would freeze over and die."

Lucy chuckled. "Dru, show some gratitude. Hannah and Harry are enormously generous opening their home this way, letting the paying public stomp

over their grounds to raise money for my campaign."
Squinting in the sun, Lucy turned to watch the long
line of cars crawling toward the house. "At ten dollars
a head it looks like a good day."

"Listen, Lucy, I signed on as your speech writer
because you're a straight-on candidate. Well, I'm
straight-on, too. You know perfectly well that Hannah
and Harry are a pair of barracudas. They don't give a
damn about the issues. They sniff a winner and they
want to be close to power when you're elected. They'd
support Jack the Ripper if they thought he was going
to be Lieutenant Governor of this State."

"Well, I'll say this much, they sure pull them in.
Three hundred paying customers today—and half of
them coming because they want to see the garden and
the Hastings, not me."

"Maybe so, honey. But when they leave, there'll
be three hundred strong raring to vote for Lucy
Lerner."

And Lucy had come through. Mouthing Dru's
words with the force of fire engines, she pocketed the
crowd long before her finish. When she was done she
stepped down from the wooden riser and, with Hannah
and Harry at her side, she moved happily among the
guests who had lingered for the refreshments included
in their admission fee.

Standing alone on the patio, Dru sighed audibly,
then looked around, embarrassed. No one had heard
her. Naturally. After the weeks of preparation for this
climactic rally, after the numerous meetings with
Hannah and Harry to make it perfect, she was, once
more, a human leftover. Lucy, Harry, Hannah, the
magical people, would go on to greater glory. She,
Drucilla Jennings, would return to her scripts and wait
for another good cause to come along.

She was turning to leave—Lucy now had dozens

of new friends to give her a lift home—when she saw
Lucy, her big breasts heaving, bearing down and shouting her name.

"Hold on, Dru. Wait a minute," Lucy was calling. And then she was there on the patio, gasping for
breath, while the lanky stranger by her side grinned
with amusement.

"*She's* the one," Lucy was saying. "Credit where
credit is due. Dru, this is Timothy Larsen, new political
analyst on the *Times*. He thinks my speech was brilliant. He congratulated me. Me! I'm just the windup
doll who spoke it. I told him he had to meet the real
genius in this campaign. Mr. Larsen, this is my ghost-
writer, Drucilla Jennings."

She looked up. Way up, because he was at least
a foot taller than she. She looked into cornflower blue
eyes that reminded her of a storybook Viking peering
over the prow of his ship into the New World. Speech-
less, she stared at the square jaw, the tanned skin, the
thick blond hair, and reconsidered. Maybe he was more
like one of those unhorsed cowboys who used to stride
across her TV screen selling virility and cigarettes.

With effort she brought her mind into focus. I'd
better describe him on paper, she told herself, because
somehow I've lost my capacity to speak.

"Dru, for chrissakes, don't stand there like a
dummy," Lucy was saying. "Give the man your telephone number. He wants to interview you about the
campaign."

"Of course," she said. "Of course . . . Here is
my business card. My secretary can always find me."

Of all places. In the domain of Hannah and
Harry Hastings, who didn't even know she was alive,
she had met Timothy Larsen and her life had begun.
Six months later, she and Tim had run up the steps of

the Santa Barbara courthouse to be married in the
book-lined office of a local judge. Together they had
settled into her little house in the rustic cul-de-sac and,
over his objections, because he couldn't pay for it, she
had built on another room so he could have a study of
his own. They had shared their political causes and
their writing problems and their love, and they had
gloried in the miracle that had brought them together.

Three years later, Tim's Pulitzer Prize had come
out of the blue. He had been a crusading journalist in
New Hampshire when he first caught the eye of William Mayberry Huntley, publisher of the *Times*.
Brought to Los Angeles, Tim had looked at the city
with unjaded eyes and had uncovered a long-festering
scandal involving municipal mistreatment of minority
women. The story had been well received when it appeared in the paper and Tim had basked in the generous praise of his readers and colleagues. When the prize
was unexpectedly announced, she and Tim had been
giddy with joy, certain that their life together, so satis-
fying already, would be richer yet.

She was not prepared for all the changes the
prize would bring. Their social life, once modest, became lively and demanding. Predictably, Hannah and
Harry Hastings reappeared, bombarding them with invitations, still acquisitive celebrity hunters seeking new
blood for their salon.

"They're vultures. I can't stand them," Dru told
Tim one evening as they were dressing for a dinner
party at the Hastingses'. "Why do we go there?"

"Because they're useful to an upcoming young
newspaperman," he teased. "And because it's research
for you. Someday you'll nail them in a script."

"Who'd believe them? They're unreal."

"Another reason we're going. Too much reality
around here. We need a touch of dazzle. I like my Dis-
neyland luxurious."

"Tim, they ignore me. They want you because all of a sudden you're a Name, a performing seal for Harry's clients."

"Not so. They want you. They love you for yourself alone."

"Bullshit—and don't deny it. Tonight you'll be assigned a seat next to some gorgeous movie star. I'll end up, as always, place-carded between the dullest man and the kitchen sink."

In time, it was not the Hastingses, or the Simmonses, or the Crichtons, or any of their new acquaintances who made the biggest change in their lives. The most important change came the day Huntley called Tim into his office and told him the newspaper, which had him under contract, expected him to take fuller advantage of his Pulitzer Prize. Tim was entering a new phase of his career, Huntley said, one that properly exploited would make him truly famous and bring fresh honor—and a great deal of money—to him *and* to his paper. Always sensitive about earning less than Dru, Tim had been immediately attentive. Letters were pouring in, Huntley explained. Universities, women's organizations, businessmen's clubs, all wanted him as a guest speaker.

"They pay huge fees for each appearance. The brass ring is there, waiting to be grabbed. But that's not the main reason I'm asking you to do this. Lecturing will make you well known all over the country. We're beginning to syndicate your column. The more familiar your name is to the public, the more widely we can sell the column. From then on, it's circular success. The greater the number of papers running your column, the higher your lecture fee becomes. Besides, there are other stories out there that will give your column a national flavor. It means being away from home a bit, but the rewards are worth it."

Dru called him a domestic absentee and pre-

tended not to mind. At first she hadn't cared all that
much. He was gone only a few days at a time and they
talked nightly, long-distance, sharing the madness of
their days. As his trips grew more frequent she would
join him occasionally, but they soon agreed that made
no sense. Her own work, with a score of scriptwriters
dependent on her guidance, was too demanding, and
the brief hours they had alone on the road were too
unrewarding.

Despite the separations, their intimacy endured.
She met him at the airport at any hour of the day or
night and they fell into each other's arms like lovers
who had been parted for years.

"I'm beginning to like our life-style," she whispered one afternoon as they lay side by side in their
tree-shaded bedroom after making love. "All these sexy
reunions. I'm sorry for couples who are free to go to
bed together every night."

Her eagerness to declare her sexual pleasure
amazed her. Although her earliest scripts had been ac-
claimed for their insights and sensuality, they were in
fact the fruits of her imagination. Girl and woman,
growing up in Montana, she had been agonizingly shy.
"Dru is a late bloomer," her worried mother had said,
defending her against friends and relatives who wondered why the child never had a date. "I'm not fretting.
She'll get there."

A few years later, glued to her TV set in Missoula, Mrs. Jennings had watched her daughter's
steamy teleplays and had been positive Hollywood had
corrupted her girl. The truth would not have pleased
her any better.

Dru had arrived on the West Coast still timid
but impatient to embark on the erotic life of the fully
liberated woman. Tiny, barely five feet tall, small-
featured, with close-cropped reddish hair and nut-

brown skin, she soon had acknowledged that she was outclassed by the brash, uncomplicated California types who cheerfully announced their availability via untethered breasts, skin-hugging pants, and turn-on language. Confronted by the competition, Dru withdrew from the race early on. She worked steadily, invested her earnings, bought the little house in Brentwood, and devoted her spare time to liberal causes.

From time to time she did take a nervous stab at the new morality. There had been one joyless romp with an overweight scriptwriter that lasted three months. The affair had ended abruptly when she told him he wrote superficial dialogue and didn't know how to structure a scene. Then there had been the night she got stoned out of her head with some ad agency executives visiting from New York and had awakened nude on the sofa of a suite in the Beverly Wilshire Hotel. That escapade hardly merited a memory. And there had been the teasing relationship between her and Patrick Smith that had never led to anything wilder than working dinners and a few drinks at Gatsby's restaurant near her house.

On the whole it was a dull life. When she fell in love with Tim she viewed herself as a virgin, and she felt like one, also.

An irritated honk from the car behind jolted her into the present. As she resumed driving, her meeting with Patrick replayed in her head like a videotape recording she was powerless to erase. She saw again the skepticism on Patrick's face as she rationalized Tim's absences. She heard the insinuation in Patrick's voice as he prodded her about Tim's activities in Washington. She tried to wipe the whole sorry scene from her mind, but it wouldn't go away.

Turning into her quiet street, her wretchedness

grew. Three years of together-apartness, she thought
bitterly. This time Tim would be away from home for
two weeks, maybe longer. His voice had betrayed his
relief when she told him she was taking a break in her
work to go to The Fountains with Gillian. Although he
did not particularly like Gillian, more and more lately
he had been encouraging her to have friends of her
own. Ever since they had settled the question of having
a baby—the verdict was No, they were much too busy
and he was away too often—he had urged her to cultivate new interests. If he wondered about other men,
he never said so.

She wondered about other women though, as
did Patrick Smith. And Patrick didn't know what she
knew—that the reunions were lousy now. She still went
to the airport to meet Tim but it was an automatic gesture, practiced, unfelt. His first night back they usually
dined at home alone. She lit candles and poured wine
and, if the evening was cool, she set a fire. In her soap
opera writing days they called that Rekindling the
Flame and it humiliated her to be playing the corny
role. It was no comfort that, just as in the soaps, it was
a futile charade.

In earlier times, after the candles, the dinner,
the wine, she would wait for him in bed, skin warm
and anointed with perfumed lotions, and he would
come to her erect with anticipation. But that was in
the past. More often now, she would lie in bed alone,
tormented in mind and body, scented, lubricated, ready.
And instead of joining her, Tim would close himself
into his study, reading, writing, she supposed, and
sometimes she could hear him pacing. On those infrequent occasions when they did make love (talk
about euphemisms) his performance was technically
correct but without passion. She was convinced he slept
with her because hers was the body at hand, but that
his desire was aroused by images of someone else.

In these darkening days of her marriage, she tried to confront their situation as she did the elements in a script. As she saw it, they were somewhere in the middle of the second act. Tim was having an affair or contemplating one. Obviously he still valued her enough to want the marriage to continue. If he didn't, he would be seeking a way out. Small comfort, but it was all she had. She didn't dare probe too deeply and risk his response. It was the third act that worried her. She could not control the way it would end. She could do nothing but wait, in dread and in anger.

The house was silent as she unlocked the front door. She was not surprised. Carrie, the lady who came in to clean from nine to five, had not expected her home so soon and had departed hours before her working day was over. The fact irritated Dru. She didn't like rip-offs, she didn't like being shortchanged. It didn't matter if it was the cleaning woman or her husband. She wanted people to be fair and they weren't.

Tears of resentment formed in her eyes as she entered the bedroom. She climbed on a chair to reach for her luggage stored in an upper closet and almost lost her balance. Damn Tim. Why wasn't he here to help? But then, if he were here perhaps she wouldn't be leaving. She was in no mood to examine the point.

When the phone rang she was choked with frustration.

"Hello," she said rudely.

"Well, you're in fine state."

"Oh, it's you, Tim. Sorry, but I've been struggling to pull down my suitcase. Carrie left early so she can't help, and I want to be ready when Gillian arrives."

"I'll make it brief then. Just wanted to wish you a pleasant trip."

"I'm not rushing you. I was only explaining why I sounded upset."

"I can't be too long anyway. It's three hours later in Washington, you know. I have to get to dinner."

"Now you're the one who's rushing. What's the great hurry?"

"For chrissakes, Dru, calm down. I simply mentioned that I have to leave soon to meet someone for dinner. It's an interview."

"Why did you bother to call if all you can say is Hello and Good-bye?"

"Take it easy, Dru. I didn't call to pick a fight. Or to get stomped into one either. Let's change the subject. What's new out there?"

"Nothing's new. Oh yes, one thing. Your friends the Hastings phoned. Or rather their secretary did. With one of those plastic dinner invitations. When I told her you were in Washington she said the Hastings would be heartbroken but they'd invite us again when you got back. Never even suggested I come without you. Love me for myself alone, do they? Next time they call, you can tell them to shove it."

"Dammit, don't blame *me* for the Hastings."

"Now you're the one who sounds mad. What's wrong?"

"What's wrong? You pick up the phone and first thing you jump down my throat."

"Look, I'm the one who's in a hurry. But you're the one who can't wait to hang up."

"You're damn right. I'm sorry I even called. And, to answer your question, a lot's wrong and you're not helping any."

She was immediately contrite. "Is it anything I said?'"

"Dru, you're impossible. It's nothing you said and nothing you did. For a woman who complains about her small ego, you're insanely self-centered. Can't you get it into your head that you're not *all* there is in my life? Other people affect me, too. I wasn't created out of your rib, you know."

"If that's the mood you're in, you could have sent a telegram: 'Having a terrible time. Glad you're not here.'"

"Next time I'll do that. If there is a next time."

And he was gone. Hung up, smack in her ear. She wanted to call him back but she had pride, also. If he was on his way out to meet one of those pushover Washington chicks, well, she had the satisfaction of knowing she had ruined his evening.

Satisfaction? She gathered up a few toiletries and an armful of sports clothes.

Then, with something considerably less than pleasure, she tossed them into her bag, and angrily snapped the locks.

V

Hurrying out of the supermarket in the Marina del Rey shopping center, Elena inhaled the pure sea air and hitched the heavy brown grocery bag higher on her hip. The sun was warm and the Pacific breeze curling around her body relaxed her. Checking the grocery bag, she could feel the bottle of margarita mix packed near the bottom. It was only a short walk to the apartment. She would head straight there, chill the mix, set out the tequila and some olives, and be ready for Barry when he got home. They would have a party, just the two of them, her first bon voyage festivity, and she was determined it would be gay.

She frowned, recalling the past months. How had Barry endured her—the black depressions, the crying spells, the drugged sleep that left her groggy in the morning? She couldn't get it together, it seemed. Not since the abortion. No, it was before the abortion, it was the night she told Barry she was pregnant—that was when everything began to unravel.

Not that she blamed Barry. He had spelled it out carefully for her before she moved into his place in the Marina. She had heard him through and nodded her head in mute agreement.

"Look, Elena, it's nothing personal. We care for each other, we can be happy together. But marriage—that's out. I've been that route. Eight years with one lousy ballbreaker. And why? Because from the day we met she drove me crazy in the sack. Biggest tits and the hottest box in history. And how she loved the fucking." He was silent a moment, remembering. "Then one day she brings me the big news. She tells me her parents are bugging her. 'There's got to be a wedding or it's all over.' Before I know it, I'm a husband. So what happens? A couple years later along comes the sexual revolution. The big free-for-all is on. Marriage is a joke. And me, I'm trapped and she's cooling down." He slapped his forehead with the palm of his hand. "Some smart lawyer I turned out to be. I needed someone to give *me* advice. Now she's liberated and putting out for free. And where am I? Still paying off dissolution fees and stuck with child support until I'm an old man. No, my little Elena, never again for dear Barry. Understand?"

She understood. She gave up her tiny flat on a side street in Santa Monica and moved into the Marina with him. The first time he brought her to his apartment she stood in the doorway, openmouthed. Her large black eyes roved over his living room, taking in the creamy white carpeting, the stark white walls hung with brightly colored geometric pictures, the red corduroy sofa, the mirrored bar, the shiny chrome-framed chairs and huge glass-topped coffee table. Beyond the window-wall, out on the sparkling water she could see the bustling powerboats and the sloops and the easygoing sailboats. She knew people lived this way. She had seen them posing in the home section of the Sunday newspapers, actors and writers, stunning models, and rising young attorneys like Barry Waterman. But she had never dreamed of actually entering such a world. Over in East Los Angeles, in the barrio where she was born and where her family still lived, you knew where you belonged and you planned to stay there until you were called by God.

Her call had come from a neighborhood employment agency. She had been working as a secretary in a local branch of the Bank of America when the middle-aged woman who ran the agency had phoned her to come in immediately.

Puzzled, she had used her lunch hour to visit her old friend, Mrs. Ricardo.

"Elena," Mrs. Ricardo said when she was seated in the shabby storefront office on Whittier Boulevard. "I have an unusual opportunity for you. That is, if you can bear to leave all this." Mrs. Ricardo waved her arm toward the noisy street and her voice turned bitter. "People like me, things happen and we get stuck here. All my life in this city and English is still my second language. Look at those signs out there. Everything Spanish. Those big advertisers, they want us to drive their cars and drink their beer and give them our American dollars, yet they condescend to us. They lock us in with language the way the city locks us in with their damned freeways. It's our fault, too. Some of us don't have the guts to fight for change." She paused abruptly. "How old are you?"

"Twenty-one."

"How long have you been at the bank?"

"Almost two years. Ever since you moved me from the insurance office on Breed Street."

"Still unmarried?"

"Yes."

"And you live in the barrio with your family? Ignore the question. Where else would you live?" Mrs.

Ricardo sighed. "How about some food? Like to go over to the Tico Tico? We can talk there."

Elena shook her head. "Thanks, I'm afraid I don't have the time. The bank doesn't like it if we're late."

"Naturally. Bankers run taut ships. Well, then—let's get down to business. This morning I had a call from an important legal firm in Century City, one of those huge ones with dozens of attorneys. They're looking for a secretary who is smart, attractive, and efficient. I'm no fool, Elena. They've never contacted me before. What they're saying between the lines is that it's good for their image to have a nice color mix around the office. I'm sure they've brought in some blacks. Now it's time to add a Chicana. The salary is very good—higher than anything I can get you here. I think you should give it a chance. You have all the qualifications and it may lead to something even better." Mrs. Ricardo's smile was wistful. "You're young. You still have options."

Elena had been thoughtful on her way back to the bank. Passing the open pool halls and cafés, the markets offering *Productos Mexicanos,* the beauty shop with the soiled placard listing its services and fees, the jumbled variety store, and the pet shop, its window still filled with lively yellow chicks—Easter orphans now that the holiday had ended—Elena had felt slightly disloyal. The barrio had always been her home. She had received all of her schooling within its boundaries. Growing up, she had often sneaked away to the nearby Robert Louis Stevenson Library, the oldest in the city, spending hours among the books she dared not bring home because Papa disapproved of females who filled their heads with nonsense. She was sorry she hadn't reminded Mrs. Ricardo of the library and the fiestas and the sweetness of the Spanish language. She thought of the *placas*, the brilliantly colored murals depicting inspirational scenes in Mexican history and religion, that were burgeoning on the once-drab walls of factories and warehouses, placed there by enthusiastic barrio artists. Apolitical herself, she sensed the fervor of young Chicano intellectuals striving right now to arouse the community to pride in its heritage and to give it backbone for its future.

Yet she had no doubt that faced with her own moment of decision she would make a dash for the exit. She knew that the following afternoon she would present herself to the personnel director of the law office in Century City, quaking but prayerful of acceptance by the Anglos that Papa detested.

The next evening as she sat with her parents around the dinner table in the weathered bungalow where she had been born, Elena told them she was leaving the bank to take a new job near Beverly Hills. Her mother said nothing, but her father was angry.

Ramon Valdez, an unskilled laborer whose harsh rule over his frightened wife and his three daughters had never been challenged, was a man who believed in the caste system and his family's place in it. "You not ask me about this new job!" he exploded, his cheeks flushing. "I say to you, don't be pushy. You don't go there."

"Papa, I told them I would start in one week."

"I tell you—you stay here. You got good job in Chicano neighborhood. Those fancy people, they laugh at you. You got dark skin and such black eyes, they say, and your hair—look at it—it's like Indian's hair."

She winced, but held fast. "They're nice people, Papa. The agency lady checked before she sent me out. It's a good place to work, beautiful, with drapes and carpets and furniture like a mansion. Some day I'll take you and Mama to see."

"No one goes there. Not you, not Mama, not me. It is settled."

"I've made up my mind, Papa. I want that job. The agency lady says I'm lucky to get such a break. There's a future for me."

"A future! Your future is here," he shouted. "You work couple years more, you get decent husband and children like Julia, that is your future!"

"Like Julia!" Now Elena was shouting. "Is that what you want for me, a life like Julia's?"

Her tone enraged him. "You forget yourself! You scream like a whore! Julia is good wife with good man who takes care of her. You get big ideas, no man will want you!"

"Julia is married to an animal. Tony gets drunk and beats her. Every time he sleeps with her, it's rape."

"You shut up your mouth this minute!"

"No, I won't shut up! Julia hates Tony and you don't think that's important. And Carmela—no wonder she locked herself up in a convent. She'd rather have no man than be a wife like Julia or Mama!"

His strong rough hand slashed across her cheek. "Get out! Make your own life! Don't come back here —never!"

Mrs. Ricardo took her in that night but it was Mama who helped her move out of Papa's bungalow and who came to visit her a few times in the little furnished place she rented on a side street in Santa Monica. When she told Mama about Barry Waterman, the young redheaded attorney from the office who sometimes dated her, Mama had been proud.

Later, when Barry Waterman found her the secretarial job with the Hollywood public relations firm of Lincoln and Rudolph, she told Mama the change was an advancement in her business career. She didn't try to explain to her mother that Barry wanted her out

of the office "for political reasons" before moving her
into his Marina apartment.

"Not good for the firm image, you know, having
a partner mixing it up with a secretary," he had said.
She never questioned his judgment. Where she came
from, you did what you were told if you wanted to
hold your man. Even Mama, looking sad, had understood.

Barry gave her a key of her own when she moved
into his apartment. "Now you've got the run of the
place, Ellie," he said. "That key opens the doors to all
the fringe benefits that come with the rent. Swimming
pool, sauna, gym, steam room, tennis courts. They're
all yours." He drew her to the window and pointed
toward the pool. "Except there's one word of warning,
baby. Keep out of the Jacuzzi. There's more whirling
around in there than the water. Down here, anyone
stays too long in the Jacuzzi, it's an open invitation to
get laid. You don't have to blink an eye, the whole
building knows you're flashing signals."

The impact of the Marina, the hedonistic, free-
wheeling life-style, was overwhelming. Elena longed
to discuss it with someone, to sort things out.

"Relax," Barry had said, trying to be reassuring.
"The Marina is nothing but a high-class barrio with
maid service. Sure there are boats and discotheques
and pickup bars, but the people aren't that different.
Everyone's just trying to get along, to have some fun.
We have more money so we try crazier things, that's
all."

The explanation hadn't satisfied her. At poolside
she had met Denise, an airline stewardess who lived
with a pilot operating out of Los Angeles International.
"It's a state of mind, living here," Denise said. "Take
Wayne and me. He's away a lot, so am I. Our flight
schedules don't always match so we have an agree-

ment. We both play around a little, nothing serious. When we're together no one else stands a chance. But when he's in Hong Kong and I'm in Boston—what's the difference?"

"Don't you want to get married?"

Denise grinned. "I've been married. To another pilot. He went to Hong Kong when I went to Boston."

Elena laughed. "You and Barry, the two of you make it sound so simple. What about Louis?"

"Louis?"

"The dentist. I hear things—"

"*That* guy. Louie the Loony. They come along like that once in a while. Poor little man. Louie spent years fixing teeth in the San Fernando Valley. After the patients went home he sneaked into his own waiting room and read back copies of *Playboy*. All that stuff about swinging singles finally got to him. One day he walked out on his wife and kids and moved down here. He was fortyish and he wanted a shot at what he'd missed. Lots of quiet men are like that," Denise mused. "Reminds me of those road signs: Last chance to fill up before you head into the desert."

"What happened to Louis?"

"The usual. He got what he thought he wanted, lots of sex. Scoring is easy in the Marina. Only it didn't change anything. Inside he still felt like Louie the Dentist. Pretty soon he was going out of his skull with loneliness. He tried to go home but his wife wouldn't take him back." She smiled pityingly. "Next thing we knew, the police found Louie out on his terrace with binoculars, zeroing in on the neighbors. They said he was sick, peeking into bedrooms every night. Louie said it wasn't like that at all, he was really looking into *kitchens*. He wasn't interested in other people's sex games. He'd had that trip. What he wanted was a part of their lives. The police didn't believe him, but I did."

Gradually Elena began to feel at home with her life in the Marina. With her name on the mailbox right under Barry's and her clothes hanging in the closet alongside his, she gained the sense of belonging she had been seeking. She and Barry frequented the Basement Cabaret, the Hungry Tiger, and Charley Brown's, and occasionally, like a pair of tourists, they dropped in to watch the action at the 2nd Storey, known to some as the biggest pickup joint in the area. Barry taught her to play tennis, and she swam in the pool every day, warily avoiding the Jacuzzi unless Barry was beside her.

Barry took her to the better restaurants in town, too, and whenever they ran into his friends and colleagues at the Bistro or La Scala, he introduced her as a public relations executive. She bought new clothes and she had her long hair shaped and smoothed. At the office of Lincoln and Rudolph she met movie and television personalities and, when invited to do so, shyly called them by their first names.

It was one night at Chez Jay's, near the beach in Venice, as the waitress placed their second margaritas before them, that she smiled at him across the candlelit table and broke the news.

"Barry," she said happily, "I'm going to have a baby."

He fixed her with a hard look. "You mean you're pregnant," he said, his tone legalistic. "That's quite a different thing."

She recoiled with hurt. "What—what are you saying—?"

"Look, Ellie, I didn't mean to sound like a bastard. It was just a shock, the way you put it. Everything can be taken care of. An abortion doesn't scare you, does it?"

"No—"

"Good. Phone your doctor in the morning. Tell him you want an abortion. First-class, no clinic. Don't worry about the bills, I'll handle everything. And for godsakes, don't worry about the operation. It's a breeze. There's this gynecologist I know—does more abortions than deliveries. Hasn't lost one yet."

"Maybe I *am* scared, a little."

He played with her fingers. "Darling Elena. Sometimes you're still the same timid kid who wandered into my office from East L.A. How long ago?"

"A year this spring."

"Hard to believe. It was my lucky day. Don't let this throw you. Tell you what—when it's over we'll go up to Mendocino for a few days. You work it out with your boss. The change will do us both good."

Remembering, she had to admit Barry had been a gentleman about everything. He never asked her how she happened to get pregnant. Nor did he ask her what happened in the hospital between the time he left her in the private room late one afternoon, and the time he picked her up late the following morning.

She appreciated his restraint. The whole subject was nothing she wished to discuss.

Feeling foolish, she had been wheeled from the hospital lobby to her room in an invalid's chair. A chatty nurse had shooed Barry out, saying it was necessary to begin the lab work.

While drawing blood, the nurse had asked if it was her first abortion.

Elena had been startled by the question. "Of course."

"Don't sound so surprised. We had one woman in here for her eighteenth. Weird, isn't it? Birth control devices available damn near everywhere, from the corner drugstore to the friendly family physician, yet we've got, maybe, a million, million and a half abortions a year in the U.S.A. alone. And worldwide—" The nurse shook her head, marveling. "Would you believe it, these days every third pregnancy ends in a deliberately induced abortion? In fact, if you add up all the money spent on different kinds of birth control, more than one half goes for abortion alone. So you see, kid, you're not so exclusive. Except you're on the luxury cruise."

"I am?"

"Sure. Most women get the job done in clinics. Decent enough. Friendly, antiseptic, efficient. But less privacy and they get you in and out in three or four hours."

"What happens here?" Elena asked weakly.

"Depends. How far along are you?"

"Nine weeks."

"First trimester." The nurse smiled comfortingly as she withdrew the syringe. "It'll be smooth as cream."

"I'm nervous."

"No need to be. Some women come in, they say it's easier than having a tooth filled."

"They can't mean it."

The nurse squeezed Elena's hand. "I don't believe them either, but you'll see, it's not too bad. In the morning you'll be given some Demerol. When you get into the operating room, you'll be draped and injected with two anesthetizing shots—one on either side of the cervix. Someone will roll up the trusty Vacurette machine—it's like a big cube with a long hose attached —and then the doctor will attach a narrow tube to the hose and insert it about two inches. He'll scrape away the matter from your uterus, and, presto, he'll suction up the remains. Takes him less than ten minutes."

"The remains?" Elena repeated.

"The broken products of conception, we call it."

"What happens to the—remains?"

"Goes to pathology in a jar." The nurse thought for a moment. "First trimester—fetus can't be more than an inch and a half long. Weighs less than an ounce."

"What do they do in pathology?" Elena's voice was barely audible.

"Routine stuff. No concern of yours." The nurse picked up her stainless steel tray. "Well, I've got what I need," she said cheerfully. "You get a good night's sleep, hon." She stood at the door, looking back. "In a week you and your boyfriend can be having relations again. It'll be like nothing happened."

After the nurse had gone, Elena had sat quietly, lost in thought. Barry had telephoned once, and later a light dinner had been brought on a tray. The tray, she observed, was covered with a paper doily bravely stamped to look like lace. White lace, like the lace on the dress she had worn for her first holy communion in Santa Isabel church when she was eight years old.

That evening there had been medication. Father in heaven, she thought as the drug began to take over, dear, dear Lord, what am I doing? In the morning, there had been more medication, and then everything had turned gauzy.

Gauzy. Like the caul that covers the head of a newborn baby. Only there was no baby. There was just the blissful dreamlike state, the undulating coming and going of consciousness as she was bumped along the hallway on a silent rolling bed. Had she slept or not slept? It didn't matter. Now she was on an operating table, smiling because she had never before felt so buttery and peaceful. Shimmering figures appeared around her. A man's voice asked if she was awake. Two women wearing green smocks glided nearby and one paused to hold her hand. Somewhere, beyond her draped and parted knees, she could hear the doctor murmuring and then his words were drowned out by the heavy hum of the suction machine, which sounded strangely like Mama's old Hoover vacuum cleaner running through the house in East Los Angeles.

Coming to, in the recovery room, she was aware of other patients, groggy or asleep on adjacent beds. Something was nipping her forehead. Reaching up, she touched the sterile paper bonnet that concealed her hair. Between her legs she could feel the bulk of the sanitary pad the doctor had said he would place there to absorb the postsurgical bleeding. An unfamiliar nurse beamed into her face and helped her to her feet.

Barry was waiting in the private room with a bouquet of pink sweetheart roses. He came toward her and kissed her and held her very close. Then he stepped outside while she dressed.

Barry kept his word about Mendocino, too. A week later they flew to San Francisco, rented a car at the airport, and drove north through verdant wine country and misty redwood forests until they arrived at the sedate hundred-year-old Heritage House overlooking the sea. At the desk in the original farmhouse, Barry registered them as Mr. and Mrs. They unpacked in a small Colonial-style cottage set apart from the others on the grounds, and then returned to the dining room in the sod-roofed white frame building to share a subdued supper and some champagne.

That night Barry made love to her for the first time since the abortion. Afterwards he tucked the covers around her and crossed the darkened room to his own twin bed.

Wide awake, she listened to the waves crashing against the wild coastline. Suddenly a terrifying sense of aloneness gripped her. She lay rigid as stone, her eyes open and unblinking, and stared at the ceiling.

A glimmer of moonlight touched the room. And then the pictures began to appear.

She saw her father first, cheerful for a change, oozing self-satisfaction and confidence in his unshakable machismo. Then his image faded and her mother's face rose before her, weary yet tranquil, her voice whispering that Yes, life with Papa was hard, but she knew she was safe and protected in her husband's home, that she belonged there. After her mother came Julia, ringed by all those demanding children but content because every one of them needed her. And finally sweet Carmela in her nun's habit, the headdress haloing her brow, radiating her serenity, her security in the loving arms of Christ.

I belong to no one, she told the vanishing pictures. *I am needed by no one. I am homeless. I am nothing. I want to be dead—very, very dead, very, very buried.*

Despair swept over her, but no tears came. Rising from some deep recess of her being she heard the terrible primitive sounds of her own dry sobs.

"Ellie, what is it? Were you dreaming?" It was Barry, hastily lighting the glass-bowled lamp that teetered on the stand between their beds.

She was sitting up now, struggling for control, wanting an end to the horrible guttural noise that only increased her fright.

"Oh, Barry, I'm so scared!" she gasped. "Barry, what can I do?"

Immediately he was beside her, on the edge of her bed. He pulled her close to him and with his free hand he stroked her face and her hair until the wracking sobs subsided.

"What is it, Elena?"

"Barry, Barry, I wanted our baby—"

He resumed his stroking but said nothing.

"Barry, I want us to be married."
"Sure, Ellie, sure. We'll talk about it."
"Someday, Barry—?"
"Sure, honey, someday."

Shortly after, they returned to the apartment in the Marina. Neither one spoke of that night in Mendocino. Several weeks later Barry came home and laid a handsome four-colored brochure before her. She reached for it eagerly.

"Where are we going?" she asked.

"Not we. You."

"But I don't want to go anywhere without you. Why can't we go together?"

"Because it's for ladies only. It's called The Fountains. It's a health spa, not far from Los Angeles."

"A health spa? Is that like a hospital?"

"A hospital!" he laughed. "Hell, no, it's more like a fantastic resort. There are only three or four places like it in the whole country. Rich women go there to shape up, tighten their muscles, lose weight, gain weight—whatever they need to make them beautiful. There's lots of exercise, massage every day, water games, dance lessons, nightly entertainment, daily beauty care. More pampering than you've had in your whole life."

"Barry, why me, in a place like that?"

"Because you deserve it, that's why. It'll perk you up, make you feel great."

"I don't want to go—"

"You *need* to go, Ellie," he said firmly. "It's all arranged. A week at The Fountains will do you a world of good. Lucky I could get you booked in. Most guests have to make reservations months in advance, but Christina Rossi is going down and she pulled some strings. You've met Christina. Remember? She used to

come into the office when you were there. She's still
one of my clients. Christina fixed it up for you. You're
leaving next week."

So once again Barry made the rules and she
obeyed them. He told her to request a week's vacation
from her job, and she did. He told her to gather up a
couple of swimsuits, some pants and tops, a sweater,
her tennis shoes, and one or two long skirts for evenings,
and she did. He told her to keep smiling, and with
some effort she did that, too. He was an angel, better
than she deserved, she reminded herself. No other man
would be so patiently supportive, so eager to keep her
enthusiasm high. This afternoon they would have their
private farewell party, and then they would get into
his car and drive down the coast to The Fountains.

She was showered and refreshed when Barry
came into the apartment and she greeted him brightly.
But as she brought him his margarita and set her own
on the cocktail table, she felt the familiar bubble of
anxiety surfacing.

"This is silly," she told him, "you spending all
that money when I feel fine. Really, I'm back to normal
again. Will they refund the deposit if we call it off?"

He sipped his drink. "Sweet Elena. Stop being
the little girl you were a year ago. A lot has happened
since then."

"Barry, I'm terrified. All those wealthy, sophisticated women. What will I say to them?"

"You'll say 'I'm pleased to meet you,' and 'Isn't
it a nice day,' same as you would to anyone."

"How will I act? They're accustomed to the best
places. Half the time I don't know which fork to use."

"Don't worry about forks, you won't get that
much to eat. Anyway, who do you think those women
are? A few discarded wives toning up before setting

out to trap a new man, a fading matron putting up a fight to keep from falling apart, some skinny East Coast model trying to get skinnier, maybe an actress or two drying out. And Christina herself—a Roman floozy until that young Count married her because he couldn't have his own mother. Think of *that* when you run into her down there."

They finished their drinks and he pulled her to her feet and kissed her.

"Ellie," he said in her ear, "don't be upset but I can't drive you down this afternoon. The damn Branigan case. I have to be on hand for an early evening conference. I've made a plane reservation for you. Your flight leaves in an hour. Get yourself together and I'll whip you over to the airport."

She was quiet on the short drive from the Marina to Los Angeles International. After he parked his car and turned her bag over to a porter, he accompanied her up the escalator to the departure gate. When her flight was announced, he kissed her again. "Stay cool, baby," he said and turned to leave.

"Barry," she called after him. "Barry, come back!"

"What is it, Ellie?"

"Barry, I won't know what to do. I—I—I've never had a massage!"

VI

Dr. Alfredo Bertini was not a *real* doctor, at least not in the sense that Americans understood the term. He did, however, encourage his guests to use the title because he believed it gave them greater confidence in his cherished Fountains and in its program.

In truth, Dr. Bertini was a lawyer. At home in his native Argentina he and others of his profession were quite properly addressed as doctor. A principled man, Dr. Bertini was scrupulously honest when anyone asked where he had studied medicine. He was less candid, even to himself, when explaining why he had made the transition from his first career to his current one.

The fact was that in Rio de Janeiro Dr. Bertini had had as a legal client the owner of a highly lucrative beauty spa that accommodated some of the wealthiest women in South America. Observing the prosperity of this enterprise over a number of years, it had occurred to Dr. Bertini that Southern California, which he had visited briefly, was ripe for another similar resort and that he, Alfredo Bertini, was the man to establish it.

With some family money, and with total dedication
to his concepts of good health, Dr. Bertini had origi-
nated The Fountains and brought it to its present
eminence.

It was rumored among the staff that Dr. Bertini
had left a wife and several children in Rio. It was also
rumored that he was entertained frequently by an
attractive socialite in nearby San Diego.

Dr. Bertini was not concerned with what the
staff thought about his personal life. All that mattered
to him was that they shared his goals for the welfare
of his guests. He wanted his ladies to depart from
The Fountains happier and healthier than when they
arrived, and oriented toward a way of life that would
sustain them in their pursuit of happiness between their
visits to his spa.

On this sunny spring afternoon, Dr. Bertini
viewed himself in his dressing room mirror and pro-
nounced himself satisfied. His body, which tended
toward stockiness, was slimmed down and taut, sternly
controlled by rigorous diet and exercise, two disciplines
he personally abhorred. His black hair had grayed
slightly in the years since he had come to Southern
California, and the silvery threads in his sharp pointed
beard and in his heavy eyebrows gave him a satanic
magnetism, particularly attractive to women who arrived at The Fountains convinced that only something
supernatural could save them.

Studying his face in the mirror, he was reminded
that his Latin good looks, like his faint accent, had
proved immediate business assets. It did not embarrass
him that he carefully avoided doing anything that
would diminish either of these advantages.

Despite his straightforwardness, Dr. Bertini did
permit himself a single deliberate, though minor, de-

ception. He often wore white slacks which he topped with a crisp linen jacket of the palest blue, a costume he knew *suggested* he was a medical doctor. It harmed no one, he rationalized, and if it had some subliminal and beneficial effect on his guests—well, so much the better.

Now, as he adjusted his tie and patted his beard, he began to prepare himself mentally for the weekly task he enjoyed the most, the confidential briefing of his staff.

Every Friday, after lunch, Dr. Bertini left the private cottage he occupied on the grounds of The Fountains and strode down gravel paths past sturdy palm trees, manicured grass, bright-blooming flowers, and the heated swimming pool to his beloved Renaissance Room.

Inspired by recollections of the eighteenth-century Teatro La Fenice in Venice, Dr. Bertini had created the Renaissance Room (bending history a bit to name it) as the cultural hub of The Fountains. Here, in this exquisite jewel box of a theater, guests who desired diversion gathered nightly for such innocent entertainment as the viewing of a movie, a stimulating lecture by an expert in astrology, wines, or precious jewels, or instruction in the art of flower arranging, gift wrapping, belly dancing, or macrame. By day, for those who wished to participate, the Renaissance Room offered yoga lessons. More often, it was used as a quiet retreat for a few minutes of meditation.

It was understood that on Friday afternoons all guests were barred from the Renaissance Room. This was the time reserved by Dr. Bertini to meet with his fifty-member staff to review the roster of the coming week's guests, known to himself and to his aides as The Batch.

It was Dr. Bertini's conviction that each in-

coming guest should be received like a welcome friend
at a dinner party rather than as a stranger arriving at
a foreign inn. Toward this end, Dr. Bertini personally
scrutinized all reservation forms for useful nuggets of
information about his guests. He also made discreet
inquiries where he could and relied upon his intuition
and experience whenever necessary. He told no one
that he kept the most recent editions of *Who's Who in
America*, the *International Motion Picture Almanac*, the
Television Almanac, and *Who's Who of American
Women* in a desk in his cottage, nor did he ever mention his secret card file, heavy with notations on past,
present, and potential guests.

He was neither nosy nor gossipy, he assured
himself, because the facts and insights that he accumulated and passed on to his staff at the appropriate
time were altruistically intended to give each guest
her own identity, and to arouse in the staff a heightened
sensitivity to individual needs.

As he approached the rear entrance to the Renaissance Room, Dr. Bertini reached for the gold-plated
doorknob, then hesitated. Today, he reminded himself,
would be different. Today he must be on guard, for
this was the first time he had broken his own rule. He
had invited an outsider to be present at a briefing . . .

Some months earlier, Dr. Bertini's secretary had
brought him a lengthy letter from the managing editor
of the noted fashion magazine, *Caress*. Dr. Bertini had
read and then reread the contents of the letter before
deciding that it merited serious consideration. The
magazine, the editor had informed him, was planning
a series of articles on the leading beauty spas in America. It had been promised the cooperation of Elizabeth
Arden's Maine Chance in Camelback, Arizona, Neiman-
Marcus's Greenhouse near Dallas, Texas, and Deborah
Mazzanti's Golden Door in neighboring Escondido,
California. No series would be complete, the editor

went on to say, without the inclusion of Dr. Alfredo Bertini's fabulous Fountains.

What the magazine proposed to do, the editor explained, was to send its highly regarded staff writer, Rita Sloane, to The Fountains to spend a typical week as a guest as well as a researcher. Knowing what they did of The Fountains, the editor and Ms. Sloane were certain the article would be immensely valuable to Dr. Bertini as well as to the hundreds of thousands of *Caress* readers who would be enthralled to learn what goes on in a world of beauty only an exclusive few might ever enter.

The letter had both warmed and worried him. It was flattering to be counted among the greats of his profession. Yet he was reluctant to subject himself— and his guests—to the exploring eyes of an experienced reporter. Business was excellent; he could scarcely accommodate all the women who wrote, telephoned, wired, and cabled for reservations. He questioned the wisdom of rocking his steady boat.

In the end, his ego had prevailed. He had admitted to himself that he would be devastated to be excluded from the company of Arden, Neiman-Marcus, and Mazzanti. He had responded to the editor in suitable time (no need to appear eager) and invited the magazine to send Rita Sloane to The Fountains. After some correspondence, a date had been set and she had arrived from New York this morning, a moderately pretty young thing (twenty-five years old according to his sources, born in Brooklyn, a graduate of Brooklyn College and the Columbia School of Journalism, and formerly with an advertising agency), looking not the least bit menacing. Still he would start out carefully. One never knew . . .

Dr. Bertini turned the doorknob and entered the Renaissance Room. Rows of fragile, gilt-finished chairs

faced the small stage and he could see that most were
already occupied. Nodding greetings, he hurried past
the mirrored walls, down the apricot-colored carpeted
aisle, notes clutched in his hand, and quickly took the
two steps to the parquet-floored stage.

Years earlier, on a trip to Italy, Dr. Bertini had
acquired a Venetian music stand, very old and delicately wrought, which he now used as his lectern.
Positioning himself behind the music stand, he spread
his notes on its tilted rack and beamed at his audience.
How he loved this moment! He was the general ad-
dressing his worshipful troops, the great leader bringing news of yet another victory.

"Dear ladies, fine gentlemen," he began. "How
delightful it is to have you gathered with me in our
little Renaissance Room. Once again I must congrat-
ulate you. Your accomplishments with last week's
Batch were, as always, remarkable. The lovely ladies
who left us today were renewed, refreshed, restored.
There *was* that one exception—but then we cannot make
miracles, can we? Those guests who are staying on—
most of them, anyway—report splendid progress and
joyfully anticipate another week of your attentions."

Pausing, he placed his hands on his hips and
grinned like a mischievous child.

"My dear staff, today I have a surprise for you.
Some of you may have noticed. We have a visitor among
us—yes, at one of our top secret meetings—and at *my*
invitation. You think I have taken leave of my senses?
No, my friends, not yet. Let me explain. She is Ms. Rita
Sloane of *Caress* magazine. She will be with us all
week." He looked about him dramatically. "And I must
warn you—she is here in her professional capacity. She
is going to write a story about us, so do be careful.
Ms. Sloane, will you please stand for a moment?"

As Rita Sloane rose to acknowledge the introduction, there was a polite spattering of applause. When it had faded away, and Rita was back in her seat, Dr. Bertini resumed.

"Rita, dear—I may call you Rita? We are informal at The Fountains—it is my purpose at this meeting to review for the staff our guest list for the coming week. As is customary, I will begin with our holdovers.

"Castle, Richards, and the Lyman twins are still here. No problems with any of them. In fact, the Lyman twins are ecstatic. When they arrived they both weighed the same. In a week, one twin has gained five pounds and the other has lost five pounds. They still look identical to me, so flat and tall and gangly. Unimportant. Each twin has set her own goal and for each we adjusted the diet accordingly. Now both are gratified. As long as a guest remains within a safe range, we strive to oblige her. Every woman must be happy with her own body. Kellogg, Coyne, Hart, and O'Connor are staying on. Rita, you will remember our agreement—no names unless I approve them. Now then, I must apologize to some of you for O'Connor. Also I beg your continued forbearance. O'Connor has been unconscionably rude all week. I am aware of that. Despite her wealth, she is a miserable woman. They say money cannot buy everything. I am afraid it does buy the right to be disagreeable to us. Sad but true.

"Coyne is another matter. A sticky situation there. She has come into my office several times to complain. She says she does everything she is told to do yet she has not lost an ounce. Yesterday, she called me a phony. Fortunately I had knowledge from the maids that they find Butterfinger wrappers in her wastepaper basket. I told her gently that I know what she is up to, and that I sympathize. I have faced that conflict in myself. We agreed she would stop by my office every evening just before retiring. There I will give her a brief inspirational talk. I cannot force her to give up her Butterfingers. That is a decision she must make for herself. Otherwise she will fall back into bad habits when she goes home. She does have a problem—her husband is wandering—she wants him back. I think she will make her own determination to slim down."

Stopping to pop a lozenge into his mouth, he scanned his audience and his glance fell on Rita Sloane. He was dismayed to see the amusement in her eyes and in her close-lipped smile. Her pencil, flying across the page of her open notebook, briefly concerned him. Recording angel or avenging angel, he wondered? He was familiar with the latter type—nasty, resentful, underpaid scribblers, ready to pounce upon his darling ladies merely because they were rich. Well, he had time to deal with this one—seven whole days to convince her they weren't all silly, vapid, pampered children.

Noisily he turned a page on the music stand. "Now to our returnees . . . Rita, dear, may I interrupt your note-taking? I think you should know this. At any time, at least eighty percent of our guests are people who have been here before. That is our finest testimonial. We desire no other. Some women have standing reservations to come to The Fountains every three months, others every six months. Still others come whenever they can fit us into their busy lives.

"So, let me tell you which of our old friends will arrive today. Jessica Haskell is coming—by commercial flight, I am sorry to say. Her husband needed his company plane to visit with associates in Barbados. That always makes her cross. No matter. She usually settles down in a day or two. Manuel—" Dr. Bertini located the swarthy young man in the audience. "Manuel, you have your instructions to meet her at the airport. I would suggest this time you wear your chauffeur's cap.

"Helen Reiser flew in from Washington this morning. Yes, another baby. Her ninth, I think. And Judge Reiser again shows his appreciation by sending her to us to get her back into shape." He shrugged elaborately. "And after we do, the Judge—well, that is not our affair. Melissa Dawes is on the night flight from Acapulco. She will remain two weeks before returning to Rome. The Texan, Sheila Henderson, also came in earlier, this time by way of San Francisco. Last night she was a guest of the Mayor at a benefit for the ballet. Leni Archer will be here. Her husband will drive her down. Same story. An important singing engagement next month. As usual, she will remain in her cottage most of the time. She's a bit—puffy. We will deal with the matter. We have before.

"Ah, Rita, your pencil is going too fast." He wagged his finger playfully. "Remember, my love, you promised to be discreet.

"Where was I? Yes . . . Once again, little Debbie Colson. As always, she will take the bus from her school in San Diego. Poor Debbie, perhaps not so little yet but thinner and happier than when her parents sent her here from Charleston a year ago. I must ask all of you to continue to extend particular kindness to Debbie. For a youngster of sixteen, she has shown extraordinary discipline in a difficult situation. Still, she needs all the support we can give her."

Seated uncomfortably on one of the absurd gilt chairs, listening to Dr. Bertini, Janet Wolfe tightened with resentment. Poor Debbie, my ass, she thought. Debbie needing support, attention, kindness. Well, to hell with Debbie. Okay, so the kid had had a bad time. Tough tittie. Janet recalled Debbie's history. At the time of her parents' divorce, Debbie had been a clumsy, lumpish child, almost sixty pounds overweight. Her

mother and father, after dividing their houses, their
cars, and their art collection, had looked at their un-
comely daughter and had not known how to dispose
of this last possession. It was then that a doctor friend
had stepped in and recommended a decompression
period for Debbie, far removed from both her parents.
After some investigation, the doctor had come up with
a boarding school in the San Diego area, close by The
Fountains. The grateful parents had immediately en-
rolled Debbie in both places—the school at once; The
Fountains whenever there was a school break. With
relief, they had shipped her to the West Coast and out
of their lives.

Debbie was thirty pounds lighter now, The
Fountains' only off-campus guest, and something of a
staff pet. But to Janet, she remained a symbolic irritant.

Janet had been a fat kid, too, but who had given
a damn? Not her parents certainly. What the hell had
they ever cared about *her* struggle to survive? They
were too absorbed in their own struggle, that was for
sure. Her weak salesman father and her timid housewife mother, forever filled with nameless anxieties, had
admitted no joy into their own lives nor into the life of
their only child. They lived meagerly, banked their
modest savings (their only extravagance had been the
purchase of adjoining burial plots), and nervously
awaited their inevitable doom.

Nor had any friendly doctor bothered to step forward to lend her a hand, Janet reminded herself. Hell,
no, just the opposite. A few relatives had opened their
traps, she'd never forget *them*. They had dared to ask
why she was going to college instead of to work. Lousy
big mouths. And her parents hadn't defended her, nor
mentioned that she *was* working, even while she went
to school. Later, when she graduated from UCLA as a
physical education instructor, she heard her parents

boast about her. Didn't she have the only degree in the whole ignorant family? And an apartment of her own?

Let's not forget the apartment. Soon after graduation she had landed a job in the Phys. Ed. department at Palisades High School, and overnight moved into a small place near the school. It had been her first taste of freedom, her first release from the stifling air she had breathed in her parents' house. She had reveled in her privacy, sought few friends, and had had no further goals.

The loss of her teaching job had come as a severe blow. The Governor of California, after numerous threats, had managed to cut the State's school budget (although leaving his own salary untouched) and many Phys. Ed. teachers had been wiped out of employment.

Janet was thirty-four years old at the time. Joblessness terrified her, and the quavering worry in her parents' voices only increased her own anxiety. Her overriding concern was that her savings would be exhausted and that, broke, she would be forced to return to her old room under her parents' roof, an event mutually feared by all three of the Wolfes.

It was her mother, of all people, who had come up with the suggestion that had saved her.

Glumly watching television one night, Mrs. Wolfe had startled her daughter by leaning forward suddenly and exclaiming, "Look, look at the movie!"

"Jeesus, Ma! What do you think I'm doing?"

"I mean look what's happening!"

"I *see* what's happening. What's the matter with you?"

"Look, the lady is getting a massage! What an idea I got for you!"

"Calm down, Ma. What are you babbling about?"

"Massage, Jannie—you—"

"Big idea. Just what I need—a massage."

"No, you got it wrong. You could *give* massages —like in the picture."

"That's revolting."

"I mean it, Jannie. You learned—in school—all about the body."

"So what do I do? Get in the movies?"

"Now you're being fresh. You know plenty people. All those no good mothers you *yenched* about. You said they didn't care even when their own kids were in trouble."

"What are you getting at, Ma?"

"You said they were so selfish, all they did was sleep late and go to lunch and shop around for new clothes and worry about getting fat."

"So?"

"So—so they would love it, Jannie, if you went to their house, like on the television, and give them a massage. And I bet the pay would be good."

"Ma, you're out of your head."

But the idea had taken root. As the jobless weeks continued to pass it became clearer to Janet that the future held no hope unless she took a drastic step. Her mother had never again raised the subject of massage. Instead, one Friday night after dinner, she had whispered, "Jannie, don't look so worried. Pa and me, we'll always have a room for you here."

The following morning, Janet had seated herself before her telephone, her old student roster on the table beside her, and had begun to make calls. The response had astonished her. She knew most of the women were lazy and self-indulgent. What she hadn't guessed was how eager they were for one more effortless time-waster.

Encouraged by the calls, she had bought herself

a portable massage table and several white nurse's uniforms and, complying with the law, she had registered with the police department. She also purchased an engagement book and a large imitation-leather cosmetics case that she filled with creams and oils and cooling eyepads. With disbelief, she found herself in business. She was a masseuse.

From the start, she loathed the demeaning white uniform and she resented lugging her massage table in and out of other women's homes. She detested clients who forgot their appointments or kept her waiting by ambling in late from some amusing activity. And she had no sympathy for those who summoned her at night to relax them when they couldn't sleep. Still, she understood that willingness and good cheer were important ingredients of her service, and she offered these without protest. The Janet Wolfe that her clients knew was an unshakably pleasant woman and every last one of them adored her.

Janet owed her present position at The Fountains to one of those grateful ladies, a certain Mrs. Holcomb. During a visit to The Fountains, Mrs. Holcomb had raved about Janet to Dr. Bertini, who was looking for a third masseuse to add to his staff. An embittered divorcée, Mrs. Holcomb was moving to New York anyway, and it pleased her to deprive her friends of Janet's services as a kind of farewell gesture.

Dr. Bertini's offer had been immediately intriguing. Janet had welcomed the distance the new job would put between her and her parents, and she was flattered by the generous salary Dr. Bertini was prepared to pay. With no regret, she had notified her clients and her landlord that she was leaving town for an indefinite period.

Four years had passed since she had come to The Fountains and they had not been too bad. Her colleagues on the staff were a decent lot, and the house she rented nearby was an improvement over the apartment in the Palisades. The women she massaged at The Fountains were, in her opinion, as vain and empty as those in Los Angeles, but they came and went swiftly and were therefore more bearable. From time to time, she encountered a real killer and then she would stalk up to Dr. Bertini to complain. Dr. Bertini was unfailingly soothing and always took her side. She suspected he then trotted off to the offending guest and took *her* side also, and the thought annoyed Janet. However, she had long ago learned to mask her irritations. She supposed she could fake her way through one more week of being polite to Debbie Colson.

Tuning back in, Janet found that Dr. Bertini was still reading from his list of returnees.

"—last summer. After Charlotte finished her stay with us she went off to France. I will refresh your memories—a slim woman, reddish-brown hair, midforties, perhaps a year or two younger, somewhat melancholy when she arrived. At the time, newly divorced after a long marriage. Her most recent letter came from the same address in Chicago—the exclusive Gold Coast, by the way—but I have been unable to learn what has happened to her in the interim. As all of you know, some women in middle life sail through divorce quite easily; others suffer the trauma for many years or forever. With Charlotte you will have to—how do you say?—play it by ear. Try to sense her needs but do not inquire into her personal life. She will tell you what she wants you to know. And, naturally, you will share with me anything you learn, so I too can strive to make her visit a happy one.

"Manuel, we are fortunate. Charlotte Caldwell's plane arrives twenty minutes before Jessica Haskell's. I think Charlotte will not mind too much if she must wait for your other passengers."

Riffling the papers on his music stand, Dr. Bertini found the page he was seeking.

"The Immigrants," he announced. "Now we come to the Immigrants . . . Rita, my dear, do put down your pencil.

"In no way is my use of the word to be construed as a pejorative description of the guests I am about to discuss. To those of us at The Fountains, the word Immigrants means first-timers—strangers to our shores. It is to them that we offer a special kind of attention. Some may be spa-wise, having visited the resorts of my honored colleagues here and abroad. They may have preconceived notions of what they will be offered at The Fountains. We like to know their expectations so they will not be disappointed. Others may be embarking on a totally new experience and be somewhat unsure of themselves. We want those women to be put at their ease as soon as possible.

"This week we have only three Immigrants. From their reservation forms I have learned that none of them has ever before visited any spa. Loretta Marshall, our hostess, will chat with each of them this evening. Rita, you think that is funny? Perhaps to you it sounds like a preoperative procedure? Let me assure you, we find that a personal talk with our Loretta is the best medicine to make a guest feel comfortable and at ease.

"So now, staff, we meet our Immigrants. The first one is Drucilla Jennings. You may be familiar with her name. A former television scriptwriter and many times an Emmy Award winner, Drucilla is now an associate producer and executive story editor at the Columbia Broadcasting System in Hollywood. Remember *Feather My Nest?* That was one of hers. Currently she is in-

volved with *Dynamite* and *Sara on My Mind*. She is
thirty-three years old and, fortunate lady, she is married
to the noted political columnist, Timothy Larsen. Their
home is in Brentwood, a section of West Los Angeles.
They have no children. Drucilla prefers to keep her
professional identity separate from her husband's and
has retained her maiden name. At the same time, she
is a rather retiring and modest person and probably
will not wish to discuss either her own work or her husband's. I foresee no difficulty with Drucilla. Responsible
professional women usually adjust very well to the discipline of our program.

"Drucilla will arrive with our second Immigrant,
her friend, Gillian Crain. The two women have asked
for adjoining cottages and will be neighbors in our
Leonardo Wing. Gillian is thirty-six years old and describes herself as a homemaker. I happen to know that
she is the only child of Lawrence Delman, the celebrated art dealer. She has one child of her own, a
daughter. Her husband—" Dr. Bertini frowned. "Her
husband is not known to my usual sources. The telephone directory describes him as a real estate broker.
The residence address in Beverly Hills is excellent. The
Crains—his name is Jason—belong to a fashionable tennis club. Gillian is devoted to cultural causes and active
in fund-raising events. The photograph in a recent
newspaper clipping suggests they are a handsome couple. Manuel, note this—Drucilla and Gillian will drive
down together from Los Angeles, so you need not be
concerned with meeting them.

"Our final Immigrant is Elena Valdez. She is
twenty-two years old and lives in Marina del Rey. The
Marina, as some of you may be aware, is one of Southern California's marvels. It is a new community, chic,
lively, famous for its population of well-to-do, uninhibited unmarrieds. Mostly professional and creative
people. I myself have never been there." He sighed rue-

fully. "I am told it is no place for a man past thirty-five—even one in top-notch condition. Elena's reservation was made by our dear friend, Christina Rossi, at the request of her attorney, Barry Waterman. Elena herself is a member of a major Hollywood public relations firm. I do not know her exact position there. According to Christina, the young lady has not been well lately. I do not know if she has been ill, or merely overworked. But treat her with your usual consideration.

"Manuel, pay attention. Miss Valdez had expected to drive down to The Fountains but there was a sudden change in her plans. Her flight arrives at Lindbergh Airfield from Los Angeles at—let me see—oh, dear —almost a half-hour after Jessica Haskell's. Impossible to bring Charlotte and Jessica here and get back to the airport in time to meet Elena's flight. Jot this down, Rita—it is one of my rules—an Immigrant must never be kept waiting. That would be a most inhospitable beginning.

"Manuel, it is up to you. You must chatter and be charming for Charlotte and Jessica. Fuss around a bit with the luggage. Make the time go by. Jessica, particularly, must not realize she is being detained. It would take all week to calm her down. Let us pray that Jessica's plane will be delayed and that Elena's will not."

Dr. Bertini began to gather up his notes. "And there you have it, our Batch for the new week. No, wait. How could I have forgotten? Christina, herself— you need no introduction to Christina Rossi. She will be here, too, in her own good time. That frivolous girl. A glorious costume party in Bel-Air tonight, and tomorrow she must stay in her bed to recover. She will join us when she can.

"So, dear ladies and gentlemen, I thank you for your time. Until our cocktail hour, I bid you adieu."

Sweeping his notes from the music stand, Dr.

Bertini prepared to descend from the stage into the rapidly emptying theater. A figure, standing alone, caught his eye.

"Rita, dear," he called out, "wait for me. May I show you over the grounds, escort you to your room, perhaps?"

"You're very kind, Dr. Bertini. But no walk just now, thank you."

He was by her side, moving up the aisle. "My talk tired you?" He registered mock horror. "Or worse yet, bored you?"

"No, no—it's my inner time clock. My body is still on Eastern time."

"But you look so rested. No, I think you must be in a hurry to reach your room and write up your notes."

"Of course, that, too—"

"A word of advice?"

"I'd be most appreciative."

"Do not waste too much time on what you have heard in this room. Our little session here—that was merely the overture. It is tonight that the curtain goes up."

The jovial, wrinkled skycap waved as Manuel slid the station wagon into the passenger loading zone of the Charles A. Lindbergh Airport in San Diego. They were old friends, these two, veterans of many meetings on this parking strip. The skycap enjoyed teasing Manuel about all the women the younger man met, never failing to joke lewdly about the fun Manuel must have at that walled-in paradise outside of town. Manuel liked the skycap's game; it enhanced his *macho* image of himself. But the women themselves were of little interest to Manuel.

A few years earlier when Manuel, recently out of California State Polytechnic Institute in Pomona with a degree in horticulture, had joined Dr. Bertini's staff, his bride had been jealous of the gilded women who moved temptingly and often half-clad over the lawns and paths of The Fountains where Manuel went about his job as head landscape gardener and part-time driver. To reassure her, Manuel had sneaked her onto the grounds and allowed her to see for herself that she was prettier than any of them, and she had gone away placated.

Only Manuel (and Dr. Bertini) knew there had been that one lapse in fidelity—with the beautiful, neglected wife of a famous movie star. Manuel still remembered how that sad creature had seduced him from his beloved flowers one hot July afternoon and, in her darkened cottage, hungrily opened herself to him. Never in all his experience had he known a woman with so magnificent a body nor one who responded so quickly. He had barely touched her and she had been off like a rocket. She had remained three weeks and, day after day, while the others rested, Manuel had slipped into her bed and made love to her. They scarcely spoke, either in her cottage or when they glimpsed each other on the grounds, and Manuel understood he meant nothing more to her than relief from her savage frustrations. She had disappeared from The Fountains without saying good-bye and Manuel had hoped she would find someone else who could satisfy her.

The week following her departure, Dr. Bertini had called him from his roses to show him a note from the movie star's wife. Manuel had tensed but he quickly saw there was no reason for concern. In sparse sentences, the lady did no more than thank Dr. Bertini for the unexpected pleasures she had found at The Fountains. The two men had looked at each other solemnly until Manuel had nodded his head and returned to his flowers.

Earlier today, in the Renaissance Room, Manuel had only half-listened to Dr. Bertini describing the new Batch, and he had been attentive only when he heard his own name. He knew he was expected to meet three guests at the airport, and he had a neatly typed card bearing their names and times of arrival. He needed no physical description of the women. He had long ago devised his own method of spotting The Fountains' guests as they came up the ramp from their landing gates.

"They wear uniforms," he had told his wife one morning at breakfast.

"You're talking nonsense."

"No, I mean it. They dress alike."

"Like convent girls? Like waitresses? I don't believe you."

"It's true. And the joke is that they don't even know it."

"If you want to pull my leg, it is better in the bedroom."

"No, I'm serious. Look in your newspapers and magazines. You'll see their uniforms—Ultrasuede pant-suits, cashmere coats, Gucci shoes, Vuitton traveling bags. If they come from a cold climate, they bring a mink coat. And the designers' initials—everywhere. On shoes, on scarves, on blouses. They are like tattooed women."

"You are teasing—"

"I am not. They devote their lives to appearing special and they end up looking like peas in a pod."

After winking broadly at the skycap, Manuel hurried into the brightly tiled terminal and headed for the illuminated flight-arrival board. Flight #61. From Chicago. On time.

Stationing himself at the gate, he watched as the

passengers from flight #61 deplaned. Almost at once, he picked out the one he wanted. It was too easy. Amid the shuffling bodies clad in permanent press and polyester, she stood out like a porpoise in a swimming pool. Carefully tailored taupe wool dress, Gucci shoes, Mark Cross handbag—and a dark mink coat over her arm.

Immediately he hastened to greet her. "Mrs. Caldwell. I am Manuel, from The Fountains. May I take your coat?"

Startled, Charlotte clutched the coat tightly. "How do I—? How did you know me?"

"Madam has been here before."

"Almost a year ago. You can't possibly have remembered."

"I remember."

Surrendering the coat, Charlotte put her baggage claim checks into his outstretched hand.

"Two bags," she said. "I'd better go with you."

"That won't be necessary." His white teeth shone between his parted lips. "I'll have no trouble picking them out."

"Where is the car?"

"Madam, Dr. Bertini asked me to explain. Three guests are coming in this afternoon. You are the first. There will be a small delay before the others arrive. Dr. Bertini wishes me to apologize. He hopes you will not mind."

She shrugged. "Where would you suggest I wait?"

"There is the San Salvador cocktail lounge, a magazine stand, a souvenir shop—"

"I have a small grandson. I'll be in the souvenir shop."

Twenty minutes later, with his peaked chauffeur's cap carefully adjusted atop his black hair, Manuel stood at the terminal gate and watched flight #11 disgorge its passengers from New York. No need to test his identification skills with this one. He'd recognize her bare-assed. Jessica Haskell. A bitch on wheels. Born to a faded foreign title, mårried to a steel-manufacturing tycoon, spoiled evil from the cradle. He could see the petulance on her face as her gaunt body descended the steps from the plane and crossed the airfield to the terminal. He checked his wristwatch. Damn. The plane was right on schedule. He dreaded telling her he could not whisk her off at once to the comforts of The Fountains.

"Mrs. Haskell—" He tipped his hat politely.

"Where is the car?"

"It is right through the door, at the curb."

"I'll meet you there after you get my luggage."

"Mrs. Haskell—"

"Yes?"

"Dr. Bertini hopes you will forgive us. An unexpected change in scheduling. We must wait for another guest. It will not be long. Perhaps—"

"This is ridiculous. I've had a terrible flight."

"I am very sorry."

"Take my baggage checks. Where is the bar?"

Something had gone wrong. Once again, he studied the typed card listing the expected arrivals. The Los Angeles-San Diego flight had appeared on schedule ten minutes ago. He had been at the right place at the right time, but he had not seen anyone who could be Elena Valdez. He considered having her paged on the loudspeaker system at the Traveler's Aid desk, but rejected the idea. Occasionally, one of The Fountains' guests desired anonymity. He could not risk broadcasting anyone's name over the whole terminal. He decided to make one more circuit of the place. He had already stopped by the souvenir shop in the Cabrillo Court where Mrs. Caldwell had finished her shopping and was restlessly thumbing through magazines. After assuring her they would soon be on their way, he had scrambled over to the cocktail lounge to deliver the same message to Mrs. Haskell. Luckily, Mrs. Haskell appeared to be getting on well with the bartender. She had ordered another drink and told Manuel she was in no hurry to leave. Nevertheless, Manuel was growing uneasy. He could not continue to hang around the airport, yet he could not take off without Elena Valdez.

And then he saw her. She was huddled on a bench near the luggage wheel, a dark-skinned young girl wearing pink cotton pants and a flowered top that exposed her smooth midriff. In one hand, she held the four-color brochure of The Fountains. The fingers of her other hand played nervously with wisps of straw torn loose from the purse on her lap. A wicker suitcase sat on the floor beside her. She looked like a lost child. He suspected she had been crying.

"Miss Valdez?"

She raised her head and stared at him. "Yes?"

"I am Manuel, from The Fountains. We are happy you are here."

"Thank you."

"I am sorry I didn't find you sooner. I've been searching everywhere. I thought you would be—older."

"It's all right."

"May I take your bag? Please come with me. I will make you comfortable in the station wagon, and then I will bring the others."

They had been riding in the station wagon for a quarter of an hour and they still had ten minutes to go. The conversation in the back of the wagon had died down and Manuel felt relief. After introducing the

women, he had taken his place behind the wheel of
the car and tried, without success, to ignore their talk
and concentrate on his driving. At the start, the queru-
lous, thickened voice of Jessica Haskell had dominated.
Good-humored when she entered the wagon, she had
soon turned surly. When the other two ceased to respond, she had fallen silent.

Manuel hoped he had made the right decision
about Jessica. He knew Dr. Bertini took a hard position
on guests who drank. Only recently he had reminded
the staff that any woman who turned up drunk was to
be escorted without delay to the nearest motel and requested to remain there until sober. With some trepida-
tion, Manuel had decided to make an exception of
Jessica Haskell. He felt personally responsible for her
overlong visit to the cocktail lounge. Also, it was his
judgment that the drive would clear her head.

With sinking heart, he heard her voice break
the stillness. This time she sounded downright com-
bative.

"Aren't you chilly, Miss Valdez?" she was asking
critically.

Through his rearview mirror, Manuel could see
the girl defensively pull the straw handbag closer
against her bare midriff.

"Just a bit, Mrs. Haskell. It was warmer in Los
Angeles. I—I didn't know what to expect."

"Clearly—"

Charlotte Caldwell turned to Elena. "That's a
charming outfit, dear. My daughter has one almost like
it."

"Thank you."

"I admire you young things." Jessica again. "It
takes a lot of nerve to dress that way."

Glancing over his shoulder, Manuel saw Charlotte place her hand over Elena's and squeeze it before

looking at Jessica Haskell. "My dear Mrs. Haskell," she said, "it takes a lot of years to *stop* dressing that way."

And, once again, there was silence.

The little red Mazda with the two women inside tooled down the highway like an overfed bug hurtling along under the late-day sun. The driver, her green eyes concealed behind dark glasses, softly mouthed the lyrics of the ballad pouring from the car's stereo, scarcely aware of the brooding companion beside her. Since leaving Los Angeles, dialogue between the pair had been sporadic and desultory. Both preferred it that way. The brooding one was afraid to speak, fearing her voice would break, inviting questions. The driver sat wrapped in some enchantment all her own and wanted no intruder.

Gillian Crain and Drucilla Jennings considered themselves close friends. They were proud of their relationship. It was free of hostility, unblemished by competitiveness. They were entities from different backgrounds, drawn to each other by genuine liking and shared interests. They loved chatting on the telephone, visiting over lunch, exchanging gossip and anecdotes, joining up on the tennis court and at dinner parties. They knew each other very well—yet not at all, for they understood the tribal rites of their social set, and especially the rules of the friendship game they played. Share, share everything—except real intimacy. Tell, tell all—but never what really matters to you. Hold back how you feel, conceal what is important, never confide what gives you the greatest joy or the deepest pain. Why take the chance? Today's friend may turn into tomorrow's viper. Cultivate a bosom companion if you must. But it's safer to keep her away from your bosom and at arm's length.

These two close friends, Gillian and Dru, had

met on the courts of the Los Angeles Tennis Club shortly after Dru and Tim were married. Thrown together for mixed doubles, the men had been mutually uninterested in developing a friendship, but the women had sparked instantly. In the years since, Gillian and Dru had grown increasingly fond of each other. It appeared perfectly natural to both husbands that their wives would choose to visit a beauty spa together. They were two babes off on a sybaritic picnic. Nothing could be more innocent.

In Gillian's little red Mazda the ballad spilling from the stereo ended abruptly and Gillian reached out and turned off the radio. The sentimental lyrics had distracted her from the more intriguing entertainment going on in her head. Like a child arranging a pageant with the contents of a toy box, she first evoked the ugly scene at home with Jason, then quickly she removed it. She was mellow now, softened by distance and by erotic fantasies of Dr. Karl. Jason was too vague, too remote to stay long in the scene. Only she and Dr. Karl were real players on her stage. The two of them in his office, the two of them at The Fountains, and in their motel rendezvous. She and Dr. Karl—and always the image of the splendid violence of their bodies, joining, parting, joining, until—

"Gillian, I'm sure we've passed it!" The brooding figure beside her had come alive. "Over there. The place with the pink walls."

"Dammit, I wasn't paying attention."

"Swing around in the side road—it's back a bit, through those wrought-iron gates. Can you believe it? The blooming Taj Mahal—and an honest-to-God leaping fountain. What are we getting into?"

VII

The idiot telephone in the bedroom would not quit. Once, twice before, it had bullied its way into her head in a series of persistent rings. Each time Gillian, lazying in her bubble bath and daydreaming of Dr. Karl, had chosen to ignore it.

Now, aware it would continue or, worse yet, bring someone to her cottage to see if she was safe, Gillian decided it had to be answered.

Tufts of bubbles clung to her skin as she padded across the carpeted bathroom floor to the telephone in the adjoining room.

"Loretta here. Found you." The voice on the other end was triumphant.

"Loretta—" Gillian sought to link the voice to one of the many women she and Dru had met since their arrival at The Fountains late that afternoon. Loretta. Loretta Marshall. Of course, The Fountains' designated hostess. Large, rawboned, New England regal, Loretta Marshall, wearing a simple black dress and lots of chains, had been standing at the entrance when she and Dru had stepped into the Reception Hall of The Fountains for the first time. It was Loretta who had indicated where they were to register and who eventually had led them to their individual cottages.

"Each suite is unique," Loretta had explained, as they followed a baggage boy down a gravel path. "We've chosen the Empire for you, Gillian, and for you, Dru, something a bit more Italianate."

In Gillian's cottage she had pointed out the closets concealed behind elaborate *boiserie,* the panel in the bedside stand with three pushbuttons for piped-in music, the array of fresh cosmetics and lotions on the dressing table, and the radiant heat in the bathroom ceiling. Finally, she had departed. Gillian had been happy to see her leave; the syrupy charm was irritating, the very presence of the woman an invasion of her fantasies.

And here was Loretta again, the nasal voice slightly reproachful. "You had me worried, dear."

"I was resting."

"It's seven o'clock. We're waiting for you."

"Waiting for me?"

"Did you forget? It's cocktail hour. We're all gathered in the Garden Room having our drink."

"I'd rather not."

"Do come, dear. It's just across the lawn. You'll enjoy it. We always mingle before dinner." The words were coaxing, the tone insistent.

"If you say so."

"Just jump into something comfy. We're casual here."

Returning to the bathroom to find a towel, Gillian passed the full-length mirror that hung on the connecting door. Her body, hastily glimpsed as she went by, suddenly fascinated her. Pivoting, she slowly came back to the mirror, gliding with the easy grace of a woman approaching a waiting lover. Self-hypnotized,

she studied her slim figure, still glistening with dampness from the bath water. Wisps of hair, escaping from
pins that held the golden mass high on her head,
touched her smooth neck. Remnants of soap bubbles
clung to her full round breasts and their rosy areolas.

Entranced, she allowed her gaze to rove over
her slender hips and lean stomach and then to her pubis.
With eyes still fixed on the mirror, she released the
hair piled on her head and let it tumble to her shoulders.
Then, like a clubwoman appraising her accessories before departing for lunch, she compared the hair tones
and noted with pride that they matched. In this era
of bleaches and tints how many women could make
that claim? Damn few, she was sure.

Dr. Karl was right. She was very nearly perfect.

Without moving from the mirror she reached for
a towel on a nearby glass-topped table. Stroking her
body dry, she felt each movement of the towel heighten-
ing her own sensuality and her need for Dr. Karl.

A loud rap on the door roused her.

"Gillian, it's Dru. Are you ready?"

"Still dressing."

"Did the headmistress call you? I fell asleep on
that heavenly bed."

"Me, too."

"Want me to wait?"

"No, pet. Hurry along. And Dru—order me a
Scotch on the rocks."

As Dru's footsteps receded on the brick porch
that fronted their adjoining cottages, Gillian turned before the mirror and contemplated the rest of her body.
The silky back, the buttocks curved like porcelain
globes, the remarkably long legs, mesmerized her.
Searching for flaws, she found none.

Still marveling at herself, she realized that Dr.
Karl had never seen her this way. How could he in the

rough-and-tumble and haste of their office encounters?
But here . . .

But here . . .

Frowning, she recalled her shock at coming face
to face with the reality of The Fountains. What a total
dunce she had been. At no time, in anticipating this
week, had she given more than a fleeting thought to
anyone but herself and Dr. Karl, and to Dru as a device
to bring them together. Only the motel and its promised
pleasures had existed for her. The noisy women flocked
in the Reception Hall, the poised hostess, the effusive,
bearded man who called himself Dr. Bertini, all of them
had taken her by surprise. Dazed, she had stared at
these rude trespassers in her private world. They weren't
supposed to be here; they belonged somewhere else,
faraway.

Pulling her thoughts together, she had confronted the facts. She was not in a secluded trysting
place. She was in a spa called The Fountains. There
would be crowded, structured days here, and dozens of
people with shared purposes. She would have to play
along if she wanted to achieve her reward.

Soberly, she had surveyed her surroundings and
dwelt a moment on her reward.

It would be worthwhile.

She drew a blue silk caftan from her suitcase and
pulled it over her head. Then she stepped into silver
sandals, pulled her hair back into a ponytail and
started across the grounds to the Garden Room.

The idea of a drink appealed to her. A good
stiff Scotch might be just what was needed to survive
the ordeal of the evening ahead.

Unlike her mother who thrived in the company
of women, Gillian had always zealously shunned all-
female society. Even the women's consciousness-raising

group she had joined in Beverly Hills had failed to involve her. She had remained aloof, contributing nothing. Within weeks she had dropped out, convinced that the solution to her own unrest was not to be found among other questing women, however earnest and intelligent they might be.

It had been soon after her experience in the women's group that Bitsy's analyst had mentioned Dr. Karl and she had gone to see him. Nothing since her meeting with Dr. Karl had aroused any need for the further group company of women. To find herself trapped, because of him, in a virtual nunnery, was the supreme irony.

Cheered by the thought of the drink that awaited her, Gillian drew a deep breath and opened the door to the Garden Room.

The high decibel level in the room assaulted her, increasing her need for the drink. A quick glance told her the room itself was quite lovely. But once again there were women, hordes of them it seemed, polluting the surroundings. They were off to her right, clustered about a huge coffee table before an unlit fireplace, chattering and laughing, providing a raucous, ear-shattering chorus.

Gillian watched as Loretta Marshall detached herself from the group and hurried forward to greet her.

"You made it," Loretta said with satisfaction. "And how pretty you look. Here, let me pin on your name tag."

"My what?"

"Your name tag. We all wear them for the first day or two until we're truly acquainted."

"Must I?"

"Nobody *must*. It's just cozier that way."

Nodding dumbly, Gillian allowed Loretta Marshall to pin the small plastic nameplate to her caftan, then looked about for Dru and deliverance.

"Your little friend? She's there in the group. Let me take you over to meet the others."

"If you don't mind, not yet. I'd like to get my bearings. The room—it's so handsome."

"Certainly, dear. How about a cocktail? Shall I bring it to you here?"

"Please. Scotch on the rocks."

Loretta Marshall looked at her oddly. "We're all having the same thing."

Then, she shrugged and went off.

Waiting for Loretta to return, Gillian studied the Garden Room. Her mother would love this, she thought. Quiet elegance (if anything could be called quiet amid the din coming from her right). In a far corner, a splendid, lacquered Coromandel screen, embedded with mother-of-pearl and jade, rose toward the high ceiling. On the walls, huge Venetian mirrors topped bombé chests. Off to her left, a single table on a dais and three or four tables below it were circled by thickly padded Louis XVI chairs. The tables were draped and set with the formal perfection of a layout in *House Beautiful.*

But it was the view straight ahead that held her. Running the length of the room was a tall bare picture window, and beyond it the garden that gave the room its name. In the deepening twilight it was breathtaking. Brilliant flower beds bordered gravel paths; fine old trees, some evergreen, others just leafing into spring foliage, overlooked lush expanses of grass; hanging baskets suspended from tree limbs spilled down their colorful plantings. And, framing it all, was the distant slate blue outline of mountains.

"Delightful, isn't it?" Loretta Marshall, glass in

hand, was beside her. "Enjoy it a bit longer before it gets dark."

Moments later, when Loretta had hurried back to the fireplace group, Gillian raised the glass to her lips, took a small sip, swallowed, then stared with disbelief at the drink in her hand.

Apple juice. Plain old-fashioned apple juice, laced with a touch of cinnamon.

What was this—the House of Borgia?

And, once again, she recalled what this was. It was a beauty spa. Alcohol would have no place in this land of trim and slim.

In some ways it was going to be a rough week.

They were very fortunate, the five of them agreed.

After a brief discourse for the benefit of newcomers, Loretta Marshall had suggested that since everyone was now acquainted, it would be appropriate to look about and choose tablemates for the week.

"Of course, if friction develops—and it *never* has—" she had said, "we can make adjustments later."

Charlotte had reached protectively for Elena's hand, and Gillian and Dru had paired off naturally. Dru and Gillian had enjoyed Charlotte's wry view of The Fountains, expressed in asides as they sat around the coffee table drinking apple juice and eating raw vegetables, and Dru had remarked that they would make a compatible foursome. They had selected the table near the big picture window, where they had been joined by Rita Sloane, and together they had formed one of the groups of five for which each table was set.

The dinner, served by candlelight and consisting of sparse portions of Dover sole, green beans, tomato aspic, and lemon soufflé, had gone well. Charlotte

had spoken of travels in France. Gillian, suddenly remembering Bitsy, had described the anguish of raising
a teen-ager in these weird times, and Dru, drawn out
by Rita (who had confessed she was writing an article
for *Caress* magazine), had modestly disclosed her position in the television hierarchy. Elena had maintained
her silence until, encouraged by Charlotte, she had revealed that she too was in the entertainment industry—
in a way. She worked in a public relations office, she
said, and had frequent contact with show business
celebrities.

Yes, they were happily met, they told each
other, and could look forward to many pleasant meal-
times in the Garden Room.

The tinkling of a crystal dinner bell in Loretta
Marshall's hand brought them to attention. Loretta,
swallowing her last drop of decaffeinated coffee—with
artificial sweetener—rose from her chair to address the
room.

"Tummies full?" she asked playfully.

Groans greeted her question. "Well, perhaps not
all tummies, not yet," Loretta said. "It takes time, you
know, to shrink our stomachs. That is one of our goals,
to shrink the stomach so the silly thing demands less
to be satisfied. Don't be discouraged. You'll all get
there. And when you do, you must stay there. The
problem is, how can you accomplish this once you
have left The Fountains? Well, let me repeat a few
useful suggestions—I cannot do so too often.

"In a week many of you will be back in your
own homes. Once there, try eating with chopsticks
whenever possible. By their very nature, the implements slow you down. The more time spent over a
meal, the more fulfilling it will seem to be. Also at
home, never permit casseroles or other serving platters

to be set upon your dining table—inevitably, they will tempt you to reach for second helpings. Instead, we recommend serving main courses restaurant-style; that is, directly from the kitchen with your meat or fish and vegetables already set upon your plate. The use of a smaller dinner plate is advisable so that reduced portions will not appear forlorn.

"For many of you, restaurant dining is a necessity of life," Loretta continued. "When you are in a restaurant—and this is of great importance—you must order a la carte only. If a table d'hôte dinner should appear on the menu and entice you, you must resist it firmly. To yield is to trap yourself into eating *everything* simply because the waiter will say 'It's included in your dinner.' And at all times, stop eating as soon as you have had enough. Leave food on your plate. *Waste* food. Yes, you heard me correctly—waste food. That is a hard lesson to learn. As children we were taught to finish everything set before us—that to do otherwise would be sinful. But now we must think as adults. And we must have no guilts. Ask yourself—does it really help a starving person who is one hundred or one thousand miles away if *you* swallow food you do not need? Whether you swallow it or leave it, you are discarding food. Does it make better sense to discard it *into* your body?

"Many of you complain about the obligation to overindulge at dinner parties. Our advice to you is this—at a party *never* admit to anyone that you are dieting. Someone is certain to say 'But *you* don't need to diet,' or 'Just a little of this won't hurt,' and then you may weaken. We suggest that you explain you are not really hungry, that you snacked before you left home. People accept that.

"And, a final word. Be wary of the enemy within your own gates. It is not unusual for a friend or mate to feel threatened by your improved appearance. Under the guise of love, someone close may unconsciously subvert your diet, urging you to eat more because they fear you are becoming too attractive. If you recognize what is happening, you will be able to protect yourself."

Loretta paused and observed the Empire clock on the wall behind her. "Dr. Bertini will be here shortly," she said. "He regrets he was not able to join us for dinner. Unfortunately, he was detained by long-distance calls. He will have several interesting things to tell us, so do let's stay together, shall we? Dr. Bertini is always worth waiting for, as all of you who know him will agree. Am I not right?"

Vigorous nods and friendly catcalls came from the tables. Loretta waved her hand, commanding silence. "Ladies, ladies, restrain yourselves," she chided. "We don't want to frighten Dr. Bertini, do we? Can you put up with me a bit longer? While we are waiting, I'd like to take a few moments to address our new guests. Those of you who are veterans of The Fountains need not listen. Dru, Gillian, Elena, Rita, my words are for you. You are in an unusual and unfamiliar environment. You must be curious about what will happen to you next."

At the table near the window, Gillian kicked Dru's ankle. "That woman drives me up the wall. Can't we get out of here?"

"Afraid not. She's looking straight at us."

"I'll be brief," Loretta was promising. "To begin —tonight and every night after dinner, we take a brisk half-hour walk. It is not compulsory—nothing at The Fountains is—but we do recommend that you try it. Walking is one of the best exercises known to man— or woman. It works off calories and it tones muscles. Whenever you wish to share our walk, return to your cottage and find your most comfortable shoes. Pick up a wrap, too; the night air is crisp. Bring along the lantern you will find on a ledge near your bed. We reassemble in the Reception Hall and start out from there as a group. I will set the pace. It's safe enough but easy to lose your way if you don't know the trail.

"After our walk, we relax with some divertissement, usually in the Renaissance Room. Nothing too strenuous, mind you. Dr. Bertini wishes his guests to sleep well. We may see an old film or have a fashion show from our own boutique, or invite an expert from town to address us on some fascinating subject. If Raoul, our chef, is in a good humor, he may ask us into his kitchen and demonstrate the secret of his fantastic omelets."

At the table near the window, Gillian shuddered visibly.

Charlotte leaned toward her. "It's not that bad," she whispered. "Sometimes it's fun."

"*Fun*—for grown women? Uh-uh, I've had it with patty-cake games. I've been to nursery school *and* summer camp."

"You're free to leave anytime you wish."

"Don't be surprised if I do."

Dru put her forefinger to her lips. "Quiet, you two. I want to hear this."

"—your exercise suits, called 'rosies,'" Loretta was saying. "Each evening when you return to your cottage, you will find a fresh set waiting for you. Terrycloth pants and matching sweatshirt. Don't anticipate haute couture. Our rosies fit like potato sacks. You will wear them for early morning hikes in the hills and for more energetic exercises throughout the day. Dr. Bertini ordered them made in the kindest color possible, a soft flattering rose. Since you will be without makeup most of the day, you will come to appreciate your rosies."

A flutter of activity at the window table slowed

her momentarily. As she watched with disapproval, she saw Rita Sloane pull a spiral notebook and pencil from her purse and begin to make rapid jottings.

Loretta drew a deep breath before resuming. "In the morning, we are up with the buttercups. We gather in the Reception Hall for hot coffee and by 7:15 we are off and marching. When you return to your cottage, something lovely happens. You shed your rosies and you pop back into bed where one of our pretty waitresses will bring you your breakfast on a tray. While you are eating, do listen to music, read the morning newspaper, luxuriate—because after breakfast the day's work begins. Each morning, next to your coffee cup, you will find a card with your personalized schedule for the day. Pin it to your rosies. It will be your guide; it will tell you where to go and when, till cocktail time. Any questions?"

"Just one, Loretta," Jessica Haskell called out. "Where is Dr. Bertini?"

Rich, masculine laughter rippled from the recesses of the fireplace area. "Dear, dear ladies, I am here." Natty in burgundy silk sports jacket and fawn beige flannel slacks, Dr. Bertini stepped forward and bounced up to the dais.

"How beautiful you all are!" he exclaimed. "Who would not envy me tonight—a lone man in such a garden of delights?"

He smiled engagingly, then turned to Loretta, now seated at his side. "I have only just arrived. Did you explain about our walks? Our entertainments?"

"I did."

"And about our Mrs. Kaplan?"

"No, I didn't get to that."

"Then I shall start with Mrs. Kaplan. Ladies, as most of you know, twice weekly we have weights and measures. Tomorrow is one of those days. So I remind our old friends and inform our new ones—when you return from your morning walk, *before* you have breakfast, go to your cottage and remove everything you are wearing. In your bathroom you will find a wraparound robe. Put it on and proceed immediately to the Lanai Room. There you will meet Mrs. Kaplan, our registered nurse. Mrs. Kaplan will take brief medical histories from newcomers. Be frank with her, I beg you. It is for your own benefit.

"All of you," he continued, "I repeat, *all* of you, will be asked to submit to the scale and to the tape measure. Do not try to hide, my lovelies. This is a most important part of our program. Weight loss is of concern to most of you. A few here may be gainers; still others, maintainers. However, at The Fountains we consider measurement loss an equally vital statistic. Frequently guests who show little weight drop will record up to ten inches in total measurement change in a single week. A narrower waist, tightened upper arms and thighs, reduced hips, stomachs, even ankles— a bit here, a bit there—all add up to enhance your health and beauty.

"For those of you who have come for the first time, let me say this to you: There is nothing to fear. Mrs. Kaplan will see each of you privately in her own examining room. Any information you give her will be held in total confidence." He smiled. "If you choose to share your report card with your friends, that is up to you."

Dr. Bertini stopped to sip some water. Stroking his beard, he set down his goblet and beamed affectionately at the faces turned in his direction.

"Are you ready for a treat, my darlings? Yes? Then I have a splendid one. Loretta has mentioned our amusing nightly attractions. Well, prepare yourselves for something special. I correct myself. I should say *someone* special. A most remarkable gentleman has consented to steal time from his busy professional life in Beverly Hills to come to The Fountains to speak to us. He will be here Tuesday evening. That gentleman, known to you by reputation, I am sure, is none other than the distinguished psychoanalyst, Dr. Karl Lorenz."

Dr. Bertini broke into a happy grin as the sweet sounds of anticipation burst about him. Once again sipping his water, basking in approval, he failed to notice the byplay at the table near the window.

"Hey," Dru was saying to Gillian. "Isn't that *your* Dr. Lorenz?"

Gillian stiffened. "He is not *my* Dr. Lorenz."

"But you told me—"

"I told you that I'd consulted Dr. Lorenz, that's all."

"Jeesus, I'm sorry."

"Are you?" Gillian crushed her napkin and tossed it on the table. "See you in the morning," she said to the others. Ignoring Dru, she jumped to her feet and headed for the door. Stung, Dru sat back in her chair. Then, embarrassed, uncertain of what she had done, she apologized to the women at the table and followed Gillian from the Garden Room.

"—has been impressed by our program," Dr. Bertini was saying. "That is why Dr. Lorenz accepted my invitation, as well as my suggestion that he address us on the subject of 'Vibrant Health: Vibrant Sexuality.' Now ladies, for the sake of both, may I recommend that you take your evening walk with Loretta, then watch our film in the Renaissance Room, and be peacefully in your beds by ten o'clock."

"How about it?" Charlotte asked. "Anyone for the Long March?"

Elena stood up. "I'd like to come."

Rita dropped her pad and pencil into her handbag. "No thanks. I think this is a good time for a chat with Dr. Bertini."

He was standing alone leaning against the railing on the porch of the Garden Room when Rita moved up to his side. Together they watched the last of the guests trickle down the path.

"Looks like a merry crew," she said.

Dr. Bertini shook his head sadly. "I wish it were so. I am sure it is not."

"I don't understand—"

"My dear Rita, you are looking at *women*. Most have problems, many of them serious. Not that we are a haven for unhappy females," he added hastily. "We are not. We merely reflect the human condition."

"Come now, Dr. Bertini. Those little lambs are some of the most privileged persons in the world. Are you asking me to believe *they* reflect the human condition?"

"Materially, their needs are met. In that sense you are correct. But as a journalist, an observer, can you say that is all a woman needs?"

"It helps."

"I will not deny that. Unfortunately it does not help enough." He gazed in the direction of the cottages. "Who knows? Perhaps this group will be different from the others. But I doubt it. Over the years, I have never followed a single one of my guests into her bedroom. Yet, I know well what happens behind their closed doors. Tonight, every night, a few will touch their heads to their pillows and immediately go off to sleep. They are the rare ones.

"Think about it. When a woman goes to bed without a man, as she does here, it is an occasion—just as going to bed with a man is an occasion. Not

necessarily an unhappy occasion but an occasion nonetheless. The absence of a man, like the presence of a
man, is felt in the bed.

"Tonight at The Fountains, we have women who
will be happy to be alone in their beds, grateful to be
apart from a despised or tiresome mate. Others, poor
creatures, will sleep very little. Their bodies will not
let them rest because of their need for a man. A particular man, or any man.

"Among those you met—some will drink, others
will swallow sleeping pills, although we discourage
both practices. Many will reach for the telephone to
call a husband, a lover, even a child. A few will hesi-
tate, decide against the call. In the morning, we will
see red eyes and we will never know why. Even you,
Rita, may not rest too well tonight.

"But we do the best we can. The activities of
the day absorb the hours and tire the body. As we move
through the week, sleep comes more easily to our
guests. That is one of the reasons for our success.
Here at The Fountains we create a womb environment,
a secure and protected place. Here women find respite
from the pressures of their outside lives. But we have
a larger purpose, too. Our real goal is to lead women
to other, more meaningful fountains. As the poet, Col-
eridge put it: 'I may not hope from outward forms to
win/The passion and the life whose fountains are
within.'"

Rita nodded approvingly. "The fountains
within," she said. "Sounds noble. But how often can
you achieve that? You must have failures, too. Today,
at the briefing—"

"Ah, that," Dr. Bertini sighed. "A well-known
actress. An amphetamine addict. She went wild one
night. Frightened the other guests. We explained she
had an emotional problem. Everyone could understand

that. Her manager came after midnight and took her away."

He touched Rita's arm and they started down the stairs.

"An unusual event," he said. "I do not think we will have such high drama this week." And then he added quietly, "At least, I hope we will not. One never knows."

VIII

It was her first morning.

Elena nestled into the quilted bedrest, savoring its silky smoothness against her skin. The movement jounced the white Lucite breakfast tray that straddled her lap and snugly bracketed her thighs. Checking quickly, she reassured herself that nothing on the tray had spilled. Everything was in place, the ten strawberries—no more, no less—topped with a sprig of mint and heaped in a clear crystal bowl, the steaming black coffee she had poured from a silver carafe, and the single pink rose in a tiny bud vase.

She raised her arms in a slow stretch, then tugged the downy blanket over her breasts. Luxuriate, Loretta Marshall had said. Elena wiggled under the blanket. It was going to be easy.

Leaning back, listening to the soft, piped-in music, her thoughts drifted to her job in Los Angeles and to the handful of wives discontentedly wed to the actors and directors who were clients of the public relations firm of Lincoln and Rudolph. Faceless women, resigned to neglect by busy husbands, cemented in marriage by the community property laws of the State of California, many of the wives fought for recognition of their own by feverishly participating in newsworthy civic events. Political, cultural, charitable, it hardly mattered. What did matter was that soon afterward they could affirm their identity by reading *their* names in the local newspapers.

Sometimes the press failed to mention one or two of these wives. It was then that Elena was expected to field the resentful telephone calls they made to their husbands' unfortunate press agents. Always the calls came in the morning and, listening to their complaints, Elena could hear the chewing and sipping sounds of breakfast and the occasional brusque interjection, "Damn, my tray's slipping."

In the office, Elena and the other secretaries had invented their own images of the clients' wives. They called them the lonely ladies of the three B's—Beverly Hills, Bel-Air, and Brentwood—and they pitied them. Over their bagged lunches and coffee-filled paper cups, the secretaries agreed that not one among them would change places with any wife in the three B's.

Munching on a strawberry, Elena decided she had news for the gang in the office. Maybe those wives were bored and miserable, but when you got right down to it, so were lots of secretaries. And thus far, there was no evidence that being broke made it easier.

Dear, wise Barry. She couldn't wait to tell him about all this. He had understood better than she how badly she needed the change. Candlelit dinner, breakfast in bed, exercise, massage. It would be a marvelously restorative week. When she went home to the Marina, her depression would be no more than a dim memory. Barry would be proud of her. It would be like old times again.

Blissfully she studied the room. Yesterday she

had been overwhelmed by its elegance. This morning, with sunlight glimmering through sheer curtains, she felt transported by its loveliness. Ahead of her, a velvet-covered fauteuil was drawn up to a Louis XVI desk made of pearwood. Butter-yellow Creil plates and eighteenth-century etchings portraying Paris adorned the lime-silk walls. From the corner, a Regency chaise longue laden with pillows stretched toward the window.

They were authentic antiques, all right. She had inspected each piece last night after her walk on the trail and had marveled that Dr. Bertini had not furnished the room with less expensive reproductions. Even the opaline lamp on the desk was a treasure.

Barry teased her about her rapturous appreciation of what he called "fancy junk." And laughingly she accused him of being jealous of Gordon Prescott, the other man in her life.

Gordon Prescott. She smiled, remembering the distinguished director who was a client of the office. A tall, striking, white-haired widower, world famous and widely traveled, Gordon Prescott was also noted as a passionate collector of rare books and paintings.

The first time Elena had been sent to Gordon Prescott's hilltop home to deliver a press release, she had stood in the vestibule of his manor house and gaped.

"Like it, Elena?" he had asked.

She could only nod.

"Then let me show you the rest of the place."

Later, after he had taken her through the house and over the grounds, he had invited her to sit beside him in his large drawing room.

"You're not like the others," he had said.

She had stared at him, petrified, fearful of what would happen next.

But Gordon Prescott had fooled her. "You are interested in what you have seen here. Would you really like to learn about it? If so, I would enjoy being your teacher," he had said, "to introduce you to the things that give me so much pleasure. It would make me extremely happy."

Observing the lingering fright in her eyes, he had added, "That is all I want, Elena. Nothing more."

Trusting him, she had relaxed. In response to his questions, she had told him about her life in the barrio, her parents, the series of jobs that had brought her to her present employment—and about Barry Waterman.

He had listened solemnly, making no comment.

"And that's it," she had concluded.

"Not quite," he had said. "I perceive more."

"What more could there be?"

"There could be the other Elena, one not so easily seen. The surface Elena seems simple, easy to read. A reticent, uncertain, often withdrawn, always insecure, mildly ambitious, striving, surviving young woman. But I see another Elena, one curious, eager for knowledge and learning, and the independence and identity and assurance that come from knowing. Am I right?"

"How did you guess?" she had asked.

"It was in your voice, the way it rose with un-asked questions. And in your eyes, the way they widened at everything, fascinated, wanting answers. Would you like to know about the things in this house?"

"Would I!"

And then and there he had begun her education.

She had left his house with an armful of books dealing with classical music and period furniture. That night, after Barry had fallen asleep, she had read hungrily. Thereafter, whenever she returned to see Gordon Prescott, he had been ready for her, waiting with more books, more exquisite *objets* for her enchantment. Under his guidance she had discovered the stunning worlds of literature, art, architecture, music, horticulture—and antiques.

Yet, although she loved everything she was learning, it had all seemed abstract, existing somewhere outside of her own life. Until this moment—

She closed her eyes. It's coming together, she told herself. I am coming together. I am not an outsider anymore. I am comfortable here. I belong in this place as much as any of them do. I am no longer a scared Chicana *niña.* I am changing. Fast.

Her first surge of confidence had come the night before at dinner in the Garden Room. Earlier, during cocktails, she had cautiously avoided the nasty Haskell woman, seating herself beside Charlotte Caldwell, who had continued to be warm and friendly. To Elena's relief the hour had passed without incident. Over dinner her tablemates had welcomed her as a peer and her timidity had begun to evaporate. After that, all of her moments had been good ones, thank God. She had returned from her evening walk with Charlotte feeling physically exhausted. And for the first time in ages, she had dropped off to sleep without reaching for a pill.

Loretta Marshall's wake-up call had aroused her before seven A.M. Stopping only to brush her teeth and splash some water on her face, she had pulled on her terrycloth suit and rushed out the door to the Reception Hall. There she had gulped some coffee from a heavy mug. Then, falling in with the other guests, she had hiked and jogged her way over a mountain trail bordered by scrub and chaparral. The exercise and the early-morning air had exhilarated her—as had the events that followed.

She opened her eyes and looked at the wall clock. Impossible. Only eight A.M. The day had scarcely started and already it had been one of the most extraordinary days of her life. Finishing off the last of the strawberries, she slid the breakfast tray to the foot of the bed, tossed the bedrest onto the floor and, dropping back against her pillows, she tried to recall everything that had happened in the past hour.

"Out of your rosies and into your robes," Loretta Marshall had instructed when they returned from their walk. "Faster you get to Mrs. Kaplan, faster you'll get to your breakfast. Hurry, ladies."

Elena had sped to her cottage and, with the single-mindedness of a relay racer, she had switched from one costume to the other. Out on the path again, she had stopped, and looked about, confused. A passing guest had pointed the way and, thongs slapping the gravel, she had almost run to the Lanai Room.

Stepping inside, she had again been overtaken by the feeling that she had been Xeroxed. The first time had been when she and the others had set out on the trail in their matching rosies, their individual sizes and shapes blurred by the baggy sweatsuits. Now they were suited up once more, wearing identical wraparound white robes, waiting in line to be interviewed by the still-unseen Mrs. Kaplan.

Peering down the line, Elena had made out a door grandly lettered *Nurse's Office*. Closer inspection had revealed the office to be no more than a small cubicle built into a rear corner of the tile-floored room. Its two milk-glass walls fell short of the high ceiling, offering little soundproofing. From where she stood, Elena had heard a muffled voice that she assumed was Mrs. Kaplan's. It had been interrupted occasionally by groans and squeals from the guest then undergoing inspection. Moving up in the line, she had watched the women entering the cubicle one by one, to emerge shortly with bright pink cards clutched in their hands.

Behind Elena, a plump-faced woman introduced to her earlier as Helen Reiser had suddenly grunted in her ear. "Look at those dummies. Built like brick you-know-whats, and still not satisfied. Me, I'm a fat slob here for a rest. Nine kids, would you believe it?"

"That's a large family. But I'm sure you have a very nice figure."

"The hell I do, and I couldn't care less. Jeesus, I'm glad I'm not like that one." Helen Reiser had tilted her head toward a statuesque redhead exiting from the cubicle. The redhead's robe had been thrown back revealing broad shoulders and firm high breasts.

"Hey, Sheila," Helen Reiser had shouted. "How'd you make out?"

"None of your damned business, Helen."

"Get off it, doll. What have you got to hide? It's all hanging out anyway."

"How'd you like my dental history, darling?"

"Bet that's good reading, too."

"Up yours."

"Cover the boobs, girl," Helen had replied. "Sun's getting hot. Wouldn't want them to melt, would you?"

"Why don't you cover your ugly head."

Helen Reiser had looked pleased.

"Push on, kid," she had said to Elena. "You're next."

Mrs. Kaplan, dumpy and middle-aged, had greeted her warmly and asked a few questions about childhood diseases, allergies, surgeries, and menstrual periods. Elena had answered fully, omitting only the episode of the abortion.

"Drop your robe, honey," Mrs. Kaplan had said and, while Elena stood nude before her, the nurse had recorded her height and weight, and checked her blood pressure and pulse. That done, Mrs. Kaplan had whipped about with a tape measure, encircling waist, abdomen, neck, bust, hips, thighs, knees and ankles, meanwhile mumbling numbers that she had scratched rapidly on one of the little pink cards.

"Good, good," Mrs. Kaplan had said. "A wee bit heavy in the thighs, maybe, but we can work that off. Beautiful bust. Beautiful. Exercise, keep it firm. Once it starts sagging, let's face it, extreme measures are necessary. You wouldn't want that, would you?"

Elena had looked at her blankly. Mrs. Kaplan had laughed. "You're a long way from there, child. You can go now."

Outside the Lanai Room, on her way back to her cottage, Elena had spotted a bulletin board. A handwritten sign thumbtacked to the board had announced the luncheon menu: Lobster Bits in a Lettuce Bed, Lemon Dressing, Sliced Tomato, Iced Tea.

She had reread the sign. Lobster Bits, it had said. That wouldn't be too bad. It meant that someone else would have enticed the juicy meat from the claws and legs and she would not be expected to cope with the strange appendages that belonged to the lobster. So many times, at restaurant dinners with Barry, she had fallen back on steak or fish or fowl rather than admit she did not know how to deal with the intimidating lobster and the funny little fork that was the weapon of attack. Bits would be easy. Lunch, like breakfast, was going to be an adventure.

"Birdshit," a voice said over her shoulder. "One thousand dollars a week and they feed us birdshit."

Elena had swiveled to see Helen Reiser standing behind her. "What—?"

"You're not one of these weight freaks, are you?"

"Not really. Mrs. Kaplan wants me to lose a little in my thighs."

"Forget it. Thighs aren't a crisis area. What about the boobs?"

"Mrs. Kaplan says they're—they're attractive."

Parting the top of her robe, Helen had gazed affectionately at her own breasts. "Udders," she had said cheerfully. "Comes from nursing nine babies. The Judge loves them just as they are. Says when he puts his head underneath, it's the only time he can't hear the kids." Helen closed her robe. "The Judge would have a fit if I had knockers like Sheila's."

"They looked pretty good to me."

"*Pretty* good? *Too* good. Picture perfect, a miracle of science. Silicone. Couldn't you tell? Of course, you couldn't. You're still an infant. Takes a jaundiced old bird like me to spot them. Next time take a real look."

"Next time? I don't expect—"

"Oh, there'll be a next time. She's so proud of them, she displays them every chance she gets. You'll see, they don't jiggle like human flesh. They're packed too solid. Hell, the law of gravity would pull them down, if they weren't phony."

"You mean they've been—treated?"

"How delicately you put it. Yeah, treated. That and more. Poor dumb Sheila. I never did like her. Not from the beginning when her ex, Joe Henderson, brought her to Washington to visit us. Joe's an old friend of the Judge's. He's one of those Texas billionaires. One day he clumped into Neiman-Marcus and there was Sheila behind the candy counter flashing the biggest pair of eyes and the softest little boobs in the State. Squishy, like week-old peaches. A real turn-on for Joe. Anyway, he married her. Right from the start Sheila was a lousy lay. That's what Joe told the Judge. He thought he could break her in but she was too stupid. A couple years later he dumped her and while he was at it he dumped a few million bucks into her settlement."

"What's that got to do with her breasts?"

"Plenty. Next time I saw Sheila she was right here at The Fountains. It hit me something was different. The peaches were gone. Must have gotten flabby. All of a sudden Sheila's got grapefruits. She's all poked out and stuffed with silicone—and, kid, that costs money. Probably figured it would change her luck. So now the boobs are bigger but packed solid like cannonballs. A man could get a concussion if he bumped into them in the dark."

Elena had drawn her own robe tighter. "Mrs. Reiser, that's the saddest story I've ever heard."

"Call me Helen. And don't worry about Sheila. She'll make out. It's supposed to be a secret but she's hired herself one of those closet press agents, some rundown socialite who's like a sponsor, too. She gets Sheila invited to upper-crust parties, and chaperones her to the fanciest resorts in the United States, Europe, and Mexico. Sooner or later, Sheila will break through. She's no different from the rest of that jet-set pack. They're all hustling something."

"How depressing."

"A lot of things are, sweetie—a lot of things."

My name is Drucilla Jennings. I am thirty-three years old. I have all my own teeth and the Pill has not made me fat. I have a fantastic husband, the handsome, celebrated journalist, Timothy Larsen. I have a career ten thousand women envy. I am the luckiest woman alive. I am so goddam lucky, I wish I were dead.

Dru slumped on the crackled brown leatherette mat, thankful for a brief respite from the body-breaking exercises. Around her on the gym floor other women griped and puffed with exhaustion. Why am I punish-

ing myself this way, she wondered? Isn't it enough that
my head is scrambled? Does nature require that I beat
my body to a pulp, too?

At the record player beside the long mirrored
wall Polly, the exercise leader, was switching platters
from Herb Alpert to Frank Sinatra. As though that
would help. Ache along with Alpert, sag along with
Sinatra. Why bother? It all stank.

She sneaked a glance at Gillian. Flat on her back
on a mat near the mirror, Gillian was as cool and exquisite as ever. How was it possible at this obscene
hour? How was it *not* possible? Gillian was downright
magnificent at all times. Furthermore, unlike the rest
of the group, Gillian had scorned the clumpy exercise
suits and had appeared in the gym wearing black tights
under an ass-hugging black leotard. Her figure was
fabulous, her face serene. Dru hated her.

Dru scowled remembering the scene with Gillian the night before. She had been concerned about
offending Gillian and had followed her from the Garden Room to apologize. For what? She still didn't know.
Her question about Dr. Lorenz had been innocently
put. Gillian's overreaction had been upsetting. But Dru
did know one thing—she loathed emotional hangnails.
She wanted messes tidied up. When she had overtaken
Gillian she had said that she was sorry, although she
did not yet understand what she had to be sorry for.
Gillian had cut her down with a curt "Forget it, I'm
going to bed," and had disappeared into her cottage.

What ensued had not improved Dru's evening.
Still smarting from her telephone quarrel with Tim, she
had decided to put *something* right by apologizing to
him, too. After some backing and filling, aware it was
after midnight in Washington, she had placed a call
to Tim's room at The Madison, his favorite hotel in
the District. Masochistically, she had counted the rings.
There had been twelve before she had given up. Tears

had stung her eyes as she replaced the phone in its cradle. Washington was not a night town. If Tim wasn't in his own bed, he had to be in someone else's.

She had crumpled into a chair. Fear and anger had drained her. Hours later, she had fallen into restless sleep.

"Dru sweet, forgive me." Gillian linked her arm into Dru's and looked remorseful. Behind them in the gym the husky voice of poor dead Janis Joplin wailed out of the record player, following them as they crossed the lawn.

"I don't know what made me fly off the handle," Gillian went on. "Maybe talking about Bitsy. Jason and I can't manage her anymore. You and Tim wouldn't like to adopt a fat, dirty, rude, useless teen-ager, would you?"

"You make it sound awfully tempting."

"You're not upset with me?"

"Why should I be? Isn't that what friends are for—to kick in the butt?"

"Never again, you have my word."

"Thanks loads. You're all heart."

"Dru—"

"Okay, it's forgotten. I have to go."

"Where to? Maybe we can go together."

Dru tugged at the card dangling from the safety pin on her terry sweatshirt. "Steam room. Downstairs."

"Beauty salon for me. See you at lunch, darling."

Dru watched the gorgeous figure recede. The beauty salon. What could they do with Gillian, she asked herself sourly. Except copy her.

Janet Wolfe was early. Alone in the room, she sat stolidly on the edge of the chaise longue.

Everything was in readiness for Charlotte Caldwell's massage. The folding table had been opened and two white sheets had been spread over it. The first sheet would protect Mrs. Caldwell from the cold vinyl surface of the table, the second would be carefully arranged to shield whatever portion of her body was not exposed for the massage. Lotions, saturated eye pads, and towels were ranged on a nearby stand. The wooden sign that said *Massage* was hung on the outer doorknob to ward off visitors and the lined drapes were drawn. The darkened room would make the massage more soothing for Charlotte Caldwell.

Charlotte Caldwell. A former guest, Dr. Bertini had said. Janet could not remember her. Perhaps Charlotte Caldwell had been assigned to one of the other masseuses on her first visit. It was of no importance. Janet barely remembered any of them. They came and went, in assorted shapes and sizes—but all alike to Janet. Two arms, two legs, ten fingers, ten toes, one neck (usually tense), back, hips, stomach. Janet sighed and extended her strong hands. What the hell, she thought as she studied them—it was a living.

Janet heard the door opening and jumped to her feet. The woman who entered was tawny-haired and of medium height. In the dim room she appeared to be no more than thirty.

"Hello, I'm Janet Wolfe. I don't think we've met before."

"Hi. Be with you in a minute." Charlotte swung toward the dressing alcove.

"Don't hurry, Mrs. Caldwell. This is your time for taking it easy."

When Charlotte reentered the room the rosies were gone. She was nude except for a robe flung over her shoulders. She appeared dejected.

Janet stood aside as Charlotte mounted the table and flattened her back against the sheets.

"Warm enough?" Janet asked.

"Just right, thank you."

"Some music?"

"I'd rather not."

"I'll have you snug in a minute." Janet circled the table, raising and tucking the top sheet until Charlotte was swathed from chin to toes.

"Eye pads?"

"If you think so."

Janet picked up two astringent-soaked pads and placed them on Charlotte's eyelids. Then she stepped to the head of the table. So this one didn't want to talk. Good. Neither did she.

"Let your mind go blank," she advised. "Try to doze. I'll tell you when it's time to turn over."

Her creamed hands loosened the top sheet and slipped behind Charlotte's back. For several minutes she manipulated first one shoulder, then the other. As the tight muscles eased, she moved on to Charlotte's neck.

Lightening her touch, she pattered her fingers over Charlotte's face. With professional satisfaction she heard Charlotte emit a soft breathy sound and saw the body beneath the sheet go limp.

They never ceased to surprise her, these wealthy, overindulged women. They had dozens of everything money could buy, yet they reacted like infants to simple human touch. Janet had observed them, mewing, squirming, even sobbing under her hands. Their primitive need and her own ability to evoke and gratify that need still amazed her.

Deftly she swept along Charlotte's jaw, curved around her ears, and rotated the tips of her fingers into the soft hair.

Another one. Definitely. Janet's trained, sensitive fingers detected it. This one had fooled her because the body appeared so young. But the face-lift scars were there. No question about that.

Who was Charlotte Caldwell? Janet narrowed her eyes, trying to recall Dr. Bertini's briefing. Caldwell . . . the divorcée. From Chicago. The one who had taken the breakup so hard.

Janet shifted around to the right side of the table. She released Charlotte's arm from the swaddling sheets and took hold of her hand. She began to massage the fingers, gently, one by one, one by one.

The noisy arrival of the Countess Christina Rossi the following afternoon created a huge stir among the guests of The Fountains. Rumor that she was expected had filtered through from the staff and even the most jaded among the guests confessed to being curious.

Christina Rossi was an amiable though legendary figure of uncertain age. Like her friend, Dr. Bertini, she was possessed of certain marketable commodities and she clung to them with passion. These commodities were her earthy Italian accent, her title acquired in the first of four marriages, and a generous pink-and-white cushiony body. Of the three attributes, it was the last that had served her best. In dozens of visits to The Fountains she was proud she had never left behind a single ounce of her flesh.

Christina came to The Fountains because her visits were free (early in his career Dr. Bertini had considered himself amply repaid each time she mentioned The Fountains on one of the television talk shows she frequented), and because she had an athlete's concern for keeping her body in good working condition.

Christina acknowledged she was a genuine celebrity although, along with her admirers, she had difficulty defining the reason for her fame. She was, she supposed, a character.

Christina made no secret of her impoverished childhood in Naples nor of the skills which, years ago, had enticed the young Count Aldo Rossi into marriage. After appearing in a few cheap Italian films, Christina had dissolved her union with the Count. Thereafter, her pilgrimage across Europe and the United States had been as well recorded as the daily tides. She had been detoured only once, by an experimental marriage for love, a misstep she had never repeated. Her groom, a hungry medical student from New York City, had freed her willingly when her larger ambitions became clear. He had returned to his less demanding cadavers and Christina had continued her migration westward.

Christina's subsequent marriages and affairs, all conducted in full media glare, were confused in her own mind. That both arrangements—affairs as well as marriages—had compensated her lavishly was due in part to the legal services of Barry Waterman. As her attorney, Barry had extricated her from innumerable liaisons while simultaneously guaranteeing that she was well rewarded for her investment of time and talent. In a period when younger women celebrated their sexual freedom by demanding nothing more than shared pleasures, Christina was a thriving anachronism.

"You keep me so busy I ought to be your lawyer-in-residence," Barry Waterman had suggested.

"No freebies," she had replied. "Not even for you, Barry. Take your fee and go away."

Like everything else she did, Christina did not make her entrance inconspicuously. She was swept into the courtyard of The Fountains by a surly chauffeur seated at the wheel of a mile-long Cadillac that scattered gravel as it braked to a halt. Prodded by Christina, the chauffeur pressed his horn and glowered as it emitted several short, loud blasts.

Christina enjoyed the Cadillac. It belonged to a close friend, a conservative aging banker who resided with his wife in the old-rich section of Los Angeles known as Hancock Park. The gentleman, belying his aristocratic mien and life-style, had surprising physical gifts and Christina called him "my secret sensualist." She entertained him weekly in her own bedroom in Bel-Air, and she left it to him to deal with his wife and with his chauffeur whenever she wished to borrow the Cadillac.

The swishing sound of wheels hitting the gravel had reached Dr. Bertini as he sat behind his office desk. Immediately, he dropped his work and dashed to the door, arriving in the courtyard while the chauffeur was still honking.

"Christina, my darling," he exclaimed as she stepped from the car. His arms went around her in a quick embrace. Standing back, he kissed her on both cheeks. "Let me look at you—you are glorious! Why do you come here when already you are so radiant?"

"Alfredo, you are a lovable fraud."

"Shhh," he admonished, laughing. "I am an artist. We are both artists—in our different ways."

"In this place you are the maestro. I am your clay."

He eyed her suggestively. "You mean that? My time will come?"

"Who knows? Tell me, how is your business? And you must not ask about mine."

"We are filled up, this week as every week."

"Who is here? Anyone I know?"

"Yes, a few people. When you have changed

your clothes, I, myself, will take you to join the others."

"Good. Where is everyone?"

"It is lunchtime. They are all on the pool deck."

"So, let us start. Mr. Smithson will carry my bags. Which cottage is mine?"

"Christina—" He hesitated. "You are always so understanding. I could not give you the Pompadour Suite this time."

Her eyebrows shot up. "Oh—?"

"Jessica Haskell is back."

"You dog. You should have warned me."

"And deprive myself of the fun? Never! It is always thrilling to see two gladiators on the field of battle."

With the chauffeur following, Dr. Bertini led the way to a cottage on a small hill. He unlocked the door and gestured for Christina and the chauffeur to precede him.

Grinning, Dr. Bertini settled himself on a tufted loveseat and watched as the chauffeur slung Christina's bags on luggage racks and unfastened them roughly.

"Thank you, Mr. Smithson. You may leave now. You will be back Friday morning at ten, not a moment later."

Christina turned to Dr. Bertini. "I must return to Los Angeles early in the day, Alfredo. I have given my word. There are last-minute details for a cocktail party at the Italian consulate. We are honoring a new fashion designer in from Milan. I am to be co-host."

"I will regret the loss of every hour."

"Do not be sad. At least I will be with you for the Gala and the Chateaubriand and Dom Perignon."

When the chauffeur had left, Christina peered after him through the window and stuck out her tongue. "He is a pain, but what can I do? I am a helpless child. I cannot order him fired, the wife would not understand."

"And who can understand you? Hurry, the guests know you are here. They will not disperse until they see you."

"What a nag you are. I am doing the best I can."

He watched, amused, as she plunged into her suitcases, examining and rejecting one item after another. There was a small mound of clothing on the floor before she found what she was seeking.

In seconds, she was stripped to the buff. "The wrong way to undress before a man," she said. "But I know—and you know I know—the right way."

Her milky-skinned body with its full breasts and ample hips and buttocks did not excite him, nor did she intend that it should. They were friends these two, no more, and they understood each other well.

It was not until she pulled a sheer chiffon caftan over her head that he stirred. "Christina, you cannot go out that way. You might just as well be naked. There are limits."

"It is you who must learn limits. To your prudery. Your guests are panting to know what I really look like. It will help them to see. They will understand there is no great mystery. I do not have three breasts nor an extra orifice." She twirled before him, then bent to tug affectionately at his beard. "They will stop to *think*. In time, they will realize my appeal is spiritual."

Minutes later, approaching the pool deck with Christina at his side, Dr. Bertini lowered his voice. "See what you are doing to them? My ladies have never appeared more bored."

"In my entire life I have never bored anyone."

"If only you would—no, you are not boring

them. They are only pretending to be unimpressed.
Secretly they are all members of your fan club."

"Then I will give a great performance."

"Please, my darling, nothing outrageous. They
are sweet—and they are my bread and butter."

"They are your champagne and caviar."

He groaned. "You are wicked. Come, let us say
Hello."

The women clustered about the umbrella-
shaded tables were sipping their iced drinks and nib-
bling what remained of their dilled shrimp salad. "Eat
lingeringly," Dr. Bertini had said the night before.
"*Experience* each bite, make it last. Then you will think
you are at a feast."

"My stomach is growling—what about that?"
someone had demanded.

"That you must think of as applause, tribute to
your splendid restraint."

"Dr. Bertini, that's a crock," Helen Reiser had
muttered.

Now, stripped of makeup, oiled hair pulled
back, the women sat scavenging their plates. Wrapped
in terry robes, fatigued from their morning's activities,
they resembled evacuees from an institutional disaster.

Dr. Bertini threw wide his arms as he neared
them. "My lovely harem—you are blooming," he sang
out. "And what a beast I am to bring yet another bride.
But this one, I promise, this one will be docile. Come,
Christina, let us greet old and new friends."

"Hey, Christina, welcome to the chain gang,"
a voice called to her.

"Helen Reiser, the Earth Mother herself. Migod,
not another baby!"

"Another baby."

"I don't believe it! How many does this make?"

"Nine. So far."

"Unbelievable! How do you do it?"

"The same way you do, honey. Only not as often."

Christina laughed good-naturedly. "Watch out, you will poison them with your mother's milk."

"Come, Christina," Dr. Bertini interrupted. "Let Helen finish her lunch in peace—and please do not spoil the day for anyone else."

Carefully weaving Christina among the guests, Dr. Bertini introduced her to strangers and he stood by nervously as she hailed old friends. He looked into the distance when she asked Jessica Haskell if she had been ill. "Your face is too peaked, my darling, you must take better care of yourself." And he coughed into his handkerchief as she marveled at Sheila's figure. "Do not tell me what you have done, I *know*. You have exercised, exercised, exercised. The change is remarkable!"

At the final table, he presented her to Rita Sloane, Elena Valdez, and Charlotte Caldwell. After seating Christina, he collapsed into a chair facing her and exhaled with the uninhibited release of a man who had successfully maneuvered his way through a minefield.

"Beware of this terrible woman," he said. "Rita, you are not to report a word she says. She lies without shame."

Christina offered a confirming nod. "He is correct. I am dreadful."

She grimaced as a waitress placed her dilled shrimp before her. "And where is the bread?"

"In your suitcase, as usual," Dr. Bertini replied. "Be quiet and eat."

"In a minute." Her eyes fastened on Elena. "Elena Valdez? Of course. You are Barry's friend. I made this reservation for you."

"Yes, thank you very much."

"I have seen you before."

"I used to work in Barry's office."

"Ah. Yes, I remember now, the little secretary —the one who poured the drinks. You have not been there lately."

"I left. I have a new job. I'm in public relations."

Christina smiled approval. "Bright girl. One does not stay too long with a man like Barry."

"I never had a problem with him. We're still friends."

"Then you are lucky. Barry is a bad boy, always using women. Even with me, he tried."

Christina popped a shrimp into her mouth. "Last night he was drinking at the Bistro with Naomi Riggins—" She shook her head, impressed. "Such a famous singer—you'd think he would not dare. Not in a public place, anyway."

"Dare what?"

Christina giggled. "Naomi is the one who is supposed to lay them in the aisles. Last night it was Barry who was trying to do that—to Naomi."

"I don't believe you."

Christina eyed her shrewdly, then understanding touched her face. "Possibly I made a mistake," she said, her voice softening. "Perhaps it was *I* who was drinking too much."

They were alone in the steam room, set in to bake like two buns in an oven. The silver-haired attendant who had placed them there had promised to return in fifteen minutes.

Sweat streamed from their bodies as they sat close together on the white-tiled ledge.

"Up there on the pool deck—" Rita began.

"What about it?"

"It was a rough moment for you."

"Not at all."

"I'm a reporter, Elena. I don't miss much. That's why I've got my job. I saw Christina lay it on you—pow, right between the eyes."

"You're wrong."

"Am I?"

"Maybe yes, maybe no. Either way it's none of your business. You hardly know me."

"Don't I? I know you as well as I know myself. We're sisters under our terry towels. Let's see. I'm maybe three, four years older than you. That's the main difference. We're two kids from simple families who worked our way up to something that looked better, right? Only today you think your whole life depends on one roll of the dice, that Barry person Christina mentioned. Me, I'm not ready to do or die for any man."

"Neither am I."

"No? You should have seen your face when Christina drew the little scene at the Bistro. Poor Christina, I thought she'd perish when she realized what she'd done."

"It meant nothing. Barry Waterman is an old friend."

"You still see him?"

Elena chewed her lip. "I live with him."

"It figures. Did he send you down here?"

"Yes. To pull myself together. Lately, I've been —moody."

"You want him to marry you?"

"I did, in the beginning."

"And he's not interested?"

"It's not his fault. Barry's been married. He had a bad experience. He's not ready to marry again. He's always been honest about our relationship. We have an understanding."

"Only you don't understand."

"I'll get used to it."

"The hell you will. Deep down you're longing for wedding bells and a little white house with a picket fence."

"Aren't you?"

"Longing? Never. My parents tried pushing me in that direction and I almost gave in to please them. Fortunately I escaped in time and moved to New York. For a while I tried the joyous singles scene. Ugh. That was even worse. Downhill all the way. Luckily Peter rescued me."

"Who's Peter?"

Rita grinned sheepishly. "He's the man who's complicating *my* life."

"All right, so we have men trouble in common. But we're different in other ways."

"Name one."

"I'm still a secretary."

"Yeah?"

"And you're a writer for *Caress.*"

"So what? My mask says chic fashion magazine, yours says public relations. But we both wind up at the typewriter singing the praise of strangers. Face it, what are we doing in this funny famine farm? We're outsiders, you and I, pretending we belong. We're here on a pass."

Elena glanced at her curiously. "Where do you come from?"

"Brooklyn. Brooklyn College, honor student. Then, Columbia School of Journalism. The magazine needed new talent and I had a little, so they hired me. I'm a working girl same as you. Would you believe it, my own family gets confused? They pick up *Caress* and see pictures of those models and heiresses and female executives, and they start thinking suddenly

I've got royal blood. It's a joke! I'm like a refugee.
Still part of the old country, sometimes uneasy in the
new one."

"Like me."

"Not exactly. When I'm with a crowd like this,
I don't try to cross their damn line. You do. Forget it,
it's not worth the price."

"What price? I wouldn't demean myself for
anyone."

"Do you think they'd notice if you did? How
many times have you seen Christina Rossi?"

"Ten, twenty—I'm not sure."

"And she hardly knew your name. She had to
reach to place your face. 'The one who poured the
drinks,' she said. Hell, all you ever were to her was
living wallpaper."

"She's not like the rest."

"Correct. She's better. She had to make it the
hard way. She's worked for everything she's got."

"That has nothing to do with Barry and me.
You heard Christina. She admits she's a liar and sometimes she drinks too much. Last night—Barry and that
singer—I don't believe it."

"Suit yourself. Let the buyer beware." She
studied Elena's dripping torso. "You've got one helluva
product there. Don't give it away."

The silver-haired attendant reappeared at the
steam-room door. "Ready, ladies?" She signaled Elena.
"You first. Time for a shower and your Scotch hose."

In the tunnellike shower room, the water hit
Elena's body from all sides. It came from a dozen spi-
gots set at different levels, snapping at her skin, making her blood tingle.

She welcomed its assault. It cleared her head,
put things back in perspective. Of course Barry had

gone to the Bistro with a date. Why not? She didn't expect him to stay home every night opening cans of tuna fish, did she? She wouldn't do that herself. When Barry went out of town leaving her behind, she telephoned old friends, men friends from other times, and visited with them over a restaurant dinner. Barry was never jealous, not when she saw Victor Origo, a barrio neighbor who was a medical student at UCLA. Or Danny Montoya, her former boss in the real estate agency, who was handsome and unmarried and a big spender. Barry didn't believe in chains, not for himself, not for her.

She soaped her body energetically. Rita Sloane was a meddler. And Christina Rossi was a careless gossip who would say anything about anyone, because she didn't care what anyone said about her.

"Finished, dear?" The attendant stood at the open door.

Elena cut off the shower.

"Time for the Scotch hose."

Elena stared at her uncomprehendingly.

"You're a new one—I forgot," the woman said. "You'll enjoy this. We do it right here. Step way back. I'll get my hoses."

Elena did as she was told. When she turned around to face the doorway, the woman was standing there holding two heavy, snakelike rubber tubes in her hands.

"Ready? Better cover yourself. These things come on with real force. Good for circulation, though."

Instinctively Elena's hands flew to her vaginal mound.

The woman laughed. "Not there. That part's already well protected. Cover your *breasts*."

Embarrassed, Elena obeyed. The water hurled against her flesh as the woman manipulated the hoses

up, down, and crosswise. She was relieved when the
woman instructed her to face the wall. The water
beating on her back stung painfully. But it was easier
to take than the patronizing smile of the silver-haired
attendant.

The night air was sharp with the scent of
eucalyptus and pine.

Sweaters buttoned high against the chill, Dru
and Charlotte strode in rapid cadence behind Loretta
Marshall. About them, they could hear grunting and
laughter as other guests struggled to hold the pace.

Dru shivered, then swore as she stumbled on
the rutted path. She grabbed for Charlotte's arm to
steady herself, straightened, and apologized before
resuming the walk. Exhausted by the grueling day,
Dru had been tempted to stay behind after dinner, to
crawl into bed, to read, to sleep. Sheer masochism had
induced her to drag her stiffened muscles onto the
path for one last bout of exercise. Masochism, and—
she had to admit it—fear. She dreaded returning to her
cottage. Face to face with the silent telephone, she
might weaken and place yet another call to Tim in
Washington. Since her first call to his hotel, she had
tried a half-dozen times to reach him and each time
there had been no response in his room. No, she had
told the concierge at The Madison, she did not wish
to leave a message; No, not even her name. Now, her
mood a murky brew of hurt, resentment, and anxiety,
she allowed a whimper to escape her lips.

Shamed, she looked over to Charlotte. "This
hike is killing me."

"You, too? I'm half-dead but I wasn't going to
admit it. At my age you don't."

"At *your* age. You're a young woman."

"I am a middle-aged woman. I have to hang in

there and keep fighting. Can't reveal I'm getting older. It's my dirty little secret."

They had turned back on the trail and were slowly descending the hill. A few puffing figures, in pursuit of Loretta Marshall, passed them as they retreated.

Dru raised her lantern to Charlotte's face and lowered it with a sigh. "You're crazy."

"Am I? I told you I'm a divorcée, a not-so-young woman put out to pasture." Her smile was sad. "Divorce—the ultimate castration, the unkindest cut of all. One's self-image takes a beating with a divorce. Unless you're the partner who wants out. I wasn't."

"Were you still in love with him?"

"In my fashion, yes. There was no longer the hot flame of youth, you understand, but I didn't expect it. Arthur and I had been married for more than twenty years. I was proud of that, and satisfied. We were in another phase, I thought. I called it contentment."

"I'd fight for my marriage. I'd—"

"Fight?" Charlotte interrupted. "True, there's a resemblance but marriage isn't the same as a go-round in the ring. It's not as fair. I was the dethroned champ before I knew I was in a contest. And I never had a crack at a rematch."

"Another woman?"

"That's one way of describing Marcy. *Girl* would be more precise. His secretary, hardly older than our own daughter."

"Sonofabitch. You should be congratulated."

"So it seemed, for a while. In the beginning it was all numbness, anyway. Arthur was decent, and I was obedient, as usual. I did exactly what the lawyers told me to do. No scenes, no bloodshed. It was civilization's finest hour."

"If a man doesn't want you, I suppose—"

"That's what I thought. After the numbness wore off, I was giddy with freedom. Answerable to no one for the first time in my life. I'd gone from my parents' home to Arthur's. Now, suddenly, no one was putting down rules or demanding accountings of my time. I ate and slept when I wanted to. And with whomever I wanted to. Yes, I went that route, also. Overnight, I became the hottest ticket in town, a newly discovered sex object. I couldn't believe it. Me, unnoticed Charlotte Caldwell, raising pulses and penises all over Chicago's North Side. Some of the men were husbands of old friends. They told me I was desirable. They couldn't understand how Arthur could relinquish such a jewel. I thought of their wives and I agreed. I told myself it was my time now.

"Then one holiday weekend—a family sort of weekend—I sat at home alone and it dawned on me. It was all going nowhere. Those men were just different versions of Arthur but not as honest. They didn't want divorce, only an available lay. So I called it quits."

"You could have left Chicago."

"I did that, too. A trip to Europe. A brief romance. Beautiful while it lasted."

"What happened?"

"I'd rather not talk about it. It didn't work out. I ran back to Chicago."

Charlotte kicked a stone out of the path. "Then came the worst time of all. I learned what divorce really is—living death, the end of the line. In a word: loneliness."

"But you wouldn't have taken that bastard back?"

Charlotte's voice in the darkness was dull. "That bastard—or Attila the Hun. Yes. It's terrible to be alone."

Dru reached for Charlotte's hand and together they entered the wrought-iron gates of The Fountains.

The tiny, kimono-clad figure fluttering her hands above the flowers might have stepped out of a Japan Air Lines travel poster. To Dru, appraising her professionally, Mrs. Narahara was perfect casting; she *looked* the part. Not until Mrs. Narahara spoke did it become obvious that she was pure American—another working girl garbed in the uniform of her trade.

"Flower arranging." Dru shifted restlessly on the narrow gilt chair in the Renaissance Room. "Insane. Here we are, dressed like Canadian lumberjacks, seated in a pseudo-Venetian theater in Southern California, learning Oriental graces from a San Diego housewife."

Charlotte shrugged. "Got a better idea? It's nine o'clock—too late for Walter Cronkite, too early for bed. You could read, watch television."

"No, I'll stay."

"Good. One more skill to take home to your husband."

"Don't need it. The old ones are wasting away."

"Huh?"

"Nothing. Let's listen. Wouldn't want to flunk eucalyptus leaves, would we?"

With effort, Dru turned her attention to Mrs. Narahara. She watched as the little Japanese woman swung two baskets onto a long wooden table upon which she had already spread her clumps of loose flowers and greenery. Chattering lightly as she worked, Mrs. Narahara dipped into her baskets and withdrew pruning shears, blocks of styrofoam, wire frogs, and an appalling collection of ceramic bowls.

"We will make beauty," she lilted. "Come closer and I will show you how."

Rising with the others, Dru trudged to the table. She gathered up a set of implements and selected an elongated shallow container to hold her arrangement.

"I see you like them straight and not too thick." Helen Reiser was at her elbow.

"I beg your pardon?"

"You a writer? Here for material?"

"Yes, I am a writer. No, I am not here for material."

"First time in Bertini's nunnery?"

"Yes."

Helen pointed to the bowl in Dru's hand. "You catch on fast. Went right for the banana, didn't you? Couple of days here and already you're like the rest of us—thinking phallic."

Dru returned the bowl to the table. "All I see is an ugly piece of pottery."

Helen snickered. "They all say that in the beginning."

Abruptly, Dru took up the bowl again and shoved it at Helen. "If it means something to you, you're welcome to it. I hope you two have a fun evening."

"Don't be upset."

Dru patted the fat arm. "I'm not upset. Kinky sex talk just isn't for me. Besides, I'd feel ridiculous fiddling with flowers and turning on with a bowl. I guess I'm not the type."

Dru turned and started for the exit. "Smart-ass," Helen called after her retreating back. "Don't bet on it."

Dru continued to her cottage, entered, slammed the door behind her, and leaned her head against the wall. Briefly, she closed her eyes. When she reopened them they were misted, blurring her vision of the room.

With the heel of her hand she dried her eyes, then pulled a tissue from her pocket and blew her nose.

Straight ahead she could see the offending telephone, squatting on a turquoise-petticoated table. Alongside the table was her double bed, covered with a shiny turquoise-and-white striped bedspread.

Like almost everything else in the room, the telephone was turquoise.

"Color coordinated." Loretta Marshall had emphasized the obvious that first day. Dru had smiled appreciatively, playing the hayseed who had turned up wearing unmatched socks.

Her gaze held on the turquoise telephone. It *was* a nice touch.

But that wasn't what telephones were for. Telephones were supposed to ring, to bring together people who were in love, who hungered to hear each other's voices, who could croon and whisper and make plans to meet and touch.

This silent monster wasn't doing its job. It was just hanging around. Impotent.

Helen Reiser had nailed it. After a while, everyone at The Fountains thought phallic. She would talk to Dr. Bertini about that, about using it for a slogan. Think Phallic. Maybe she could do it up in needlepoint. A pillow perhaps, in varying tones of turquoise to coordinate with the telephone and the bedspread.

Flinging herself on the bed, she kicked off her shoes and began to tear open her sweater. Too jittery to lie there, she got to her feet and headed for the bathroom, the sweater flapping loosely behind her. She was reaching for the bathtub tap when she heard the ringing of the telephone in the bedroom.

Please God, let it be Tim.

It was.

"Tim, it's been ages."

"For me, too. I miss you, Dru."

"You do? You mean that?"

"On my honor."

"Tim, I tried to reach you."

"I'm out most of the time."

"I know that." She couldn't conceal the implied rebuke.

"What's that supposed to mean?"

"After midnight—" the words trailed off.

"That's why I'm in Washington, remember?" His voice tightened. "I came here to work, to see people, to do my job."

"Certainly, darling," she said, signaling retreat. "I'm not complaining. It's just this place, it confuses me. I needed to talk to you."

"My wife doesn't confuse easily. What's wrong?"

"Nothing. That's what's confusing. I'm in a cradle of opulence. They're pampering me like an empress. I'm getting healthier by the second. And I can't take it. I guess it's the old puritan ethic disapproving of me again."

"Dru, you've earned this treat."

"That's what I tell myself. 'Dru,' I say, 'you work hard, you deserve life's luxuries. If not you, who? If not now, when?' That's what I keep repeating—but I'm not getting through."

He was laughing now. "You can take the girl out of Missoula—"

"It's not just that. It's my damned social conscience. Yesterday they gave me a pedicure—I looked at my toes and I saw unemployed field workers." She groaned. "After lunch they wrapped me in steaming sheets and told me to loosen up."

"Did you?"

"How could I? I thought of famished children all over the world and I felt guilty."

"Dru, that's silly. You can do more for your causes by being strong and well so you can help in your own way."

"Who's arguing? I guess that's just my cop-out. Something else is bothering me."

"What's that?"

"I miss you."

"I told you, I miss you too."

"Tim, I still have the rest of the week. Why don't I cut out of here and join you in Washington?"

She counted the skipped beats.

"That's a lousy idea," he said at last. "I'm too tied up. You'd be bored."

"I'll poke around the Smithsonian. I'll visit the FBI Museum. When you have a minute, I'll be there."

"Not this time, Dru." He sounded drained. "There's too much going on. There are problems, things that need working out."

"I could help. You know I'm good at research. I'm even better at story problems."

"Another time. Maybe at the end of the week I'll grab a flight from Washington to San Diego. I can rent a car and we can drive home together. Right now, I want you to stay where you are. Soak up everything they give you. Somebody's got to be strong in this family."

"Tim, there's trouble. I can tell."

"Nothing that concerns you. I need more time. When I get back to California, everything will be solved. It's late, Dru. I need my shut-eye."

"Tim, do you love me?"

"I love you."

"Say it again."

"I love you. It's you and me, Dru—forever."

Long after she had hung up, Dru continued to lie back on her pillow, trying to make sense of her life with Tim.

It was futile.

"I love you—stay away," was the message she'd received. And "—everything will be solved," was what he had said.

Great. A solution was what she was waiting for.

But what the hell was the problem?

IX

It was midafternoon, and Gillian was glad she had stayed behind. Lying flat on her stomach, the pool mat damp beneath her body, she needed this time to herself, to think about Dr. Karl, about the adventure ahead. For today was the day, tonight the night. If Dr. Karl held to his schedule—and he *always* did, even when she wanted to go on and on—he would be there at The Fountains soon.

After the brisk sunrise walk and breakfast in bed (one insipid, soft-boiled egg—disdained—and a cup of black coffee), her morning had been crowded with group activities: gym class, yoga, vegetable juice break, and a return to the gym for a workout on the automatic toning machines. Lunch had been followed by an hour of modern dance, then more exercise and a volleyball game, this time in the heated swimming pool. A strong swimmer, she had longed to break free in the water, to stretch her limbs, to experience every movement, her way. But there had been no escape.

She smiled, recalling the surprise on the other faces when she had announced she was skipping the tropical fruit snack about to be served on the patio of the Garden Room.

"You're kidding!" Helen Reiser had yelped. "Nobody passes up food in this dump. Next to sex, it's all we have to think about. If you don't have one *or* the other, honey, you're dead."

"Color me dead."

"I did that the minute I laid eyes on you."

The sun was hot and she could feel the tiny beads of perspiration rising on her skin. She thought of the foamy lilac negligee still boxed and hidden in the trunk of her car. She envisioned herself wearing it, coming toward Dr. Karl as he stood near the waiting bed in his motel room. The picture she evoked made her tingle and she responded to the sensation between her legs by pressing hard into the mat and squirming pleasurably.

"Down there, it's like the epicenter of an earthquake," she had murmured to Dr. Karl following one of their better sessions on his office carpet.

Now that remarkable epicenter, spurred by her imaginings, was beginning to throb. Involuntarily her hips struck their own rhythm. The to-and-fro motion increased her need and the rush of feeling filled her with wonder. She was real, she was a woman like other women, not the bloodless, frigid stick-figure Jason accused her of being. She adored Dr. Karl for making this miracle. Tonight, with no patient buzzing at the door to cut short their lovemaking—tonight she would show him how much.

Footsteps crunching the gravel path broke her reverie. Turning on her side, she watched lazily as the two men approached. Dr. Bertini, sleek and immaculate in his pale blue jacket and white slacks, reminded her of one of those toys Bitsy had played with when she was a little girl—a dapper Ken doll readied for a date with Nurse Barbie. And beside him, white hair mussed, dear Dr. Karl, a rumpled Mark Twain, wearing a suit she had never seen, a baggy seersucker obviously selected for travel.

She came to her feet quickly when she heard Dr. Bertini call her name.

"Mrs. Crain, Gillian, what a pleasure. You have had your snack?"

"No, not today. I wasn't hungry."

Dr. Bertini's black eyes scurried over her body. "Naughty child, you need your strength."

"Your guest looks healthy enough," Dr. Karl interrupted.

"Ah, forgive me, dear Gillian. Mrs. Crain, may I present my good friend, Dr. Karl Lorenz."

She offered her hand. "Dr. Lorenz, I am privileged. Everyone is excited about tonight. Speaking for myself—I can hardly wait."

"I will try not to disappoint you."

With that, he and Dr. Bertini moved away.

"Who was that?" Christina Rossi had appeared beside Gillian as she stood watching the two men enter Dr. Bertini's quarters.

"Dr. Karl Lorenz."

"Who is sick?"

"No one is sick. Dr. Lorenz is a famous psychoanalyst. You missed the announcement. He's here to lecture us tonight."

"That funny man? What about?"

"His subject is 'Vibrant Health: Vibrant Sexuality.'"

Christina threw back her head and laughed. "I hope he has good recall."

"That's bitchy."

"Did you get a good look at him? He's sixty-five years old, at least."

"What of it?"

"A man that age—I think he must suffer from
terminal libido." She laughed anew. "There is a saying:
Those who can, do. Those who cannot, teach."

Gillian's jaw tightened. "Those who can, also
teach. You're the expert—why don't you deliver the
lecture?"

"Someday I may do that." Christina's high humor
was unshaken. "Meanwhile, I am a willing pupil. Tonight I will fold my hands in my lap and listen quietly
to the fuddy-duddy."

Although the masseuse had forgotten to hang
her sign on the cottage door, Charlotte knew the
woman—what was her name?—Janet, that was it—was
already in the room.

It was amazing how divorce had sharpened her
senses. In the years with Arthur she had been almost
childishly trusting, blissfully unaware and naive. In a
word, *dumb.* It had been a family joke that for three
years running Arthur had actually succeeded in surprising her with a birthday party.

Cynicism and loss of innocence had been unwel-
come bonuses, extra goodies hidden away in her divorce
papers like stale jellybeans in a birthday basket. She
sighed, then sought to console herself, recalling that
the divorce agreement had offered other, more favor-
able, features as well—like the financial settlement that
made it possible for her to be here in this extravagant
beauty spa, about to enter her own suite for a delicious
massage.

The day had been rigorous but she had enjoyed
it, even the teasing she had been subjected to in the
pool when she had missed the volleyball and lost the
game for her team. "What can you expect from a grandmother?" she had said, and Elena had hugged her, saying, "I hope I'm as terrific as you when I'm a mother."

Now it would be pleasant to lie on the massage table, eyelids closed beneath the cooling astringent pads, and give herself up to the undemanding strokes of the large, silent masseuse.

The white-clad woman rose as Charlotte entered the room. "I was resting," she apologized.

"Can't blame you. It's five o'clock. You must be beat."

"Not at all. My work keeps me in condition."

"I can see that. How many bodies have you done today?"

Janet raised her hands and crooked her fingers one by one. "You'll be the sixth."

"Any more before you go home?"

"You're the last."

Charlotte yawned. "How long does each massage take?" she asked without interest.

"It depends."

"Depends? On what?"

"That's a professional secret."

"Sorry, I didn't mean to pry." Charlotte slipped off her robe and moved toward the table.

"Oh, I don't mind telling you. It's Dr. Bertini's idea, the way we do massages at The Fountains. He insists we repeat each stroke ten times, no more, no less. The neck, the back, the arms, legs, fingers, toes—all to the count of ten. He believes there's something hypnotic about repeating the number. The guest is often counting along subliminally. If you stop at nine or run over to eleven or twelve, the guest is jarred without understanding why."

"Then you *do* know how long each one takes."

"No, that's the point. You can't know—not until you're familiar with the individual body. Ten strokes on the stomach of a fat woman will take more time than ten strokes on the stomach of a thin one. Long legs take more time than short legs. Bony arms go faster than flabby ones. Massage time can vary from ten to fifteen minutes."

Charlotte stretched her back against the massage table.

Janet's glance swept over her calculatingly before she switched off the lights. "You're a small one," she said. "You won't take long."

Minutes later, eyes closed, enveloped in sheeting from the waist down, Charlotte felt the masseuse's creamed fingertips pattering gently over her face. Another rule of the game. She knew that one without asking: Easy on the facial muscles, they collapse soon enough as it is; save the hard rubs for where they are needed, the limbs and the extra padding on the backside and hips.

In the darkened room, she tensed slightly as Janet's deft fingers slid over her ears, stroked her neck, then slid into her hairline. Two years, and she was still sensitive about the face-lift. She knew she was being foolish about the scars. The woman had probably encountered them dozens, maybe hundreds of times; a masseuse would think nothing of it.

"Relax, dear," the voice behind her was low. "Let yourself go. It's good for you."

Charlotte stretched voluptuously as the lotioned fingers slid forward to her throat.

Skin on skin, migod, how she craved it! Once she had read an essay on skin hunger and thought it rather funny. Sharing a bed with Arthur, night after night, year after year, comfortable against his body, she had accepted human warmth as she did her own breathing. Later, after the separation, she had wept in that same bed and asked herself why a civilized society could not provide a neighborhood depot where the tactually deprived could stop by for a handout of simple touching. As she saw it, it could be a sub-branch, possibly under the Department of Health, Education and Welfare which, conscientiously administered, need not be too costly to the taxpayer.

She felt the masseuse's fingertips playing across her shoulders. This was a lighter massage than before. She supposed the woman was tired after all. Just as well. She preferred the smooth gliding motions to the heavy poundings.

Outside the cottage the final exercise class of the day was going through its paces to the tunes on an old Andy Williams record. The music was soothing and she felt her muscles loosen. Drowsiness crept over her and she seemed to be drifting.

She wasn't quite sure it had happened.

The distant music, the dark room, the rhythmic stroking, the unseen woman reaching from behind the table, had come together to induce a dreamy, hypnotic state that was not quite sleep, not quite wakefulness.

She was in this shadowy place when she felt smooth hands cupping her breasts. Soft fingers seemed to be gliding slowly around their fullness, and soon there was a gentle squeezing on her rising nipples.

Of course it was a dream . . . or a fantasy. Straining to consciousness, Charlotte raised her hand to the moistened pads and pulled them away from her eyes.

When her eyes were opened, the woman was by her side; her profile, vaguely perceived, was impassive as she bent across the table and vigorously slapped at Charlotte's hips.

Charlotte shuddered.

The woman nodded her head. "Best thing for the circulation, if you can take it."

"I can take it."

After the woman had gone, Charlotte sat swathed in her bathrobe, a cold cigarette between her fingers, and tried to sort it out. Except for that dreadful moment, the massage had proceeded routinely. Beyond the usual instructions—relax, turn over, try to sleep—Janet Wolfe had spoken little. She had kneaded and oiled and towel-dried, performing as efficiently as before. She had departed after promising (threatening?) to return the following day.

In the still room, Charlotte frowned (a certifiable crime at The Fountains), forcing deep lines into her brow and around her mouth.

Something had happened. Was it her own imagination or had the woman dared, actually *dared* to fondle her? Angered, Charlotte drew on the unlit cigarette and then, in disgust, she crushed it into an ashtray. Dammit, she'd report the incident to Dr. Bertini, that's what she'd do. He ought to know what was going on at The Fountains, practically under his own nose. He was harboring a sex fiend, a menace to the community, a woman-molester, no less. She visualized herself marching into Dr. Bertini's office and Telling All. Telling what? If Janet Wolfe had made overtures, how could she explain that she had remained upon the table permitting the masseuse to continue stroking her? Any woman with her head screwed on right would have thrown the pervert out.

Unless it was what she wanted.

That is, if it had really happened . . .

The ringing of the telephone was a welcome interruption.

"Cocktails, dear." Loretta Marshall was a trilling bird. "Ten minutes from now, in the Garden Room."

"I'll be there."

"And Charlotte, don't forget—tonight Dr. Lorenz speaks to us about 'Vibrant Health: Vibrant Sexuality.' " She tittered and she was gone.

Charlotte glared at the dead telephone. "Damn

you, Loretta, is this a beauty farm or a sex farm?" she thought indignantly. "I'll worry about my sexuality when I get out of here. Meanwhile you worry about yours. And you can stick *that* up your four-color brochure!"

For the first time, Gillian was feeling doubts about the anticipated rendezvous with Dr. Karl.

Dinner had not gone well. From the dais, Dr. Bertini had introduced his guest and Dr. Karl, somewhat clumsily Gillian had to admit, had come to his feet from his chair at the host table. There had been an unimpressive smattering of applause and Dr. Karl had bowed like the Old World Viennese that he was. He had said a few words about meeting them later in the Renaissance Room. Then he had dropped back heavily into his seat.

At the table near the window, Elena had been glum. Rita and Charlotte had appraised Dr. Karl coolly and then made gleeful references to the charismatic deficiencies of professional sex experts. Drs. Masters, Johnson, Reuben, and Comfort had been discussed but Dr. Lorenz easily had walked away with top honors in the lack-of-sex-appeal division. Dru, after glancing at Gillian, had chosen to say nothing. And Rita Sloane had made further jottings in her notebook.

Dinner ended, Loretta Marshall had announced that in recognition of the uniqueness of the evening, there would be no night walk in the hills. They had filed from the Garden Room to the Renaissance Room, settled onto the impossible gilt chairs and, with varying degrees of expectancy, awaited Dr. Karl Lorenz's thoughts on the subject of "Vibrant Health: Vibrant Sexuality."

Seated between Dru and Rita, Gillian studied Dr. Karl as he stepped up to the Venetian music stand centered on the stage. Dr. Karl's single-buttoned blue suit, the style so dearly familiar to her from their office encounters, was enlivened this evening by a neat red vest. His jacket stood open and his sizeable paunch flared on either side of the graceful stand. As he tipped his head toward his audience, his thick-lensed glasses slid to the bulb of his nose. Fleetingly, Gillian saw him as the others did and, for an instant, she lowered her eyes.

"Why am I here?" Dr. Karl's tone was self-deprecating, his smile benign. "I look about me and I see only healthy faces and bodies that are excitingly alive. I ask myself—what have I, a doctor of the mind, to say to women so knowledgeable, so conscious that they inhabit the most sublime temple of all, their very own bodies? Knowing the special kind of woman I would find here, I nevertheless accepted Dr. Bertini's invitation to come before you. Why? I think many of you can guess."

Abruptly, Dr. Karl's smile vanished and with it, Gillian was gratified to see, his unaccustomed air of modesty. "I come because I know, as many of you know, that even within the healthiest womanly flesh there may dwell a sick, frightened child, a little girl, hurt, inhibited psychically, fearful of the natural arousal that could permit her to release her innermost physical self.

"Sometimes, the frailest bodies have sheltered the most ardent natures. Elizabeth Barrett Browning comes to mind, but we need not deal with her here. Neither circumstance is ideal. What we strive for, we humble doctors, is a joyous harmony, the fullest realization of the many aspects of our being. And we must achieve this, for to do any less is not to be alive. We all know—"

"*I* certainly do." Rita Sloane unlatched her purse and dropped her notebook into it. "I've written that spiel a thousand times."

Gillian spun toward her. "You could be polite and listen. Maybe you still have something to learn."

"Well, pardon my blubbering lips. I didn't know you take this stuff seriously."

"I do."

Gillian looked down at her hands, trembling in her lap. That had been a damn fool thing to do, ripping into Rita that way. Dr. Karl had pointed out her tendency to overreact. "A displacement of feeling," he had said, "easily recognizable to anyone with insight." She grasped the edge of her chair in an effort to control her anger. Another flare-up and she would disgrace both of them.

Looking up again, she surveyed the faces around her. Dr. Karl had his audience now, she noted. Suddenly, pride of possession warmed her—her shameful moment of disloyalty became an aberration of the past.

Christina, caustic earlier, sat deeply absorbed. Helen Reiser, the loud mouth closed for once, leaned forward, attentive to every word. Debbie, the fat teenager, was flushed. The Lyman twins inexplicably held hands. And stupid Sheila, a secret chord touched, seemed close to tears.

Gillian wanted to cry, too. Returning her attention to the stage, her love and gratitude became overwhelming. To the other women, Dr. Karl's words were impersonal. It was she alone who knew their true meaning. She understood that the lost child he had described was Gillian, before she had become his patient. Only Dr. Karl on the stage and she in the audience knew that when he spoke of deep passions to be acted out, he was speaking of their own exquisite affair. However veiled his references, she exulted that he had chosen this platform to proclaim their love.

She wanted him desperately. When his gaze roved the upturned faces, lingering briefly on her own, her breathing accelerated and the crazy pulse between her legs became unmoored. His ability to arouse her was awesome. This wonderful man, without touching her, was lubricating her vaginal vault, readying her for his entry.

She felt like breaking into laughter, remembering the cerebral precision that she and Jason had brought to their bedroom in Beverly Hills. They had purchased stacks of books about the art of lovemaking and together they had perused them like playmates studying the instructions on the box of a complicated game. Putting aside their books, they had performed without technical error—and without emotion.

Tonight she would show Dr. Karl something of what she had learned in her studies. She would not be content to revel in her own sexuality. She wanted to share, to give to Dr. Karl every sensual pleasure she was capable of offering.

The fussy sound of chairs being moved, and a light touch on her knee, brought her back to the present.

"It's over," Dru was saying. "Didn't you hear the applause? Dr. Lorenz has a smash act."

"Yes, I liked him very much."

"How about a quick walk around the grounds before going to sleep?"

"Not me, I'm ready to drop. Must be close to ten o'clock. Just enough time to call Jason and Bitsy before I collapse into bed."

Sauntering back to her cottage with Dru at her side, Gillian carefully weighed her alternatives.

She could phone the house in Beverly Hills, risking another unpleasant scene with Jason, or just as likely, a drawn-out entanglement in Bitsy's crisis of the day. Or both. Whatever was happening at home, she reasoned, was certain to break her ecstatic mood.

On the other hand, she could take a warm bubble

bath, cream her body, arrange her hair and apply a bit of makeup before pulling on slacks and shirt and driving off to the motel to meet Dr. Karl.

It was no contest.

Throwing off her clothes, she hastened to the bathroom and began her ritual.

Dr. Bertini was alone in his bedroom preparing to undress when he heard footsteps crunching on the gravel outside his cottage. Switching off all his lights, he strode to his sitting room window and stealthily parted the drapes. The merest slit would do, he knew from experience, just enough to allow him a view of the illuminated parking court ahead.

Peering between the drapes, he saw a long-legged blonde moving toward the little red Mazda wedged between The Fountains' station wagon and his own black Buick. Mrs. Crain. He never would have guessed it. He had had Gillian Crain pegged as the original Snow Queen, beautiful without doubt, but desirable only if a man was courting frostbite.

Dr. Bertini was disappointed. Another one. The fifth this year. And it was still spring. Momentarily, he dwelt upon his profession and wondered if his colleagues at other spas endured what he did. True, these night wanderers presented no serious problem to him. He did, however, harbor some resentment each time one of them sneaked off for an assignation. Not that he was jealous. He was not. His own needs were charmingly met by the divorcée in San Diego. No, it was something else. What he actively disliked was the knowledge that he was being used. After all that he did for them. Didn't they know that he, Dr. Alfredo Bertini, made it a practice to review each guest's record card personally? That he consulted regularly with the spa's dietician and nurse and exercise staff? Didn't they appreciate that he de-

voted hours to working out individual schedules designed to bring maximum benefit to every woman who
became his charge? Didn't they understand that he
cared?

Yet, too often, his ladies betrayed him. They
broke training, which was disgraceful.

Experience had taught him that although a tru-
ant guest did not always stay the night with a man,
she would devote at least part of her evening to eating
too much and drinking too much. And following dinner,
he was sure, she did not sleep too much, either.

Dr. Bertini took no moral position on anyone's
sexual activity. He did, however, resent the unsuper-
vised and unhealthy calories a woman ingested in the
hours she was away from The Fountains. And he deplored the loss of her necessary sleep. He knew that
in the morning the guest would appear red-eyed and
cranky, if she bothered to appear at all. She would drag
around having a depressing effect on other guests, and
invent ridiculous stories about the cause of her fatigue,
lying with an ease that would astonish him. Eventually,
appearing before Mrs. Kaplan for her final weigh-in and
measure, she would be noisily disappointed to discover
the efforts of the week had not achieved her goal. If
she was truly brazen, she would blame Dr. Bertini and
the regimen of The Fountains.

But that was only part of what troubled Dr.
Bertini. What he disliked the most was having The
Fountains used as a way station, a contrivance to escape
a husband or lover left behind.

Dr. Bertini treasured his spa. He was fervently
committed to it. In a sense, he felt *he* was the one who
was being cuckolded.

He was about to drop the drapes when he saw
Mrs. Crain doing something odd. As he watched, she
headed for the rear of her car, looked over her shoulder

furtively, and then, inserting her key, raised the lid of the Mazda's trunk. Using both hands, she withdrew a large cardboard box tied with ribbons that met to form an elaborate bow. She snuggled her face in the bow, then, with great care, she replaced the box on the floor of the trunk and quietly closed the lid. Taking a last look around her, she hastened to the driver's seat and started up the engine. In seconds, she was gone.

Dr. Bertini released the drapes and they fell closed. Women, they were mad. But no madder than the men who awaited them. This time, he would not permit himself to be annoyed. It had been too fine a day to spoil.

He turned the lights back on, lit a cigarette and reviewed the day . . .

His invitation to Dr. Karl Lorenz had been inspired. The analyst had been in splendid form. The guests, even the most skeptical such as Christina Rossi, Jessica Haskell, and—before the evening was over—Rita Sloane, had become adoring converts, many of them gathering around the white-haired analyst, beseeching answers to questions suddenly grown urgent. Dr. Lorenz had been patient, graciously attempting to respond to each of them until, sensing that the older man was growing restless, Dr. Bertini had intervened, separating him from the persistent women.

Crossing the grass, going toward the spa's station wagon which was to take Dr. Lorenz to his motel accommodations near San Diego, Dr. Bertini had been effusive.

"Karl, you were admirable. If my guests remember nothing more of their visit, they will remember you."

"I am the one who was privileged. They are an extraordinary group."

"You think so? Then you have special vision or a

generous heart. Some of them are horrors. Shall I tell
you which?"

"No need, I recognize them. The important thing
is that even the horrors can be helped. There is always
hope."

"Ah, hope, but what about time?"

"Time? It is the enemy of all of us. What are you
getting at, Alfredo?"

Dr. Bertini had broken into a sheepish grin. His
strong white teeth shone in the moonlight.

"Karl, this is unfair of me, but it is a rare opportunity when I have you to myself."

"You have a problem?"

"Not yet a problem, but a fear. Perhaps every
man's fear. Tonight you spoke about 'Vibrant Health:
Vibrant Sexuality.' Vibrant health I will always strive
to provide for myself. But—vibrant sexuality—for a
man—as he grows older? Is that attainable?" He continued to smile, embarrassed. "I have experienced no
lessening of my abilities, not so much as a hint of
failure. Still, in my profession, one is trained to think
of the future, to plan ahead if it is possible."

Dr. Lorenz was amused. "My dear Alfredo, it is
possible."

"Diet? Exercise?"

"Exercise."

"Good. You will send me some literature, something you have written on the subject?"

"There is no literature, my friend. You must
merely exercise as you have been, that one muscle, that
vital muscle. The penis may take brief vacations but it
should never be allowed to take a long sabbatical."

"I do not see that happening."

"Then you have nothing to worry about. I, at
my age—"

"Please, Karl, I did not intend for you to be personal."

Dr. Lorenz removed his glasses and waved them in the direction of the Renaissance Room. "Back there, one of your horrors, I heard her as I approached the stage. 'Dr. Lorenz,' she was saying, 'he can dish it out, but can he get it up?' "

"Unbelievable! I apologize for the insult."

"Not at all. She cannot provoke me. I am secure. I know my own strength. I do not mean to boast but today, as always, I am the match of any man."

They had reached the station wagon. Manuel, wearing narrow blue jeans and an open-necked western shirt, had been waiting to chauffeur Dr. Lorenz to his motel. As the two men approached, Manuel had leaped from the driver's seat and swung open the passenger door.

Dr. Lorenz had eyed Manuel. Turning back to Dr. Bertini, he had winked. "Of *any* man," he had repeated. "Good night, Alfredo."

Now musing in his sitting room, Dr. Bertini took a long pull on his cigarette. He would break his regular routine, he decided. He would telephone the divorcée in San Diego and tell her he was leaving The Fountains immediately. Additional exercise could not hurt.

Spirits high, he carried his ashtray into the bathroom and flushed away all remnants of the cigarette. No need for the hard-working maids to clean up behind him.

Besides, as everyone knew, he did not approve of smoking.

The moonlight sifting between the trees lit the path in an irregular checkerboard pattern. Unthinking,

Dru stepped from one dark patch to the next, making ragged progress back to her cottage. She did not know how long she had been on her solitary walk nor how many times she had circled the quiet grounds.

After leaving the Renaissance Room, she and Gillian had strolled to their cottages and parted on their shared brick porch. Troubled by Dr. Lorenz's lecture, Dru had tried to lose herself in reading, but the books and magazines scattered about the room had irritated her. A quick circuit of the radio dial had disclosed nothing but junk.

Too restless to sleep, she had again pulled on her clothes and returned to the deserted grounds hoping the fresh air would clear her muddled head. It had not.

There was no escaping the truth. Dr. Lorenz's lecture had struck hard. Repeatedly, as she walked, she had gone over the analyst's numerous suggestions for the betterment of a woman's life. She had explored each nugget of wisdom, examining it minutely for some clue to her own misery. She had come up with nothing—at least nothing that seemed relevant to Tim and her.

She did not blame Dr. Lorenz for her present confusion. It was unreasonable to expect one man, in one evening, to straighten out the lives of twenty screwed-up women. And they were screwed-up, every one of them, in different ways, to differing degrees. If she was certain of nothing else, she was of that. She considered telephoning Dr. Lorenz when this week was ended to seek an appointment in his office, but she doubted that she would do so. Her tidy Missoula mind clung to the precepts of her childhood, to her mother's firmly held belief that the Lord helped those who helped themselves. "Be yourself, be healthy," Mrs. Jennings would declaim when coming upon her daughter sunk in depression. "I don't know what's worrying you, Dru, but remember, everything happens for the best."

Does it, Mama? her brain demanded. Well, fuck you, Mama, unless you can explain to me, and very clearly, how all that chin up, hold-a-good-thought crap is going to help my pain.

Yet, she thought, reversing herself, Dr. Lorenz might be the answer. Look at what he had done for Gillian. Granted, Gillian had never confided her reasons for consulting the analyst except for mentioning the skirmishes with Bitsy. If Gillian was to be believed, Bitsy was still a trial and, Dru suspected, Jason was, too. Yet Gillian did seem happier now. In recent months, her skin and hair and eyes had taken on a new glow. She laughed more easily, her mood was light and sweet. Only in the past few days had Gillian regressed, revealing the nastier side of her character.

Still, Dru understood that was the way it went in therapy—and after therapy, too, when the patient had been terminated by the analyst. It was not unusual to suffer through a few letdowns. The important thing was that you mellowed out over the long pull.

She wondered if Gillian still saw Dr. Lorenz. She wanted to question her about the old gentleman but she knew she didn't dare. Gillian had chosen to be secretive about that aspect of her life. She, Dru, had no right to invade her friend's private world simply because she could not cope with her own troubled marriage.

She was nearing her cottage when a new sound, unheard on her earlier rounds, caused her to pull deeper into the shadows. Frightened, she looked off in the direction of the sound. It was a door, she realized—a cottage door that someone was opening and closing with caution.

Unsure of what to do next, she slipped further into the dense shrubbery and waited. Seconds later she heard footsteps descending a porch.

And then she saw Gillian.

Breathless and eager, her yellow hair bouncing on her shoulders, Gillian was moving rapidly into the motor court and heading for her Mazda.

Puzzled, Dru suppressed an impulse to call out. And then, in an instant it all came to her and she understood.

So that was it, that was why they were here—so that her true friend, Gillian Crain, could sneak off into the night to get laid. She had no doubt, not a shred of doubt, that Gillian was going to meet a man, and she was sure the man was not Jason.

Watching, she was surprised when Gillian did not go directly to the driver's seat of the Mazda. Instead, Gillian raised the trunk lid of the car and withdrew a bulky box. For an instant she held the box close before replacing it carefully on the floor of the trunk. And only then did she get behind the wheel and drive away.

The bitch—the lying, scheming, two-faced bitch. The *sleepy* two-faced bitch—who was too tired to take a walk.

Dru stepped from behind the shrubbery intending to return to her cottage, but anger immobilized her. She stood stock still, swearing under her breath. She was a fool, a dupe, a dimwit, lured into dropping her work and coming to The Fountains because Gillian had a lover nearby and she was going to him tonight. Every night, for all Dru knew.

And she, Drucilla Jennings, the big brain, she had been conned into playing the beard. She hated the word but she could not think of a better one. The beard

—the graphic Hollywood term for the third party who didn't have any fun, who tagged along to make everything appear respectable until the two who mattered went off to ball.

A thousand dollars a week and all the carrot juice she could drink, so Gillian Crain could sneak away and have a love affair.

She began to swear.

The highway stretched ahead, deserted save for an occasional rumbling truck. Gillian pulled into the slower lane each time she heard another truck approaching, moving out again only when the vehicle was gone from view. She was resolved not to hurry.

Dr. Karl had left The Fountains more than an hour ago. Heart pounding, she had observed him in earnest conversation with the fatuous Dr. Bertini. Then he had departed, seated alongside Manuel, in the big station wagon.

Several times, while preparing herself for this miraculous night, she had looked out her window to see if the station wagon was back. When she saw it at last, safely returned to its usual slot, she stole a look at the wall clock. Sternly, she put her plan into motion. She was determined to delay her own leavetaking another twenty minutes. She wanted to give Manuel time to deposit the wagon keys with Leslie, the night switchboard operator, and to gossip a while, which seemed to be his style, before quitting the premises himself. The delay would be excruciating. It would also be prudent.

Too, Dr. Karl might want some time for himself, to shower, to rest, to read or drink, or whatever it was a man like Dr. Karl did while waiting for a woman to join him for the night.

She tightened her grip on the steering wheel to steady her shaking hands, then abandoned the effort. It was a vain exercise in control. Her body seemed all jelly and nerve ends, and her foot on the gas pedal jiggled.

It was ridiculous; she was like a quivering virgin. The analogy seemed comical. Virgins—if there were any around these days—could never feel like this because they did not yet know the mind-boggling joy that awaited them.

It was almost a physical relief to see the neon lights of the Spindrift Lodge up ahead.

She would have to be a good girl, a lady really, to carry this off without embarrassing Dr. Karl. She would hold back her imaginings and concentrate on the immediate objectives: checking into her own reserved room, and getting to Dr. Karl's room as inconspicuously as possible.

With the Juel Park box containing the negligee under one arm and the large canvas tote dangling from her shoulder (the saleswoman at Saks had assured her it could double as a weekender), she entered the lobby.

The night clerk, a chubby, balding young man wearing an outlandish plaid sports jacket, was absorbed in a car repair magazine as she marched purposefully up to the reception desk.

"I am Mrs. Delman," she announced. "You are holding a room for me."

At first, it had struck her as uncreative to have made the reservation in her maiden name. Once, in a discussion with her father, who was a true crime buff, she had heard Lawrence Delman mention the peculiar fact that criminals seldom looked much beyond their real names when inventing pseudonyms. If she was following a criminal pattern, all the better. She liked the idea.

Absently, the clerk shoved a vinyl-backed reservation pad at her.

"Please fill it in, ma'am," he said, barely looking up.

"Of course. Oh, do you have a Dr. Lorenz registered? Dr. Karl Lorenz?"

The clerk reluctantly put aside the magazine and scanned his records. "Yup," he said. "Room 18."

"I'm a patient. I'm not well—"

"Sorry to hear that, ma'am. Any luggage?"

"Just what I'm carrying."

He picked up his car repair magazine. "You won't be needing any help. Here's your key. Room 12. Out the door. Turn left, past the cigarette machine."

She decided not to go to her own room first. She stood nervously before Room 18 and waited for Dr. Karl to respond to her rapping.

"The door is open," she heard him say. "Come in."

He was hunched in a scruffy velvet chair, clad in a dressing gown of nondescript blue. Crushed red bedroom slippers completed his costume. A shaded floor lamp shone on the papers in an open folder spread across his lap. Beyond the arc of lamplight, nearby the chair, she could make out a turned-down double bed. A Navajo-patterned bedspread hung over the footboard. The rest of the room was not illuminated.

Dr. Karl remained seated, his face expressionless, as she uncertainly closed the door behind her. Then he removed his glasses, put aside his folder, and lifted himself from the deep chair.

"I am happy you are here."

She was briefly confused. "Didn't you expect me?"

"I have been waiting for you."

Gently, he removed the tote bag from her shoulder and placed it against the wall.

"What is that?" He pointed to the gold box under her arm.

Her voice was low. "It's a surprise—for you."

"Shall I open it?"

"No, it's for later."

She came through the door into the bedroom wearing the foamy lilac negligee. At her back, the dim bathroom light silhouetted her nude body just as she had planned it would do. Dr. Karl was waiting for her. Now that his heavy-lensed glasses had disappeared somewhere, the excitement she had anticipated was clear in his eyes.

Also clear, disconcertingly, was the thick, curly white hair on his chest, visible for the first time as he began to undo the blue bathrobe. Involuntarily, her eyelids closed. When she looked again, Dr. Karl stood naked before her, his broad belly overhanging his erect penis.

Jason, she thought in panic, who is this stranger? What am I doing here in this awful motel, with a homely, fat old man? Jason, you sonofabitch, why did you let this happen to me?

Dr. Karl was running his fingers over her face, her throat, reaching for her breasts.

"You—are—magnificent." His voice was blurry. His fingers fumbled at the single pearl button that held the negligee together.

She stood, unmoving, observing him as he manipulated the fastening.

When he had parted the negligee, he stepped back and stared at her.

"You—are—overwhelming." In seconds he was all over her, his lips suckling her nipples, his hands exploring her breasts, her hips, her stomach, her buttocks.

She could feel herself responding. Her lips parted as her breathing accelerated, and her vagina dampened and pulsated. This man was incredible—she wanted to dissolve completely into him. Her hands grasped at his thick body and—bending slightly to accommodate herself to his height—she pulled him to her, tighter and tighter, pressing her pelvis against his, welcoming the thrusting organ between her legs.

"I love you, migod, how I love you," she said.

Impatiently, she pulled at the lilac negligee. It was a nuisance now. It fell to the floor and she kicked it aside. Body free, she dropped to her knees and, clutching at his thighs, she took his engorged penis between her lips. Her tongue and her lips encircled it wildly.

He pushed her loose of him and brought her to her feet, emitting strange wheezing sounds as he drew her to the bed. Throwing himself on his back, he guided her until she was locked above him, riding and rolling with his fierce, quick movements.

Then, suddenly, he was above her, swaying, tantalizing, a playful pachyderm eluding her until her groping fingers caught his organ and drove it into her body.

Even then, he held back, gliding in and out, slowly, teasingly. She raised her hips and beat against him, forcing him to accelerate, to match her rhythm.

Her orgasm—or was it his?—shot through her being, enduring an eternity. *So this is why I was born, to know this ecstasy.* She seemed detached from her own body, off somewhere in another consciousness, filled with mindless joy.

Again and again he pleasured her. When it was finally ended he pulled the sheets over them and kissed her for the first time that night. Then he cradled her to him and she slept.

One morning over breakfast Tim had chided Dru for awakening in a ferocious mood.

"If Shakespeare had met you, he couldn't have written that line about how sleep—"

"Don't nag me," Dru had said crossly.

He had dipped his head into his newspaper. "I hope someone feeds you happy pills today."

Tim knew her well. Whenever she went to bed angry, she unfailingly awakened with her anger un-abated. No sleep ever knitted up *her* ravel'd sleave of care.

This time it was no different.

The clanging telephone had barely roused her when the recollection of Gillian's double-dealing trick flooded her mind. The fluorescent wall clock informing her it was barely three o'clock did nothing to improve her temper.

Her caller was Leslie, the switchboard operator. "Gee, Ms. Jennings, I'm sorry—I shouldn't be doing this to you—not in the middle of the night—but it sounds important."

"What does?"

"There's this man. I'm holding him on the line."

"What man?"

"He says his name is Jason Crain. He wants to speak to Mrs. Crain."

"Well, let him speak to Mrs. Crain then."

"She's not in her room. I buzzed her maybe twenty times and she didn't answer—that's what I told him."

"You didn't!"

"Yes, I did, and he got mad and made me go

over to her cottage." Leslie's voice was choked. "I'm not supposed to do that. I'm not allowed to leave the board but this man was hollering so, and Dr. Bertini is away tonight—"

"Did you find Mrs. Crain?"

"No, she's not in her bed. She's not *anywhere*. And now he's yelling and asking to speak to you."

"Put him through."

"Thanks, Ms. Jennings. You're a sweetheart. He's really raving!"

Dru turned on the bedside lamp. After a short wait, she picked up the receiver. "Jason? It's Dru. What's wrong?"

"Goddammit, everything's wrong. Where's Gillian?"

"In San Diego." She hesitated. "There was trouble with the car. She has to stay there overnight till the garage gets the part. She's at some hotel, I can't remember the name."

"What the hell is she doing in San Diego? I thought you dames were supposed to stay on the premises!"

"Jason, stop shouting at me. We're not inmates here, you know."

He was immediately contrite. "I'm sorry, Dru, I shouldn't be taking your head off."

"Forget it. Gillian said something about a prescription. She needed a refill . . . Jason, what's so urgent?"

"It's Bitsy. I've got a problem with her."

"Is she all right?"

His voice rose again. "How the hell do I know? That's what I want to talk to her mother about."

"Jason, settle down. Tell me what's going on."

"Well, you see, I was out pretty late tonight.

Business meeting. When I got home Bitsy wasn't here and Ada was having hysterics. She had phoned all around and Bitsy's friends didn't know where she was. Anyway, that's what they said. I was getting ready to call the police when Bitsy walked in."

"You're phoning at three in the morning to tell Gillian *that?*"

"You don't understand. You should see her. She's a wreck. Her hair's all tangled, her clothes are a dirty mess. She looks like the victim of forcible rape!"

"What's new about that?"

"She won't tell me where she's been—and I think she's sloshed. She's locked herself in her bathroom with the water running."

"Maybe she's taking a bath. Wouldn't that be nice for a change?"

"Dru, this is serious. It's a matter for her mother."

"Jason, Bitsy is home, she's safe. Gillian can't be reached. Naturally you're upset. But why don't you get off Bitsy's back for tonight? It doesn't sound like the best time for rational talk anyway. Get some sleep. I'll tell Gillian you called."

Later, after hanging up, she wondered why she had done it. Gillian had deceived both of them; she didn't deserve protection.

It was, she decided, a conditioned response. No matter what, the sisterhood stuck together.

The thin fingers of dawn were creeping around the edges of the blinds when Gillian opened her eyes. Dr. Karl's back was turned to her now. She curled against him, spoon-fashion, feeling his warmth, then sliding her free arm over his body, she began to fondle and tease him.

Aroused, he faced her and smiled. "I'll be right back," he said, and left the bed.

Her eyes followed him as he entered the bathroom and shut the door. Stretching lazily, she heard the unexpected noise of the toilet flushing, and then the dribble of water at the porcelain sink as Dr. Karl rinsed his hands. The sounds offended her. As the dreamer of this dream, she had failed to include bathroom duties. Other men urinated—not her Dr. Karl.

She was being ridiculous, she told herself. By the time he returned to bed, she had forgiven him.

Shed of the nervousness and doubts of the night before, she gloried in their new lovemaking, wanting it never to end.

"I'm not leaving," she said when it was over.

"My adorable child, you will dress and go at once. Only by using discretion can we hope to be together like this again."

"When will that be?" she wailed. "And where?"

"Now I am the one who has a lovely surprise for you," he said.

She reached for his flaccid penis. "Have I found it?"

"Do not be mischievous. Take your hand away or I will not tell you."

Dutifully, she removed her hand and raised herself on one elbow, leaning way over him till her breasts touched his face.

"And take those away, too," he ordered. "Listen to me. It is a dangerous thing we do and you must not be flippant. This morning I want you to be in your bed at The Fountains when the maid brings your breakfast. If anyone asks where you have been, you must say nothing, *nothing*. Do you understand?"

"I understand."

"Good. I want you to go through your day normally. And, then, my little one, I want you to come back to me tonight."

"Tonight!" She was overjoyed. "I thought you had to be in your office today."

"My patients have been informed. Their time will be made up."

"Then we can spend the day together. I'll think of some excuse—"

He cut her off. "No. I will be busy all day with colleagues in San Diego. Out. Out now. Leave. I will be waiting for you tonight. Shall we say nine o'clock?"

She picked the lilac negligee off the floor and put it on. Then she buttoned it modestly and started for the bathroom.

On impulse, she returned to the disheveled bed and kissed the top of his head.

"I love you," she said, her expression serious. "This has been the most beautiful night of my life."

X

The young Mexican maid reaching across the bed to remove the breakfast tray eyed Gillian curiously. Most guests tore into their food like hungry street dogs. This one was different. She had not so much as touched her grapefruit—the only solid food on the tray—and she had barely sipped at her black coffee.

Something else was different, too. This woman had a special drowsy look on her face. The maid recognized the look. She had seen it on the picture screen in Tijuana when a neighborhood theater had played that old movie, *Gone With The Wind*. It was the look of a woman who had just been with a man.

But how was it possible to have that look at eight o'clock in the morning at The Fountains? The maid had been recently hired by Dr. Bertini but already she had many questions about the strange people who came here. She would add this question to her list. Someday she might have all the answers.

The maid was backing away from the bed when she heard a rapping on the door. She glanced questioningly at the guest. The woman in the bed had buried her cheek into her pillow and appeared to be asleep.

When the rapping was repeated, the maid spoke. "Ma'am, shall I see who it is?"

Gillian turned her head slowly. "Did you say something?"

"There is someone at the door. Would you like me to open it?"

Gillian slid under the blanket. "Would you, please? I'm not ready to get up."

Carefully balancing the tray against her hip, the maid swung the door inward. The woman at the door was another guest, dressed in her Fountains exercise suit. She did not look at the maid, nor did she greet the occupant of the bed. She just stood there, glaring. Then she stepped inside.

Loco, the maid decided—they are all loco.

Gillian lifted her head and looked at her visitor. "Hi, Dru," she said, and yawned. "How're you?"

When Dru did not answer, Gillian brought herself to a sitting position. As the blanket slipped from her breasts, she tried again. "Good to see you, pet. Is it nice out there?"

"It's nice."

"Anything special going on?"

"Nothing special."

"Then, why—? Dru, what's the matter? You look ready to explode."

"We missed you this morning on the walk."

"And you're in a snit about *that?*"

"In a way."

"You're joking. Yesterday—all that exercise— it wiped me. I needed more sleep."

"Still sleepy?"

"You know how I am. If I don't get my eight to ten hours, I'm useless."

"Gillian, I have something to tell you." She paused. "Jason phoned this morning. At three A.M."

"Here? Why?"

"Something about Bitsy. Don't panic. I talked to Jason. Bitsy is okay. He had this problem with her and he wanted to discuss it with you."

"At three in the morning?"

"Bitsy stayed out late. He was worried."

"Someone should have awakened me."

"Someone tried. You weren't here."

"That's absurd. You saw how exhausted I was. I conked out completely. I never heard a thing."

"Is that what happened?"

"Of course, that's what happened. What are you suggesting? What did you tell Jason?"

"I said you weren't here. I told him you had to pick up a prescription in San Diego. I said you had car trouble and had to stay in town overnight."

"Well—that was decent and chummy. I should say Thank you, I suppose. But you needn't have lied. I was right here in my bed."

"Gillian, stop the bullshit. You weren't here in bed. You were out. I watched you leave last night. I know what time you left, and I know what time you came in this morning."

"Why—why—how dare you—" She caught herself, then asked warily, "What else do you know?"

"That's all I know. And it's more than I want to know."

"You were spying on me. That's contemptible."

"Stop it, Gillian. I have better ways to spend my time. I couldn't fall asleep after the lecture, so I left my cottage and went for a walk around the grounds. I was still out there when you got into the

Mazda and drove away. I dozed a bit, but after Jason woke me I couldn't fall asleep again. Around six I heard you pull in, and I heard you open and close this door."

"So that's the way it is. All right, I'm stuck with your story. But from now on, do me a favor. Stay out of my personal life. It's no concern of yours."

"But Jason—I was trying to protect you with Jason."

"You needn't have been so noble. I can handle Jason. There happens to be someone more important than Jason—or me."

Dru stood at the foot of the bed, glaring.

"Dammit, Dru, get out of here," Gillian said furiously. "I want to call my husband."

The door, slammed shut by Dru, was still shuddering when Gillian lifted the phone and gave the operator the number of the house in Beverly Hills.

Jason caught the call on the first ring. "Hey, what's going on?" he demanded.

"I'll get to that. What's this about Bitsy?"

"You first, what happened to you?"

"Didn't Dru explain? I needed something at the drugstore. And then I had car trouble. Nothing serious. It was the fuel pump or carburetor or whatever. I'm so dense about those things. An early-bird mechanic fixed it for me. Now will you tell me about Bitsy?"

"I don't know the details," he said angrily.

"Just the highlights then—"

"Highlights," he hissed. "How the hell do I know? She won't talk to me. I came in around two and she wasn't home. Ada said that dopey kid, Jerry, picked her up at nine. She stayed out half the night. I was about to call the police—"

"Jason," she said pleasantly, "where were *you* until two in the morning?"

"Don't start anything, Gillian. You know I have business. Anyway, that's not the point. She finally came in stinking from booze and looking like she'd been gang-banged. She wouldn't tell me where she had been. She took a bath and went to her room and locked herself in. She's only coming out now. I haven't set eyes on her since last night."

"Let me talk to her."

"Bitsy!" he shouted. "I've got your mother on the phone. Would you like to tell *her* what the hell you've been up to?"

Gillian held the receiver at arm's length. When she could no longer hear Jason, she returned it to her ear.

"Mom?" Bitsy sounded like a six-year-old. "Mom, I'm sorry to spoil your vacation."

"It's not spoiled, darling. Tell me what happened."

"Nothing happened. I don't know why Dad is carrying on this way. He told me he'd be out late. Ada was in her room watching one of her dumb TV shows. I was just hanging around and I guess I got lonely. You know Jerry? Well, he called and said he was getting a few of the kids together at his house so I asked him to pick me up. All we did was sit around and drink a little wine. It got late and he brought me home. Geez, you'd think I committed a murder or something."

"I understand, baby. That doesn't sound too serious. Let me talk to your father. I'll get it all smoothed out."

"Thanks, Mom."

"Have a good day at school—and Bitsy, I miss you."

"I miss you, too, Mom."

Waiting for Jason to take up the telephone, she

had no difficulty identifying the real villain. It was Jason, the miserable bastard. If he had remained at home, fulfilling his fond father role as he had promised, none of this would have happened. Bitsy would not have left the house. There would have been no theatrics back in Beverly Hills. And she, Gillian, would not have suffered this crashing ending to the happiest night of her life.

"Jason?" She was pleasant, warfare postponed. "Were you listening? Really, honey, it's nothing more than a tempest in a teapot. You shouldn't worry so. Mind if I make a suggestion?"

"Go ahead." He was still surly.

"Why don't you take Bitsy out to dinner tonight? Nothing fancy. Just the two of you. A father-daughter thing. A good talk will patch it all up. You'll both feel better. And I know I will."

He hesitated. "I'll have to call a client—"

Call your client, she was tempted to say. Tell her you'll be by to fuck her before six. Tell her you'd love to make a night of it, but you have to get home to your daughter.

Instead she said, "I'm sure your client will understand. I'll speak to you and Bitsy later. And Jason—"

"Yes?"

"I kind of envy you. It gets awfully boring at this hen party."

Elena looked down at the slim package lying across the palm of her hand. It was addressed to Ms. Elena Valdez, no mistake about that, and its taut paper wrapper was brightened with a red stamp informing anyone concerned that the contents were valuable enough to have been shipped by registered mail. The sender's name and address were imprinted in the upper left-hand corner. The package had been mailed by Tiffany and Co. of Beverly Hills.

Minutes before, like a band of Pavlovian pets, Elena and the others had responded to the nameless tune over the loudspeaker which they had come to recognize as mail call.

With their scheduled activity scarcely ended, all had reported to the Reception Hall where Loretta Marshall was stationed behind a desk, waving a handful of mail. Most of the women, anticipating nothing, were lined up at the sideboard awaiting their turn at the silver coffee urn.

Elena, having filled her cup with the hot coffee, stood aside as Loretta sang out names and bestowed the mail with the air of a benefactress. For Helen Reiser, there was a fat folder stuffed with scribbled notes and crude drawings from several of her children at home in Washington. For Debbie Colson, there was a color postcard from her father vacationing in the Virgin Islands. For Sheila Henderson, there were three or four invitations to couture showings in New York and Dallas department stores that had been forwarded to The Fountains. Christina Rossi was laughing raucously over a note she said was too depraved to share with anyone. In a corner, Charlotte Caldwell had settled on an ottoman, opened a buff-colored envelope, and begun to read its contents.

Elena had been refilling her coffee cup when Loretta Marshall had called her name.

"The best for the last," she heard Loretta say. "For our little Elena, a mysterious package from a not-so-mysterious shop—Tiffany's, no less."

Mystified, Elena had accepted the package and now, with a circle of women about her, she tentatively turned it over in her hand.

"Open it, you goose." Christina was impatient at her side. "Take pity. I am fainting from the suspense."

"I—I—need a scissors."

"Nonsense." Christina grabbed the package from her and tore off its wrappings. "Quick, look inside," she said handing it back. "Is there a card?"

"Yes. Christina—it's from Barry!"

"Barry? Barry Waterman? You sly kitten. I never suspected you were so close. What does he say?"

"He says, 'I want you to be happy.'"

"*How* happy? What is in the box?"

Awkwardly, Elena removed a long blue velvet case from the cardboard shipping box and unsnapped the lid. "It's a bracelet," she said, awed. "It's gold with diamonds—and colored stones."

Christina took the velvet case from Elena and carefully examined the bracelet. "Fifteen hundred, two thousand dollars, I'd guess. The colored stones are sapphires." Christina's expression was thoughtful. "Expensive jewelry from Barry Waterman? I don't understand this. I know men. I know Barry. What is going on in his head?"

Elena spoke in a murmur. "He says he wants me to be happy. It's his funny way of telling me so. And Christina, I am—I am very, very happy."

When everyone else had left the Reception Hall, Charlotte, still seated on the ottoman, remained behind and reread her letter.

"Mother dear," Nina had written. "You've always said I was such a miserable correspondent. Remember way back when I went to summer camp and didn't answer your letters, how upset you'd get? Well, I thought I'd surprise you and show you I've changed. Yesterday Ned and I were talking about what a sensational lady you are, and only this morning when I yelled at Charlie for spilling his orange juice in the living room, he cried and said he wanted his Grandma Charlotte.

"See how much we love and appreciate you? I thought you'd like to know.

"Mother—Mother, darling—that is not why I am writing this letter to you, although you are loved and you are appreciated. That part is true. I'm writing because there is something I must tell you, something I hate telling you.

"Mother, Marcy is going to have a baby.

"I'm saying it straight out—I don't know any other way. They broke it to us—Marcy and Dad did— last week at dinner when they told us about the safari—the night before you left for California. Maybe I should have told you right away but you were high about your trip, and Ned and I figured news like that would keep. Only now we see it hasn't.

"You know how Marcy adores seeing her name in the newspapers? Well, instead of being quiet for awhile, next day she called all the gossip columnists in town and told them she was pregnant. And today everyone in Chicago knows that Mrs. Arthur Caldwell, the *new* Mrs. Arthur Caldwell, is going to present her loving husband, etc., etc., etc. You can imagine the rest.

"Right now, I hate both of them. I know what this news will do to you. I hate them because they are the ones who are stabbing you, and I am the one who is twisting the knife.

"Ned and I talked it over for hours. We finally agreed we couldn't let you come home, or get a phone call or a letter, and hear the news from someone else. That would be too cruel.

"Mother, Mother darling—I love you more this minute than I ever have in my whole life . . ."

Charlotte slowly folded the letter and replaced it in its envelope.

At lunch she poked at her salad and gazed out at the pool and the florid flower beds beyond. When Rita asked if she was feeling well, she said she had a slight headache. The peculiar thing was, she couldn't summon tears. There was just this leaden feeling that wouldn't go away.

Lunchtime over, she consulted her daily schedule card and dutifully made her way to the sunny yellow and white beauty salon. Two salon operators greeted her. Alternately, they administered a shampoo-blow-dry and a pedicure. Leaving the salon, it occurred to her that her hair and her feet were ready for anything. It was just the rest of her—the part in between—that was wreckage.

Afterwards, wearing a leotard, she performed the exercises in the gym like an automaton—bending, twisting, reaching, rolling to the music from the record player. Suffused with hopelessness, she observed her partners in the class. Gillian, a remote smile on her lips, was more fluid and graceful than before. Elena, her sweetly curved body outlined by a red leotard, had a new spring in her movements. Sheila, siliconed breasts rigid, her limbs flabby, puffed and gasped, yet appeared determined to stay the course. Dru, figure taut, face grim, followed instructions with military discipline. Christina Rossi and Helen Reiser, losing their balance, stopped to laugh and rest, and gallantly resumed.

All were purposeful, all were committed to the hard physical effort. All were readying themselves for *someone.*

And she, Charlotte Caldwell, discarded wife, freshly humiliated by the morning's disclosure, painfully reminded of Arthur's resurgent virility—why was she here, submitting to this jumping-jack ordeal? To

whom would she present her toned, tightened, in-
vigorated self? To those balding, faithless, middle-aged
husbands in Chicago, or to the smoother, younger, more
attractive escort-types a woman alone could pick up in
New York and Paris and Rome?

She was relieved when the exercise music
stopped. Pulling a robe over her leotard, she once
again consulted her schedule card. Sauna next. That
was better. Ten or fifteen minutes of solitude was what
she needed to throw off the deep depression that was
spreading inside her like sludge.

Avoiding the others, following arrows, she
walked down a breezeway until she arrived at a small
detached redwood hut. She opened the door and peered
inside. Empty, thank God.

Leaving her robe and leotard in an adjoining
dressing stall, she wrapped a towel around her and
slipped into the sauna room. The redwood shell was
dimly lit and humid. Eucalyptus branches stacked in a
corner scented the air. Slatted benches built into facing walls were the sole furnishings.

Charlotte dropped her towel, seated herself cautiously, and folded her hands in her lap. She did not
stir as moisture rose on her naked body. Once, touching
her palm to her forehead, she discovered the newly
done hair falling limp. Someone on the staff had erred
in the day's scheduling but she didn't care. Perhaps, if
she sat here long enough, she would melt away. The
notion had a certain appeal; it was a tidy way to go.

A sudden draft from the direction of the door
roused her. Disappointed, she realized she was not
going to be alone after all. She had hoped to find a few
moments of solace in this sultry cell, to empty her head,
to experience blessed blankness. Now, to her regret,
she had a companion.

Squinting, she identified the intruder. Sheila

Henderson, the big redhead from Texas. That wasn't too bad. In fact, it was almost as good as being alone if the imbecile didn't attempt a conversation. She was familiar with Sheila's story—the candy counter in Neiman-Marcus, the marriage, the divorce, the record-breaking settlement, the famous surgery. She had no further curiosity about the woman.

Grudgingly, she returned Sheila's nod, saying nothing. She was about to look away when Sheila plopped down opposite her and slowly removed her robe. Mesmerized, Charlotte stared at the notorious, doctored breasts. The damned things *were* beautiful—round and high and solid—unflawed marble. Even when Sheila bent forward to remove her paper slippers, the breasts held rank, refusing to slosh in any direction.

A few years before, Charlotte had been told that a woman could test herself for mammary gravity by standing straight and placing a pencil beneath each breast. If the pencils were trapped, too bad. If they rolled out, the woman could claim to possess youthful firmness. Charlotte had experimented before her own mirror. By throwing back her shoulders, she had succeeded in making the pencils drop to the floor. Satisfied with the result, she had never dared repeat the experiment.

"So you heard about them," Sheila was saying.

"Heard—about what?"

"These—my breasts." Sheila was stroking them fondly. "You were staring. Don't be embarrassed. I know people talk."

Charlotte shifted on the bench and did not speak.

Still stroking, Sheila went on. "That Helen, she's a bitch. She told me to stay in the shade because of my breasts. She said the sun would melt the silicone. I called my doctor. He says she's crazy. And Christina, she's worse than Helen. She wants to know if I paid more for the left one than the right one. She says the left one's bigger. What do you think?"

"I think—I think they're a perfect pair. I'm sure Christina was teasing."

"*She* was teasing. She's the last one who should open her mouth. They say she's had the zipper."

"The what?"

"The zipper. Some people call it a tummy-tuck. That's my next one. The doctor makes an incision in the pubic hair and removes fat all the way up to the navel. Makes the stomach nice and flat and the scar doesn't show. Actresses like that one. But you have to watch yourself and diet and exercise or it all comes back. Like Christina's did. She's a lazy cow." Sheila smiled shyly. "It's all kind of silly, don't you think?"

Charlotte closed her eyes. I've gone down the rabbit hole, she thought. This woman is mad. Do I laugh or do I cry?

I cry.

Because we are alike, we two. A perfect pair, like her breasts. We are both desperate, floundering women, casting about to make our lives real. With or without silicone, we are sisters under the skin.

She wanted to empty her head again. She hoped Sheila had said all she had to say. There was silence for a while. Charlotte was conscious only of the heat and the pungent scent of the eucalyptus branches.

Then Sheila spoke. "You had any work done?"

"I beg your pardon?"

"I said have you had any work done—on your face, your body?"

"I—why, do you think I need any?"

Sheila's eyes narrowed. "You look pretty good. I only asked to be social. Around here, it's Topic A. Everyone's getting pretty open about it." She patted her breasts again. "Did you know that up in L.A. there's a doctor who takes off every year for a month in Palm Springs? They say he does about thirty face jobs while he's there."

"No, I didn't know that."

"Yeah, it's true. And there's this other doctor in Beverly Hills—I heard a rumor that the Shah of Iran brought him over to his country and had him trim all the royal noses in one visit."

"You do keep up on world events."

Sheila nodded. "I try," she said seriously. Then her bland face brightened. "Hey, where are you going from here? After this week, I mean."

"Home, to Chicago."

"Got a husband?"

"We're divorced."

"Thought so. Who've you got in Chicago?"

"Lots of people."

"I mean anyone special?"

"My daughter, her husband, their son."

"That's *their* home. Who's at yours?"

"My housekeeper—"

"Figures. A cook, a country club, a canary."

"I don't have a canary."

"Just a joke. So you're unattached."

"I like it that way."

"Don't be so defensive. *Nobody* likes it that way." The bland face was animated now. "How would you like to go to Acapulco with me? Be my houseguest. I have a gorgeous place, right on the bay. Lots of parties. Lots of men. Augusta says this time it'll be better than ever."

"Augusta?"

"Augusta Padget. She's my social relations adviser."

"Your *what?*"

"Social relations adviser. Sort of like my manager. Augusta doesn't handle my money, of course. The lawyers in Houston do that. Augusta handles my time. She's like an agent—best in the business—only she doesn't get me jobs. She gets me parties. And she helps me give them, too."

"Sheila, what are you talking about?"

"Not so smart, are you? And all along you've been thinking I'm the dumb one." She held up her hand. "Okay, don't say anything to that."

"I didn't intend to. Tell me more about Augusta."

"Augusta Padget is this real elegant English-woman. She looks to me about fifty, but Augusta has too much class to discuss age. Some of her ancestors were dukes or something, and they used to be filthy rich. You know what happened to *those* families. Flat on their asses, most of them. Financially, that is, what with taxes and inflation and all that. They've still got their connections, though. Augusta was feeling the pinch herself, so one day she got this bright idea and now she's in business."

Charlotte was bewildered. "What idea? What business?"

"It's simple. Augusta takes over people like me, men and women loaded with money, but—let's face it —kinda short on breeding, and she launches us in international society. Her job is to dig up Italian counts down to their last silk suits, a few broke princesses, a handful of South Americans who'd rather play than work, and then she makes sort of a stew. She brings us all together and keeps everyone moving. We go from continent to continent, from one resort to the next—in season, of course—having fun. Those of us who have the money, we don't mind paying for those who don't. It's one great big party."

"Sheila, are you inventing this?"

"Hell, no. I'm not that bright. Augusta's no phony, either. She delivers."

"However did you find such a person?"

"Augusta's clever. She found me. Read about my divorce settlement in the London papers." Sheila's face shone with pride. "It was a *fantastic* settlement. Newspapers all over the world picked up the story. One of those British rags ran a headline: *Oil Yields Bread!* Augusta was in her West End flat eating crumpets or something, and she read about me. She phoned long-distance, and we talked, and I liked how she sounded and next day she was on the plane to Houston to sign me up as a client."

"You have a contract—?"

"Not exactly. It's more of an understanding. I pay her X-number of dollars every month and I buy her gifts from time to time, and she takes care of the rest."

"Sheila, she sounds like a pimp."

"Uh-uh, no sex. That part is strictly up to the client. Two people like each other, they take it from there. Augusta just starts things rolling and sees to it that people get to know each other."

"You *pay* for that?"

"Sure, lots of people do. Augusta's not the only one in the business. Naturally, it's a hush-hush operation but there are professionals like Augusta in New York, Paris, Los Angeles, Rome. For all I know, they're working out of St. Louis and Pittsburgh, too."

"But, who—"

"Who'd want them? I'll tell you who. Big-shot Hollywood brass, f'r instance. They've had it with movie stars—they're not impressed with them. They want something different like princes and lords and barons and oil sheikhs. They get jollied when some foreigner with a title and an accent calls them by their first name. Rich businessmen and their wives want them,

too. They've made their pile—now what? They've got
six houses and they've cleaned out Harry Winston, but
nobody knows how important they are. They've got
time and money and they want to keep moving—up.
They want to read about themselves in the newspapers
and magazines. Augusta, and people like her, take care
of that also. Theater openings, charity balls, elegant
restaurants—how do you think people you never heard
of suddenly get invited into society, to all those social
events?"

"I never thought—"

"No one does. Hey, guess what?"

"What?"

"Augusta thinks it's time to give me a more
serious image. She's gonna get me on the board of some
symphony orchestra or museum. That's why I went to
San Francisco last week. I write a big enough check and
—" She whooped with glee. "Me, Sheila Henderson, a
patron of the arts. The kids at Neiman-Marcus will flip
out!"

"I suppose you'll like that?"

Sheila was silent for a long while.

"Can I tell you something private?" she said
finally.

"Of course."

"It's all shit."

They didn't speak again until the buzz of a distant time clock announced the end of their sauna period. Immediately, an attendant appeared, bearing fresh
terry robes for their damp bodies.

Sheila rose from the slatted bench. "The invitation still goes," she said quietly. "You'd like Acapulco."

"You're sweet to ask me—I mean that. But I'm
not sure it's my style."

"Don't say No yet. It beats going back to Chicago to feed your canary."

"I told you—*I don't have a canary.*"

* * *

Weary, depressed, Charlotte made her way up the walk in the direction of her cottage. Sheila's portrait of jet-set social life had been briefly diverting, even amusing, but later, standing beneath the cold shower that had followed the sauna, her despondency had returned. She had reflected on the maneuvers of Sheila and her friends, and the emptiness of their games had saddened her. Her despair had deepened when she discovered she was actually considering Sheila's invitation to join the house party in Acapulco.

Yet she didn't want what they wanted, she told herself. She wanted someone to care about her, to love her so she could love back. She wasn't interested in *places*. Acapulco, Capri, Sardinia, Taormina, Marrakesh —the names were exciting, but they weren't flesh and blood. They couldn't talk to you and hold you tight, and take you to bed.

Marcy is going to have a baby, Nina had written. The message marched before her eyes and she began to grow nauseated. A drink was what she needed, that would fix her up. But at The Fountains you didn't step up to the bar and order a short one.

If only—but she did—she *did* have a small amount of liquor in her cottage. On the plane from Chicago the stewardess had given her an extra minibottle of rum to add to her Mai-tai. Fuzzy enough at the time, she had accepted the bottle but dropped it, still sealed, into her traveling bag.

She glanced ahead at the cottage. The masseuse's sign was not yet on the doorknob. If she could get there first, she could have her drink and once again induce the desired fuzziness.

She entered the cottage and closed the door behind her, shutting out the sunlight. She was alone. In the dressing room she located her traveling bag. Rummaging through its contents, she found the little bottle. She emptied the rum into a bathroom glass and, grimacing, she swallowed it in a gulp.

When she returned to the bedroom the drapes were drawn and the masseuse was waiting. She said Hello to the woman but did not hear her reply. She tossed her terry robe on the bed and climbed onto the draped massage table.

She sensed the drink taking over, warming her. She squirmed beneath the sheet the masseuse had wrapped about her body. Still restless, she threw back the sheet, welcoming the cool air on her skin. She was not listening when the woman apologized for causing her discomfort.

The woman's hands, gentling the tight muscles of her neck, were soothing. As they moved across her shoulders and slid down her arms, Charlotte felt the tears coming at last. So she needed this touch of kindness—was that wrong?—didn't everyone?

For a moment she dwelt on Arthur and herself, then on Arthur and Marcy. Then she thought of what had happened in France. Then she tried to think of nothing at all.

Dimly, she was aware the masseuse had decided on a soft massage again, and she was pleased. Even the stomach strokes were coming slow and easy. She knew she couldn't bear the heavier pounding that improved the circulation and made the blood tingle. For a precious little while she wanted the sensuous pleasure of delicate touching.

When a light tap on her hip signaled it was time to turn over, to lie on her stomach so the masseuse could work on her back and legs, she could not conceal her disappointment.

"So soon?" she whispered blearily, regretting the massage was already half done.

The masseuse's hand casually brushed her pubic mound. "There's more to come. Relax, dear."

Lying on her stomach, cheek resting on one arm as she faced the wall, Charlotte heard the masseuse above her, pouring oil from a jar and rubbing it between her palms. She shivered slightly as the oil touched her skin. As the woman's hand slid up and down her back in long sweeping strokes, she sighed voluptuously.

"Feel good?"

"*So* good. I wish it would never end. Must it?"

Without responding, the woman poured more oil onto her hands and returned to her stroking, gliding now across the smooth back.

"You have beautiful skin," she said.

Dropping her hands to Charlotte's buttocks, she began to knead the flesh more vigorously.

"Too hard," Charlotte said weakly.

"Thank you for telling me."

Resuming her stroking—delicately, this time— the woman massaged first one buttock, then the other, each to the silent count of ten.

Finished with the buttocks, her hands slid to Charlotte's parted thighs. Insinuatingly, her fingers slipped along their warm inner surfaces. Upward and upward. Teasing, arousing. Almost accidentally—or so it seemed—her fingers touched the dampening vagina and darted away. When Charlotte said nothing, she sought and found the throbbing clitoris and rubbed it lightly.

"Please, please—" Charlotte whimpered. Woozy from the rum, she was not certain what she was pleading for.

"Please," she begged. "Please—"

The woman touched her again. Half-repelled, half-grateful, Charlotte capitulated. Rotating her hips against the woman's artful fingers, harder, harder, faster, faster, moaning, sobbing, she felt it coming, the soaring, longed-for climax, the blessed physical relief. Her face twisting in anguish, she clutched the table pad and groaned.

I needed this, she told herself. I needed it so very much.

They were in near darkness as the woman reached beneath her and began to caress her breasts. Dazed, Charlotte rolled over onto her back. She wanted to rise but she couldn't. The woman stood over her, large and shadowed. She looked down at Charlotte and understood. Wordlessly, she trailed her hands over Charlotte's breasts, drawing her fingers through the well that separated them—down, down, past the tensed stomach, past the pubis, until she found the hungering clitoris. Again and again, her skilled fingers brought Charlotte to orgasm.

Only when the woman lowered her head to kiss her, did Charlotte protest.

The woman stepped away from the table. "You are the loveliest creature I have ever seen," was all she said.

Unsteadily, Charlotte climbed down from the table and groped for the robe she had flung on the bed. She pulled it around her protectively.

The woman had turned on a small table lamp. While Charlotte watched, she gathered up her oils and efficiently folded her sheets and massage table. She started for the door.

"Until tomorrow," she said, looking over her shoulder. "There are two of us now. You *and* me."

The troupe of waitresses moving among the candlelit tables in shiny black-and-white uniforms reminded Dru of the choreographed penguins she had once written into a network variety show. Dipping before each guest, the waitresses swept away cups that had recently held hot bouillon and replaced them with gold-rimmed plates bearing lamb chops, a dab of mint jelly, and diced carrots. In time the penguins would be back, according to the menu, for a finale of lemon sherbet.

At the table near the window, conversation had sagged, then died.

Still smarting from the morning's scene with Gillian, Dru had rejected Gillian's pretense that nothing had gone wrong between them. Dru had been infuriated further when Gillian had accepted the rebuff with a shrug, and had then withdrawn into herself with a serene smile on her lovely face.

Across the table, Charlotte was a case study in misery. Merely dejected earlier in the day, she now appeared bogged down in despair. When Dru had looked at her questioningly, Charlotte had stared back, hollow-eyed, and volunteered nothing.

Only Elena, new bracelet gleaming on her wrist, had come to the table in high spirits. She and Rita had begun dinner gaily enough but had gradually succumbed to the heavy moodiness of their companions.

No one was sorry when Loretta Marshall's dinner bell diverted their attention to the table on the dais.

"Ladies, ladies," Loretta began. "We had announced a surprise film for your entertainment this evening. Regretfully, that pleasure is not to be ours. Through Dr. Bertini's connections in Hollywood, we were able to obtain an old movie that our dear friend, Christina Rossi, made in Italy early in her distinguished career. Sadly, the film that arrived is not suitable to be shown." She smirked. "Not *technically* suitable, that is. I am told Christina's performance is delightful. Unhappily, the custodian of the reels did not protect them and the condition of the negative is impossible. Christina has promised that one day she will bring us a film from her personal library. I hope all of you will be here to view it.

"Dr. Bertini and I are as disappointed as you must be," Loretta continued. "However, we do have a film tonight—a western starring John Wayne. For those of you who are interested, our screening will begin sharp at nine in the Renaissance Room. For others, there is our cozy television lounge next to the Reception Hall. Perhaps there you will find something more to your taste."

John Wayne. Dru shuddered. She had endured his pious patriotism for years. She winced each time she saw his face or heard his voice. She would not voluntarily expose herself to an additional ninety minutes of that face and that voice. Mindful that she could encounter John Wayne in a film rerun on the tube, she nonetheless mentally opted for the television lounge.

Her wristwatch told her it was exactly eight o'clock. She would join the others on their evening walk, and drop in later to view some television. A political news freak, she had gone days without her usual input—had, in fact, neglected to ask Tim for the inside stories he usually picked up in the nation's capitol and passed on for her avid consumption.

She was annoyed to find Helen Reiser clumping at her side as the hikers started up the trail. The vulgar, loudmouthed woman was a distinct pain in the ass. Anywhere else, she would cross to the other side of the street to avoid Helen Reiser. At The Fountains, guests were expected to be a big, jolly family. With one feud going—Gillian's self-satisfied smile was still vividly before her—she could ill afford another. Besides, in a few days it would all be over and she need never again see Helen Reiser.

They were barely onto the trail when Helen nudged her. "What's happening at your table, honey? I've been sizing up your group. Some of you look mortally wounded."

"Nothing's happening. We're tired, that's all. We're not accustomed to so much exercise. Dr. Bertini says we each have hundreds of muscles. Well, every one of them hurts."

"That's only the first day or two. C'mon, tell Helen what's going on."

"Don't you ever let up?"

"Okay, don't tell me. I can guess. It's the sexual tension thing, just like I told you. The energy's building, the sap is running high, and there's no natural outlet till you get home to your man. We oldtimers at The Fountains, we understand. We can kid about it. Your bunch is still uptight." Helen mused a moment. "Except that leggy blonde—what's her name?"

"Gillian?"

"Yeah, that's the one, Gillian. Came to The Fountains stiff as Sleeping Beauty. Now she looks like some prince laid a wand on her. Or in her." She sniggered. "Anything going on there? What with the new kitchen crew and the groundskeepers, Dr. Bertini's rounded up some real studs since the last time I was here."

"Helen, I don't know how you get through the day alive."

"Touchy, touchy—"

Safe in her cottage, having escaped from Helen Reiser, Dru fell into a chair and yanked off her walking shoes and heavy socks. She spotted the evening snack the maid had left on a table—three tiny cubes of jack cheese garnished with a sprig of parsley—and she pulled the plate toward her. She nibbled at the cheese and slowly finished it. Still hungry, she polished off the parsley, too.

Television could wait. She needed time to rest, to vacuum Helen's voice from her head. She sprawled in the chair, intending to relax, then had a better idea. She would go into the bathroom, empty all the remaining bubble crystals and bath oil into the tub, and take a long, lazy bath.

By the time she stepped out of the tub, she was humming. She felt cleansed in body and brain and ready for a witless evening of television. Even John Wayne—if that was what the fates held in store.

Dressed in denim pants and a floppy cashmere sweater, she stepped onto the porch. The surrounding greenery filled the air with delectable scents. She lingered on the porch breathing deeply to the count of five as she had been taught to do during lawn exercises.

Concentrating on her breathing, she did not hear the door of the adjoining cottage open and close.

"Hi," Gillian called out. "Gorgeous night." Large weekender hanging from her shoulder, full gathered jersey skirt swinging below a low-cut silk blouse, Gillian approached her jauntily.

"Going somewhere?" Dru regretted the question at once.

Gillian smiled. "Moon makes me restless. I thought I'd take a drive. See where the road leads me."

"And what do I tell your husband when he wakes me in the middle of the night?"

"No problem, my sweet." Gillian's smile widened. "I spoke to Jason before dinner. He and Bitsy were on their way out to a nice family restaurant in Malibu. Good food, good talk, a table overlooking the water— they'll have a grand time, get to know each other. Best thing that's ever happened to them."

"It's a touching scene."

"Isn't it? As for you, there's nothing to worry about. You'll sleep well tonight." She grinned wickedly. "It's going to be a *glorious* night."

Furious, Dru watched the tall, slender figure descend the stairs from the cottage and half run toward the Mazda. When Gillian paused once to wave in the direction of the porch, Dru did not wave back.

A single lamp in the corner of the television lounge illuminated the viewers riveted before the set. Dru could make out Helen Reiser, busily belaboring a wad of chewing gum, Jessica Haskell, the Lyman twins and, strung lumpily across the floor, the fat teenager, Debbie Colson. Off to the side, Charlotte Caldwell occupied the room's lone wing chair.

On the small screen a special starring Sammy Davis, Jr., shone in candystick colors and Sammy himself was reprising a familiar number from *Porgy and Bess.* Sammy's past political excursions had confounded Dru, but she continued to admire his talent. Tiptoeing across the room, she slid to the carpeted floor near Charlotte's chair, folded her legs under her, and settled back to enjoy the show.

With professional appreciation, she watched Sammy tap and strut, laugh and twirl, chat and sing, and soon she was lost in his performance.

She did not hear the rapping on the sliding glass door that separated the television lounge from the patio.

"Over there." Helen Reiser slapped Dru on the shoulder. "Outside, someone wants to see you."

"What?" Dru followed Helen's pointing finger. Beyond the door she could make out Leslie, the night telephone operator, beckoning frantically.

She rose immediately. "Excuse me," she said,

and passing quickly in front of the others, she hurried to join Leslie on the patio.

"Ms. Jennings, I'm sorry—"

"What's wrong?"

"It's that man again, the crazy one—Mrs. Crain's husband. He says he's got to speak to you."

"Leslie, get yourself back to that damned switchboard and tell him you can't find me."

"That's impossible. I already told him you were here. I told him it's Mrs. Crain I can't find."

"Tough luck, Leslie."

"Please, Ms. Jennings, he's raving again. Will you talk to him for just a second, please? It'd be a real favor."

"Leslie, I'm getting tired of this. Okay, where's the nearest phone?"

"Follow me, I'll hook you up."

In an enclosed booth adjoining the business office, Dru wearily lifted the receiver.

"Jason, it's Dru."

His voice was strident. "Well, where is she this time?"

"Gillian? I don't know."

"Of course you know. She tells you everything. You're lying!"

"And you're shouting! Godammit, Jason, I'm not my sister's keeper. She's out—that's all I know."

His tone flattened ominously. "And last night, where was Gillian last night?"

"Ask her yourself."

"Dru, were you lying to me last night?"

"Ask her yourself," she repeated, and hung up.

She was on the footpath, returning to the television lounge when she heard Leslie again, calling her name.

"Ms. Jennings, Ms. Jennings, please come back!"

"What for?"

"It's Mr. Crain. He says you hung up on him. He wasn't finished. He says he *must* talk to you. It's urgent!"

In the phone booth once more, she sagged onto the narrow plastic seat and, still angered, lifted the receiver.

"Okay, Jason, what's so damned important?"

"Bitsy. I've got to talk to Gillian about Bitsy."

"I thought Bitsy was with you."

"She is, but something's going on, something serious. Her mother's got to know about it right away."

He was obviously distressed. Dru relented. "Bitsy's not sick, is she?"

Jason hesitated. "No—no, she's not sick exactly. But I must talk to Gillian immediately."

"Jason, we've been through that. Gillian's gone, vanished into the gorgeous moonlit night. I don't know where the devil she is. And I don't want any part of whatever's going on."

"Do something for me then," he implored. "Leave a note under her door. Tell her to call me the second she gets back, at any hour. I'll be sitting here, waiting."

"I'll leave the note," she promised. "But, Jason—"

"Yes?"

"Go to bed. You have time enough to get your sleep." And she hung up once again.

When Dru reentered the lounge, Sammy Davis, Jr., was gone from the television screen, replaced by a toothy newscaster from San Diego who was happily recounting local and state disasters.

Dru crossed the room swiftly and returned to her place at Charlotte's feet.

A devastating fire, a bomb scare, an extortion plot, and the cheerful newscaster faded from the tube after bidding his viewers a good, good evening, and urging them to stay tuned for the national news soon to follow.

Focusing on the ensuing barrage of commercials, Dru tried to put Jason's calls out of her mind but failed. A niggling sense of loyalty told her she should have invented another cover story for Gillian. Yet common sense informed her the ploy would not work a second time. Jason was properly suspicious. His outrage was in full flare. It needed no additional fuel from her.

Furthermore, she owed nothing to Gillian Crain. Her protective gesture, her lies to Jason the night before, had earned her nothing but abuse from both Crains. Well, screw them, she told herself. From now on she would wash her hands of that pair of ingrates. Tim would survive the loss of their friendship; he'd had little fondness for the Crains from the beginning.

She recalled Tim had said something about taking a direct flight from Washington to San Diego. He had suggested renting a car at the airport so they could drive back to Los Angeles together. At the time she had not encouraged the idea, feeling obliged to return with Gillian in the Mazda. Now she no longer had that obligation. She would phone Tim's hotel in the morning. If he was not in, she would leave word with the concierge that Mr. Larsen's wife had changed her mind and hoped Mr. Larsen could meet her on Friday at The Fountains.

When she returned her attention to the television set, the national news was coming in from Washington. The newscaster was an old friend. His warm, reassuring voice, slightly tinged with cynicism, strove to bring reason to the host of world dilemmas he was reporting, and she listened intently. Persistent confusion in the Middle East, political scandal in Italy, desperate factory workers in Chile, continuing famine in India, the tragic pageant went on.

From the corner of her eye, she saw Helen
Reiser fidgeting on the sofa, a *TV Guide* in her hand.

"Oh, God, let's get rid of this crybaby," Helen
was saying. She riffled through the magazine. "Hey,
here's an old Liz Taylor flick. On Channel Eight. You
remember, girls? The one where Liz goes to Switzerland for all that medical magic and the doctors make
her over from head to tail, and her own daughter
doesn't recognize her, she looks so divine? Let's switch
channels."

Dru opened her mouth to object, then decided
it would be useless. Helen Reiser was a force she did
not wish to contend with this evening. She rose part-
way, and was preparing to leave the television lounge
when, before her on the screen, she saw the earnest,
handsome face of Jonathan Ring.

"Hold it, Helen," she said, reseating herself.
"Senator Ring is on the Foreign Relations Committee.
I want to hear what he has to say about India."

She never did hear about India.

Overriding Jonny Ring's voice, Helen began to
laugh loudly.

"That one," she hooted. "It's okay for him to shed
tears for Indian kids, but I sure wouldn't let him near
one of mine."

"Why not?" Dru asked, annoyed. "Senator Ring
is one of the most sensitive, compassionate men in the
entire Congress. Everyone knows that."

"Maybe so. But the Judge and I, we live in
Washington, in the middle of the action. What everyone
doesn't know is that Senator Ring is also a closet faggot."

"You're out of your mind. You don't know what
you're saying."

"Don't I though? Sure, he's not the kind that
wears high heels and corsets. He's the discreet type.

Quiet little cocktail bars, meet-you-later-at-my-place. That kind of queer."

"You're making it all up. Jonathan Ring is an outstanding man, he's been married, he has children."

"What of it, writer lady. You never heard of guys who swing both ways? He's one of those. The Judge says Senator Jonathan Ring is having a heavy affair right now. With some newspaper guy he romanced in prep school. After graduation, the boys cooled it. They found wives and went straight for a while. Then they rediscovered each other, and now they're a flaming item."

Dru's tone was dull. "You can't mean that."

"Would I make up anything so juicy?" Helen feigned hurt. "Of course I wouldn't. The lover lives out of town somewhere but he shows up regularly and they're *this* close." Helen made a circle of the thumb and forefinger of her left hand. Then she ran the forefinger of her right hand through the circle and wriggled it suggestively.

"You—are—making—me—ill," said Dru.

"Hear that, ladies? An old-fashioned girl in our midst. Hell, do you know the joke going around about those two? They're saying it used to be Washington, D.C. Now it's Washington, AC-DC."

On the television screen it was all over for Elizabeth Taylor. After enduring terrible torture in Switzerland—all those lifts and scrapes and nips and tucks, and the painful shots of serum made from the glands of baby lambs—there was poor Liz, more gorgeous than ever, standing alone on the snowy railroad platform in Cortina in the Italian Alps, waving good-bye to the only man she had ever loved, the husband who was forsaking her forever.

When the tube went dead, Dru continued to stare at the blackened screen. Throughout the film, as through a wall, she had heard Jessica Haskell, Helen Reiser, and the Lyman twins gasp and sigh and thrill as the star underwent her metamorphosis from wrinkled matron to creamy-skinned bedmate of a younger man.

It was Jessica Haskell who turned off the set and, after some tart comments about youth and men, invited them to her cottage for a brandy nightcap.

"Dr. Bertini knows I break his damned no-drinking rule. Those stupid little maids tell him everything. But what's he going to do about it, expel me? I'd badmouth him in eight countries. Some of his best clients would take their checkbooks elsewhere." She picked up her sweater. "Come on everyone, grab some paper cups, let's drink a toast to Dr. Bertini."

They were gone at last and the room was quiet.

"Dru?" Charlotte tapped the younger woman's shoulder.

Dru turned her head. Her eyes were empty as they looked into Charlotte's. "I didn't know you were still here."

"I couldn't leave you like this, Dru. Helen is a fool. She doesn't always mean what she says."

"But Jonny Ring—that's impossible."

"Do you know him?"

"I know him—and I know his ex-wife, also. Last year, in Georgetown, we had lunch. She was trying to tell me something. I cut her off."

"Why?"

"Because Jonny Ring is a family friend. I didn't want to hear. I ran away from the truth, but tonight I was trapped. I found out about Jonny—and about the other man."

"And you think you know him, too," Charlotte said evenly.

"Yes. How could you tell?"

"I watched your face. I saw the shock—and the pain." Charlotte reached down and took Dru's hands in hers. "I'm a student of pain, I told you that."

"Then you guessed. That disgusting woman—she was talking about my husband."

"How do you know for sure? Maybe it was someone else."

"Because I know. I just know." Dru sat shaken. "What can I do?" she asked hopelessly.

"Did you have any idea?"

"I've known things were terribly wrong between us. Lately, after his trips to Washington—Tim—he's been different, withdrawn. It used to be so perfect. Now he locks himself into his study at night—he paces. He seldom comes to bed with me. Our personal life—it's like a battlefield between actions. We're both tensed, waiting—for God knows what."

"That happens in marriages. There are times when husbands and wives march to different drummers. It doesn't necessarily mean—this."

"But, Tim, he's been so unhappy. He's working something out. He told me so."

"What did you think it was?"

"Another woman. Someone sexier, prettier, than I am."

"You could accept that?"

"Accept it? No, I've been miserable. But I've consoled myself. I've been thinking, yes, he's having an affair but he's shielding me from it because he still loves me and wants our marriage to go on."

"What were you going to do about it—I mean, if it had been another woman?"

"Nothing. I've been praying it would pass. I love him, desperately."

"And he—?"

"He says he loves me. Yesterday, on the telephone, he said he wants us to be together forever."

"Do you believe he does?"

"Yes—No—I don't know!" She placed her head on Charlotte's lap. "I can't handle this. Another woman, ten women—I'd figure it out somehow. But another man? My husband, a *homosexual*."

"Are you sure? Are you really sure?"

"*You* believed Helen. I can tell you did. What are you saying?"

"I'm saying your husband—he may not be a homosexual. He may be a bisexual."

"That's horrible!"

"Is it?"

Dru raised her head. "What do you mean? Don't you think so?"

Charlotte shrugged. "We know so little about our true natures. We allow ourselves to live by taboos. Long ago, in other cultures—before we became so wonderfully civilized—there was a certain acceptance. Not of faithlessness, of course—everyone suffers when a beloved person turns to someone else—the humiliation, the fear of loss, of the future, that's universal. But same-gender sex, is that where we must draw a heavier line?"

"We have to draw it somewhere. We have to behave like different sexes."

"I'm not sure anymore. Sometimes—the other way—it fills a particular need at a particular time. It begs for understanding, not outrage."

Dru sat up straight. She studied Charlotte carefully.

"You've given the subject a lot of thought."

"Yes. Here. Tonight." Charlotte smiled at the

younger woman. "You're wondering if I am a bisexual? The answer to that one is No—but a qualified No. Have I had a homosexual experience? Yes, I have—recently. Once I'd have said, Yes—I plead guilty, but I don't feel guilty. Something happened. It had to happen when it did."

"Charlotte, you're lying. To make me feel better."

"No, it's true. Another woman—made love to me. At first I was stunned. But I've been sitting here, thinking, and now I can face it. Because I learned something from the experience. I learned there are hidden areas of myself I never dreamed existed. I know I'm not a different person, not a worse person, because they do exist. It's not even a matter of forgiving myself. There's nothing to forgive. I'm accepting myself. That done, I'm ready to accept others. I urge you to do the same."

"But if it were your husband? Can you imagine how you'd feel?" Dru covered her face with her hands and her body shook. "Damn, I can see them now—*doing* it!"

Charlotte's voice was harsh. "Stop that!" she commanded. "Stop making pictures! Keep going this way and you'll end your marriage."

"I have no marriage."

It was six A.M. when Gillian swung the little red Mazda into its parking slot in The Fountains' forecourt. As the car ground to a halt, bits of gravel erupted against the hubcaps, making clicking sounds like pebbles on a windowpane. The noise startled a squirrel who scampered up a palm tree, then sat, stony still, staring down at her.

It had drizzled in the night and mist still hung in the air, cooling her face as she stepped from the car. She held back, inhaling the sweetness of the dawn.

Off in the kitchen, cooks and maids were busily preparing the breakfast trays and she could hear the clatter of dishes and silver rising above the soft Spanish voices. She thought she saw two or three pairs of eyes peering out at her, but she didn't care.

Her happiness had made her bold.

Slamming the car door behind her and starting up the path to her cottage, she hoped she would awaken everyone. She was proud of herself, proud of her love for Dr. Karl. Most of all, she was proud of Dr. Karl's love for her.

He had finally admitted it. After a shattering orgasm, his heavy little body had flattened against hers and he had murmured, "I love you." Moments later, he had rolled off her stomach onto his back and fallen asleep, but she had not moved. She had lain there, hands folded across her pubis, a grateful smile on her lips. Beside her, Dr. Karl whistled in his sleep but she heard only his words, replayed in her head: I love you . . . I love you . . . I love you.

Throughout their affair, in their most ardent wrestlings in his office in Beverly Hills, even the night before in the motel, he had withheld the final gift, the spoken admission of his feelings—the commitment of himself. Always she had been afraid to ask directly if he loved her, sensing the question would irritate him, that he would resist being pressured.

Then, in the early hours of this morning, in violent, convulsive abandonment, he had permitted the words to escape his lips.

"I love you," he had said.

Once inside her cottage, she leaned against the closed door and hugged herself with glee, rocking back and forth, laughing quietly.

It was a while before she spotted the white notepaper at her feet. She picked it up and carried it to the bedside night light.

"URGENT," it read. "(Jason's word, not mine.) He wants you to call him as soon as you get in. He's waiting by the phone." It was signed: Dru. In small numerals alongside the signature it said 9:37 P.M.

Jason. She had forgotten about him. He was more remote than ever now, a figure on a distant planet, someone she had met in another incarnation.

She crumpled the note into a ball and aimed it at the wastebasket. Then she loosened her clothes and let them drop to the floor. Exhausted, she pulled back the blanket and fell across the bed. Within seconds she was asleep.

XI

The phone jangled in her ear. Pulling the blanket over her head, Gillian burrowed into her pillow and waited for the ringing to stop. When the room was still again, she lowered the blanket to her chin and, cat smile on her lips, began reliving the night just past.

At the appointed hour, she had appeared at Dr. Karl's motel room door. He had greeted her wearing the same blue robe. It was apparent he wore nothing beneath the robe and that anticipation had made him ready for her. His close embrace had confirmed her observation and she had been jubilant. Nonetheless, she had pulled away from him and gone to the tiny bathroom. There she had shed the jersey skirt and her blouse and slipped into the lilac negligee which had been crushed into her shoulder bag.

Without speaking, she had reappeared before him and, in silence, he had removed his robe and come toward her. He had drawn off her negligee, taken her hands into his hands and, glazed eyes holding on her eyes, had stiffly led her to bed. There she had fallen back, legs wide apart and he, with surprising agility, had mounted her. This time he had not teased. As her hips rose and her long legs encircled him, he had plunged deep inside her, blending his grunts with her moans.

Now, she trembled under the blanket, remembering what had followed. Still bemused, she heard the phone ring again and languidly she brought the receiver to her ear.

"Hullo," she whispered.

"Gillian, f'rchrissakes—!"

"Jason—"

"You're goddam right it's Jason. It's been Jason for the past eight hours!"

"I'm sorry, dear. I just got your message. Dru forgot to tell me."

"Don't lay it on Dru. I'm not buying that crap. Where've you been all night?"

"Right here, right in this bed."

"The hell you were. I called you fifty times and no one could find you."

"Because I was sleeping. You know how charged up I get sometimes. I took a walk after dinner and when I got back I was still wide awake. I took some pills, the big ones. They knocked me out."

"And you're telling me that was it?"

"I am."

"Why, you lying bitch! You filthy, lying bitch!"

"Jason, stop the sweet talk. Why are you calling?"

"Damn you! I'll get to you later! First we've gotta talk about Bitsy."

"What about her?"

"Bitsy—our darling baby daughter—she's pregnant."

"You're joking!"

"Am I? If you were any kind of mother, she'd have told you herself."

"I don't believe it."

"You can start believing it right now. Last night in the restaurant, she was sneaking my wine and we were getting confidential and—bam—she let me in on her little secret."

"Who—who's the boy? Does she know?"

"Does she know? What kind of question is that? There's only one boy, that skinny kid with the pimples."

"Jerry?"

"Yeah, Jerry." Jason's voice cracked with fury. "She's been screwing him for a year. She's been on the Pill! Since she was fourteen! Did you know that?"

"Of course not. I never suspected. How far along is she?"

"Not very. What are you going to do about it?"

"What am *I* going to do about it? First of all, I'm not going to lose my head. When I get home in a few days, we'll all sit down and have a talk. Then we'll arrange for an abortion and I'll see to it that she has a sympathetic doctor, someone who will convince her she must take proper precautions at all times. She probably forgot to take her pill. You know how sloppy Bitsy is."

"You mean you'll help her go on this way, fucking whenever she feels like it—at her age?"

"Jason, don't be childish. What's so wrong about what she's doing? She's having a good time, isn't she?"

"She's fifteen years old," he shouted. "When did you get so casual about the rules?"

Gillian snuggled into her pillow. "Just recently. There's a lot to be said for fun in bed. I wish I'd discovered it earlier myself."

His voice dropped menacingly. "Gillian, what's going on down there? Where have you been the last two nights?"

She decided to be reckless. "I had some business out of town. Surely you understand that, Jason."

"You lousy cunt! What are you telling me?"

"I'm telling you nothing," she said. "I'm letting you figure it out for yourself—the way you've been letting me figure it out for years."

"It's not the same thing!"

"It isn't? Why not?"

"It's different," he sputtered. "You can get pregnant, that's why. You could bring me someone else's kid."

She thought that was funny. "Don't worry, darling. I remember to take my pill."

"Bitch! No wonder Bitsy's knocked up. She learned it at her mother's knee."

"Jason," she laughed. "It's not done with knees."

"I want you home immediately. Get the hell out of that place. Right now. We have a lot of things to settle."

"I'm not ready to leave," she said reasonably. "Just a second, let me tell you my schedule. Today, I'm probably down for yoga, personalized exercises, sauna—"

"Don't give me that crap. Are you coming home today?"

"I am not."

"Then I'm coming down there. And you damned well better be on the premises."

"It's always nice to see you, Jason."

"I'll leave after I pick up Bitsy at school. That kid's not going to be deserted by me. She's got to know she has one parent who cares."

"Jason, you're boring me," she said, and replaced the receiver in its cradle.

*　　*　　*

In Modern Dance class, Elena and Rita compared their day's program cards. Both read "11:15—Herbal Wrap."

"Meet you there," Rita said.

"Where's there?"

"The Harem Room. Off the lanai. The place with the smoky glass door. Dr. Bertini gave me the rundown. We get out of these sticky leotards and grab a shower. Then we hustle over there in our robes. Get moving. See you soon."

When they arrived simultaneously at the entrance to the Harem Room, they stood at the open door and stared into the exotic interior. Sheer blue curtains billowed at floor-to-ceiling windows. Mosaic tiles in brilliant blues and greens decorated the floor and walls. Overhead, bell-shaped filigreed brass light fixtures swayed from slender chains.

A female attendant, pudgy and pink-faced, greeted them. "Come in, come in, dears. Been here before?"

"First time out. We're babes in the wood." Rita looked into the colorful room again. "So to speak," she added. Elena, wide-eyed, nodded her head in agreement.

"You'll love this," the attendant said. "It's another of those nice things we do for you after you've worked so hard. This way, please."

The attendant preceded them into the spacious room.

"Where are the eunuchs?" Rita wanted to know.

The attendant turned around. "I beg your pardon?"

"Nothing. It's breathtaking. Who designed it?"

"Dr. Bertini, personally. He visited Istanbul once. He calls it his little Blue Mosque."

"It figures. No prayer rugs?"

"We considered that. Dr. Bertini decided there was too much moisture in the room. It would be bad for the rugs."

Trailing behind the woman, Elena and Rita observed two stainless steel tubs from which clouds of steam were rising. Several cots draped with heavy rubber sheeting were ranged, dormitory-style, against the walls. A lone wooden chair and a record player on a stand completed the furnishings of the Harem Room.

"Just give me your robes, girls," the attendant instructed. "All you have to do is lie flat on your backs and put your hands by your sides. I'll take care of the rest."

After selecting adjoining cots, Elena and Rita complied.

Fascinated, they watched as the woman wrapped the sheeting around them, sealing them in like mummies. Their eyes followed her as she strode to one of the tubs, plunged her chunky hands into the near-boiling water, and pulled up a pair of dung-colored linen cloths. Vigorously, she wrung out the cloths and carried them to the cots.

"Eucalyptus tea," she explained. "Sweats out all the impurities, eases the muscles."

Working rapidly, she swathed them in the tea-drenched cloths. Next she fetched cold towels and covered their brows. Then she placed the cast album of *Kismet* on the record player and went off into a corner to read a paperback.

"We're a pair of houris," Rita said delightedly.

"A pair of what?"

"Houris. Women who dwell in Muslim heaven."

"Don't let my father hear you say that."

"Nor mine. He'd bust a gut back in Brooklyn."

They were silent awhile, listening to "Strangers in Paradise."

Then, "Elena?"

"Yes?"

"How do you like it here? Happy you came?"

"I am now in spite of what Christina said about Barry. It's surprising because—" she hesitated.

"Go on, Elena. Because what?"

"When I left L.A. I didn't expect to be happy anywhere. You see I—I'd just had an abortion."

"So that's it. Big deal. I've had three. That was before I met Peter."

"Mine was my first. I was pretty depressed afterwards."

"You mean you *wanted* the baby?"

"Some of us do. I guess I wanted Barry's baby."

"And naturally he said No?"

"He was sweet about it. I respect his feelings. Barry and I—we're not in the same place right now. Maybe some day he'll change his mind. Barry is sensitive. This week at The Fountains, the bracelet—it's his way of saying he's sorry."

"Hmmm. I never got that much. One of my guys brought me a bottle of Scotch. Another paid half the medical bills—he said I was responsible for the other half. The third never called again."

"Weren't you bitter?"

"Hell, no. I finally learned the rules of the game. In football, you wear a helmet. In sex, if you're not on the Pill, you wear an IUD or a diaphragm. Leave off the equipment and you get hurt. It's that simple."

Elena laughed. "You're right. Thanks for the toughness lesson. I can use it. Barry says I bruise too easily."

The attendant was nearing with a fresh set of cooling cloths for their brows.

"Stand back, Barry." Elena laughed again over

the strains of "Baubles, Bangles and Beads." "Because ready or not, here I come—a stronger, braver, more independent woman than the one you sent away."

The voice from the loudspeaker summoning her to a long-distance call brought Charlotte out of the pool in a wet rush. Long-distance calls were unexpected and they promised no good. Seizing her robe from the flagstone deck, she ran across the grass to the main office and picked up the telephone receiver.

Nina's voice came through, loud and frantic. "Mother, I thought I'd never get you."

"What's wrong? Is it Charlie? Ned?"

"No, no, we're all okay. Mother, it's *you*."

"What about me?"

"There's a cablegram here at your apartment, from Paris. It sounds crazy. I think the man's dangerous!"

"Stop dramatizing, Nina. Read it to me."

"Are you ready? It's addressed to Mme. Charlotte Caldwell and it says: 'You are still the stupidest woman I have ever known. But I love you. Come back at once or I will take desperate steps.' And it's signed Jean-Claude. Mother, who is this person? Why don't you answer me? Mother, are you all right?"

Charlotte clung to the phone, striving to find her voice. Over the wire she could hear Nina, shrilly demanding reassurance.

"Yes, Nina," she said, "I'm fine. I don't think I've ever been better."

"But, Mother, who is this person—this Jean-Claude?"

She thought about him, and it brought a smile to her lips. "A friend," she said, "an old friend. Someone—special—I met in Paris. I'll tell you all about him when

I get home. Right now I'm in the middle of a million things. Thanks for calling. I'm so glad you called. I love you and all of you. Good-bye, dear."

Turning away from the phone, she found she was still smiling foolishly. My God, when was the last time something—someone—had made her smile?

Wrapped in the damp robe, she wandered slowly around the room, remembering, then she sought a secluded corner of the office, curled into a soft chair, and thought back to last summer. To Paris . . .

She knew it would work. Paris had never let her down.

In the old days with Arthur she would come to the city troubled by some escapade of Nina's or the illness of an aging parent or even by the vague malaise of her own life, and unfailingly the beauty and vitality of Paris had restored her.

Her two-day stopover in New York, en route from Chicago, had been a brilliant idea. Old college friends, accompanied by present mates or lovers, had come together to give her a boisterous farewell celebration at La Caravelle. The following day, one of the party husbands had sent flowers to her suite at The Plaza, then had telephoned to invite her to meet him in the hotel bar. Parched for attention, she had been tempted to accept but her loyalty to the man's wife and memories of her experiences in Chicago had intruded and she had declined, settling for the doubtful flattery of being asked.

Now, as the Air France 747 lofted above the John F. Kennedy Airport and positioned itself for the flight over the sea, she listened with pleasure as the pilot's voice came from the public address system, offering instructions and words of comfort in French. Hearing not the words, just the melody of the language,

she closed her eyes and was content. As the plane rose
above the clouds into the twilight she experienced a
delicious sense of removal from her past. Hours later,
with the plane sweeping into a new zone, she witnessed
her second dawn of the day and she read it as a good
omen.

At the Hotel George V off the Champs Élysées,
the same suite she had always shared with Arthur was
ready and waiting for her. Back in Chicago, Charlotte
had considered the advantages of moving to another
hotel, then decided against the change. Old ghosts
would seek you out wherever you hid, she had reasoned;
it was best to banish them on their own grounds.
Moreover, there were familiar faces here, friendly staff
faces that would brighten when they saw her, making
her feel less alone.

The hotel director, M. Traynor, was standing in
the entrance as her taxi rolled under the porte cochere.
After an exuberant greeting, he personally escorted her
to her suite, tactfully making no mention of Arthur. In
the suite, a bottle of champagne lay cooling in a silver
ice bucket. M. Traynor's discreet card was beside it.
Near the telephone on the Louis XV desk she discovered a stack of messages from friends living in the
city, promising her a round of festivities to come.

For a few moments, Charlotte sat at the desk,
perfectly still, savoring the warmth fanning through
her body. She was in Paris, at peace, almost happy.

She was out of the pit at last. The insult of the
divorce was behind her.

Confidently, she reached for the telephone and
began to return her friends' calls.

Reality seeped in gradually.

Everyone had been marvelous really, and for the
first week she had barely had breathing time. Then,

like a carousel grinding to a halt, the welcoming parties
slowed, and stopped. Her own reciprocal invitations
ran their course. Further overtures, she felt, would be
embarrassing. French friends departed from Paris for
their own vacations in Italy, Spain, and Switzerland,
or returned to the demands of their day-to-day existence. She had dropped into their lives and they had
been kind but they were not committed indefinitely
to the healing of her wounds.

Overnight, Paris became Chicago; the Place de
la Concorde, the Loop with statues. She was alone.

She considered moving on. Her plans called for
a month in Paris and she did not know how she could
endure the emptiness of the remaining weeks. More
painful would be the necessity of notifying Nina and
Grace and all the friends with whom she had left her
itinerary that she was departing from Paris earlier than
she had expected. Whatever explanation she gave would
be interpreted for what it truly was, an admission of
failure.

Fighting off depression, struggling to think it
through, she anguished and she vacillated. In the end
she opted for the lesser of the miseries. She would remain in Paris until her sentence was served. She would
fortify herself with demanding lists of Things To Do,
daily assignments, as many as she could contrive, until
her time was up and she could escape.

First she scheduled a day on the Left Bank. Clad
in sensible shoes and a simple dress, she spiritlessly
roamed the once-enchanting streets. This time, the
jumbled windows of bookstores and boutiques held no
attraction. Wandering in and out of exquisite antique
shops and dusty *brocantes* on the rue du Bac and the
rue de Seine merely left her exhausted.

Out of remembered ritual, she decided to lunch
at the raucous Drugstore-Publis on the boulevard St.
Germain. Climbing the curving stairway to the balcony

restaurant she murmured, "Just one," to the hostess who came forward to seat her.

Huddled alone in a tiny booth, poking at her *salade Niçoise*, she felt absurd among the vibrant, blue-jeaned young people who filled the neighboring booths. With envy, she watched the intense byplay among groups of students, the frank affection of the homosexual couple in the booth ahead, and the mutual adoration of the biracial pair in the corner. Finally, choked with loneliness, she asked the waitress to hold her seat while she descended the stairs to the newsstand to find something to read.

In a few minutes she was back with a magazine the salesclerk had urged her to buy. Called *Paris Connection*, it was published in English and proved to be a guide book of sorts. But she was an old Paris hand and it offered little she did not already know.

Discouraged, she closed the magazine. As she pushed it across the table, an overlooked cover-line caught her eye. In white lettering on a black background it announced that somewhere within the magazine the reader would find something called Pleasuring Tips. Curious, she pulled the magazine back to her, located the table of contents, and ran her forefinger down the listings until she reached the page number for an article entitled, simply, "Pleasuring."

The opening lines told her that Pleasuring was, as she had suspected, one more exploration of the subject of prostitution in Paris. With a difference. *Paris Connection* was a guide for the discerning consumer. Its purpose was to serve. Treating with a commodity called prostitutes, it cheerfully offered readers the same practical information it reserved for its chapters on foods and wines. Charlotte began to read:

> There are 40,000 professional hookers in Paris, and many more "amateurs." There are 200 hotels in Paris which cater to "short stays," and around 19

"maisons de rendez-vous." Male prostitution is climbing and to date, six establishments offer bored and rich women male services at prices around $60 . . .

The business today mixes the real pros and the "debutantes" . . . The "debs" are in it to pay their rent, their overdue boutique bills, or a weekend at some smart country hideaway . . . These girls are not prostitutes.

The "pros," on the other side, are in it strictly for the money. They have numbers, and agents and appointments like a mutual fund salesman . . . They work as if they're punching a time clock. You can meet them through legwork on the boulevards or through hotel concierges, doormen, bartenders, and cab drivers . . . Simply ask directions like you're looking for the Eiffel Tower . . .

Helpfully, *Paris Connection* volunteered the names and addresses of some of the better hotels available (adding the reminder that obtaining your lovemate was your own responsibility) and went on to offer a few suggestions for those with tastes running to the gay scene (active), group romps (try the suburbs), or the more passive diversions of the sex shops ("standard fare").

Clearly, Paris hadn't changed that much. Prostitution was still as French as crepes suzette, and any number could play. Even bored, rich women.

Charlotte closed the magazine and left it on the table alongside her tip.

Back on the street, she found a taxi in front of the Brasserie Lipp and returned to her hotel more depressed than when she had left that morning.

Abandoning the Left Bank, she planned days of couture-hopping and gift-shopping in her own *arrondissement*. She bought at-home gowns (for whom?) at Givenchy and dresses and suits at Valentino and promised to return for lengthenings and shortenings of hemlines although she did not remember and did not care which was to happen where. When a salesman at Charles Jourdan quickly removed a new shoe from her foot, explaining that it was too narrow and he did not want her to have anything that would give her pain, his kindness so overwhelmed her, she broke into tears.

One late afternoon, fatigued from her exercises in futility, she asked her cabdriver to drop her at Fouquet's on the Champs-Élysées. Weaving her way through the close-packed tables of the outdoor café, she located a table that was unoccupied and wearily dropped into a wicker chair.

After ordering an espresso, she looked about hopefully for a familiar face. It was August, the swarming season of tourists. In the past, it had not been unusual to encounter someone from back home. Today there was no one. Around her sat men and women plunged into their newspapers. Others ate and sipped and talked to companions. Still others, like herself, sat alone, glumly. No one returned her weak smile.

Wretched, she swung her gaze beyond the tables to the Champs-Élysées spread before her, taking in the sweep of the avenue and the demented maneuvers of the motorcycles, buses, bicycles, and cars. When the sight dizzied her, she narrowed in on the pedestrians moving past Fouquet's, rushing, sauntering, hobbling, bumping, apologizing, swearing, chic, ragged, casual, young, old, male, female.

Then young and male, young and male, young and male.

Mesmerized, she blocked out everyone and everything else. Only the young men held her riveted. Smooth-skinned, slim-hipped young men, wearing unbuttoned, chest-revealing cotton shirts that disappeared into pants so tight they became second skins over flat stomachs and taut behinds and faintly mounded gen-

itals. The feral movements of their bodies seemed deliberately insinuating, and her breathing quickened.

Some returned her stare and she knew they were
reading her mind. A few, smiling smugly, signaled their
own availability.

Suddenly, she felt sickened.

Christ, what have I come to? she asked herself.
I am nothing but a horny, frustrated, middle-aged bitch.
A dirty joke. As bad as Arthur, seated here in a sidewalk
café leering at kids no older than my daughter.

She wanted to scream out her despair and caught
her lip between her teeth to keep any sound from
escaping.

Tossing some franc notes on the table she
jumped from her seat and clumsily made her way
across the café to the Avenue George V side, determined to reach the refuge of her suite before breaking
down.

M. Traynor was standing in the hotel lobby,
hands clasped behind his back, as she rushed in. Immediately, he hurried toward her.

"Mme. Caldwell, I have been waiting for you.
Will you join me for a drink?"

"Another time, if you don't mind."

He bowed slightly. "Another time as well, of
course. But today we must have our first drink together.
There is something we must talk about."

"Can't it wait?"

"It would be better if it did not."

She gave up. "But just a quick one, please. I've
had a busy day. I must dress for dinner."

"There will be time for that, I promise."

His fingers touched her elbow lightly as he
guided her beyond the concierges' desk, around the
corner past the vitrines, to the large, deeply carpeted,
dimly lit bar. Waving off the smiling maître d', he chose

a secluded red leather banquette, indicated where she was to sit, and slipped in beside her.

When they had ordered their drinks and the waiter had withdrawn, she looked at him, waiting for him to begin.

"In a moment we will talk," he said. "After we are served. What I have to say is rather personal."

She was losing her control. She wanted to escape the bar, reach her own bed, and sob into her pillow. She opened her mouth to say she felt ill but closed it again as M. Traynor pointed to the approaching waiter.

In a moment the waiter was gone, leaving them with bowls of olives and nuts and two tall glasses.

Gratefully, she reached for her gin and tonic. "Now?" she said.

"Now." He shifted his body to face her fully. "Mme. Caldwell, this is a delicate matter. Do not be angry with me. I must tell you—I have been studying your bill."

She tensed instantly, despair replaced by indignation. "You know my credit is good. Even without a husband."

He covered her hand. "Dear Mme. Caldwell, there is no question about your credit. I said I have been *studying* your bill, not worrying about it."

"You're making no sense."

"Madame, a hôtelier is like a detective. Every item provides a clue."

"Clue? What clue?"

He sighed. "I look at your bill and I see that you have room service charges. Every night. You, a beautiful woman, have your dinner in your room, every night, by yourself. It is not so difficult to deduce that you are lonely here, and unhappy."

"That is no business of yours."

"Perhaps not. Certainly not in my role as hôtelier. But we are old friends. We have known each other many years, since you and your husband first came to Paris, when your daughter was small. It is a long time."

She took a large gulp of her drink and waited for him to go on.

"You were so gay then. I thought your husband the luckiest of men. I would like to see you gay again."

She laughed nervously. "M. Traynor," she said, pointing to her glass, "you must talk to your bartender. Only one drink and I'm giddy. I do believe you are offering me your body."

He lifted his shoulders. "How I wish it were true and that you would have me. But I am a married man. I also have a mistress. Both are demanding. Unhappily I suffer certain human limitations."

She fell silent, mortified by her assumption, feeling rejected by a man she didn't even want.

"What I have in mind is a young man who—"

The magazine story about prostitution leapt into her head. What was it she had read there, something about male whores for bored, rich ladies?

"How dare you," she said. Her voice rose and the few people scattered about the room turned to watch.

Unperturbed, M. Traynor went on "—a young man, a chauffeur. Jean-Claude Severn, who can serve as a guide, too."

"A guide! Thanks a lot. I've seen the Eiffel Tower." She was simmering.

"No, no, not a guide to show you Paris. You must leave Paris, that is what I am suggesting."

"Leave Paris?"

"This is not a good place for you, not at this moment in your life. And that is all it is, a moment, but a bad one."

She was wavering. "Where would I go?"

"Have you seen Normandie? The châteaux country? The Côte d'Azur is lovely this time of year. Jean-Claude can take you anywhere. His English is fluent, he is multilingual. Only yesterday he returned from Spain with two ladies, sisters from Canada. He is available to accept a new client. His fee is moderate, it can be added to your hotel bill."

"I can't travel with a strange man."

"No need to decide now. Meet him first, let him drive you around the city for a few days. If you like him, you can discuss a longer trip. Will you think about it?"

She sat morosely. "I'll think about it."

After all, she had nothing better to think about.

The first thought that crossed Charlotte's mind when she saw Jean-Claude was that his pants were tight. Not too tight. Just tight. Just right. He was standing in the lobby near the newsstand, a slender, tall, dark-haired man, thirty-three, thirty-four at the most, listening intently to something being said by M. Traynor. Both men looked up as she approached. She heard introductions being made and acknowledged, and in minutes she was on the curb and Jean-Claude was helping her into the rear seat of a black Mercedes bearing the legend *Taxi* over its windshield.

The Mercedes was unexpected. In a final spasm of guilt, Arthur had insisted she take his Mercedes as part of her divorce settlement—one more sacrifice to assuage his own stricken conscience. Six months later when Arthur purchased a new Mercedes for his young wife, she wondered what he was atoning for so soon.

Charlotte wanted to say something to Jean-Claude about the extravagance of using a Mercedes as a taxi but resisted, fearful of sounding patronizing. In-

stead, as he looked over his shoulder from the driver's
seat, his chocolate-brown eyes questioning, she reached
into her handbag and pulled out a fresh list of Things
To Do. Agreeably, he accepted the list and put the car
in gear.

He drove her to her fittings at Valentino's and
Givenchy, and to Angelina's, a *belle époque* tearoom
where she stopped briefly for a snack. He dropped her
at Brentano's bookstore on the avenue de L'Opéra and
when she emerged an hour later he materialized at her
side to relieve her of her packages. He was amiable
and attentive, neither obtrusive nor subservient.

Another day he took her to the Marché aux
Puces, that zany complex of stalls and street merchants
known as the Flea Market of Paris. Because her French
was faulty (and because he was beginning to be fun)
she invited him to accompany her through the old alley-
ways and shops of the Market where together they
marveled and hooted and bargained over the jumbled
displays of priceless artifacts and appalling junk. At a
little bistro in the Marché Biron he joined her for a
lunch of cold chicken and white wine. He made no
move to pick up the check.

One afternoon, on impulse, Charlotte asked Jean-
Claude to take her to the Jardin d'Acclimatation in the
Bois de Boulogne. Charlotte had never forgotten the
noisy, colorful amusement park, part playground, part
zoo, where she and Arthur, hard put to entertain their
daughter, had spent so many tiring hours with the
young Nina.

Now, shed of the need to please someone else,
Charlotte opened herself for the first time to the childish delights of the Jardin. With Jean-Claude encouraging her, she bull's-eyed the cardboard characters in the
shooting gallery. She giggled when the pink cotton

candy he brought to her stuck to her nose and chin. And she shamelessly licked her fingers one by one after gobbling a crepe suzette hot off the griddle and filled with sticky strawberry jam. Hand in hand they circled the giant bird houses, enthralled by the exotic captives. At the monkey pit, they bent forward against the iron railing and talked solemnly to an ancient chimpanzee which dove for their peanuts and chatteringly demanded more.

In the House of Illusions, they stood before the distorting mirrors and laughed until they hiccupped watching their stomachs ballooning on toothpick legs, turning them into joyful Humpty-Dumptys, and they were uproarious children as the next mirror reflected them grotesquely elongated like two emaciated El Grecos.

Still laughing as they left the fun house, she told him it was ridiculous for him to call her Mme. Caldwell while she called him Jean-Claude.

"I insist," she said, "this very minute. You must say Charlotte. Try it. Char-lotte."

"Charlotte, Charlotte, Charlotte," he repeated. "Enough? I can say it now, naturally."

"Perfect. What do we do next?"

He bought two tickets for a ride on a tiny boat, a two-seater tub really, operated by some invisible engine. Facing each other, they drifted down a narrow stream. Leafy willow branches touched the water. Rounding a bend, they were alone in the world. Leaning forward, he cupped her face in his hands, and kissed her.

On the drive back to the George V she told him she would like him to chauffeur her to the south of France. A month earlier, in Chicago, she had made her reservation for a week at the Carlton Hotel in Cannes.

She would be ready to leave on Monday. He said he would be ready, too, and would find his own place to stay until she was prepared to return to Paris.

"Monday at ten?" she said as they drew up to the hotel.

"I'll be here."

"Have a good weekend."

"I intend to," he said. "I'm going on a Sunday picnic."

"Sounds nice."

"You'll love it. Be ready at noon."

"*Me?*"

He eyed her trim navy blue linen skirt and dyed-to-match silk shirt.

"Designer clothes aren't happy on picnics. Wear something more comfortable," he ordered. "Cotton pants or a loose skirt, old shoes if you have them. We're going to the country, to the forest of Fontainebleau. I want you to see how the French spend a holiday afternoon."

Paris was a deserted village, silent, hot, the sky a clear blue bowl. They headed south for Porte d'Italie and the old road to Fontainebleau, passing small towns with shuttered shops and houses, and unmanned gasoline stations. On a dreary street corner, Jean-Claude pulled his car to the curb and slammed on his brakes.

"What's wrong?" she wanted to know.

"What's wrong is that my date usually sits up here, in front with me."

"I thought you'd never ask," she sighed happily. As he opened the door for her, she popped into the seat beside him. "Mmm, much better," she said. "In a democracy, no one rides in the back of the bus."

The avenue du Fontainebleau, ribboning through the lifeless towns, held little promise until they reached

the suburb of Bicêtre. Like an oasis in a desert of dull-
ness, Bicêtre with its gaudy miniature Flea Market
bordering the highway, teemed with families that surrounded stalls offering everything from raincoats, re-
frigerators, and rubber tires, to pizzas, antique chests,
and new-born puppies.

Excited by the spectacle, Charlotte wanted to
leave the car and join the crowd but Jean-Claude held
her back.

"Not here. There is another place I want you to
see."

Obediently she fell back in her seat. They were
both quiet as the drab towns continued to roll by.

When they reached Corbeil, a town little different from the others, he slowed the car.

"I want you to take a good look at this place.
Look at it hard. Try to remember what you see."

"But why?"

"I'll tell you in a minute."

Charlotte observed the main street and the side
roads leading off to the left and to the right. What she
saw was row after row of two-story houses, all made of
limestone, all under red-tiled roofs supporting red-brick
chimneys. The sole variation was in the color of their
trim. Some had red shutters and some had green. But
mostly the tones were beige and buff and tan. The few
shops facing the street were concealed behind gray
metal shutters and they seemed as melancholy as the
houses. At a distance, she could make out a gray church
steeple.

"What do you think?" he asked.

"Levittown," she replied.

"What does that mean?"

"No individuality," she said carefully. "All the
same. But why does it matter to you?"

"Because Corbeil is my town. This is where I was

born and grew up. My mother and grandmother are
still here in Corbeil."

"Are we going to visit them?"

He found that amusing. "No way. I don't think
they would want to see you. And I know they would
not want to see me."

"I don't understand. Why not?"

"Because they think of me as my father's son,
and he's the one they want to see least of all."

"Where is your father?"

"Like your old American song title: 'Back Home
Again in Indiana.'"

"Indiana!"

"An unlikely place? You're right. But then, they
were an unlikely pair."

"Indiana," she repeated. "How on earth did he
get here?"

"His own father came first, in the twenties. My
grandfather was an automobile engineer working for
the Cord Motor Car Company in Indiana. Cord ex-
ported cars to Europe and twice a year my grandfather
would come over to road test them. He'd bring them
down from Belgium and test them on this very road—
it was cobblestoned then—and he'd get them into condition to be sold to Frenchmen. He was a big, tough
man, half Irish, half Welsh, who had spent most of his
life in the Midwest. France dazzled him and he thought
Corbeil was romantic."

Jean-Claude paused. "In time the Cord Company called him back to Indiana to stay, and because
he was a dutiful employee he followed orders. But he
never forgot Corbeil. He told his sons about it and
when my father came to France during World War II,
he headed for Corbeil.

"Pop was big like his father, lusty, and full of

juices, ready to burst. When he saw my mother—she was a prim little waitress working in her widowed mother's pastry shop—he tumbled. He had never known such demure innocence, and she was swept away by the force of his personality. I don't know if they were ever in love. I think they were hypnotized by their differences.

"After they were married, my father moved in with the two women—temporarily, he thought. Pop was an experienced automobile mechanic. By the time I was born he had saved enough money to buy a house for his own family. That's when he discovered that the two women were tougher than any of the steel in his shop. They would not be separated. They were a team, a man-hating team, united against him. He was an intruder. His lustiness shamed them. All physical contact ceased when my mother told him sex sickened her.

"Poor Pop. He couldn't get me away from them —what would the town think?—and he wouldn't leave me alone with them, so he stuck it out as long as he could. I was eleven years old when he went back to America, to Indiana.

"He was a great guy." Jean-Claude smiled, remembering. "Never forgot my birthday or Christmas. But that was the last I ever saw of him."

"How awful for you."

He grinned down at her. "No, that was the good part. After Pop went, the two women removed every sign of him. Except me. There I was, a dirty little biological souvenir left behind by that damned American. They had hopes though. They thought they could make me one of them, a tight-assed prig who would neither drink nor swear, nor—God forgive the thought —touch a woman. They froze me out. They were harsh and critical and they relished cataloguing my sins and reporting me to the school priests. The only father they wanted me to know was the father who heard my weekly confession.

"When I finished school—ninety percent of the kids in Corbeil still go to Catholic schools—I took a shot at the University of Paris, even tried studying the law for a while. But I'd had enough regimentation for a lifetime. I knew I didn't ever again want someone telling me what to do. I broke the news to my mother and my grandmother that I was leaving school, and they washed their hands of me. They'd just been looking for the excuse.

"After that, I thought hard about my future. I had to be satisfied with my decision. And I am. What you see before you today is that rarest of creatures, a truly free man, a taxi driver. Don't comment, dear Charlotte, you won't come up with the right thing to say, anyway."

"I think it's fine what you're doing. I mean that."

"My sweet lady, you are appalled. You were certain a young man of my obvious charm and ability was just biding his time, waiting for something worthier to come along."

"I didn't say that."

"You didn't have to. How could you suspect that behind the wheels of this Mercedes is a man who has fulfilled his highest ambition?"

"Well, there *are* better things to do."

"Not for me. There are fifteen thousand taxi drivers in Paris. Half work for private companies, maybe ten hours a day. The other half are men and women like me, drivers who own their own cars, independent drivers who answer to no one but themselves. Think of it. I work when I want to. I sleep, loaf, drink, copulate whenever it pleases me. For long jobs, I choose my clients although they think they choose me. I am more in control of my life than the President of France."

"Who gave you this car?" she asked suspiciously.

He began to whistle and she recognized the strains of "Back Home Again in Indiana."

"Not your father?"

"None other. I had scraped together four thousand dollars to buy my taxi license. When I wrote and told him I had chosen my career, he was so amused he cabled me the money to buy a Mercedes. He wanted me to have the best. He never said it but I know he was proud I had beaten the two biddies of Corbeil and he wanted to be part of the game."

"Those poor women," she said. "You and your father—you're a fine pair of bastards." But he could tell she did not mean it.

Corbeil was behind them now and in a mock-guide singsong he began to comment upon points of interest along the way.

"Back there, Madame, we passed Ris-Orangis where you may see a home for retired artistes, donated by the great Maurice Chevalier and still maintained by the terms of his will. To your right you see fields of wheat and sugar beets; to your left, fields of corn. The wheat and sugar beets are for humans. The corn is for cattle. We French think corn eaten from the cob is an American eccentricity, just a bit gauche. The man by the side of the road who is selling fresh peaches is—"

"Stop that," she said sharply. "Don't do that to yourself, or to me."

When they reached the storybook village of Barbizon on the fringe of the forest he changed his tone and told her with pride that this had been the creative home of the famed Barbizon School. To this place, he explained, had come the painters, Rousseau, Corot, and Millet, and then Paul Verlaine and Alfred

de Musset with George Sand, all seeking inspiration.
Many had dined at the ancient Café Ganne facing the
road.

Deep in the forest of Fontainebleau there was a
stillness in what had once been the hunting grounds
of kings. They picked their way among the shiny ferns,
careful not to tread on new shoots, until they came to a
grassy spot beneath the old oak trees. Jean-Claude
spread a blanket he had carried from the trunk of his
car and on it he placed a wicker basket with its picnic
lunch of crisp baguettes, cheeses, pâté, and wine. They
nibbled at the cheese and pâté, finished off the wine,
and spent the rest of the afternoon side by side on the
blanket, saying little.

Their journey to the Riviera, begun the following day, was over too soon although they held to a
leisurely pace. They toured the châteaux country, stopping at Chambord, Chenonceaux, and Tours. From the
ancient Château d'Artigny, rebuilt as a private mansion
for the Coty perfume family and now an exquisite hotel,
she mailed her first postcards to Chicago, wanting everyone to know she was happy. As they continued south,
they sat close for long hours of each day, gradually revealing fragments of their secret selves, testing carefully
to be certain each new confidence would be received
with the sensitivity it deserved, and they never disappointed each other.

Charlotte knew the idyllic interlude was over
when, after lunching at L'Oasis, in La Napoule, a small
town on the Mediterranean, he told her the time had
come for her to return to the patron seat in the rear of
the Mercedes.

"Cannes is less than a half hour away," he said.
"You are an American divorcée arriving with your

French chauffeur. People can be unpleasant. I do not want anything to embarrass you."

She protested, and she obeyed.

An aging *bagagiste*, bent by years of toting the belongings of the rich, shuffled behind Charlotte, carrying her single suitcase into the air-conditioned lobby of the Carlton Hotel.

Outside in the driveway, Jean-Claude was in gesticulating conversation with the doorman about where to park the Mercedes.

At the lobby desk the chef de reception welcomed Charlotte, handed her a pen, and pushed the registration pad toward her. She was engrossed in filling out the registration form when a shrill, female voice calling her name crashed across the lobby.

"Charl, Charl Caldwell, I don't believe it!"

Charlotte dropped the pen and swiveled in the direction of the voice, flinching as she recognized to whom it belonged. Shirley Shelby, of course. Shirley Shelby, the scourge of Chicago society, wife of a wealthy insurance broker, distasteful leftover of her old life with Arthur, was hastening toward her.

"Charl, what a surprise! I mean, I never expected to see *you* here again. I mean, after Arthur and that young girl and everything. Wait'll I tell Joe."

Ten years earlier, in a futile pursuit of beauty, Shirley had submitted to a disastrous nose job. Now, as she rattled on, the foreshortened snout quivered among her thick features like a yo-yo gone mad. The yellow beach robe she clutched over her swimsuit could not conceal her sagging breasts or the brown, sun-dried skin of her arms and legs.

"It's nice to see you, Shirley. I wasn't expecting this either."

"Poor Charl," Shirley went on, "Joe and I were so sorry to hear about the divorce. It's always old faithful who gets the dirty end of the stick isn't it?"

"There's nothing to feel sorry about, Shirley. I'm quite adjusted, really I am."

"You do *look* great," Shirley conceded. The lidless eyes narrowed and studied Charlotte carefully. "My God, Charl, you've had your face lifted!" she exclaimed. "Who's the genius who did it? I always say, when my time comes I'll march right in for a few nips and tucks myself."

Over Shirley's shoulder, Charlotte saw that Jean-Claude was ascending the steps to the lobby.

"If you'll forgive me, Shirley, I'd like to go upstairs. I could use a shower after the drive from Paris."

"Drive? From Paris? You come alone?"

"In a way. I hired a car and chauffeur."

At the lobby entrance Jean-Claude slowed, appraising the scene. Then, his manner formal, he strode up to the two women.

"Mme. Caldwell, are you settled?" he asked. "Is there anything more I can do?"

"Nothing, Jean-Claude, thank you. Shirley, this is Jean-Claude Severn. Jean-Claude, Mrs. Shelby and her husband are old friends from Chicago."

"Then I leave you in good hands. I will telephone in the morning. Perhaps you will wish to use the car."

As Jean-Claude crossed the lobby to the exit, Shirley Shelby's eyes followed the easy swing of his body and her heavy face grew shrewd.

"Nice-looking chauffeur," she said. "Must have been a fun trip."

Jean-Claude phoned faithfully each morning as she breakfasted alone on the terrace of her suite over-

looking the Mediterranean, and each morning she told
him that he was free for the day, that she and her
friends had made plans.

Pressured by Shirley, helpless to resist, Charlotte allowed herself to be absorbed into the Shelbys'
social routine, the same unvarying routine she and
Arthur had shared on their vacations together. First,
breakfast in her suite, delivered by room service. Then,
hours on the crowded Carlton beach, stretched on a
canvas chair, oiled and immobilized in the sun. Later,
lunch at the lavish snack bar that was sheltered from
the heat by a woven bamboo roof. For the men in the
group there was, as always, a special treat, a close-up
view of the professional hookers down from Paris for
their annual working vacations.

With the cooling of the afternoon, Charlotte
joined Shirley on witless rampages through the expensive boutiques along the boulevard de la Croisette, or
the tackier but more diverting shops behind the hotel
on the rue d'Antibes.

Evenings meant cocktails on the hotel terrace
with the Shelbys and their crowd, followed by the time-
honored game of Our Turn, in which one couple among
them selected the restaurant for dinner and, following
ritual protests from the others, picked up the check
for the entire group. When Charlotte proposed the
restaurant, the protests were louder than usual but in
the end the check came to her.

Charlotte had never felt fully comfortable on the
Riviera, although she had voiced no objection when
Arthur put Cannes on their itinerary year after year.
After all, it was *his* vacation, wasn't it? Hadn't *he*
worked hard, earned the money? And wasn't everyone
else having a great time?

Habit and apathy had led her to instruct her

travel agent to add Cannes to the itinerary once more. Without Arthur (and without Jean-Claude) she liked the place no better than before.

The Shelbys and their crowd were a mystifying breed to her, relentless travelers who journeyed thousands of miles every year only to meet up again in such places as Hawaii, Palm Springs, the Caribbean, and the Côte d'Azur. Wherever they met, they resumed running in the same pack. Invariably, they arrived at their destinations with luggage stuffed and heads empty, devoid of interest in the language, the customs, or the people of the region. Weeks later, departing, they were enriched by nothing more than their own deep tans.

On the Côte d'Azur, Charlotte had observed, this same hearty band made their obligatory pilgrimages to the art centers of the area. Just once. They visited the Fondation Maeght in Saint-Paul-de-Vence, the Leger Museum in Biot, and the Matisse Museum in Nice. They gasped appropriately at the treasures they viewed, and mentally pocketed a few famous names and bits of jargon that would knock them dead back home.

Their obeisance to culture paid, they hastily returned to their striped chairs on the jam-packed beaches and to their tables at the best bars, to talk about things that mattered: the stock market, the cost of the new yacht in the harbor, and who was laying whom.

Except for the morning telephone calls, Charlotte never spoke to Jean-Claude. Once she saw him on the beach, tossing a ball with a lithe, string-clad brunette whose small, close-cropped head and long, slender neck announced she was a dancer or a model. Charlotte had returned Jean-Claude's cool nod and prayed that Shirley Shelby, sprawled beside her, had not noticed the exchange. Another day, on the rue d'Antibes, Jean-Claude and the same brunette had pressed back against a shopwindow to allow Shirley and Charlotte to pass on the narrow sidewalk. Again they had barely nodded.

One day, watching Jean-Claude and his brunette lying together on the wood-slatted jetty that extended into the sea, she began to grow ill. The two young bodies, glistening after a dip in the water, made her own body feel worn and ugly. She hated herself and even more she hated Arthur—for casting her off, for stripping her of her self-esteem.

Arthur, you bastard, she thought, why did you do this to me at this awkward age in my life, when I'm too young to be old and too old to be young?

And she knew the answer. "Marcy makes me feel like a kid again," he had told her. "That's what I like; that's what I need." She had wanted to kill him then because he had accused her of the one crime for which there was no atonement, her crime of growing older.

The small moan that escaped Charlotte's lips roused Shirley from her doze. Hoisting herself on one elbow, Shirley glanced toward Charlotte and then, her little eyes unblinking, she followed Charlotte's gaze to the pair on the jetty.

"Cute, aren't they?" Shirley smiled wickedly.

Charlotte leaned across her chair and pinched hard on Shirley's cheek. "Not as cute as you are, baby," she said. "You take the prize."

On the sixth morning of her stay in Cannes, Charlotte waited nervously for Jean-Claude's call. When it came, she told him they would have to leave for Paris that day.

"It's Nina, my daughter," she apologized. "She phoned from Chicago. There's a problem. I must go home."

"Nothing serious, I hope."

"No, I'll explain later."

"Ten o'clock? I'll have the car checked out by then."

"Ten o'clock will be fine." She paused. "Jean-Claude, I'm truly sorry if this changes your personal plans."

"I have no personal plans," he replied.

An hour later, on the Carlton terrace, Charlotte looked past Shirley Shelby, and said good-bye to Joe and Peggy and Phil and the others as the pack prepared to file across the heavily trafficked Croisette to the beach on the other side. She saw Shirley glance back once and wave as Charlotte took her seat in the rear of the Mercedes and Jean-Claude moved in behind the wheel.

Shirley, you bitch, she wanted to cry out. You cruel, empty, stupid bitch. Can't you guess how much I hurt?

They were on the road, safely clear of Cannes, when Jean-Claude slowed and stopped the car. He leaned over and opened the passenger door to his right. Without comment, Charlotte left the back of the car and joined him on the front seat.

"Now tell me what it is with your daughter," he said.

"Usual thing. Husband trouble. Must run in the family."

"What does it have to do with you?"

"Nothing. Everything. I'm not sure. Ned is threatening to leave her. They fight a lot, about money. Nina doesn't know how to manage. It's not her fault. She wasn't taught. Arthur and I never stopped competing for her approval. We thought we scored points when we bought her everything she asked for. The most casual hint—wham, there it was in her lap. And that, in brief, is how we gave her the biggest gift of all—a lousy marriage."

"For *that* you are leaving France?"

"It's important. She needs me."

"She's a grown woman, a mother herself. And you are going back to hold her hand?"

"I don't want to talk about it."

They were driving through the rich greenery of Provence when he drew her to him, brushing his lip across her cheek.

"You're lovely," he said, "even when you're miserable."

"I'm a bore and a drag. I'm ruining your day. I'll try to think of something funny to say."

"No one has asked you to say a word."

With one hand still on the wheel he raised the other to her dark, curly hair, then slowly dropped his fingers to her neck and began to massage her tense muscles.

"Better?"

"Much better." She closed her eyes and moved into the curve of his arm.

It was not until he turned the wheel abruptly that she sat straight up and saw that they were off the autoroute and on a rustic country road. He drove the car under a tree and cut the engine.

"Exercise time," he said. "Let's walk."

Standing beside him on the road, she raised her arms high in a long stretch. Her small breasts beneath the thin T-shirt rose with the gesture and his eyes glinted approval.

"This way," he said, and taking her hand he led her down the dirt road. When they came upon a narrow footpath, almost invisible from the road, he stopped.

"Feel like exploring?" Without waiting for an

answer he turned onto the footpath pulling her deeper into the woods, through brambles and tangled vines, until they arrived at a small, shadowed clearing. Overhead, the mingled treetops, filtering the early afternoon sun, formed a distant leafy canopy.

Edging her toward one of the darkened tree trunks that ringed the clearing, Jean-Claude took Charlotte into his arms and pressed his body hard upon hers against the rough bark. Unaware, her own arms drew him tighter.

"I love you," he whispered. "I've been out of my mind needing you."

"Me? You need *me?* But that young girl in Cannes—"

"Nothing. I want you, now."

"You don't know what you're saying."

"I know what I'm saying and I know what I'm feeling. Now, Charlotte, now."

"This is crazy, impossible." Her tone was miserable.

"But why—?"

"I love you, I want you, too. But look at me. Can't you see? Can't you understand? *I am older than you are. I am at least ten goddam years older than you are.*" She stifled a sob. "Nothing adds up in this stupid world. Nothing but those goddam birthdays."

He heard her out and then he released her. Leaving her leaning against the tree weeping quietly, he took several steps backward into the clearing, his eyes never moving from her face.

Pained, she watched his retreat.

Then, with wonder, she saw him unbutton his cotton shirt and cast it off. His eyes still on her, he kicked off his shoes, loosened his blue jeans, and tossed them aside. Unbelieving, she watched his penis slowly rise.

"For me?" she whimpered. "*I* make you feel like that?"

He attempted a smile. "There are certain things even a Frenchman can't pretend." But there was no humor in his thickened voice or clouded eyes.

"It's up to you now, Charlotte. I'm not going to rape you."

Her eyes scanned his face, then dropped again to his penis.

Dazed, she found the edge of her T-shirt and pulled it over her head. She stepped out of her sandals, untied her denim skirt, and let it drop away, and then she stood before him nude.

As she waited, he studied her body with joy, the small conical breasts, still firm, the tiny waistline, the slight roundness of her belly. When she saw him approach, nearly forgotten waves of arousal started upward from the dampness between her legs, making her tremble.

She was aware of his strong fingers on her shoulders, pressing her to the ground. The carpet of fallen leaves, moist in the deepness of the woods, felt soft and spongy beneath her body.

When he entered her, her orgasm came so quickly and violently it left them both startled.

"You're unbelievable," he groaned. "Fantastic. We'll never stop."

Her body arced into his and as he resumed his thrusting, first slowly, then faster, her endless moans rose into the trees and she peaked again. When they had satisfied each other, they lay entwined in the clearing.

"Never again will you be wasted," he promised. "It would be an offense against nature and me."

In the car, headed toward Paris, he kept her close beside him.

"We're going to be married," he announced. "Immediately."

"You know that's impossible."

"But you love me."

"I've never loved anyone more."

"Then what's to stop us?"

"Bad timing, that's what. What happened back there, that will always be the most beautiful moment in my life. But nothing can change the fact that I am still ten lousy years older than you are."

He listened, pretending solemnity. "True, true. And you are also smaller than I am, and rounder and prettier. And I believe you play the piano. But this is no time for irrelevancies. What matters is that I love you and you love me. We will be married and we will leave the arithmetic to the mathematicians. Agreed?"

Running her fingers between his inner thighs, she reached his crotch and with the palm of her hand stroked it gently. When he responded, she nodded and said, "I agree to everything." Then, throwing back her head she began to laugh in hysterical bursts.

"What's funny?" he demanded.

"I am. I, Charlotte Caldwell, am very, very funny. I am forty-four years old, a responsible Chicago matron, a grandmother. And I have just been laid in a glade! Don't you think that's marvelous? Jean-Claude, you laid me in a glade and I love you insanely!"

By the time they arrived at the George V, it was after midnight and Charlotte was back in her patron seat in the Mercedes. Plans for the following day had been made. In the morning, she would pack her bags for the return flight to Chicago. At noon, Jean-Claude would fetch her in the Mercedes and she would finish off a newly inspired list of Things To Do. For the evening, he would have a table reserved at his favorite restaurant, Tong Yen on the rue Jean Mermoz, and they would dine together openly, for the first time, as lovers.

At midafternoon she had already dashed in and out of a half-dozen shops on the rue de Rivoli opposite the Tuileries Gardens, ticking off small, last-minute purchases. Hurrying under the arcades, headed for Galignani's to buy a book for the plane, she found herself on the corner of the rue de Castiglione, captivated by the displays in the windows of A. Sulka & Co., Shirtmakers and Haberdashers. A gift for Jean-Claude. Why hadn't she thought of it before? Excited, she studied the luxurious items in the windows: pure silk pajamas, leather belts with stunning silver buckles, suede jackets, even handbags for men.

She decided upon the suede jacket and tentatively opened the glass door. A swarthy, moustached salesman, obsequiously rubbing his manicured fingers together, padded across the red carpeting to offer his services.

"I'd like to see a jacket for my—my husband," she said. "Brown suede, I think. Yes, he'd look good in brown."

"Certainly, madame. His size, please?"

"His size?" Her confusion was obvious. "His size?" she repeated. "I'm really not sure. He's—he's been dieting, you see. Yes, that's it, he's been dieting and he's lost a lot of weight."

The salesman smiled knowingly. "Of course, madame. Men do change. I understand perfectly. Would you say he's about my size?"

His oily smirk irritated her. "He's taller than you are, and thinner than you are, and broader in the chest."

"And luckier, too, if I may say so, madame."

"Please show me the jackets."

When she had made her selection and paid for it, the salesman disappeared briefly. He returned with a large box.

"I'm sure your, uh, husband will enjoy his new jacket," he said, handing her the box. "And if he finds the arms too long or too short, do tell him we stand ready to make any alteration."

"How would you like to be altered yourself?" she snapped, and slammed the glass door in his face.

Her anger had cooled by the time she reached the rue Cambon and found Jean-Claude waiting beside the parked Mercedes.

"A present for you," she said shyly, handing him the box. "Something soft for you to touch until I come back to Paris."

Jean-Claude, wearing the new suede jacket (the sleeves *were* too short), had met her in the hotel lobby. Together they had strolled down the gaudy Champs-Élysées to the Rond Point and turned left into the rue Jean Mermoz.

The hostess at Tong Yen, recognizing Jean-Claude, had seated them in a quiet booth along the restaurant wall. Between them, tucked in a niche, sat a chubby Buddha, throwing off a soft light that touched their faces. Warmed by wine, they held hands and made plans for their future.

"Skiing in St. Moritz," she said.

"Scuba diving in the Caribbean."

"A farm in Vermont."

"Summer on the Riviera."

"Uh-uh, too many beautiful girls."

"I've heard good things about Pittsburgh."

"Jersey City's nicer."

"Lapland."

"Costa Smeralda."

"My apartment. Right after dinner."

"Best idea yet."

Stroking his wrist, bared by the shortness of the jacket sleeve, she remembered Sulka's and jokingly related the incident with the salesman.

"My poor Charlotte. You encountered a provincial, something brought in from the outskirts, probably Corbeil. No Parisian would treat a lady that way."

He had moved to refill her wine glass when, suddenly grown serious, she grabbed his hand, forcing him to return the bottle to the table.

"Jean-Claude?" She hesitated. "All our plans, how will we pay for them? What will we live on?"

His surprise was genuine.

"I have a little money, I'll earn more. You have a great deal. You told me so yourself."

Her face crumpled with disappointment.

"You mean you would take my money? You would let me support you?"

"I didn't say that, you did. I'll always have enough money to take care of two people, my way. But if you want to live like the wealthy woman you are, then you will have to pay for it. That is your decision, not mine."

She looked doubtful. "You make it sound so logical."

"Then nothing is changed? You'll return to Paris quickly and marry me?"

"Yes, I guess—"

From the restaurant foyer, she heard her name being shouted.

"Charl, you little devil! I don't believe my eyes! And I thought you were tearing home to Chicago!"

Shirley Shelby, a bit drunk, her porcine features jiggling, was bearing down on them.

"Joe and I flew up for a few days of shopping and—" she stopped and stared at Jean-Claude, at his dark good looks, at his ill-fitting jacket, and the wine glass he was raising to his lips.

She returned her attention to Charlotte.

"Why, Charl, you rascal," she said. "You sweet ol' Venetian, you. Guessed it, didn't I?"

"What did she mean by that?" Jean-Claude demanded after Joe Shelby had appeared and dragged his wife off to another table. "What in the hell did that mean?"

"Nothing really. A private joke, something we had between us once."

"Then why do you look as though you've been struck? Tell me the truth."

"Please—"

"Start—now."

"It was years ago. Arthur and I, Shirley and Joe, we went to Italy, to Venice. At the hotel, on the beach, in Harry's Bar, we began to notice older women escorted by good-looking, attentive young men. At first we were naive, we thought it was beautiful that sons and nephews could be so devoted. Then we learned the women were from the States, rich widows and divorcées who had booked escorts for the summer, sometimes a year in advance. By prearrangement they met up with the escorts in Venice. They sent money ahead so that the young men could buy themselves expensive clothes and jewelry—or other young men. Those pathetic ladies. We thought it was so bizarre then. Anyone would have, don't you think?"

"Go on," he said coldly.

"It's not important."

"Go on."

"It—it was handled quite nicely. For an entire summer the young men would devote themselves to their patrons, always be by their sides, thoughtful, concerned, making dinner arrangements, picking up checks—in public anyway—accompanying them to concerts or to parties given by other ladies in the same situation, all of them pretending they were there because of mutual attraction.

"The young men were decent about their jobs, too. I never heard one joke or snicker. They were honest about their work and dedicated to it.

"I doubt that they ever slept with their ladies. That wasn't part of the job. At the end of the evening, the women would trot off to bed, and the young men —they would hurry out to the Piazza San Marco and rendezvous with other young men. That was the best part of it for them."

She looked into his glowering face and continued lamely. "Oh, it's not that uncommon. It's happening in America, too. They're called 'walkers.' In New York—people who live in apartments—they hire someone to walk their pets in the park. The name must have carried over. Now it means escorts. That's what they are really—men who keep women company, take them to parties. They're not paid, except for an occasional expensive gift." She glanced at his new jacket and faltered. "They—they have their own personal lives, together. They like being 'walkers' because they can go to glamorous places, meet successful people who may help them get ahead."

"I've heard enough," he said angrily. "You think I'm one of them, a hired leech, a lover of men?"

"Some of them like women, too."

His voice was low and furious. "You are a fool," he said. "Let's get out of here."

The following morning Jean-Claude was in front of the hotel, waiting grimly at the wheel of his Mercedes for the drive to Charles de Gaulle Airport. He stared straight ahead as two porters loaded Charlotte's luggage into the trunk of the car and the hotel doorman helped her into the rear seat.

This time he did not pull up to the side of the road so that she could join him in the front, and they did not speak.

At the airport, he helped her through customs and deposited her bags at the airline weigh-in counter.

When a uniformed official reminded him that for a few francs he could accompany the lady up the escalator to the passport desk near the departure gate, he declined.

Charlotte hurried through alone and never looked back.

Nearly a year. For her, a time of loneliness and longing. She had never dreamed she'd hear from him again. Or rather, she had dreamed it—but on waking had never believed it could come true. And now this cable. He loved her, he wanted her to come back. It was not a dream. It was real.

Did he mean it? Did he love her? Or had he sought and failed to find another rich woman?

She would never know for sure. But what difference did it make? If she never knew, that was all right, too.

She walked out of the office toward her cottage. She would pack and leave this place. She started to giggle and she felt very, very young.

She thought: What will we wear in St. Moritz?

XII

Elena wondered what they would do if she threw up, right there, over dinner in the Garden Room.

She had said nothing to anyone about the letter. When the maid had brought it to her cottage door, she had accepted it eagerly, recognizing the name of Barry's law firm embossed on the envelope. She had apologized to the maid for making the trip necessary, explaining she had lingered in the shower after her herbal wrap, and must have missed the mail call.

Clad in her bikini, she had taken the letter into the sunshine, sat yoga-fashion on the grass, and begun to read.

At first, she hadn't understood. Barry couldn't do this. Not Barry. Not after all this time, loving her the way he did.

She had reread the letter—several times in fact. Then she had folded it roughly and, hands shaking, had forced it back into the embossed envelope. She had sat on the lawn, mind deadened, until she heard her name on the loudspeaker summoning her to exercise class. She had come to her feet, walked the few steps back to her cottage, and shoved the letter to the rear of a desk drawer.

A robot, she had gone through all the exercises, even grimacing for the new instructor who stood before the group teaching them how to tighten their facial muscles. The grotesque, distorted faces reflected in the mirror wall had had an hilarious effect on the class. Elena had felt nothing.

She had avoided the letter for the rest of the day but, dressing for the cocktail hour, she had been drawn back to it.

She had pulled it from its hiding place in the desk and started to read it once more. There it still was, written in Barry's own hand:

Ellie dear,

By now you've had a few days to enjoy that great place. How I envy you there in the sun, living it up. You must be right back on your feet—or should I say on top of the world—and that makes it the best time to tell you what's on my mind.

Ellie, you haven't been too happy with our arrangement lately and, to tell you the truth, neither have I. So, let me say it for both of us. This is the time to break it up. If I didn't think it was the best time for you, believe me, I wouldn't raise the issue.

In a way, I feel a little guilty. You were a healthy, happy girl when we met, and Ellie, you weren't either of those things when you left the apartment. So here's your chance to become again what you once were.

On Friday, I'm leaving for Europe. Some client work in London and Rome. (Remember Branigan?) When you get back to the Marina, I'll be gone; for a month at least. Here's what I want you to do. Stay in the apartment. It's yours, rent-free, Barry-free, as long as I'm away. I'll drop you a note before I come home so you can move out in time. Until then, feel free to enjoy the place.

You'll be receiving a small memento from me, from Tiffany's. Whenever you wear it, think of me— fondly, I hope.

Ellie, I'm really sorry about this, for me as well as for you. We had a fun thing going for a while, didn't we? I'll always remember it.

Keep in touch. As ever,

Barry

Her features as she read had remained expressionless. She had allowed the letter to slip from her fingers to the floor and had not troubled to pick it up.

She had reached for a sweater and woodenly made her way to the Garden Room.

Charlotte's suitcases, zipped and strapped, rested on matching luggage racks. Her dark mink coat and handbag were thrown across the bed.

She had already informed Dr. Bertini, Loretta Marshall, and The Fountains' bookkeeper that she planned to depart for Chicago as soon as travel arrangements could be made. There was an important matter that required her personal attention, she had said, something she had neglected far too long.

No, she had assured them when they had looked at her anxiously, it was not a *problem*. It was, in truth, a happy affair. Tonight she wished to join her tablemates at the gala dinner in the Garden Room, and following that, she hoped to take the earliest possible flight from San Diego to Chicago.

Dr. Bertini had raised his eyebrows quizzically. Loretta Marshall, good breeding overcoming curiosity, had held back questions. Charlotte had pointedly ignored both of them. She had waited for the bookkeeper to compute the incidental charges she had accumulated in The Fountains' boutique—a few lipsticks, thong sandals, a scarf—and had briskly written her personal check. Then she had hurried back to her cottage to pack for her leave-taking.

There was, however, one piece of unfinished business. There was Janet Wolfe.

Now, packing accomplished, attired in travel dress, Charlotte stood erect at the foot of the bed, hands folded loosely before her, and faced the door.

When she heard the expected rap, she was composed. "Come in," she called. "I'm ready."

She did not stir when she saw Janet in the doorway. "You may leave your table and kit on the porch," she said. "You won't be needing them."

Janet tilted her table against the porch rail and set the kit beside it. Without speaking, she stepped into the room.

"Please close the door," Charlotte requested. "We're just going to talk today."

Janet did as she was told. Her face was impassive as she glanced at the fastened bags and the mink coat—the unmistakable accoutrements of departure.

Charlotte moved toward a chair. "I think you'll be more comfortable if you're seated."

Charlotte waited until Janet's large body was settled. Then she found a second chair and drew it around until she was face to face with the masseuse.

"About yesterday—" she began. "That was an —*unexpected* thing that happened. Embarrassing. You shouldn't have—I don't know how—"

A glimmer of amusement lit Janet's eyes.

"Unexpected," Charlotte repeated. "I'd had something to drink. Why did you—?" Her voice faltered. "I—I hope you'll forget it. I know I intend to."

Janet's eyes were unblinking. Without looking away, she pulled a cigarette and matches from her uniform pocket and lit up.

"Look," Charlotte began again. "I'm not really like that. You understand, don't you?"

The woman was silent.

"I—I'm not one of you. It was my first experience." Charlotte was growing nervous. Her voice rose. "All right," she said, "so I let it happen. I admit it."

She ran her fingers through her hair. "Goddammit, say *something!*"

Janet leaned forward and placed her chin in her hand. Gertrude Stein by Picasso. "You're the one who called the meeting," she said.

Charlotte let a long moment pass. "May I have a cigarette?" She waited until Janet found another cigarette in her pocket and allowed the masseuse to light it for her. She accepted the cigarette, then fell back in her chair.

"Please forgive me," Charlotte said. "I regret what happened here yesterday but it's unfair of me to play victim. I was no victim. I misled you and I accept my share of the responsibility. I was lonely and miserable. I let you see that. I guess—well, I guess I wanted to be—serviced." She laughed uneasily. "You sensed it, and you did what you were invited to do."

"And you got scared. You liked it, and got scared. You're running away."

"No, no. It's not like that. I have a friend, a man. There was a misunderstanding between us. It's fixed up now. I'm going to him."

Janet came to her feet heavily. "I wish you luck," she said.

Charlotte studied the masseuse's face. "You do believe me, don't you?"

Janet was at the door. "I believe you." She smiled wistfully. "I meant what I said when we were together. You're very, very beautiful. If you ever change your mind—"

And she was gone.

Dr. Bertini adored weekly Gala Night at The Fountains. It was his own creation—in truth, a recreation—reminiscent of the fabulous Captain's Dinners he had enjoyed as a first-class passenger on the S.S. *France*. In a way, the analogy was not too farfetched. Here at The Fountains, he was the captain. It did not seem inappropriate to celebrate regularly the completion of yet another successful crossing.

Dr. Bertini meticulously supervised every detail of Gala Night, scrutinizing the gleaming porcelain, examining the heavy silver, and holding each crystal goblet to the light before permitting it to be placed upon a table. He met with the florist who designed the centerpieces and he carefully coordinated the table linens and candles.

He also let word be passed that guests were welcome to wear their most glamorous clothes. Women who traveled with jewels were not discouraged from displaying them.

When Christina teased him, saying Gala Night was a carefully constructed homage to his own achievements, he denied it. He contended that women liked the fussing, and secretly wished to preen for each other.

Of course, Gala Night did not always proceed according to plan.

This evening, for example, as he had stood in his bedroom adjusting his jet cuff links, he had heard raised voices in the motor court. He had peeked through his drapes and seen Gillian Crain, propelled by a youngish, dark-haired man, step into a Jaguar sports car. Although he could not hear their words, he had had time enough to see the anger in their faces.

Once they had driven away, Dr. Bertini had sped to his desk, unlocked a deep drawer, and withdrawn one of his private folders. After leafing through the folder, he had come upon the item he sought, a clipping from the *Los Angeles Times* portraying Gillian Crain, victorious at the net, at the conclusion of a tennis tournament. He looked closely at the figure beside her. Not unexpectedly, he saw that it was Jason Crain, the husband, the same furious man he had just observed take the wheel of the Jaguar.

Dr. Bertini sighed. Usually, he groused to Loretta Marshall when a guest left the grounds on Gala Night. On this occasion, he saw no point in opening up the subject with Loretta. He was mindful of Mrs. Crain's previous nocturnal absences and he had received a fully dramatized account from Leslie, the switchboard operator, of Mr. Crain's telephone calls to his wife and to Drucilla Jennings. Dr. Bertini had no doubt that Gillian and Jason Crain were headed for a showdown. Predictably, they would seek out one of the finer restaurants in San Diego. They would down a couple of drinks and order well, but he did not think they would eat very much. They would most certainly continue their quarrel. If tempers got out of control, they would create a disagreeable scene.

He was thankful it would not take place on his turf.

Gillian yanked the screeching seatbelt across her lap and fastened it into silence. Then she turned to observe Jason.

Unfailingly, it surprised her that even under stress Jason retained the immaculate good looks of a male fashion model. Despite the long drive from Beverly Hills, his fawn-colored trousers were spotless and unwrinkled. His single-button maroon jacket was fastened, and beneath the jacket, his open-necked white sports shirt was still crisp. Only the hardened chords of his throat revealed the intensity of his fury.

Had he bedded down with anyone during the afternoon while he waited for Bitsy to finish her school day? Conceivably. She knew Jason was as serious about his fornicating as he was about his tennis. Neglect of either sport could spoil a man's game. Jason was not likely to be guilty of such neglect.

After their move to California, she recalled, Jason's dalliances had tormented her. Over the years she had passed from torment to mere resentment. In time, she had settled into indifference. In the beginning, they had quarreled bitterly and inconclusively whenever she learned of a new affair. Yet hours later, while she still brooded, he would stand before her smiling, the ugly scene behind him. If she dared reopen the unresolved subject, he would react with irritation, accusing her of belaboring the past, although the past might have been as recent as yesterday. For her, confrontation had been a loser's game and, long ago, she had stopped playing it.

Now, in the car, waiting for Jason to speak, she felt a rush of triumph. This reversal of their roles was exhilarating. She evoked Dr. Karl and their motel rendezvous the night before. The warming images, and his remembered words, made her feel secure, like an urchin with a penny in her pocket.

When Jason spoke, his rage rendered him nearly inarticulate, and she was delighted.

"Gillian—" he began. "What the hell—?"

"Where are we going?"

"I'll find something. I know the area."

"I bet you do."

"What does that mean?"

"Nothing," she said. "You must be tired from the trip. You needn't have bothered, you know."

"You'd have liked that, wouldn't you? Well, I'm here. And this may be the most important talk of our lives."

"Jason, you're being theatrical. Don't worry about Bitsy and the abortion. She'll survive. Thousands of kids have."

"Bitsy!" he exploded. "To hell with Bitsy!"

She threw back her head and laughed. "The loving father. All those noble noises. 'Bitsy's got to know she has *one* parent who cares,'" she mimicked.

"I *do* care, and we'll come to that. But first you and I have got to get a couple of things straight."

She pointed to his crotch. "Is that one of them, Jason? Have you been getting that straight? For anyone I know?"

"Damn you, Gillian! So I have played around a bit. It never meant anything. Maybe you have, too."

"Maybe I have."

His eyes left the road and held for an instant on her mocking face. "You telling me something?"

"Could be."

He swerved the Jaguar toward the dirt shoulder of the highway. "Gillian, we're going to have it out, right now."

"Not here. Get off the highway," she ordered. "Let's find one of your little trysting places—someplace where we can have a drink and talk like adults."

"I don't want a drink."

"You may need one."

He gunned the engine and shot the car toward

an off ramp. His slender body was tense, his jaw set.

After driving in silence for several minutes, he swung toward her furiously. "How many men?"

"Later."

"I want to know. This minute."

She smiled, ready to oblige. "Only one man. A beautiful human being."

"Since when?"

"Oh, six or eight months, maybe."

"Who is it?" he demanded.

"Jason, be careful. You almost hit that car."

"Who is it?" he repeated, fiercely.

She shrugged. "You asked for it. It's Dr. Karl. Dr. Karl Lorenz."

Now it was his turn to laugh. "You can't be serious."

"I'm serious."

"That gnome! That repulsive, old gnome?"

"How dare you! Dr. Karl is the most exciting man I've ever been with! He makes me come alive!"

"You've been sleeping with him—with *him?*"

"Why not! He's ten times, a thousand times the man you ever were!"

Jason's knuckles whitened on the wheel. Involuntarily, his foot drove into the accelerator.

"You're making it up," he shouted.

"Oh no, I'm not."

"Then you're having a revenge fuck, to get even with me!"

"You fool, you fatheaded, conceited fool! You can't believe it because it's Dr. Karl. If it was getting even I wanted, I could have done that years ago. There are men everywhere. It's easy. I don't want *men.* I want a man, a real man. I want him—and I have him. In his office—last night and the night before, in a motel.

What's more, I intend to have him—again and again and again!"

"Gillian—" Jason's hand left the wheel. "Gillian—" He twisted violently in his seat and his fingers clawed for her throat. "I've heard all I want to! I'm not going to let my wife . . ."

A brightly lit gas station, painted in cheerful blues and yellows, loomed before them.

The white-uniformed attendant, panic distorting his face, jumped back as the car spun out of control.

The attendant's broad mouth, hanging slack in horror, was the last thing Jason and Gillian saw as the Jaguar exploded headlong into the forward pump and, still hissing, ground to a standstill like a smashed accordion.

Dr. Bertini observed the vacant seats at the table near the window and frowned. Two empty places and the waitresses had set the table for five. The irregularity of the arrangement was, in part, his fault. He had not informed anyone that Gillian Crain had gone off with her husband and probably would not return to join the gala party. However, he was not responsible for what had happened to the timid Chicana. Elena Valdez—looking quite lovely in a simple cotton blouse and skirt—had taken her seat with the others, but after a few whispered words to Rita Sloane, had agitatedly pushed aside her caviar and departed in a rush.

The general disorder at the window table, as well as the break in symmetry, unnerved Dr. Bertini. Charlotte Caldwell, dressed for travel, was a jarring figure among the prettily gowned women. Rita Sloane appeared deeply troubled and continued to watch the door through which Elena had exited. Drucilla Jennings, face tragic, toyed with the floral centerpiece and made meaningless designs of rose petals as they dropped to the cloth.

The window table was a mess.

Dr. Bertini looked about for reassurance. At his own host table on the dais, members of his staff—females all—selected on a rotating basis for the weekly honor, were garbed appropriately for the occasion. Their dresses were subtle, their grooming perfection and—bless them—he knew they could be relied upon to deport themselves like ladies.

At the other tables, he was gratified to see that most of his guests were decently gowned and chatting happily as they crunched their toast triangles topped with caviar and sipped their champagne from the Baccarat goblets. As usual, there were several exceptions to Dr. Bertini's notion of good taste. But then, he knew, he could not advise his guests how to dress and garnish themselves unless they sought his opinion.

Now he wished some of them had.

Christina Rossi's melon-colored jersey shift was suspended from narrow braided straps and dipped dangerously to a point barely above her nipples. Christina had a habit with which Dr. Bertini was familiar. When amused, she pressed forward, using her hand to suppress her mirth. It was apparent that Helen Reiser, seated opposite Christina, was in particularly fine form tonight for Christina was having an uproarious time. Her hilarity was reflected in the swooshing of her splendid breasts and was accented by the frequent emergence of the dark nipples which she casually recovered for comfort rather than decency.

Dr. Bertini deplored Christina's unabashed exposure of flesh. In his opinion, Christina's endowments were so widely known that it was somehow unseemly for her to display her wares like some newcomer in the marketplace. He was tempted to lecture her once more before she departed from The Fountains, but he rejected the idea, recalling an earlier exchange on the subject.

"Christina," he had begun. "You are a legend. It behooves you to conform just a little—"

She had stopped him. "We are both professionals. We are like shoemakers working at different lasts. You do not need my help, and I do not need yours."

"But you are a woman alone."

"I shall manage without your protection."

Her unfettered breasts had swung before his eyes as she spoke. He had agreed then that he would never again interfere and had sat back to enjoy the fleshy spectacle.

Guiltily, he did so now.

When he felt he had stared long enough, he forced his gaze to travel to Helen Reiser. Mentally, he apologized to Christina. In contrast to Christina's naked landscape, Helen's body was totally concealed within a hibiscus-splashed orange muumuu, incredibly overprinted with fern-shaped purple leaves. The coarse face, the blasting voice, the upswept hairdo that resembled the crown of a pineapple, made him shudder.

For visual relief, his gaze moved on to the adjoining table. With satisfaction, he studied Jessica Haskell. Flame-colored chiffon flattered her sallow skin. Emeralds at her ears and throat attested to her good judgment in the employment of her wealth. The total picture she presented was a tribute to The Fountains and to himself. Admittedly, the looseness of her gestures revealed Jessica had nipped a few from her private stock before coming to the Garden Room, and the realization displeased him. Jessica knew he disap-

proved of alcoholic indulgence beyond its occasional
social use. Nonetheless, even drunk, Jessica had style.

Flanking Jessica, the Lyman twins were still a
pair of matched marvels. With a second successful
Fountains week behind them, in which, again, one had
gained weight and the other had lost, they remained
lean-faced and bony shouldered, displaying concave
chests and stringy arms that terminated in fingers like
bleached fossils. The Lyman twins, Dr. Bertini recalled, were well-to-do Southerners who, as young
women, had gone north to Bennington to study the art
of the dance. In New England they had met and
married brothers from Harvard, men who, according
to Dr. Bertini's file, were presently partnered in an
influential Boston law firm. Contemplating them now,
Dr. Bertini found it extraordinary that anyone, anywhere, could have found these two appealing enough
to wed and presumably bed. But then, Dr. Bertini conceded, he had never had the privilege of meeting the
husbands.

As the waitresses removed the caviar and service plates and replaced them with platters of Chateaubriand and baked zucchini, Dr. Bertini's eyes
continued to rove the room. Little Debbie Colson, the
perennial undergraduate, appeared no slimmer than
she had earlier in the week. Yet according to Mrs.
Kaplan, with whom he regularly consulted, the child
would certainly register a five-pound loss at her
weigh-in tomorrow.

The pleasant humming in the room, induced by
the flow of the Dom Perignon, was agreeable to Dr.
Bertini's ears. Earlier, he had rationalized the lavish
Gala Night dinner for his guests.

"Dieting," he had told them, "should not be an
orgy of deprivation. Occasionally all of us must let
ourselves go—but not too far—in food and drink as

well as other areas of pleasure. Our appreciation is keener if we indulge our hedonistic side from time to time. It is Nature's dictate."

It was, he reflected, also good business. Tomorrow there would be a tapering off of activities and a few of the ladies would leave. By the following day, anyone not remaining for an additional week, would be gone as well, making way for a new Batch. For each of those present, this dinner must be made unforgettable, an event slightly indulgent and especially gay.

Dr. Bertini raised his goblet to the four staff members seated at his dais table. "We've brought it off again," his glance told them. And each of the staff women lifted her glass in silent acceptance of his unspoken praise.

Dr. Bertini took several more appreciative sips of his champagne and was about to approach his Chateaubriand when his attention was caught by a stirring near the window. He saw Rita Sloane slap down her napkin, speak a few words to her remaining companions, Charlotte and Dru, and shove her chair away from the table. From his place on the dais, it appeared to him that all three women were suddenly talking at once. Whatever was happening eluded him.

With a surge of annoyance, he saw Rita Sloane jump to her feet. His eyes tracked her as she rushed across the floor, and out the door of the Garden Room.

At the window table, Dru had been abruptly roused from her own misery.

"Elena worries me," she said.

"She worries me, too."

"Maybe we can help." Dru started to rise.

"No," Charlotte held her back. "Those two have a special rapport. Rita can handle Elena without us."

She tipped her head toward the dais. "Our bearded friend up there, he's watching our table. He'll have a tantrum if we all leave."

"I really don't care."

"I don't care either. But I do want to talk to you."

"If it's about Tim, forget it. There's nothing more to say. I've made up my mind."

"Oh?"

"I was awake all night. I thought it through. Tim phoned again. He wants us to go away—together—the way we used to."

"What did you say?"

"Nothing definite. Tomorrow when he gets here, I'll tell him I want a divorce, and I'll tell him why."

"And that's your decision?" Charlotte looked about at the other tables. Assured they could not be overheard, she turned back to Dru.

"Yes," Dru was saying, "that's it. Final, irrevocable. Anything else would be impossible. I could never, ever—"

"Come now, Dru, you don't mean what you're saying."

"There's nothing else I can do."

"Isn't there? You could go on with him. Had you considered that?"

"Continue this—this marriage? With a *homosexual?*"

"You keep using that word." Charlotte was impatient. "By any definition, Tim is not completely homosexual. He fell in love with you, didn't he? He married you, didn't he? From everything you've told me, he still loves you."

"But—"

"Hear me out, Dru. I'll be blunt. If Helen is telling the truth, it's obvious Tim isn't completely heterosexual, either. But put to the test, with all defenses down, many people are not all one thing or the other—more than you might suspect. I told you about myself."

"You said it was a single experience."

"It happened, didn't it?"

"Could it happen again?"

"I doubt it. Still, I'm not that sure of things anymore."

"And the man in France—will you tell him?"

"No, I won't. Because it has nothing to do with him and me. If he learned about it, well, I'd hope he could understand that only part of me was involved." She smiled. "No double entendre intended. I mean only a part of my emotional makeup—a spur road, going nowhere."

"Whatever it was that happened with you, it's different with Tim."

"Probably. But last night after you went to your cottage, I stayed on in the television room. I remembered that Dr. Bertini keeps a ragtag library there, a weird assortment of books, mostly left behind by previous guests. But he has others, too—his own collection, with his personal bookplates pasted in. There are books about sex, and loving, and relating. Dr. Bertini is not a foolish man. He put them there for people like us—women who don't turn their minds off when they come to The Fountains, women who know there's more to life than weight and measurements."

"What are you getting at?"

"Remember the word I used yesterday? Bisexuality? I looked it up in the books last night. Don't wince. It's not some vile disease. It's a fact of life, not necessarily an abnormal one. Attitudes depend on where we stand in history. The ancient Greeks accepted dual sexuality—Socrates and Demosthenes are examples. In Napoleon's time, Mme. de Staël, who was a devoted mother, and Mme. Récamier, a great beauty who also was married, were widely admired despite their love affair. On the other hand, two husbands, Oscar Wilde and Paul Verlaine were vilified when they took male lovers. Today, there are new flickers of understanding. And tolerance, if you will. Even in a growing number of churches."

"But it's not natural."

"Natural? Who are the authorities? Freud himself firmly believed in 'the natural bisexuality not only of all human beings but of all living creatures.' In fact, he once wrote, 'I am getting used to regarding every sexual act as one between four individuals.' And Jung. He believed that *everyone* is essentially bisexual."

"Most of our society won't buy that," Charlotte went on. "Worse, they reject the possibility that such things exist. Their minds are caves—they feel safe in their dark beliefs—they refuse to admit any light.

"Consider Senator Ring's wife. She divorced her husband. Is she happier because of her decision? Are her children better off? Could be. But maybe not. Some day Nancy Ring will meet someone else and remarry— a totally heterosexual man this time. When all the returns are in, will she have done the right thing? Possibly, for her. Along the way, her new husband may have affairs with other women. By then she may be resigned to his occasional lapses and even indulge in a few of her own. When she thinks of what he's doing, she will console herself, saying—at least he's with a *woman.*

"Yet, it's a curious fact—attested to by patients to their doctors—that some women are relieved to discover their unfaithful mates are sleeping with partners of the same sex. What it means to the wives is that as women they have not failed their husbands. To a husband who learns his wife is bisexual, it means that while he may satisfy that aspect of her nature that requires a man, her desire for a woman is something he was never intended to fulfill. Therefore he cannot suffer a sense of failure or emasculation.

"Husbands, wives, even parents have learned to turn their thinking around out of love for someone close. Once upon a time, a wayward daughter and her illegitimate baby were banished into the snow. Can you imagine writing *East Lynne* today?"

"It's not the same thing," Dru said.

"No, it isn't. But the lack of understanding, the rigid prejudice—that's the same. And the selfishness, that's the same, too."

"You're accusing *me* of selfishness?"

"Yes, I am. So far, you've considered only what the situation means to you. What about Tim? Doesn't he count?"

"Of course he counts," Dru protested. "I love him."

"You said he was unhappy."

"Yes, he is. But if I shut my eyes, try to go on— can I take the risk?"

Charlotte sat bemused. "Risk," she said finally. "Isn't it always a risk? Years ago, when Arthur and I were married, we'd have laughed at the suggestion of risk. We were sure things, blue-chip investments. Same age, same church. Similar backgrounds—culturally, socially, financially. And we were in love. Risk? If there was one thing we were certain of, it was that there was no risk."

"You told me yourself, you were very young."

"And now I'm older. And about to marry again. Only this time I have full knowledge of the risk. In all of my excitement I didn't tell you very much about Jean-Claude. He was my chauffeur in France. You're surprised? I hired him to drive me around Paris. That's how we met. There I was, a lonely, rejected, middle-aged woman. Vulnerable, available—and rich. And Jean-Claude? Ten years younger than I am, handsome, never married. Today he's still a chauffeur. He owns his own car, but beyond that his life's savings couldn't pay for a week at The Fountains. Risk? Tomorrow in Chicago I'll meet with my lawyer. I'll tell him I'm going to be married. He'll ask for details and I'll tell him everything. He'll study the prospectus—it won't take him more than a minute—and he'll be horrified. He'll point out the risk. 'Risk?' I'll say. 'Show me a marriage without risk. Tell me why I should play it safe.' No, I won't go that route again. I'll take my chances. I'll take the risk." Charlotte folded her napkin. "When is Tim coming in?"

"His plane arrives in San Diego at eleven. He's renting a car at the terminal. I guess he'll get here about noon."

"I'm sorry I won't be around to meet him." Charlotte looked up. "Manuel's waving from the doorway. Must be time to leave for the airport. Dr. Bertini will have to forgive me. Say good-bye to the others. Tell them I'll write."

She kissed Dru on the cheek. "Give him a chance. Give yourself a chance."

"A toast to Dr. Bertini!" Jessica Haskell, weaving slightly, stood before her seat, champagne goblet held aloft. "We thank you for making us beautiful." She looked about and her gaze held on Helen Reiser. She snickered drunkenly. "Or at least for trying."

"Jessica, that was lovely." Dr. Bertini acknowledged the toast.

"I'd like to say something, too." Fat Debbie Colson was on her feet, glass in hand. "It's only ginger ale," she confessed bashfully. "California law says kids can't have anything stronger. But I want to express my appreciation to Dr. Bertini, and to his super staff." Her face reddened. "And to all the marvelous guests. You've been like a family to me. I want everyone to know The Fountains is the best home I've ever had—and that's all I want to say."

"Debbie, I am deeply moved," Dr. Bertini responded. "I know everyone else is . . . Debbie! Debbie!" His voice rose in distress. "Don't cry! Please, child, don't cry *here!*"

"Alfredo." Christina wriggled her shapely body out of her chair. "Let the little one weep. You see how we are all in your debt? From the youngest"—she paused meaningfully—"to the oldest, whoever *she* is. As I am the one who has known you longest and perhaps best, I wish to . . ."

"*Bella mia,* be seated." Dr. Bertini was jovial again. "It is my turn to offer the toast: to each of my ravishing guests, to your continuing good health and happiness, and to the fortunate men who await you."

A sudden burst at the door stopped him. Turning, he was dismayed to see Rita Sloane, out of breath and distraught, rushing toward the dais.

"Dr. Bertini," she was gasping. "*Someone,* please help. It's Elena! Something terrible has happened! Please come, *please!*"

It was two hours later when the town doctor summoned by Dr. Bertini clicked shut the lock on his medical bag and faced Rita Sloane.

"Good thing you kept the others out of here," he said approvingly. "Alfredo has had experience dealing with these things, but the rest—they just soak up oxygen the patient needs."

Chester Richlin, M.D., was a drab, lanky Midwesterner whose blue-tinged skin suggested he had been deprived of oxygen himself. He had appeared in Elena's cottage, tieless and rumpled, after what had seemed an age of waiting. With Dr. Bertini and Rita standing by, he had swiftly checked Elena's blood pressure and pulse, listened to her heart and lungs, and tested her reflexes. Then, seated on Elena's bed, he had looked up at Dr. Bertini.

"She's going to make it," he had said. "Fortunately she didn't swallow all the pills in the bottle. I suppose she hadn't made up her mind for sure she wanted to die."

Dr. Bertini had smiled crookedly. "The Fountains always pulls them through."

"What did you do for her?" Dr. Richlin had wanted to know.

"The usual." Dr. Bertini had looked despondent. "What you instructed me to do the first time something like this happened, eight, nine years ago. She was groaning, stuporous, when I got here. I slapped her face hard. I forced her to drink water until we could get hot, black coffee for her. I put spirits of ammonia under her nose. I gave her syrup of ipecac to induce vomiting and I stuck my finger down her throat to help it along. And Miss Sloane and I, we kept her walking and talking, walking and talking—"

"You did as much as I could have done."

Dr. Bertini's shoulders had sagged. "Chester, I cannot accept it. I do everything in my power to teach them to revere their bodies and still, with no hint, every now and then one of them tries to destroy herself. In The Fountains, in this life-loving place." He had shaken his head in bewilderment. "I don't understand."

"Alfredo, we go through this every time. You mustn't feel it's your failure. You know you're not responsible for the problems they bring with them."

Dr. Bertini had looked appealingly at Rita. "You heard Dr. Richlin? It is what I told you the first night we talked. They come from everywhere, with secrets

I cannot guess. Some young, some successful, some wealthy, some all three. Their bodies are relatively healthy. We examine them to be certain. But what goes on in their heads and in their hearts, ah, that we can never know."

"This one," he had continued, indicating Elena on the bed, "this one was so sad when she came. But soon she began to be happier. And yesterday, after the mail—yes, Rita, I heard about the bracelet from Tiffany's—yesterday she was cheerful as a bird. Who could expect this?" He shook his head mournfully.

"She's going to recover," said Dr. Richlin. "She'll sleep much of the night, off and on, in a natural way."

"You're sure?"

"Stop worrying. But I'd like someone to stay with her."

"That's me," Rita had said.

"Fine," Dr. Richlin had replied. "Alfredo, you need some rest. Why don't you go to bed? I'll leave instructions with Miss Sloane here."

With Dr. Bertini standing by, Dr. Richlin had jotted down a few notes and handed them to Rita. Satisfied his patient was in capable hands, he had taken Dr. Bertini by the elbow and together the two men had left the cottage.

Now Rita sat on Elena's bed and patted the sleeping girl's hair.

"Poor, dumb baby," she murmured.

Reaching into the pocket of the long dinner skirt she still wore, Rita pulled out Barry's letter and reread it. Bastard, she thought, dirty, rotten bastard. Thank God, I found this filthy thing before anyone else did. Those savages out there, they'd have jumped on the jungle drums to spread the news.

She thought about the letter.

When Elena was fully conscious the two of them would cook up a logical story, something that would head off questions and forestall humiliating answers—something acceptable like a death in the family or a crisis at the office. Whatever. They would say Elena had been upset and had wanted to sleep on her problem. She, Rita, had come upon the groggy girl and misread the scene. With her writer's impulse, she had created a drama where none had existed.

She would apologize to one and all for disrupting the gala in the Garden Room.

A movement under the blanket warned her Elena was returning to wakefulness. Rita shoved Barry's letter into her skirt pocket.

"Hi, honey," she said. "Feeling better?"

"Mmmm—"

"Don't try to sit up yet. There's coffee on the hot plate. Dr. Richlin wants me to get more of it into you."

Elena's voice was thick. "Dr. Rich—who's he?"

"I'll explain in a minute. Coffee's coming up. Black, no sugar, no cream. Doctor's orders."

"Who's Dr. Rich—?"

"Chester Richlin. He's The Fountains' unofficial rescue squad. He comes around when someone pulls a dopey stunt like you did."

"The pills, the sleeping pills—Rita, what happened?"

Rita stood over the hot plate, coffee pot in hand. "You tell me. I was worried when you left the dinner table. Time was passing and you didn't come back. I came looking for you. I found you on the floor near that old desk. First I thought you had fainted. Then I saw the prescription bottle. I couldn't believe it. I figured you were smarter than that. I went for Dr. Bertini and he located Dr. Richlin and we marched you around and—what's the dif? You don't need the details. What matters is that you're okay."

Elena's black eyes widened. "The letter, did you find the letter?"

"Sure."

"Did—did you read it?"

"Of course I did. I'm a reporter. I read everyone's letters."

"Then you know why—"

"The hell I do. Some rat decides he got himself into the wrong nest and wants out. And *you,* a sweet, sensitive doll like you, *you* decide you can't live without him. It's crazy."

"Rita, please, you're so cold about it. You don't understand."

"Don't I? Do you think I, or any of those broads out there, made it past twenty-one without some jerk splitting just when we thought we'd found true love? Don't you know there are jokers in the deck for everyone? But suicide. That's not for anyone, ever, and it's doubly not for you—especially not over an asshole like your pen pal here."

She removed the letter from her pocket. "Mind if I tear it up?"

Elena shut her eyes. "Go ahead," she said. She listened as Rita ripped the letter into smaller and smaller pieces, and she lay perfectly still as Rita moved to the bathroom and flushed the scraps of paper down the toilet.

She was crying quietly when Rita returned.

"Now what's going on?" Rita demanded. Her voice softened. "Elena, Elena dear, I'm truly sorry. Dr. Richlin told me to be supportive. Instead I'm scolding you. Forgive me."

Rita poured black coffee into a cup and handed it to Elena.

"Drink it," she said. "It's good for you." She poured a second cup for herself and sat down on the bed. "So, where do you go from here? I've been thinking while you were asleep. *Caress* won't mind if I hang around for another week or so. I'll tell them I need more material for my story, that I want to be close to The Fountains. I'll help you move. Where will you go?"

"Barry said I could stay in the apartment for a month. I'll start looking for another one—"

"A month. I won't let you stay there overnight. You're cutting out immediately. The question is—where to?"

"I don't know."

"Parents?"

Elena smiled weakly. "Impossible. Papa predicted this. He said Barry would throw me out. And Mama, if she ever heard about the sleeping pills, she'd have to tell the priest. It would break her heart."

"Other relatives?"

Elena wrinkled her nose. "Two sisters. Remind me to tell you about them sometime. The answer is No."

"What about friends?"

"A few, but they've got their own troubles. I can't burden them with mine."

"You telling me there's no one, absolutely no one, you can turn to?"

Elena looked away. "There is one man, an important man. He lives in Bel-Air."

"Who is he?"

"Gordon Prescott."

"The director? He's *your* friend?"

"In a way. He's more like an uncle."

"An uncle? How did someone like Gordon Prescott get on your family tree?"

"I met him through the office, Lincoln and

Rudolph, the publicity firm I work for. They sent me to his house to deliver some press releases. He became interested in me."

Rita snorted.

"It's true. In *me*. It moved him somehow, this funny barrio kid falling in love with his art collection and antiques and everything." She placed her coffee cup on the bedside table. "I'm so sleepy. Can't we talk tomorrow?"

"Sure, sure. But tell me a little more about Gordon Prescott."

"He called me a discovery. He said I was 'educable'—that's his word." She yawned.

"And he never laid a hand on you?" Rita was still skeptical.

"Never. He said he was happy to find someone who felt the way he did about the arts. He said—his own friends—had no honest passion—" Her voice was growing blurry. "He gave me books and sent me to lectures and museums and to concerts." She smiled ruefully. "Gordon mustn't find out about this. He'd be so disappointed. All his time and trouble—almost down the drain." She yawned again. "Sorry," she mumbled. As Rita watched, Elena's eyelids dropped and her mouth relaxed. In seconds she was asleep.

Rita bent over the quiet form. She was relieved to hear the breathing coming evenly.

"Poor baby, I hate to do this. But you'll thank me for it later."

Moving swiftly, Rita opened and closed the few drawers in the room. It did not surprise her that most were empty. She recalled that Elena had apologized for her sparse wardrobe, explaining she had followed the advice in the brochure, and all the belongings she had brought to The Fountains had fitted into a single wicker suitcase.

Rita opened the closet door. Inside, on the floor, she found the wicker suitcase and raised the lid. Nothing. She surveyed the clothes on the hangers—a few blouses, a skirt, pants. She fumbled through the pockets. Zero.

Frustrated, she was about to shut the closet door when she spotted a woven straw handbag.

Glancing toward the bed, she confirmed that Elena was still sleeping soundly. She pounced upon the handbag and thrust her hand inside. The address book was there.

She checked her wristwatch. Nearly one A.M. She hoped Gordon Prescott was as understanding as Elena had said he was.

Tiptoeing back to the bed and muttering a prayer, she pulled the telephone to her and asked the operator to get the number in Bel-Air.

"Hullo?"

"Mr. Prescott?" she whispered. "My name is Rita Sloane. I'm a reporter for *Caress* magazine."

"Are you mad?" the hoarse voice barked. "Do you know what time it is?"

"Yes, I do, but—"

"Call my secretary in the morning. Better yet, don't call at all."

"Mr. Prescott, please, please, don't hang up. I'm a friend of Elena's—Elena Valdez. She's in trouble."

"What do you mean? Where are you?"

In quick, short sentences, Rita told him about Elena.

"Dear God," he said, almost to himself. "I didn't teach her a damn thing." He raised his voice. "Say, you —what's your name again?"

"Sloane. Rita Sloane."

"Listen to me, Miss Sloane. I want Elena taken care of. I want her to stay with me at my house."

"Wait a minute, Mr. Prescott. Elena's not going to be in such great shape. She's going to need someone supportive—"

"Damn it, woman," he broke in. "Do you think I haven't figured that out? Do you think I'd do anything to hurt her?"

"No, but—"

"Look here. This is a big house. You can stay, too. It may take both of us to give her the help she needs. When can you get her out of there?"

"The doctor says she needs another day to rest."

"That's it then. Day after tomorrow. What time?"

"I don't know. We'll have to find out about the plane."

"Call me from the airport. I'll be waiting."

Gillian Crain returned to consciousness reluctantly.

The sickly green hospital walls, the blurred, dark-clad figures shifting in and out of focus at the foot of her bed, were ominous portents of things to come, unsafe harbors after the directionless cruising of her clouded mind.

"Gillian, can you hear me?" Her mother's voice was strained. Gillian struggled to bring the anxious face into sharper relief. Then, fearful, she painfully turned away her head.

"Gillian—it's Margo," her mother was saying. "Lawrence and I—we came as soon as we heard."

"How do you feel, dear?" her father asked.

She refused to look at them. "Heard—what?"

"About the accident, about you." The voice faltered. "And about Jason."

Gillian's head felt heavy. She supposed it was bandaged. She forced herself to look toward the foot of the bed.

Her mother was wearing black. A triple strand of pearls circled her throat. *You must always keep a black dress in your closet,* her mother had taught her. *You never know when you'll need one—and there isn't always time—*

But it was the pearls that were most frightening. She recalled them from her childhood. They meant something terribly serious was going on. Serious and unpleasant.

"Jason. Where is Jason?"

"Not now, dear."

"I want to know about Jason."

It spilled over her now—the bitterness of their quarrel, the taunting admission of her affair, Jason's maniacal rage, the car going out of control. And—oblivion.

"Tell me—where is Jason!"

Her mother was blocking out the window, lifting her into warm arms, cradling her, rocking her.

"Jason is dead, dear."

Gillian closed her eyes.

"Darling, we're so sorry." Her mother was beginning to weep.

"Gillian, do you understand?" Her father was beside her, holding her hand.

"I understand."

"It was over in an instant. Cars, you never know what will happen next." His voice trailed off helplessly.

"It's a blessing you weren't killed, too." Her mother this time. "The doctor says it's a miracle you're alive."

"Where am I?"

"In the Palomar Memorial Hospital. Near San Diego."

"Where is Jason?"

Her father stroked her wrist. "We don't have to talk about that now."

"I want to know. *Where is Jason?*"

"Later, dear."

"Now, please."

"He's in a—a mortuary. Near the hospital. Everything's been taken care of. Services will be held in Beverly Hills. We thought it best not to burden you. His parents are coming tomorrow. They were too upset to leave earlier."

"I want them to stay at the house."

"We reserved a bungalow for them, at the Beverly Hills Hotel. We felt—with Margo and me—it would be too much."

"No, you shouldn't have done that! He was their son, Bitsy's father! They have a right to stay in their son's home if they want to!"

"Shhh, dear," her mother soothed. "Of course, we'll do as you say. We'll arrange it."

"Jason, Jason," she moaned. "What happened—whatever happened?"

"It was an accident, Gillian. It was no one's fault."

"An accident—" She pulled herself free and covered her face with her hands. "An accident," she repeated. "That's it—an accident."

She began to tremble and her sobs, when they came, were so fierce and abandoned her parents fled into the hospital corridor to find someone to help.

When Timothy Larsen entered The Fountains at midday, it looked empty, deserted. He hoped there was one guest left. His long strides carried him quickly across the Reception Hall to the desk on the right.

"Hello," he said to the young blond woman who

appeared after he had pressed the call bell. "I've come
for Drucilla Jennings. Will you tell her her husband is
here?"

"Certainly, Mr. Jennings."

"I'm Mr.—"

The young woman waited.

"Oh, never mind. Just tell her I'm at the desk."

"Sure thing, Mr. Jennings. Care to sit down?"

"No, thanks. Which way will she be coming?"

The blonde pointed beyond the patio. "That's
her cottage over there. 'Scuse me, the switchboard's in
the other room. I'll call her."

As the blonde doubled back and disappeared behind the paneled door, Tim walked to the window-wall
and stared out.

The long-postponed, long-dreaded moment was
here.

The past months had drawn him into hell. No,
not all of it had been hell, he conceded grimly. There
had been joy, too. The gradual reawakening of the old
attraction between him and Jonny Ring, the increasingly frequent dinner dates—just the two of them—in
dim, intimate restaurants, the accidental touching, the
searching looks, the embarrassed lapses in conversation.

And then, their first night together. It seemed a
hundred years ago.

He and Jonny had agreed to meet at the end
of the day in a bar near the White House. They had
stayed too long, drinking quietly, and had almost
missed their reservation at the Sans Souci in Georgetown. Over dinner they had continued to drink—wine,
this time—and they had talked sporadically. When the
waiter had been dispatched for the check, Jonny had
casually asked Tim to accompany him to the apartment
to review a resolution he was preparing to submit to
the Senate. Despite his alcoholic state, Tim had recog-

nized the invitation for what it was—the classic come-and-see-my-etchings overture. He had known, and Jonny had known, where it would lead.

That first erotic encounter in Jonny's apartment had been an exquisite experience. Even now, as he stood watching for his wife, he could not deny that. Jonny and he had come together as eagerly as they had in their prep school days—but more expertly because they were older and practiced and had learned so much of the art of loving from their wives.

Tim removed a cigarette from his pocket. As he lit it, he remembered . . .

After their lovemaking, he had fallen into a deep and dreamless sleep. The following morning he had awakened in the bed alone. He had hurried to the bathroom and showered and dressed. Troubled, repentant, he had stepped into Jonny's living room. To his surprise, Jonny had been calm and relaxed. Wearing pajamas and dressing gown, Jonny had looked up from his coffee and morning newspaper and greeted him with a smile.

"Hungry?' Jonny had asked pleasantly. "Won't take me a minute to rustle you up some eggs."

"Thanks, I don't want anything."

"Coffee?"

"Okay, coffee."

"C'mon, Tim, sit down. I see the way it is. I'll fetch you a cup and we can talk. Back in a jiffy."

While Jonny was gone from the room, Tim had tried to do what he had been attempting to do ever since he had awakened in Jonny's bed and looked about the handsome, masculine room. He had tried to comprehend what had happened.

Under the shower, with icy water from multiple spouts hitting his body, he had blamed it on the booze. His adolescent involvement with Jonny was ancient his-

tory. Throughout college and during the many years of
their adult friendship, neither of them had referred to
their early homosexual affair.

Tim had expected, when he entered the living
room that morning, that Jonny would make a couple of
embarrassed jokes and that he, Tim, would counter
with a few of his own. Then, he had expected, Jonny
would pour each of them a stiff pick-me-up—it *had*
been quite a night, they would agree—and after that he,
Tim, would grab a cab back to his hotel and check up
on his messages.

But Jonny had had something else in mind.

Reseating himself, Jonny had wasted no time.

"Tim, our liaison in the bedroom—that was no
accident. I've been looking forward to it for a long time.
And so have you."

"Hold it, Jonny—"

"Yes, you have. But you couldn't face it. Last
night, I watched you put away the booze. You were
building your courage. The pressure was growing and
that marvelous he-man control of yours was looking for
an excuse to collapse."

"I'd had a hard day. I was drinking—"

"True, but all that the liquor did was release
what was seething inside of you. I didn't plant it there.
God knows what did. But, man, you were ready."

"I—I—didn't mean it."

Jonny's eyebrows had shot up. "You think not? I
think you did. Maybe you're not all the way over on
the other side the way I am—there *are* degrees in these
things; scientists make studies—but last night, fella, you
meant it." He was thoughtful for a moment, and then
resumed. "Me, I've faced up to my degree. I am a committed, practicing homosexual. I've made peace with
myself on that score. Marriage got to be agony for me.
In my fashion, I cared for Nancy, and I adore my children. I'll always be a good father, but I realize that I

can never be a good husband. Nancy couldn't cope with what was happening to us. I don't know if she suspected what it was. All she said was that she was miserable living like a nun. When she asked for a divorce, she blamed the demands of my career. I told her she was right."

"I suspected what it was, Jonny," Tim had said. "There was some talk around town. But it's different with me. I love Dru. I need her. My marriage is going to last. I don't know what possessed me to come back to the apartment with you. But that was it. Period."

Jonny had put down his coffee cup and grimaced. "I never dreamed I'd be somebody's one-night stand."

Jonny had not been a one-night stand.

Back in California, Tim couldn't get Jonny out of his mind, out of his system. Every time he traveled to Washington—more and more often, it seemed—he telephoned Jonny. He went to the apartment, downed a strong drink, and then he followed Jonny into the bedroom and they made ardent love to each other. After a while, Tim didn't need the drink. The craving took care of everything. The desire was there.

And so was the guilt. Because of Dru. All along, she had suffered, the way she was suffering now.

Tim stood at the window and his eyes followed the lively young man—Mexican, he thought—who entered Dru's cottage. Moments later, the young man reappeared, carrying Dru's luggage. Dru was behind him. The first sight of her saddened him. Her footsteps were slow, listless. She looked so fragile, even tinier than before, and his heart went out to her. He could see her clearly, coming closer.

This was the moment. He would have to tell her. But tell her what?

On the flight from Washington, only one fact

had held true: He did not want to lose her. He would do battle with her, with Jonny—and, hardest of all— with himself. But he would never let her go.

Ironically, it had been Jonny who, this week, had insisted upon some resolution to their affair.

They had been lying side by side, their bodies touching, in the now-familiar bed, smoking cigarettes after their lovemaking.

Suddenly, Jonny had moved away from him.

"Look at me, Tim."

"Wh—what?"

"I said, look at me. It's time for a man-to-man talk."

Tim had flinched at the choice of words.

"About what?"

"You, me, Dru. You know how I feel about you. First love, and all that," he had observed wryly. "But you're the one who can't decide which way to go. You want me, yet part of you holds back. At the risk of sounding Victorian—Tim, I must know your intentions." Jonny had considered what he had said so far, and then he had resumed. "I want us to go on. I want you to belong to me. I have never stopped loving you. You want me too. You come to me voluntarily. You make love with passion. But when it's finished, you spoil it with your remorse. You think of your wife and you anguish. It's not easy for me either, having to share you, never knowing where I'm at."

"I'm sorry, Jonny. I didn't mean to make you miserable, too."

"But you do. You're turning something beautiful into something—well, most difficult. More important, it pains me to see you tortured. And I doubt Dru can go on living this way." Jonny had fallen back on his pillow. "In the vernacular, old boy—it's time to piss or get off the pot."

Neither of them had slept much that night. Nor had they touched each other again.

In the morning, after a subdued breakfast together, Tim had called for a cab and had returned to the Madison Hotel.

Alone in his suite, he had slumped on the sofa in the sitting room and tried to sort out his feelings. When the floor maid, using a pass key, had let herself in to fix up the rooms, he had ignored her knowing look as she needlessly smoothed the unused bed. He had also ignored the accumulated messages the concierge had thrust into his hand along with his key.

After the maid had left, he had thrown himself on the bed and wept. Later, emotionally depleted, he had telephoned Jonny at the Senate Office Building to say good-bye. He had been brief and cryptic. Jonny had understood. Wonderful, compassionate Jonny—he had wished him a safe journey to the coast and sent his regards to Dru.

The sorrow in Jonny's voice had left no doubt that he knew it was ended.

Before boarding the plane from Dulles to San Diego, Tim had loaded his arms with newspapers, books, and magazines—diversions for the hours ahead. The device had not worked. The agony of parting with Jonny was somewhere deep inside. He told himself he could deal with it in time. He had no other choice.

More immediate was the reunion with Dru. He yearned to tell her the truth, to implore her forgiveness, even to beg for her help in bringing him through this period of torment. But how much could she accept, this straightforward, wise, prim, talented, small-city girl, this trusting emigrée from Missoula, Montana?

He had to tell her *something*. She would be suspicious of his sudden decision to give up his trips to Washington, to remain at home to write the political novel he had been putting off for years. And how would he explain his break with Jonny? Jonny had a speaking engagement scheduled in Los Angeles next month and Dru had tentatively planned a dinner party in his honor.

Wretched, uncertain, he watched her approach. He had given her a rotten time but eventually, he hoped, the tension between them would lighten and, as a couple, they would endure.

Today she appeared diminished. The stamp of sorrow was on her face. He wondered what was on her mind.

Dru looked past Manuel toward the Reception Hall. The screened window formed a silver wall and she could not see beyond it. Around her, the buildings were silent. Except for Manuel leading the way, no one was in sight. A number of the guests had departed, or were shut into their cottages packing to leave. A few of the holdovers, with the week's routine suspended, had gone into town to shop. She felt like a lone figure forsaken in a surrealist landscape.

Earlier, she had rapped on Elena's door to say good-bye. Rita had let her in and the three of them had hugged and kissed and promised to stay in touch. They had talked in low voices about the tragedy that had befallen Gillian. Dru, as Gillian's closest friend, had volunteered to pass on to the others all news of Gillian's progress as well as the time and place of Jason's funeral.

Because Elena was moving from the apartment in the Marina that very day (a circumstance Dru had fleetingly found odd but, too preoccupied with her own problems, had not pursued), and because Rita's plans were vague, they had agreed Dru's office was their logical point of contact.

To dispel the grimness, they had talked of how

happy they were for Charlotte and, after another round
of hugs and kisses, Dru had said she must be going.

Going.

Presumably when one was going, one took leave
of a specific location and headed toward another. At
this moment, placing one foot before the other, she
was a woman without destination.

Manuel opened the screen door and she stepped
into the Reception Hall.

Tim held out his hands. "Hi, Dru," he said.

"Hello, Tim."

"Ready to leave?"

"Whenever you say. Where's the car? Manuel
will need the trunk key for my bag."

"Oh, sure." He fumbled in his pocket and handed
a set of keys to Manuel. "Over there." He pointed to
the blue Ford outside.

Minutes later, when they were seated in the car,
he turned to her and smiled wanly.

"You look terrible," he said.

"Thanks a lot. You don't look too good yourself."

"They've been starving you in this place. Let's
pull out and find some joint where I can get a ham-
burger and some French fries into you."

"Whatever you say, Tim."

The drive to the roadside diner had been painfully silent. Now they sat opposite each other in a
corner window booth. The afternoon sun poured
through the glass, highlighting the cracked leatherette
upholstery and the scratched formica tabletop that
separated them.

The waitress who had taken their order had
placed brimming coffee mugs before them, then gone
off to a nearby table.

"Dru," he began, nervously.

"Yes?"

"These past weeks—months—we have to talk about what's been happening."

"I have nothing to say."

"I suppose not. But I do." He pushed aside his coffee mug. "Dru, believe me, believe this, I love you—I always will. I've hurt you and I'm sick about it. It's been a nightmare for me, too. I have no right to ask but I want to go back to where we were—you and I, Dru and Tim—complete with each other."

She looked into his face and was silent.

"Dru," he pleaded. "Will you give me a chance? I did something I'm ashamed of—"

"I know that," she said quietly.

"But you don't," he said with despair. "It's not what you think. You don't know the truth."

"Is it over, Tim?"

"God, yes. It's over."

She placed her forefinger across his lips. "That's truth enough. It's the only truth I want to hear, ever." She reached for her bag. "Let's go home, Tim. Seems we've been away for years."

Manuel draped himself over the switchboard and flashed his even white teeth at the blond telephone operator.

"Circles under your eyes," he teased. "Missed your sleep again. What is happening to American womanhood?"

"*Macho* pig," she replied happily. "I wasn't alone, you know."

"And the fortunate man, who is he?"

"I'll give you a clue. Today when you go to the bank look around at the tellers. Maybe you'll see someone else with dark circles."

He looked up at the wall clock. "I don't know if

I'll get to the bank today. I have another run into the airport. Some going, some coming."

"Who are you waiting for?"

"Two of them. Valdez and that reporter, Sloane. They're leaving together."

The blonde leaned forward. "Did you hear what happened?"

"Manuel hears everything." He glared at her, pretending disapproval. "But I do not gossip. I leave such games to women."

"You clown—" The switchboard buzzed and she answered it. "Yes, he's standing right here. I'll send him over." She replaced the receiver. "Manuel, on the double. Your ladies are waiting."

The little Chicana appeared drawn, Manuel thought as he placed her wicker bag alongside the reporter's leather suitcase in the rear of the station wagon. The maids had told him about the pills and the doctor from town, but they knew no more than that about the incident.

Manuel wanted to say something comforting but decided against it. Instead, he smiled warmly as he helped the two women into their seats and then took his place behind the wheel. He was pleased to see that this time Elena Valdez was in good company. He remembered her arrival a week ago when Jessica Haskell, drunken and arrogant, had sat in the car and sniped at the defenseless girl.

"Manuel—hold on a minute!" Dr. Bertini was running toward them. "I must say good-bye to my dear guests."

Seated behind Manuel, Rita pressed a button and the electric window moved downward.

"I tried to reach you, Dr. Bertini," Rita said.

"Your line was tied up. I wanted to thank you for everything. This whole week, it's been a remarkable experience."

He put his head through the window and studied her worriedly. "I hope your editor will be satisfied. We hid nothing from you. If there is more you wish to know—"

"If there is, I'll telephone you. I'm staying in the Los Angeles area for a while." She nodded in the direction of Elena who, eyes closed, was huddled beside her. "I won't leave until Elena is settled."

"How is she today?"

"Stronger. Tomorrow she'll be even better."

Dr. Bertini looked forlorn. "A sad event. But rare, quite rare. And the Crains . . ." He shook his head dolefully. "A great tragedy. That beautiful couple. What a week this has been. I can imagine what you are thinking—"

She interrupted. "The story will be a success. Our readers will lap it up."

The worry on his face deepened.

Rita smiled. "It will be an *inspirational* story, I promise. Nothing I have seen or heard at The Fountains has been less than delightful."

He continued to look doubtful. "You mean that?"

"I do."

Dr. Bertini withdrew his head and straightened up. "Manuel," he called briskly.

"Yes, sir?"

"You have your new list?"

Manuel picked up the typewritten card lying atop the dashboard of the station wagon.

"Jasper and Obendorf, this afternoon," he read. "This evening—Benson, Lyons, and Nakura." He replaced the card. "The new Batch."

✿   ✿   ✿

Dr. Bertini watched the station wagon disappear beyond the wrought-iron gates of The Fountains. He sighed, wistfully. Each week, as his lovely ladies bade him good-bye, he suffered the same sharp pangs of separation.

He rubbed his beard and turned back to the grounds. He wondered again, as he always did: What would happen to them when they returned to their own real worlds? Had he really helped them discover the fountains within?

XIII

It was a perfect day.

Outside, the rain beat heavily on the trees and walks and flower beds of the Bel-Air Hotel. In front of the hotel, a narrow stream dimpled under the pelting water and the swans who dwelt there crouched beneath the curved wooden bridge that crossed the stream.

Charlotte stood at the window and observed the downpour. Behind her, in the cozily furnished sitting room, she could hear Jean-Claude bantering in French with the waiter who had come to remove their breakfast table.

When the waiter had departed, Jean-Claude came to her side and his arm encircled her waist.

"Must you go out?" His lips touched her cheek and he indicated the bedroom. "Must you?"

"Lecher, you know it's all arranged. Gillian, Dru, Elena—they'll be waiting for me at Scandia. It's been—" She used her fingers to count. "—five, six months."

"And what am I to do while you are gone?"

"For a couple of hours? You did well enough for thirty-four years."

"That was before I married you."

"Let me think. After you drop me at Scandia, you can visit the arboretum at UCLA. That should keep you out of trouble. No, don't go there, it'll be too muddy. Wait, there's a smashing street in Beverly Hills. Called North Rodeo Drive. Like the Faubourg St.-Honoré. Art galleries, antique shops. Hermes, Courrèges, Gucci. Buy us a present."

He feigned disapproval. "Spend, spend. You think of nothing else."

"That's what the money is for."

"*Your* decision, remember? It is not so easy, being a kept husband. You have no idea what I endure."

"Like what?"

"Like your friends in New York. They examined me as though I were a rara avis, indecently captured."

"So you are," she said kissing him. "And so you shall remain."

"As for your friends in Chicago—"

"What about them?"

"The men, so suspicious. The women, lusting. I felt unsafe. But your lawyer, he was the worst."

"Ed Butler? What about him?"

"He knows to the penny how much money your bank transfers to mine every month, yet he was dying to know how I could afford such a fine suit. I refused to tell him what it cost. I said we stopped in London on our way to America and you insisted upon buying me a new wardrobe. You know what? I think he would like to see you committed."

She placed her hands on his buttocks and squeezed them. "Let Ed pinch pennies—" She started for the next room. "There's still time," she said. "Let's go to bed."

Scandia, the restaurant on the Sunset Strip, was crowded at lunchtime. Charlotte had phoned ahead, reserving a table for four. She had asked for a table near the window.

When she arrived, a bit late, the others were already seated. She rushed ahead of the maître d' and, going around the table, she embraced each of them—Dru, Elena, Gillian.

She was pleased to see that their drinks were already before them. She asked the hovering waiter to fetch her a Mai-tai.

"You were marvelous to come, busy as all of you are," she said, settling into a chair. "Pity Rita isn't with us. I cabled her from Paris inviting her to lunch in New York. There was a note waiting at my hotel. She said she was off to Florence to cover Italian couture for *Caress.* She said something about seeing to a personal matter, too."

"Peter," Elena said. "Peter Welles. He's a think tank economist. He lives in Florence."

"Peter?" Charlotte was curious. The others grew attentive.

"An old friend. He wants her to leave *Caress* and move to Florence."

"Jason and I honeymooned in Florence," Gillian appeared saddened. "I'm so happy for her."

"Are you? Well, there's more to it than that. Rita wrote to me before she left. She said I could share her letter with all of you. Want to hear it?"

"Of course," Charlotte said. "Start reading."

Elena drew several sheets of paper from her handbag. The familiar *Caress* logo was strung boldly across the tops of the pages.

"She begins with some sweet, personal remarks to me. Nothing special there. Then she goes on to report about The Fountains article. It was a smash. Dr. Bertini was thrilled. He considered it an honest representation of The Fountains as an earthly paradise. Requests for reservations are spilling in. More than he can handle. But he promises he'll always find a place for her."

"I don't suppose she'll come back," Gillian said. "Not if she's going to live in Italy. I'll never forget Florence—it's a wonderful place for being in love."

"Better listen to the rest," Elena said. "Rita writes, 'I'm still madly in love with Peter. These six months of separation have been wretched for me. Elizabeta Stanford, my editor, knows how confused I've been. When she offered me the couture assignment she said it was because I might enjoy the change. But I know the real reason she's sending me to Italy. She wants to give me one more face-to-face meeting with Peter, to try to accomplish what our letters have not—the solution to our future.

" 'Elena, darling, it's settled in *my* mind. I've gone over it endlessly. At times I've thought my head would crack. But always I've come out the same door. I cannot give up my job for Peter or anyone.

" 'The Fountains taught me more than I realized. While I was there I thought—Rita, you're not like the others, you're detached, a cool observer. But back in New York when I began to think about our Batch, I had to admit that The Fountains taught me more than how to flatten my stomach and make low-calorie mayonnaise. I came to know myself fully there, to realize that for better or worse, I can never be one of those women who hands her life over to a man. I cannot sublimate, I cannot be a camp follower. I've even wished I could make myself over. It might be so much simpler to fit into a traditional mold instead of being stuck with this self-expression virus. In saner moments though, I'm thankful I have a brain that's hollering to be used and damn grateful I have an exciting job to take it to. Elena, can you imagine me as Penelope at the loom, waiting for my hero to return from his adventures on the other side of town? Impossible. I'd come all unglued and have to be carted away.

"'That's what I must communicate to Peter. I've got to make him see that if I domesticate with him I'll turn into a different woman—an irritable, nagging, snarling stranger. What he appreciates in me now is the aliveness that comes from being my own person. He couldn't live with the woman I'd become. Upstairs in his head, where he reasons, Pete gets the message. But in the seat of his understanding—wherever *that* is— he still doesn't grasp it fully.

"'What I'm hoping is that we'll hit on some compromise, an ongoing, long-distance arrangement with frequent visits in between until Peter returns to New York permanently. If he insists on a final break, I'll be shattered. But there is no other way. I don't expect that to happen. Still, it could. And then I'll be back at The Fountains, bruised like so many of the guests, to get my poor spirits bandaged. I'll let you know.

"'Meanwhile, explain to the others and give them my love. Ever, Rita.'"

At the Scandia table near the window there was silence for a few moments and then Dru spoke.

"And you, Charlotte, are you ever going back?"

"I don't expect to. Not that it isn't a fabulous place. I'd recommend it to any woman who can afford it. Any woman but me, that is."

"I don't understand."

"There are great spas in Europe, too. Forest Mere, Henlow Grange, Abano, San Pellegrino. Not as lavish as Arden's and Bertini's and the others—but they have something that suits me better."

"Like what?"

"They accept men and women at the same time."

"You're very happy, aren't you?" Dru asked.

"Very," said Charlotte. "And superstitiously afraid it will end. I never expected to feel like this. How could I? I never had before."

"Why should it end?" Dru asked. "It may change—things do—but they don't have to end."

"Dru's right," Elena said. "It's no secret at this table that six months ago I was at the bottom of the well." She shook her head, remembering. "I can't believe I did anything so foolish. I owe my life to Rita and to Gordon Prescott, and to all of you for being my friends." She smiled shyly. "And to Victor."

"Who's Victor?"

"The man I'm going to marry. He's Chicano, too. We were neighbors when I was a kid. He graduates from medical school next summer. I'll let all of you know when we set the date."

Charlotte put down her drink. "You look strong enough, so I'll dare to ask. Whatever happened to what's-his-name?"

"Barry? He calls occasionally. Invites me to lunch. I never accept. It would be meaningless. He belongs to another age."

"And your work?"

"I'm still in the publicity office. Only now I'm an account executive. By the way, Christina Rossi became my client soon after we left The Fountains. She gave me some good advice."

"What's that?"

"She said '*Cara*, keep the Tiffany bracelet.' "

"Did you?"

"I certainly did. When the time comes, I'll trade it in for a stove, refrigerator, some carpeting, and a color TV."

Charlotte laughed. "Smart girl."

She turned to the quiet blonde at her side. "Gillian, what about you?" she asked softly.

"I appreciated your letter from Paris, Charlotte. Not a pleasant chore for a new bride."

"Please—"

"I'm managing. Jason was so—vivid, I miss him terribly. But I have Bitsy and my art gallery. They keep me busy."

"I heard something about the gallery. A branch of your father's, isn't it?"

"Yes. After the accident, Lawrence and Margo wanted us with them in New York but I decided against the move. Bitsy has her school and her friends here. Jason's death was such a terrible blow, I couldn't disrupt her life more than it had been. And I have friends of my own—Dru, others." She paused. "Lawrence—my father—he was a dear about it. He had suggested opening a gallery for me in the past, but I was never interested. When he saw that I was grasping at straws, he brought it up again. This time I accepted, although what he offered was not exactly straws. He sends me his best acquisitions: Chagalls, Miros, Picassos. I'm doing quite well, too. For the first time, I'm learning I have some value. Not that Jason wasn't marvelous about making me feel worthwhile. He was. But I needed the experience of independence. God knows, I didn't want to get it this way."

She glanced at Dru, who was absorbed in talking to Elena. After a moment, she addressed Charlotte again.

"I used to be in therapy, you know. Once I was on my feet, when I was trying to put things together, I went back to my analyst. He helped me to see that I had to break my habit of dependence. We terminated my treatment. It's Bitsy and me now, growing up together."

Gillian remembered the day she had left the hospital.

Seated between Lawrence and Margo in the rear of the hired limousine, the subject of her therapy had come up.

"How can I ever thank you? All you've done. The arrangements. Taking care of Bitsy—"

"We'll stay as long as you need us," Margo had said. "Lawrence may have to return to New York, but I'll be here."

"No, Margo, you've done more than enough. Lawrence needs you as much as I do. I insist you go back with him."

"But you're alone, dear."

"I have good friends. And I have my analyst if things get too rough."

"Dr. Lorenz," Margo had said. "There's a letter from him at the house. I put it in the hall with the other messages."

Lawrence Delman had been thoughtful. "A fine man, Dr. Lorenz. You're fortunate to have him. Dr. Lorenz treated some of my colleagues when he practiced in Manhattan. You must see him as frequently as necessary. Don't concern yourself with the expense. It will help your mother and me knowing you're in his care."

The letter from Dr. Karl, like the others Margo had stacked on the entry hall console, had been a routine expression of sympathy for her loss. It was polite, impersonal, and she had left it with the rest for her parents to read.

Dr. Karl had not called her, nor had she called him.

A month later, after driving Margo and Lawrence to the airport, she had returned to her home and dialed Dr. Karl's office. An answering service operator had taken her name and number and asked if she wished to leave a further message. She had replied that she would like to schedule an appointment for the following day. The operator promised that Dr. Lorenz would receive the message.

The next morning, the answering service had called back to tell her Dr. Karl could see her at one o'clock.

After a late breakfast, she had soaked in a perfumed bubble bath, then toweled herself dry and smoothed matching-scented lotion over her body. The day had been warm—too warm for pantyhose. She had selected a wraparound skirt and coordinated button-front blouse from her closet and tossed both onto her bed.

At her dressing table, she had brushed her long yellow hair and applied her makeup carefully. Her tongue had swept her rounded mouth and her heart had beat faster. She had looked into her mirror a minute longer, her transformation from grieving widow to eager mistress fascinating her.

It *was* sad about Jason—tragic for his parents and unspeakably shocking for Bitsy. But she had known Jason for what he was. Death had not ennobled him, nor blurred the unfortunate truth of their marriage.

Dr. Karl had taught her to rip away false sentiment. That was precisely what she had done.

❋   ❋   ❋

"My darling child," Dr. Karl lifted himself on tiptoe and kissed her lightly.

Gently, as though she were convalescent, he led her to her usual chair and sat down opposite her. His fingers were locked in a pyramid. His glasses perched on the bulb of his nose.

"Dear Gillian, I am happy to see you."

"I thought, you know, a decent period of mourning."

"That was wise. You needed time to gather your strength."

"I received your letter. Thank you."

"It was the least I could do. How is Bitsy?"

"Subdued. She still cries a lot. Her analyst says it will take time."

He leaned forward, his elbows on his knees, his hands under his chin. "And you, what do you have to tell me?"

"I wanted to see you."

"And I am pleased to see you. But it is always better when the patient takes the initiative."

"Patient? Initiative?"

His hands left his chin and made a small, fluttering motion. "I am your doctor. I am here to help you. You have not forgotten so soon?"

"I haven't forgotten anything." She was growing apprehensive.

"And your future, have you given it any thought?"

"Yes," she said. "A great deal."

He nodded approval as she told him about the art gallery, about how splendid her parents had been, of her intention to stay on in the house in Beverly Hills, of the devotion of her good friend, Dru, now that their quarrel was a thing of the past.

"And—" She stopped.

"Go on," he said.

"And—and I'll be—well, freer."

"Freer?" He seemed genuinely curious. "For what?"

"Freer for you—for us. I mean, you know, without a husband."

His smile was benign. "Ah, that," he said coolly. "You must put all that behind you."

"Behind me?"

"My dear Gillian, I am a married man, a careful man."

"But you said—"

"Said what? I promised nothing. Only that I would try to make you well."

"I thought—"

"Listen to me. You had an experience. A maturing one, I hope. You are young, beautiful. There will be other men. Remarriage. You must think of building your personal life in a new direction."

"But I don't want—" she began plaintively.

The buzzer grated in her ears, announcing his next patient.

"I am sorry." Dr. Karl rose from his chair. "The session is ended."

Numb, she allowed herself to be led to the door.

"Call me," he said brightly. "Any time you think I can be of help."

Gillian stepped into the waiting room.

An overblown redhead, wearing tight blue jeans and a sleeveless T-shirt, put down the magazine she had been reading.

"Excuse me," she said, brushing past Gillian. "Guess I'm next."

The Scandia waiter rolled the blackboard up to

the table. The day's luncheon menu was chalked on its surface.

As Gillian and Elena discussed their selections with the waiter, Charlotte bent toward Dru.

"How are you?" she whispered. "How are you *really?*"

"Busier than ever. Patrick and I have another TV series debuting this season."

"Fantastic. And Tim, how is he?"

"Fine. Working hard. His book is coming along well."

"I can't wait to read it. Will you tell him I was always a fan of his columns?"

"I'll tell him. When he gets back."

"Oh?"

"He needed additional research for his novel. He had to go out of town."

"Where is he?"

"Washington," Dru said. "Shall we order lunch?"